OLYMPIC NEMESIS

Dedica

This novel is dedicated to the memory of that greatest of British thriller writers, the late John Buchan, who created the Republic of Olifa.

Credits

I offer my gratitude to so many friends who helped and advised me for this and all my previous four novels. To Michael Glanister my proof-reader and Jo Smith who set up the final text. I am grateful to Brian Grimwood of Frensham Pond Sailability who let me see the great work they do in competitive disabled sailing, and to former Olympian, Cathy Foster. Special thanks to Hilary Johnson who read the final version and gave me good critical feedback. To Rebecca Marriott who advised on Olympic match racing, and for an insight into an all girls racing team. Once again I thank Petersfield Writers' Circle who listened to me reading aloud and picked up repetitions and inconsistencies. Last and in no means least my thanks to fellow writer, Sarah Lucas, for her advice and support in the marketing of my work.

This book is a sequel to *Emily's Hour* and includes characters from all my previous novels. In particular I wanted to follow Emily into adulthood and see how her character had developed following the terror of her childhood abduction. I wanted to follow her father, Steve, through the ordeal of his stroke to his rediscovery of competitive sailing. Unkindly, I have put this loving, and well bonded family, under sinister threat from an event that happened long before most of them were born.

I repeat again if anyone recognises themselves among the good characters then they may keep the illusion. However no character bears any relation to anyone in the real world. Nor does any company, club or other organisation in the story exist.

The exotic Republic of Olifa I owe in its entirety to that greatest of thriller writers: John Buchan. Olifa city, the Gran Seco and the Olivarez family are all his creations. This book is in his memory

Author

Jim Morley has sailed and raced small boats all his life. He spent forty years in farming and forestry, combining this with a career in freelance writing.

He has published four novels, reflecting his interest in boats and also rural matters. He lives near Petersfield in Hampshire and sails a small family cruising yacht on Chichester Harbour.

Cover design by Guy Nicholson. Central photograph by Alan Franklin. Jacket by Cradduck Design Alresford.

To Roger and Barbara
with best wishes
Jim Morley.
September 2011.

OLYMPIC NEMESIS

James Morley

Olympic Nemesis

First published 2010

Published by Benhams Sea Mysteries, 1 Fir Cottage, Greatham, Liss, Hampshire GU33 6BB

Typeset by John Owen Smith

ISBN 978-0-9548880-4-6

Printed and bound in Great Britain by CPI Antony Rowe, Chippenham and Eastbourne

PART 1

CHAPTER 1

The villagers of South Marshall had never seen anything like this sombre occasion. Their long village street filled with parked cars and lines of spectators, leaving only a narrow centre space for the funeral cortège. Television cameras stationed inside and outside the church recorded the scene for that evening's news. Local residents both proud and voyeuristic watched as the distinguished guests, amidst heavy security, walked the last few yards. Today, Group Captain Gerald Pembelty, DSO, DFC, GM, Battle of Britain veteran and hero of the sun cult siege was making his last journey at the age of ninety-two.

Everyone knew that it was the memory of the fire siege that was attracting national and even some world attention. Nobody knew better than Emily. She stood with her parents, Steve and Kirsten, half-sister Sarah and Sarah's daughter Christine. How puzzled these pressmen had been to discover that Christine and Emily, niece and auntie, were both twenty-year olds. For the tenth time Emily glanced at the text on her mobile.

Be strong – U can do it
Love Tom xxxxxx

The hearse and attendant cars were moving slowly up the slope towards them led on foot by the town undertaker in his black suit and top hat. One by one the ex-service groups lowered their banners in respect.

Emily's throat felt dry and she began to panic. She was central to this ceremony and in a short while she must speak in front of all these people. She wanted to do it; she had asked to do it. Nobody here had a closer bond with Gerry than she. The two of them had survived those days imprisoned inside the derelict cottage that the sun cult had intended as their funeral pyre. She had then discovered a strength she never knew she had, while Gerry had reverted sixty years to the days when he had needed all his wits to survive in combat.

Emily had sat by the old man's bedside as he lay, face covered in a breathing mask. There had been no one else there. When Gerry's wife "Aunt" Dolly had passed away, everyone guessed that it would not be long before her husband followed her. Gerry's family were speeding towards the hospital but it was Emily who witnessed the old man's final moments. Gerry, who had once cheated death in battle, accepted it now with serenity. Six years ago he would willingly have sacrificed that life to save a little girl from being burned to death. That same little girl, now a grown woman, had been the one who sat holding his hand as the last flicker of life was extinguished.

They were inside the church now as the service drew to its conclusion. The vicar signalled to Emily, her mother gave her arm a supportive squeeze and, dreamlike, she walked up the three shallow steps to stand beside the coffin. The vicar passed her the hand microphone as the congregation rose to their feet, and for a few seconds Emily looked at the sea of expectant faces. In the front rows were her own and Gerry's family with the distinguished guests: the government minister, bored and looking at his watch, the Chief of Air staff and the royal Prince both in Air Force blue uniform. The Air Marshall grizzled but kindly, the Prince, gorgeous, but not for her. Suddenly she noticed she was looking straight down the lens of a TV camera. Resolve flooded into Emily; she owed this moment to the man who had saved her life, and to the memory of his friends and fallen wartime comrades. She drew breath and spoke her words clear and bright through the building.

'They shall grow not old as we that are left grow old
Age shall not weary them nor the years condemn
At the going down of the sun
And in the morning
We will remember them.'

The response from the congregation washed back over her. Emily passed the microphone back to the vicar and laid a hand on the coffin: how beautifully crafted it looked with its dark wood and bright metal handles.

'Goodbye, Gerry,' she whispered.

It was now that she understood for the first time in her young life utter desolation and grief. With Gerry's son and her own mother supporting her, Emily, face wet with tears, followed the coffin from the church while the assembly sang the hymn *Abide With Me.* In the sunshine of the graveyard she watched as the coffin was lowered into the earth. Then Gerry's family had beckoned her to join them by the grave and she had dropped a red rose and a sprinkling of earth onto the wood below.

The wake party was a much smaller affair. The great and powerful had returned to London immediately the service was over. The media had packed their bags and departed, and a select forty guests had made the short trip to Firs Farm, the Simpson family home. Kirsten, Sarah and Emily had prepared something of everyone's favourite buffet snacks. Steve had been amused to see his daughters take over the proceedings and greet each guest on arrival, shaking hands, and Emily bending down to kiss Gerry's ninety-nine year old former Hurricane mechanic in his wheelchair.

The occasion had proved too daunting for her young brother John-Kaj who had slipped upstairs to his computer.

Steve remembered his younger days when all the invitations had been to weddings, shortly followed by christenings. Now he was aged sixty-six it was nothing but funerals. He had just heard he must attend another next week. Wolfgang Bartels, close friend, work colleague, and fellow Olympic medallist, had suffered a massive heart attack. Nothing, not even the efficiency of German medical services could save Wolfgang, and he had died within the hour. In two day's time Steve must take the flight to Kiel. The funeral would be sad and the memories strong, but it would be against the background of Kiel sailing regatta. Perhaps someone would give Steve a crewing berth in a race. Wolfgang would approve of that.

'You OK, Em?' Christine touched Emily on her right arm.

'I'm fine – it's over now. I suppose it's what they call closure.'

'It's news on the telly in a minute – you'll be on there.'

Emily shook her head. 'Not now, Chris, maybe I'll look at the recording tomorrow.'

Emily felt tired: her stress had dissolved into what – depression? She really couldn't say. Probably the correct word was weariness. The old man who had saved her life was gone, and she would always feel this emptiness. But now more than ever she wanted to put the little girl from the fire siege behind her. At first it had been therapeutic, almost fun, to be the centre of attention. The hours of interview with that book writer had paid off. The thousand pounds had eased her way through uni and let her go sailing. Already she was a figure on the competitive scene with a world championship under her belt. She had enjoyed her place in Chloe's match racing crew even though they had missed out on Olympic selection.

The girls had gone their separate ways for the rest of this summer and Emily had no alternative other than to return home to Sussex.

They wouldn't be in these Olympics, but there was always next time. That would be where? In South America she had been told. She didn't care as long as the racing was on a warm stretch of sea with a decent breeze.

CHAPTER 2

Emily lay face down on her bed. She didn't know why she was in such a foul mood.

She hadn't meant to be so tetchy but her brother Johnny had wound her up to the point where she had screamed and slapped him. The little rat had run straight to Mum sobbing and howling. A fourteen-year lad shouldn't react like a little kid. It would not amuse Dad if her brother turned out to be gay. Then Tom had rung her mobile and she had snapped at him. Immediately it had been her turn to run tearfully to find Mum. That had been stupid as it played straight into her parents' protective obsession. Why couldn't they see she was a woman now, twenty-one in two weeks time. True, she still had nightmares or visitations of her abduction and the hell she had shared in that cottage with old Gerry. Now Gerry was gone and those memories, still fixed in her mind, returned less often in her dreams.

Mum and Dad were off to Germany for another funeral. Mum was Danish and still didn't trust Germans, but apparently this Wolfgang was an old friend of Dad's and he'd been a racing helmsman with an Olympic medal. Emily had looked him up on the web and seen his picture, and it didn't fit with the balding old guy she'd met at last year's Kiel Week. The picture had shown a young man with floppy blond hair. Now he was dead, and Mum and Dad were away for the second funeral in a fortnight.

Her parents' bags were packed and sitting by the front door. Emily saw a car roll up the driveway and recognised it as her half-sister's.

'Sarah's here,' she called.

'I know,' her mother replied. 'She and Chris are staying to keep you company.'

'But, why?' Emily was annoyed. It seemed her overprotective parents were determined to ruin her week.

'Somebody needs to keep Johnny in order and also…' Kirsten paused. 'Your father says that Tom will sleep in the spare room – no arguments.'

'We're both over eighteen and we're careful.'

'I know, I don't mind and I trust you, but your father is becoming a bit of a puritan in his later years.'

'With me it's like he's in the bloody Taleban, and Sarah's not much better.'

'Sarah is Miriam's daughter – she had a severe Catholic upbringing.'

Emily looked out of the window. Her father had greeted Sarah and Christine and was carrying their bags towards the front door. 'Forecast says it's going to be hot for the next five days,' she mused.

'That's nice – so what.'

'Chris and me can go nude in the pool and around the house. That'll wind up Sarah, and it'll make Tom go all red face and embarrassed.'

Kirsten laughed. 'Quite right, defy the prudish English. I'm glad you're keeping that part of your Danish heritage. Just remember don't overdo the sun, and plenty of high-factor screen or you'll end up with skin like mine.'

The Kiel funeral was a contrast to the one in South Marshall church. The gathering in the little Lutheran chapel had spilled out onto the forecourt with the service relayed by a sound system. Steve recognised so many old friends from his great days on the water. It was an unusual service; the pastor began and ended the proceedings with prayers, while most of the ceremony was taken up by music and readings. Steve couldn't follow the German, apart from odd words and half sentences, until it was his turn to read in English a short passage from Uffa Fox's 1930s book: *Crest of the Wave.*

It was all over in little more than an hour and the coffin had been borne from the chapel to the jaunty music of Brahms 1. The close family had departed with the cortège to a crematorium while everyone else dispersed. Steve knew that the wake party was due at their own hotel, and earlier he had watched the staff preparing a gargantuan German food and beer fest. No doubt Kirsten would see he stayed reasonably sober.

The next duty was the difficult one for both of them. The act of reconciliation was Sarah's idea. Steve had consulted the Royal Navy Association in his hometown. They had been divided on the matter but having understood Steve's connection to Wolfgang they had raised no further objection. So it was that following the funeral they had taken a taxi to the U-boat memorial. Steve had been awestruck by the scale of the massive wall studded with thousands of names that seemed to stretch into eternity.

They both knew that this would be a psychological challenge. Steve's father, whom he never knew, had died on arctic convoys at the hands of a U-boat. Kirsten's Jewish father had only narrowly escaped the Holocaust. Steve knew that the names of the men who had killed his father were somewhere on the wall in front of them, but for Kirsten this simple act was much harder to take.

'Come on, love,' he said quietly. 'It was a long time ago.'

They walked hand in hand to the centre of the wall and placed a little bunch of red roses. 'I don't think the Germans go for flowers like us so they'll know there were Brits here today.'

Kirsten looked at him. 'That poem that Emily recited – how does it go?'

'There you are, Steve. She is all yours now,' Wolfgang's son, Dieter, pointed to the tiny keelboat sitting on a launching trolley. 'Dad only sailed her a few times. We would like you to have her.'

Steve was both touched by the gesture and now mildly excited. He had assumed that his competitive sailing days were long finished. Now he had been bequeathed this little single-hander racing yacht and it would be churlish not to have a go on the racecourse. Dieter and a yard hand wheeled a set of metal steps beside the boat.

He and Steve climbed them and looked inside at the helming position. The foot steering and secondary central tiller gave the setup an aircraft feel. Once, on a visit to Branham, Gerry Pembelty had likened the cockpit of a similar boat to that of a World War One aircraft: a Sopwith Camel. The resemblance was illusory: no engine controls or instruments, only a baffling array of cleats and rigging lines.

Dieter looked out across the waters of the Schilksee. 'We put her afloat – you try her.'

Steve was surprised: he was hardly equipped to go sailing, dressed as he was in shirt, shorts and flip flops. He had left his bag of sailing gear in the hotel and he didn't have so much as a buoyancy aid. So what: the sun was shining, the temperature was rising thirty centigrade and only a light breeze tickled the smooth stretch of water beyond the slipway.

'OK, Dieter, I'll give her a try.'

Dieter gave the little boat a push from the pontoon while Steve settled himself into his seating position. He tested the steering pedals: good, left pedal took the boat to port and right to starboard; great, that relieved hands free for the lines. At that moment he spotted them: two other boats of his type working to windward. All his competitive juices stirred – he would go after them. Gently he pushed the starboard pedal and wound in the mainsheet and finally, too late, the jib.

A gust of wind struck the little yacht, and a few drops of water slopped in over the cockpit edge. This was no good, the boat would only slip sideways. He remembered: de-power with backstay tension and steer into the gusts. But which was the bloody line to pull? He swore again as he watched the other boats way ahead of him turn a mark and run down towards him.

Slowly at first, and then with increasing confidence, Steve began to understand his new boat and he loved her. He had no problems holding his own in an impromptu race with the other two identical boats. Suddenly it was if the long years of ageing and slow decline had flown away. Yes, he would sail in this regatta – old man though he undoubtedly was he would give it his best shot.

'Em, come here, quick!' Sarah shouted. 'I've got Kiel on the screen – I just do not believe it.'

'What's up?' Emily asked.

'Dad's won a race.'

'Oh come on – you're winding me up.'

'No, really – come and look yourself.'

Emily ran downstairs to find Sarah staring at the office computer screen. On it was the Yachts and Yachting web page with the results from Kiel Week.

'Listen to this. *Veteran Olympian, Steve Simpson took the sixth race with a decisive win in the 2.4R class, following a tight fought tactical battle with Nik Kalkkinen of Finland. This result places Simpson in fourth place in the competition with two races to go. Simpson at 66 is almost certainly the oldest helm in the regatta…*'

'That's fantastic.' Emily found herself dancing around the room. 'I didn't even know he was sailing and where did he get a 2.4 from?'

'Your mum phoned while you were out. She said Wolfgang's son had given him a boat but she didn't say what kind.'

'Yeah, a little boat like that – you know: can't capsize and all that stuff. Just the thing for a doddery old bloke. Good on, Dad, I hope he slaughters them in the next race.'

'He can't win the 2.4 event, your friend Megan has got that sown up.' Sarah switched off the screen. 'They'll be out on the water for that right now.'

'Hey,' Emily protested. 'Don't turn it off yet. Who's winning the women's match racing?'

'Sammy's just knocked out the Slovenians. She's racing the Italians next.'

‘She and those other two fat cows,’ Emily snorted. ‘They’ll never cut it when it comes to the big one.’

‘Jealousy will get you nowhere,’ said Sarah. ‘Much better you girls regroup and concentrate on four years’ time.’

‘In Olifa. I don’t even know where that is.’

‘It’s in South America – not far from the equator so it’s hot.’ Sarah glared at her younger sister. ‘Look, it’s nearly half past five, I’m serving supper at seven. For heaven’s sake, girl, put some clothes on before then.’

‘If you and Tom took yours off we’d all be equal,’ Emily giggled.

‘You can get lost. Where is Tom anyway?’

‘Gone out with some biker mates.’

‘How long have you two been seeing each other?’

‘Must be five months now. Tom’s a good sailor but Dad doesn’t like him.’

Sarah screwed her face into what was supposed to be a scowl. ‘I’ve been ordered to see that that young man sleeps in the spare room.’

‘Well, he has done every night.’

‘And you sneaked along the passage and joined him,’ Sarah was almost grinning now. ‘Don’t deny it. I heard you squealing like a stuck pig. What do I tell Dad when he asks for a report?’

‘If I get dressed now, will you acquire a temporary deafness?’

‘I would prefer that if it happens again you stuff a condom in your mouth as well as on the other place.’

Emily was gazing through the window. ‘That bloke’s there again – the one that said he was a journalist.’

‘Emily, girl, stand back a bit. If he looks this way he’ll see you’re starkers.’

‘That’ll be his fault,’ Emily giggled. ‘OK, I give in. I’ll put some jeans and a top on – satisfied?’

‘You do that,’ said Sarah. ‘The guy is trespassing on our drive. I think I’ll go and give him an earful.’

Sarah, surgeon’s wife and ward sister, could be formidable when she chose to be. She marched towards the intruder and was annoyed when the man stood his ground. ‘You are loitering on private property in a suspicious manner. Either explain yourself or leave.’

‘Are you Mrs Kirsten Simpson?’

Sarah was annoyed now, considering that Kirsten was ten years her senior. ‘It’s none of your business, but no, she’s my step-mother.’

‘Who are you then?’

‘I’m not telling you anything as I don’t know who you are, except you’re boring me and you’ve no manners. Now push off!’

The man shrugged. ‘I’m Karl Hammersen, I’m a historian and journalist. Here’s my ID.’ He handed Sarah the square of card.

She stared at him. ‘Your name sounds Danish but I would take you for English.’

‘I was born in Norway as it happens, but I’ve lived most of my life over here. So I’m very like your Kirsten Simpson, or should that be Elgaad?’

‘Mrs Simpson’s maiden name was Schmitt – what’s it to you anyway?’ Sarah was suspicious now, and for the first time she took a good look at this man. He was impressive in a way. Wearing jeans and an open-necked shirt, he had an athletic frame and with short fair hair could be described as good looking.

‘As I said, I’m a historian…’

Sarah interrupted him. ‘It says on your ID you’re a journalist.’

‘That’s my day job, but I am a historian. Don’t want to sound conceited but I’ve a Cambridge history degree, rather a good one as it happens. I specialise in Twentieth Century and World War Two in particular. I’m writing a book on the Nazi occupation of Copenhagen, and I find the Elgaad family interesting.’

Now Sarah understood. ‘All right Gerda Elgaad was a Nazi collaborator, but let’s face it she was a raving nutter and nobody here ever met her.’

‘The rather gorgeous sun-tanned young lady I saw by the window. There’s Elgaad blood there I would say.’

‘Right, that’s it. You out now or I’ll ring the police.’

‘All right, farvell, as they say in Denmark. You know you’re rather a pretty lady too when you’re angry.’

‘Just get out!’

Sarah was both fuming with anger and worried. She had a nasty feeling she knew where this tiresome scribbler was digging. A car was driving in off the road and it was Christine’s battered Fiesta. Her daughter had been in Petersfield stocking up for the weekend. Sarah was baffled and a bit envious of the amount of food the two girls could put away in a week and still remain lissom and fit.

‘I’ve done the shop, Mum,’ said Christine. ‘Say, that bloke I passed just now – has he been here?’

‘Yes, nosy reporter, I got rid of him.’

‘Another one trying to get Em to talk about the fire cult?’

‘No he’s trying to stir trouble for Kirsten over her grandmother.’

Christine grimaced. ‘Gerda Elgaad and the war you mean? That’s old hat now – who cares?’

‘The man says he’s a historian,’ Sarah replied. She suspected there might be more to it than that but neither Christine, Emily nor Johnny knew the full story.

‘I saw him in Petersfield library yesterday and again this morning in One Tree Books,’ said Christine. ‘He was drinking a coffee in the café there. There was a weedy looking girl with him.’

‘Never mind for now; supper at seven.’

Steve could not remember being on such a high for years. His body ached, his hands were sore from pulling these thin rigging lines and sheets, but psychologically he felt like a small boy at Christmas. The little 2.4 keelboat had been a revelation. He had fumbled a bit with her during the first two races and then after an evening spent tweaking the mast and rigging he had discovered a boat that would snake to windward with hardly a touch on the rudder. Steve had not raced at Kiel since his twenties but he remembered the good and bad points of that water and he still retained his tactical sense. He climbed painfully ashore following the final race to discover that by discarding his disastrous thirtieth place in the first race he had finished fourth in the competition, just missing out on a medal. He hadn’t minded that too much as Megan, the British girl, had won the event and the bronze had gone to a charming young local man with multiple sclerosis, who was already Germany’s selection for the Paralympics that autumn.

Steve climbed on to the quay and, pulling off his sunglasses, tried to focus on the blurred crowd of wellwishers that surrounded him. He heard only an odd singing in his ears, as in a swirl of giddiness he fell flat on his face. What the hell was happening? He tried to get on his knees but fell back on one side. He could feel his face contorting, nothing would work: his right leg was quivering, racked with pins and needles, and the knee wouldn’t bend. Anxious faces were peering at him. Closest of them was Kirsten, and her expression reminded him of that time in the rescue helicopter at Hayling: but that was long ages ago, wasn’t it?

He heard voices now; harsh male voices barking orders in German, just like the old war films. Someone gently rolled him on his back and he sensed he was being lifted by a team of hands that he could just see in front of him: large hairy male hands and one pair of girlie hands with bright red nails. A plastic mask was rammed over his face as he sank into a sleep of oblivion.

Consciousness returned in slow waves. He could hear a steady bleeping sound. He'd heard it before somewhere but he couldn't think when. He wasn't sure where he was, and for a few seconds he couldn't think who he was – only that he'd been at a funeral and he couldn't remember whose. Was it his funeral? Had he died and been resurrected somewhere else? He felt peaceful and slightly drunk and he recalled that he'd sailed a race in a little boat. He'd always done that but something this time was different.

Kirsten was talking softly in his ear. 'You must lie still. The doctor says you're going to be OK. Steve, I love you.'

He tried to reply but the words were lost in this irritating thing strapped over his face.

CHAPTER 3

'Mum, oh Mum, will he get better?' Emily had seized the phone from Sarah. The news from Kiel had stunned her and she felt sick.

'It's all right, sweetheart.' Her mother's voice was calm. 'Your father's had a stroke, that's all. But he's got be nursed carefully for a while. Now, will you pass the phone back to Sarah; the doctor wants to brief her on the medical details.'

Emily obeyed and ran tearfully from the room and into Tom's arms. She sobbed on his shoulder, and sensibly, he held her until the tears dried, then gently he released her grip and laid her on a sofa. She had been so excited by Dad's sailing triumph and now this. That she might lose him was something beyond comprehension; something that even in her darkest thoughts she had never contemplated, until now.

Sarah came into the room. 'Emily, it's going to be all right. Yes, Dad's had a stroke but it's more of a warning shock than life-threatening. The doctor says his blood pressure was way over the limit and his cholesterol levels are bad. His speech is slurred and he'll probably walk a bit odd for a while but he's going to be OK.'

'We must fly out there tomorrow.'

'No, Emily; your mother says he should be released in a few days, but he's not to be excited. I want you to stay here with Chris and make the house nice. I'm to go out there when he's ready and I'll look after him on the flight home.'

'You're sure he'll get better?'

'I've spoken to the doctor in Kiel. He says Dad will need nursing care and nothing stressful. If so he'll make a reasonable recovery. Tell, me: how often has he been to his doctor here? When did he last have a check up?'

'I don't remember him ever going – he's never been ill before.'

'He had the hip replacement – they wouldn't have done that if his blood pressure was way up.'

Emily was struggling with tears again. 'That was three years ago and they wouldn't do it at first. They sent him home and I think that was because of blood or something.'

'He took pills after the hip job and he hated them,' said John-Kaj. Emily hadn't noticed her little brother enter the room.

'What do you know about it?' she snapped.

'I know lots,' he replied. 'I'm going to be a doctor.'

'That's good,' said Sarah. 'You might do worse – you're a clever boy.'

John-Kaj stood legs apart, his face composed. 'He said the pills spoilt sex.'

'You cheeky little sod,' Emily was outraged. 'You can't say things like that at your age.'

'I'm fourteen, and anyway I bet I'm right.'

'You may have a point, Johnny,' said Sarah. 'There is some evidence that the treatment lowers male libido.' She grinned now. 'Maybe we should dish them out far and wide.'

Emily caught the expression on Tom's face and now she laughed. 'Poor Mum.'

Steve sat in the chair staring at the window in the door of his room. He was alone, since the hospital staff and his friends had insisted that Kirsten eat some food and take a rest. Steve tried to count the passing figures: medical staff, walking with speed and purpose, visitors slower and seemingly aimless as they searched for room numbers. He was just beginning to come to terms with this latest predicament. He supposed he should be glad that he was alive, but quite honestly he was indifferent. He had been assured he would recover to normality. His illness was a warning, they said. He would have to lose weight, he would have to assume a new diet, a new life style: all of this and he would get better. "Soon you will be able to sail your little boat again," the bespectacled young doctor had assured him. Steve couldn't see that far ahead. He only knew he had become a cabbage in a wheelchair unable to speak coherently.

Mention of boats only increased his worries. He was pulled back to thoughts, not of competitive sailing but of work. He was the managing director of a European-wide sailmaking and yacht equipment company, slap bang in the middle of an economic crisis. The wheel had gone full circle, and they were once again in the dark days that he remembered. This time Easterbroke Europe should be able to reduce canvas and ride out the storm. It was not like the nineteen eighties and there would be no predators like Kenneth Lindgrune, hungry to strip Steve's life's work assets.

They wouldn't dare with Kirsten as chairperson overseeing the accounts.

Disembodied faces were peering through the window. The door opened and into the room came Dieter, his wife Louisa, and miraculously, Steve's own eldest daughter, Sarah. He knew instinctively that she was about to revert to the bossy nurse of twenty years experience.

'Dad, what the hell have you been playing at?' Her tone was both reproving and fond.

Steve tried to reply to say hello Sarah, but it sounded like, 'Hosh-srah.'

She stood looking down at him. 'If I didn't know the facts I'd say you were pissed.' She knelt down and gave him a hug. 'I've seen your blood and cholesterol readings; what have you been doing these last few years?'

'I idnrelis,' he gabbled. Didn't realise, he'd tried to say.

'No, too right you didn't. Now I'm flying you home, and then I'm taking you in hand. It's strict diet, medication, muscular and speech therapy for the next two months.' Sarah's sadistic expression mellowed. 'Did you like sailing the 2.4?'

He nodded.

'I've spoken to Sailablity at Branham. Brian says when you're fit again they'll work on you. You see, after this you'll be eligible for the Paralympics. Your performance here at Kiel last week has got the yachtie fraternity buzzing.'

'Nrr gottamuddle,' he muttered.

'Never got a medal! Hell, Dad, you get in an unfamiliar boat in the biggest regatta in Europe and you whinge because you didn't win anything.'

She was laughing as were Dieter and Louisa. 'Mein Gott, he will not change,' said Dieter. 'I say you get better soon and we see you in a boat again.'

Steve wondered about that. If he was in for months of misery under his authoritarian daughter's supervision, then sailing again might be his salvation. He recalled the Laser race in Copenhagen; the magic week that had brought Kirsten and him together. For Steve, still consumed with grief at the death of Miriam his first wife, that one hard race had been a rebirth. Right now he didn't feel like sailing any boat. He was desperately tired and he wanted to go home.

CHAPTER 4

'I'd better clear out,' said Tom. He had made up his mind. Steve Simpson did not approve of Tom; probably did not approve of any boyfriend for the feisty impulsive Emily.

'You don't have to,' Emily had her arms around his neck while she stared into his face with that doleful expression.

'Yes, I do. Your dad needs you and I know what he thinks of me.' Tom knew he had mixed feelings. The hostility of Emily's father had hurt him. Tom was a sailor and Steve Simpson had been a boyhood hero. But the man was so possessive it wasn't true. Tom liked Kirsten, a bit abrasive sometimes, but far more welcoming than her husband.

'Dad doesn't approve of public schoolboys,' said Emily. 'But give him time…'

'It's nothing to do with where I went to school – it can't be. You were always complaining that when you were a kid he wanted to take you away from the comprehensive and send you to Roedean.'

Emily buried her face into his chest. He wished she wouldn't cry, or at least not switch on the tears like a tap and wet his shirtfront. Here he was, doing his best for both their futures, and for her grumpy old father, and she just didn't get it.

He tilted her head back and kissed her. 'Come on, help me pack my kit on the bike.'

Half an hour later Tom was astride his beloved Ducati speeding down the long straight between South Marshall and Petersfield. Why on earth should he feel so relieved? Emily was great, Emily was fun, but she carried too much mental baggage. Whatever she did in the future she would always be the little girl saved from that mad sun cult. He too remembered those ten days from six years ago. He, with his parents, his friends and the world, had followed every news bulletin with apprehension. The newspapers could print nothing else but the story of the little girl and the mad people intending to sacrifice her life by fire.

Tom had this much in common with Emily. At the age of ten he had been the victim of abduction by a mad person, for an hour his life too had hung in the balance. He still had total recall of every second of that trauma and, like Emily, he had visitations in his dreams. It should have brought the two of them closer, but on the contrary it was a mutual embarrassment that neither wanted to talk about.

When Tom had first met Emily at university he hadn't realised she was the same Emily, the sacrificial victim whose picture had been on every front page: the little fourteen-year old picnicking beside some water. Seven years later Tom had met this lovely nubile, tactile woman; danced the night away with her at a disco and four days later had welcomed her into his bed. But there was early tension in the relationship, quite apart from shared experiences. Tom was a good helm with his Laser but he wasn't top notch. Twenty-fifth in the nationals wasn't much to boast about. Emily had been Cadet Dinghy world champion, and her women's match racing team had only just missed out on Olympic selection. It was galling for a macho guy to admit his girlfriend was a better sailor than he. He couldn't quite swallow her closeness to her all-girl crew. Erin the little blonde bow girl was sweet, but Tom couldn't stand Chloe. What the hell was a New Zealand Maori doing trying to represent Great Britain? Emily said Chloe served in the army, and she had a residential qualification. All Tom could ascertain was that Chloe, however good at sailing, was transparently butch and not one for the boys.

The week spent at Firs Farm, Emily's parents home, had not been an entire success. Their clandestine lovemaking had been great, but much as he adored having her naked body curled up in his bed, he couldn't stomach her daytime nudism. Emily and Christine would jump in the pool every morning after breakfast and then walk around the place stark naked. Emily had claimed that this was normal Danish custom in a heat wave and acceptable in the privacy of one's home. Danish custom maybe, but didn't the wretched girl know that she was British and that sort of behaviour was offensive. What if his mates found out?

He was steering the Ducati through the narrow series of bends before he reached the outskirts of the town and he could do without this red Audi tailgating him. He had overtaken the car on the straight a mile back and presumably whatever prat was at the wheel had been offended. Well, he wasn't in that much of a hurry. As they reached the last stretch he slowed and waved the Audi past him. The car cruised slowly by; the passenger window was open, not surprising in the heat. Then, what bloody cheek; the man was pointing a camera at him. Tom jabbed a gloved finger in the air.

He thought no more of the incident and rode on into Petersfield, found the car park with the bike slots and, carrying his helmet, made his way to the nearest pub, The Drum. He couldn't quite analyse his feelings. He knew deep down he was being a coward by running away. He was a man who to all intents had just dumped a very desirable girlfriend. He was hot dressed in leathers, and the street was full of girls in light summer wear. The sight didn't really cheer him and he felt hungry. It was mid-afternoon, so of course the pubs were closed. He knew there was a chippy in Lavant Street, so he would try that instead. He had been aware for some minutes that a guy had been walking behind him and had followed him from the car park. He turned quickly and now he knew him. He was the same bloke who'd been hanging around Firs Farm claiming to be some sort of writer.

The stranger held up a hand and smiled. 'Tom Stoneman isn't it? I'm Karl Hammersen.'

CHAPTER 5

Of necessity Steve's return home was not the flag-waving celebration it could have been. The famous racing sailor might have scored a minor triumph in his comeback regatta but now he was returning in a wheelchair. For Kirsten the shock, the panic and the mounting apprehension of the last week had changed to a new reality. Sarah had been a rock around which the chaos of the last few days had swirled. She had taken control of the situation with her professional knowledge and reassured Kirsten that her beloved man would live. She couldn't expunge the guilt that Kirsten felt and Sarah had been brusque and dismissive. No, of course Kirsten couldn't have foreseen this calamity, wives never did.

'Look, if Dad wouldn't go for a regular check up for absolutely basic things like blood pressure then, I know it sounds a cliché, but he was a ticking time bomb. It only needed some extra excitement like Kiel Week to be a trigger.'

Kirsten was not convinced. 'But shouldn't I have made him see a doctor?'

'Oh sure, and would he have taken a blind bit of notice? I know I could have lectured him until I was blue in the face and it wouldn't have made a bit of difference.'

Kirsten had been reassured then, but now she worried again. Steve slept most of the time, on the flight home and again in the final car journey from Gatwick. But it was this one-way communication that she couldn't cope with. Steve could understand her, but his painful, slurred speech was difficult for her to comprehend. If Kirsten were to tell the truth she would admit she was scared. Though Sarah was clearly concerned for her father, Kirsten knew that as a trained nurse, this crisis was something she saw every day of the year. She knew the form and the remedies. But Sarah had her own husband and a job to return to; Kirsten could not rely on her support for much longer.

They arrived at Firs Farm soon after midday. Sarah unfolded the wheelchair and between the two of them the women helped him into it.

'That's a good sign,' said Sarah. 'He's got a little bit of mobility down there already.'

Emily had run across the gravel followed by Christine. Sarah was relieved to see the two girls were decently clothed in bright-coloured sundresses. Emily flung her arms around her father and kissed him. Steve smiled and ruffled a hand through his daughter's hair. Sarah beckoned her own daughter to one side.

'Chris, is Tom still here?'

'No, he's pissed off and Emily's a bit down about it. Not sure if she's been dumped and I don't care to ask.'

'I like Tom and he seems good for Emily, but there's something about him that riles Dad and I can't think what.'

Christine smiled. 'Granddad wants her all to himself – thinks she'll be a nun and look after him in old age. Fat chance!'

'Well, she's going to have her hands full with him for a few weeks. I've got to go home to sort out your father and then I've work. Kirsten is going to need all the backup she can get.'

'Mum, can I stay on here?'

Sarah thought about it. Why not? Chris was on holiday but would be returning to university in the autumn to start her postgraduate course. If the girl was sensible she could be a real support; do the shopping, help around the house and maybe cheer up a lovesick auntie. 'OK, but you'll have to pull your weight – this won't be a holiday camp.'

Sarah let Kirsten wheel Steve across the gravel. 'We won't get up those steps.' She pointed at the front door.

'Go round by the garden and into the conservatory,' said Emily. 'We can get somebody in to a make a little ramp but it's not too bad.'

They reached the door and, leaving the midday heat behind them, entered the relative cool of the house. Sarah and Kirsten left Steve with Emily and Christine, while the elders conferred in the office.

'I'm going to select an agency nurse to live in,' said Sarah. 'No Kirsten! Professional help is going to be essential. Your job is moral support. The next few weeks are going to be difficult for everyone especially for Dad.'

Kirsten opened her mouth as if she wanted to argue but said nothing.

Sarah changed the subject. 'What is it that Dad has against Tom? I like him and I'm worried. If Dad has driven Tom away it's going to breed a bad atmosphere.'

Kirsten nodded. 'Steve tends to be stupid about Emily's friends and then this boy appears. He's a keen sailor, his parents run a yacht harbour, and you know Tom had a similar bad experience to Emily. When he was ten, he was seized by some crazy woman who threatened to throw him over a cliff – his step-father saved him and it was all filmed from a police helicopter.'

'So what's the problem with him? I would have thought the two were ideal for each other: good-looking pair, shared interest, shared experience. What could be better?'

'To Steve, that's probably the trouble. He can't bear the thought of losing her and the fire cult abduction had a terrible post-traumatic effect. In some ways it hurt Steve and me more than Emily. She's got amazing powers of recovery, but Steve's become obsessive.'

Sarah agreed. 'I'm not a psychiatrist but Dad's got to let go, and this is a bad time for him to hurt her.'

'He's a bit irrational about Tom. When he first appeared Steve got Paul Matheson to check on his background…'

'You mean Frank Matheson's son?'

'Paul's his son and he runs the investigative agency now Frank's retired. Anyway, Steve was most put out by what Paul found, although I say it's a load of rubbish.'

'What was it?'

'Tom hardly knew his birth father; he's been brought up by his mother and stepfather. But the wretched Paul turns up the fact that the birth father was a criminal who died in a motorboat accident. So that was just the excuse that Steve needed to damn the poor boy.'

'But Tom can't help his background, and you say he never knew his father?

'His father ran away to Australia when the child was six. Anyway, Tom's been with his mother and her new husband and they're one close family. As I said, it's the new father who saved the boy's life.'

'Kirsten, you're right about this and I don't like it. Emily and Dad have been close. This is the wrong moment for him to drive a wedge between them.'

Kirsten made up her mind. 'Never mind, Steve's got a massive problem to overcome so I doubt he's much time for Emily's love life. But, Sarah, you're not abandoning us just yet?'

'No fear, I've mapped out a recovery programme. I don't think we need send him to a long-term stroke clinic. We'll see if we can treat him in home surroundings. First your GP has to be alerted and call here in person. Give me the name of the practice and I'll do that for you. They can help me find a reliable nurse to administer the medication and generally keep an eye on things. We will also need a physio and some gym kit.'

'What sort of kit?'

'I can order that for you. It'll be a treadmill with secure hand bars and one or two other things. They'll go in the conservatory nicely. I'll drive over at least once a week.'

'Thanks, Sarah. I don't know how we'd have coped without you. Tell me,' she hesitated. This was the real question that she's hardly dared to ask. 'Will he get back to what he was before? I mean will he speak properly and walk normally?'

'I can't foretell the future, but I would say he'll relearn speech but there will likely be walking difficulty. Just remember this stroke was like an earth tremor, a warning. If Dad doesn't heed the warning and co-operate then the next one could be the earthquake'

'Why the hell should I talk to you?' Tom stared at the man. He was angry at the cheek of the bloke in following him. 'If it's about Emily Simpson and the fire cult I know no more than the rest of you – OK? You bloody tabloids only twist everything you're told.'

'I don't work for any tabloid. I am a freelance writer and I am a historian. I only care about Miss Simpson's Danish connections and those of her mother.'

'What about her mother? She adopted British nationality years ago.' Tom was still angry but he was also curious. This Hammersen character, whatever he was, didn't seem like Tom's conception of a nosy reporter.

'I'll come clean,' said Hammersen. 'Like Kirsten Simpson, I too have dual British nationality. I'm foreign correspondent for the Norge News Agency, but I research past history; at the moment I am planning a book on the German wartime occupation of Denmark and Norway.'

'Bit before our time I'd have thought.'

Hammersen smiled. 'Most of history is before our time. If you would let me buy you a cup of coffee I will explain. I am interested in the Elgaad family because their name keeps cropping up. Look, honestly, Tom, I'm not a muck-raker but no one can escape their involvement in these crimes.' Hammersen spoke in an undertone that was just clear through the buzz of conversation in the café.

'All right, punish the guilty, but why persecute Emily and her mother? Kirsten wasn't alive in World War Two, let alone Emily; she's only twenty-one.'

'You don't understand the psychological scars the Nazis left behind in my country, even to this day. No, Tom, if it is true that these people carry the blood of the beast then the world needs to know.'

This was more than Tom was prepared to take. 'What blood and what beast – man, you don't make sense.'

'How much do you know about those times, Tom?'

'Only what I've read.'

'Your own grandfather made a signal contribution to winning that war. The D-Day landings might have been badly disrupted but for his bravery.'

'Hey, you've been checking up on me – you've no business. Anyway granddad Wilson was my step-dad's side. He was quite a guy apparently – bit of a nutter ... killed himself sixty years ago.'

'So, my point. If he was really a nutter, you couldn't inherit his nuttiness because you don't have his blood.'

'My step-dad most definitely has his blood and he's anything but a nutter, and my stepsister is amazingly sane – quite scarily sane. Anyway, Dad Peter was a ship's captain for most of his life.' Tom didn't like any of this. He knew he ought to walk out at this point, but inwardly he was intrigued.

'Tom, I understand you are fond of young Emily?'

'You've got a bloody cheek, man. I don't think I should answer that. I met Emily at Bristol. I had no idea that she was the same as the kid in the fire siege.'

Hammersen stood up. 'I am not going to ask how close your relationship is; but a warning. It would be better for the world if that line were to die childless.' He held out a hand. Tom ignored him.

He watched the man walk from the shop. All right, Tom could spot a clumsy hint when he heard one. If this bastard was telling him to dump Emily then Tom wasn't going to play. But he was worried. If there were dark events in Emily's family past then he would like to know the truth of them.

Steve was bewildered. He had tried to get up out of the chair and had failed miserably. His left leg moved normally after a fashion. His right leg, not so long ago totally disconnected, was beginning to respond to intense mental effort. He supposed he had to thank that bloody physio woman for that. He hated to think how much more torture she would dish out until he could stand up again. He still had difficulty articulating a clear phrase let alone a whole sentence. It seemed he was a dumb cripple and would remain one unless he obeyed every command of these bossy women. The lovely double bed upstairs that he had shared with Kirsten for years was out of reach. He now had a single bed in the office with bars like a baby's cot, and most humiliating of all a hydraulic hoist to get him in and out.

He was a helpless child in the thrall of this bunch of female harridans. Sarah and Kirsten totally ignored his pleas and Emily seemed to be permanently cross about something. They were nothing compared to the great dictator who now ruled the house. Gwenda, the huge black Zimbabwean nurse, had taken over his life. Gwenda was unfailingly cheerful as she sadistically forced medications and injections into him and took his daily blood pressure readings. Between the three of them they stripped him naked twice a week and pounded him with merciless bed baths. It was utter and complete humiliation, and he was helpless to do anything to stop it.

'Man, you do what I tell you, everything I tell and then you get better,' was Gwenda's mantra.

But Gwenda was a saint compared to the female physio. Elsa came from somewhere in Eastern Europe. In Steve's eyes she was cruel and humourless and her exercise routines left him sore and exhausted. He compared her to Rosa Klebb, the twisted assassin outwitted by James Bond. As he lay on the hard cot bed he mentally planned the retribution he would bring to the whole lot of them.

His granddaughter, Christine was an angel. She sat patiently listening to his attempts at speech and cooked the foods of his choice. She would sit beside him as he ate and spoon up the last bits into his mouth. Steve could manage a fork and spoon, but it was rather nice to be baby-fed by this pretty girl. Next week he had been promised another ordeal. The speech therapist, evidently another bloody woman, would be working with him. With him was Sarah's description. On him was more likely, he mused.

He found visitors embarrassing. Many were from the world of sailing and few of them could conceal their feelings at the sight of him in the wheelchair. Steve hated this vile contrivance, but at the same time he felt a thrill of success when he found his arms were now strong enough to move the thing across the room. The doctor was another woman, although she seemed competent and knowledgeable about his condition.

Then there were the clergy; thankfully neither the village vicar nor the town's Catholic priest, ushered in by Sarah, actually went as far as praying over him. The vicar, a hearty ex-military, public school type, was rather good company. Steve wasn't so sure about the priest. The man was cheerful, but for Steve the notion of a fifty-two year old male virgin was disturbing.

The ultimate humiliation was the toilet. He had to be hauled onto a bedpan to do a faeces dump or feed his private parts into the neck of a urine bottle. In neither case could he perform his function without manual help from one or other of the bloody women. That meant Kirsten, or Sarah if she was present. Emily was squeamish and for some reason had become increasingly surly. This hurt Steve. He loved all three of his children, but having so nearly lost her, Emily had become especially precious to him.

Gwenda wasn't supposed to do physical lifting; her agency's rules said so. The first few times they had to call on the grumbling handyman-gardener. Then, rules or no rules, Gwenda had pushed the man aside, lifted Steve as it he was a child and whisked the bedpan beneath him. The women stuffed sleeping pills down his throat most evenings, and these had sparked surreal dreams. Often he dreamed that he was young again, playing football for the Saints youth team. Then he was sailing his Cadet dinghy with Miriam's kid brother as crew. Sometimes he would reprise that dramatic last leg of the Olympic race that won him his gold medal. It was then that he would wake up and stare at the ceiling as cloying depression seized him and then he would cry; weep real tears, until he fell asleep again.

Next the dreams would take a sinister turn and he would see faces. Lindgrune's thugs chasing him, and he was unable to move or lift a finger to save himself. Sometimes dead people would appear: his first wife Miriam, old Gerry, Wolfgang, and Steve's authoritarian Irish mother, all mixed up with historic characters like Churchill or Jack Kennedy. Then, if he was lucky, he could fall spinning into a vast pit and his sleep would become kindly, enveloping, and dreamless.

CHAPTER 6

Steve staggered off the treadmill and flopped into the wheelchair.

'Good, most good,' Elsa shouted. 'I think you have turned a corner as you English say.'

'If you think so,' he muttered. Elsa, or Rosa Klebb as he secretly called her, was staring at him as if he was some half-trained Labrador.

He supposed he should feel grateful. The woman was a sadist but he had to face the fact that she knew her trade. He could talk again and he was as close as damn it to walking again, and walk again properly he bloody well would. Already he could stagger around the garden paths supported by elbow crutches, but his attempt to throw them away had ended with a fall, then a screaming reprimand from Kirsten and a kiddies'-style telling off from Gwenda.

The speech therapist was a delight: a slim girl, dressed in a yellow frock with long blonde locks swirling around her bare shoulders. Her name was Stacey, and she spoke with a lilting Scottish accent. Her twice-weekly calls were at last something he could look forward to, although Kirsten treated the poor girl with a polite coldness.

Stacey helped him to breathe properly and then slowly adopt words that he could articulate correctly. Following six weeks of Stacey he could speak almost normally.

'Why are you talking like a worzel, Dad?' Johnny asked one day. The boy looked troubled rather than cheeky.

'How did he speak before his stroke?' Stacey asked.

'Well, not like that,' said Emily. 'He used to talk semi-posh, but now he sounds as if he's crawled out of a bog in Somerset.'

'It happens,' Stacey smiled. 'I had a patient with no speech whatever. She had to start again from scratch. We got her talking eventually, but her accent was American – pure Californian in fact, and she's never been to the States in her life.'

'Do I get some say in all this?' Steve spoke. 'I'm not some kid that you can talk over.'

'See what I mean,' Johnny laughed. 'Oi be from Zummset, oi be.'

'At least your father can talk again,' his mother reproved him. 'He can learn the Queen's English later. Steve, do you want to eat with the rest of us this evening?'

'Yes, I'd like to, but what am I eating?'

'Ham and chips for us – boiled fish and salad for you,' said Emily, 'and you can have a whole pint of … water!'

'Oh bloody hell, girl.'

Emily looked at her mother. 'OK, you can have real orange juice.' Emily parked the wheelchair in the office and handed her father the daily paper. Her mother stared at her and then indicated the door with a jerk of the head.

'Eight weeks,' said Kirsten. 'That's a great recovery but I suspect we haven't had the worst of it.'

'I know,' said Emily. 'Stacey warned me that he'll start to get really grumpy now. He's done ever so well but he'll start to fret because he can't do any of the things he's been doing before he got ill.'

Kirsten caught her daughter by the shoulder and stared into her eyes. 'Emily, you've been hiding something from me. You've been seeing Tom again.'

'I don't want Dad to know,' she muttered. 'I thought he'd dumped me – Tom that is, but then not long after Dad came home he began to text me.'

'All right, Em, don't get upset about it. In this I'm on your side.'

'Mum, Tom and me,' she tried to form the words. 'We're not as close as we were, Dad's won in that way, but there's something else and I don't know how to tell you.'

'We've got an expression in Danish, but the equivalent in English would be; don't prevaricate, whatever it is spit it out – are you pregnant?'

'God no – not that! It's something quite different, but it's worrying me sick. Mum, what is it about the war that Johnny and me are not allowed to know? You see, there's a writer bloke who's been worrying Tom. The man told him we're a bad family and Tom should dump me because I shouldn't be allowed to have children.' Now she had said it and instantly she wished she hadn't. Her mother had a mobile face but now it had screwed into horrid expression of pain, no not pain – grief surely.

'Oh, Em,' her mother was crying as she hugged her daughter. 'I'm sorry. We've tried to protect you from all this family shit – I'm so sorry, but there's things I can't tell you. I'm so sorry.'

'Mum, I'm sorry too, but no scummy little journalist is going to tell me I can't have children.'

Kirsten hugged Emily and kissed her hair. 'Of course you can have children, we dream of the day, but only when you meet a guy you can be happy with for life. Just like me and your father.'

'What did the man mean – why does he think we're bad?'

'Emily, this is very painful for your father and me, but we're not bad. All I can say is that your great grandmother had a child out of wedlock…'

'Is that all?' Emily interrupted. 'I know society was a bit stuffy about that in those days, but it doesn't make us bad.'

'No, Em, not us. That child was a lovely, gentle boy, but his father was evil – totally evil. This journalist must have found something we thought was safely buried, but he's got the wrong end of the stick.'

'You're talking about Great Uncle Kaj aren't you?' said Emily. She didn't know what to think. All her life there had been this family secret, these whispers among the adults – this terrible secret she wasn't allowed to know. Now she wasn't sure she wanted to know it.

'Mum, whatever it is, the man's not told Tom. He's hinted that I've got the bad blood, but Tom doesn't think it's a big deal. He told me that his own real dad was a crook but that doesn't faze him. I don't care about that war. Gerry won it for us when he fought the Battle of Britain.'

'Sweetheart, you've had a bad time these last few weeks. Why don't you take a break – go sailing.'

'Chloe's in New Zealand, Erin's in France, and we haven't got a boat.'

'Yes, you have – *Puffin's* on her mooring. We can't use her as things are, she's all yours.'

'I haven't got a crew.'

Kirsten smiled. 'I think you should ask Tom to go along. You two need a quiet interlude to sort yourselves out.'

Emily felt a little flash of joy, before reality came crashing back. 'I don't know that he'll want to go.'

'You can only ask him.'

'What if Dad finds out Tom's with me – *Puffin's* his boat?'

'Your father is drowning in his own troubles. He's not mentioned your Tom since he came home. I don't think he'll ask questions if you go away for a few days, and I am a very convincing white liar. He's never seen through me yet.'

Emily laughed. 'Mum, I do love you – wicked.'

Emily still wasn't sure if Tom would be up for a sailing trip. She had seen him once, briefly and painfully, in a Petersfield pub. It had been difficult for her; she couldn't sum up her feelings for Tom: love, lust, laughter and companionship. Tom had given her these and she believed she had given them to him. But there were other considerations. Tom didn't have wealthy parents. He was the adopted son of a harbour master and couldn't afford to spend an idle summer. Emily had wanted to pay for both of them to go on a gap year experience. Tom had been keen, but he had insisted on paying his share with money she knew he hadn't got. That wouldn't do. Tom had done his extra years as a post-graduate student. Emily knew he was up to his neck in student loan debt. She knew he had been looking for work locally but at their last meeting he had said something about going home to Dorset.

See u 5mins – ur place.

Tom's text took her by surprise. *Ur place* was their code for a meeting at the gate of Firs Farm and five minutes! Wow, he must be almost there. Emily looked around. Gwenda was stringing Dad's washed jamas on the drying frame, Mum was nowhere to be seen and Dad was indoors finishing his lunch.

It was a hot humid early August day and for once Emily was fully clothed, or at least she wore her jeans and a long-sleeve top. She knew she'd overdone the sun this last week, despite Mum's warnings and litres of screen ointment: her skin needed rest. She wanted everyone to see her shine at the ball in that expensive strapless gown, and she didn't want to reach old age like Mum – all wrinkly. Five minutes, Tom said. That was now. She sprinted down the gravel drive; she was still barefoot but her feet were hard enough. She reached the gate and stared up the road towards the village. She couldn't see the motorbike but a smart Renault was cruising towards her and the driver was Tom.

'Get in,' he said pointing at the passenger seat door.

'How come the car?' she was puzzled.

'Goes with the job,' Tom grinned at her as he put the car in gear and sped away up the lane towards the Downs.

'What job – how come?'

Tom showed her an identity disc. 'The company have hired me to programme all their systems in the South.'

He glanced sideways at her with a smug grin. Emily felt that sinking sensation: disappointment. It seemed her sailing cruise was over before it had begun and with it any hope of saving this relationship.

'Well done,' she forced a reply and tried to smile. 'So your degree has paid off.' Tom was a whiz at maths as well as computer theory.

He'd just received his PhD at the age of twenty-four. Maths was a blank for Emily, even though her brother was a walking calculator.

'Where can we go for a stroll?' Tom asked. 'I think it's time we talked this thing out, somewhere away from your family and anyone else.'

'And your journalist friend?'

'Hammersen, is not a friend.' Tom slowed the car before pulling over into a layby. He turned off the engine and for a few seconds he was silent.

'Emily, please believe me I will never gossip about you or your family. Also, please believe me when I tell you I don't believe a word of any of the stuff that creep has been implying.' Tom's usual macho bantering tone that so often irritated her was absent now. She felt a huge relief – he meant every word and she knew he still cared for her. But she wasn't going to let him off lightly.

'That sounds pretty bloody formal – how do I trust you?'

He didn't try to kiss her but he reached across and took both her hands in his. 'I've never lied to you, Em, you mean too much to me.'

'You sound like a Mills and Boon lover boy.'

'I wouldn't know – I don't read fiction.'

'And I don't read that kind of crap either, so don't say you've never lied. What about that time you got stoned out of your skin and Connie threw herself at you. Don't pretend it didn't happen – I've got witnesses.'

'I see,' he grinned in that annoying chauvinist way that she loved and hated. 'I see you're still set on being a barrister.'

'Yeah, I've got my degree, I've done the vocational course and I'm going to work in a law chambers this autumn.' She smiled in return.

'Lawyers are the only people who benefit from the recession – admit it.'

'Could be. I'm not going into the yacht business, that's disaster – Mum says we've got to tighten our belts next year.'

'I wonder – your family shops in Waitrose, my mum shops in Somerfield – vive la difference.'

Emily squeezed her long fingernails into his wrist until he winced. 'Let's go for that walk.'

Tom turned left into the approach road to Harting Down. He had been here before, several times, although he had never told Emily. This was the place where dad Wilson had been snatched, drugged and put in that helicopter.[*] Tom could remember every detail of those days at the age of ten when, for his own protection, he had stayed in the Eriksen's house with Alix and her dad, the film actor. To this day no-one, not even Alix, was certain who had done the snatch.

He had never told Emily about Alix, his childhood sweetheart. Alix now moved in more exalted circles, an actress in her own right, with a regular part in a soap. A pretty miserable role too – every time he'd watched it her character was either in tears or screaming abuse at some luckless man. The Duddlestone experience had cemented a bond between the two of them. It was a good bond, never to be romantic and sexual, but close, and he'd much rather Emily knew nothing about it.

He found a space at the edge of the car park that looked out across the flat landscape between the Downs and Petersfield. To the north-east they could see miles of open country, all the way to the far horizon and the Hog's Back above Guildford. If they walked along this ridge they would reach Beacon Hill and see Chichester Harbour seemingly at their feet and beyond it, Hayling, then the Solent and the Isle of Wight.

'How's your Dad?' he asked.

Emily turned to him and grimaced. 'He's a bear with a sore head.'

'What did you expect after everything he's been through?'

'Yeah, but he's ninety percent cured now but he just sits all day; he's so depressed he's almost suicidal…' Emily paused, and Tom knew she'd realised her gaffe.

He diffused the tension. 'That's the next part of his recovery, the mental part. You'll have to get him sailing again. Has he got that little boat over here yet?'

'The 2.4? Yeah, Dieter had it shipped over in a container along with three others. Brian from Branham rang last night – it seems it's been there for over a week.'

'What do the medics think?'

'They're not completely happy with his blood pressure but the cholesterol's down. They've told him to do a lot of walking on the treadmill – you know, build up the muscles.'

Tom opened his driver's door. 'Come on, it's time for our walk.' He reached across and stroked her cheek, and then for the first time he saw that she was shoeless. 'Will you be OK, walking barefoot?'

'Of course I will, haven't had anything on them for weeks – man,

[*] See *Rocastle's Vengeance* by James Morley.

I'm one hard cookie.'

Tom gave her a deliberate cold stare. 'At least you've got plenty of cover on the rest of you.'

Emily was out of the car now as she rested her hands on his shoulders. 'Once we get away from this car park there'll be no one around – then I can strip.'

'No, you won't. We're not bloody Scandinavians, and anyway, I'm right up to here with sodding Danes. You know Hammersen's a Dane or Norwegian – not sure which.'

'Yes, he told Sarah he was – come on, let's walk.' She provocatively waved the grubby sole of her left foot in his direction and began to sing in a watery contralto.

'And did these feet in ancient times
Walk upon England's mountains green'

'Yes,' she continued. 'Gilbert White called the South Downs a range of mountains, but I don't suppose you've ever heard of him.'

'Of course I have. He invented the science of natural history, the man had a really intuitive mind and he was a bloody vicar – can't understand that. Anyway, I wouldn't call these mountains green. The heat wave has scorched them to dirty yellow.'

'No they're not. They're golden – you've no romance – atheist!'

'Agnostic if you please – I've an open mind but I like scientific proof.'

'Which you won't get.'

Tom paused and took in the scene. The sun beat down but was not oppressive. The heat was diffused by the light breeze blowing in off the sea. 'Do you believe in God?'

'Yes, I think I believe in something out there. I prayed like crazy when I was shut in that cellar and I did feel something. I had made up my mind I was going to die, but I did feel some sort of presence – if I died it wouldn't be the end of everything.'

'When I nearly died I only remember being scared witless. That Jolene was going to throw both herself and me over a one hundred foot cliff…'

'I'm sorry, Tom, I didn't know; you've never spoken about it before.' Emily looked so downcast that instinctively he put an arm around her.

He knew he should have talked about his ordeal but it was something he could never bring himself to do. Emily was different, almost blasé about her experience and to be honest it must have been a much worse experience than his. He had suffered at the hands of a deranged female for a few hours. Emily, imprisoned for ten days by cold-blooded madmen, must still have demons, but one would never know it.

'I don't think any God saved me that day, but my step-dad put his life on the line. He saved me and it's funny, no not funny, but rather strange. You see when it happened he was shot, wounded, lost a lot of blood. We know he saw something. Mum says he calls out in his sleep, but he'll never talk about it.'

Emily swung round to face him. 'Then he should, and so should you. I'll never get over what happened, but I put it behind me when I went back to the place again and talked about it to that writer.'

'Come on,' he took her hand. 'Let's climb the hill.'

'Go away,' Steve snapped. 'I'm working.'

'No, I am not going away,' Sarah glared at him. 'I've had a lousy trip snarled up in traffic and I've only just got here.'

'Where's Emily?' he asked.

'I don't know; she went out hours ago.'

Steve wasn't satisfied with that. 'I want her here.'

'You can want all you like. She's got a life of her own.'

'What about me? I'm stuck here and none of you care. It would be better if I'd died, that's what you'd like.' He knew this wasn't true. He had no business taking his misery out on everyone in sight but he couldn't help it.

Sarah seemed completely unfazed by all this, which irritated him even more. He loved his eldest daughter, but he didn't care for her side as the bossy opinionated nurse. Gwenda had departed, although she still called twice a week. Kirsten wouldn't tell him how much all these fee-charging medics were costing him. Rosa the physio still came once a week to torture him, but pretty little Stacey had declared his speech restored and had left him with a list of therapeutic exercises. He hoped Stacey's departure had not been speeded by Kirsten's irrational dislike of the girl. Steve had no doubt all these medics were costing a bloody fortune and that cash would come from money Kirsten had salted away over the years. He knew half the shares they had bought in good faith were now worthless.

Easterbroke Europe had been forced to close three branches, one in Iceland for God's sake. Six unhappy Icelanders had lost their jobs. There had been loud protests from Iceland's tiny sailing community.

But Icelanders were hardly in a position to lash out money on yacht sails.

Steve had become obsessed with economy. He had taken to staggering around the house on his crutches turning off lights. Then Kirsten, Emily, or some other silly woman would turn them on again. They had tried to cheer him up by driving down to Itchenor to watch the sailing. Sarah had wheeled him around the sailing club and he knew everyone was pointing him out, gossiping and sniggering behind their hands. Sarah had denied it and told him he was paranoid. It was odd that his closer friends had chatted with him as if nothing had happened.

The first casualty of the recession had been the family sailing yacht *Traveller.* This traditional wooden boat had been expensive to maintain and was a ship that held bad memories. Kirsten and Steve had only just survived the attempt to sink *Traveller.* The police were certain that sabotaging the gas cylinders was the work of the sun cult, but that was a theory that had never been proved. Anyway *Traveller* was too big and too little used. Steve had sold her to a youth charity that had received a lottery windfall. The same week he had replaced her with *Puffin,* a little Hunter 27 from the same stable as *Glorfindel,* Sarah's old boat.

Steve had mixed memories of *Glorfindel* every time he saw her still sailing on the harbour. This had been the boat with which Sarah and he had retrieved the dead body of Per Elgaad and sparked a chain of events that had found Steve a new wife, and nearly caused a violent end for all three of them.

'What do you want for supper?' asked Sarah.

'Nothing – leave me alone.'

'All right, you can have sauce with your fish and I'll steam some broccoli.'

'I'm not hungry.'

'I don't care. You will eat your food because that is vital to you getting better,'

'I'll never be better – this is the end. The sooner I go the easier it'll be for all of you.'

Sarah stood arms on hips staring down at him. 'Do you want me or Gwenda to stuff more Prozac down your throat?'

'He glared back. Just you try and I'll spit your eyes out.'

'That is no way to talk to your own daughter,' Kirsten's voice was cold and angry. 'We are all doing our best for you. Why can't you see that?'

Steve knew he shouldn't lash back but he couldn't help himself. 'I'm tired, I'm a cripple, our business is failing and I wish I was dead.'

'If you are tired we can put you to bed, but don't forget I am the chairperson of your board. I am watching the finances and production is up in five out of eight branches and next April I predict a profit.'

'What do the bank say?'

'We closed the duff branches and they like that. So, no problem.'

'I wish I could believe you.'

Emily and Tom reached the top of Beacon Hill and stopped to take in the view of the Solent and the distant Isle of Wight. Emily loved this place, and today it was even more special. She flopped down on the ground and picked a strand of grass, which she began to chew. The air was warm and bumble bees buzzed among the wild flowers. It was all so peaceful and it smelt good. This was the moment she would use to drop a few hints.

'If we had powerful binoculars or a big telescope we might see *Puffin* on her mooring.'

'We haven't got a telescope, and one with that magnification would be too heavy to lug up here.'

Oh, you bloody insensitive git, Emily muttered inwardly. I love this man but sometimes he can be a complete moron.

There was nothing for it but to come straight to the point. 'Tom, darling, would you like to come sailing – just you and me on *Puffin*?'

At first he didn't answer. He too had picked a length of grass to chew. 'What sort of boat is this?'

Thank God, he was interested. 'Not a real racing boat – she's a cruiser, a Hunter.'

'Which version, British or Yank?'

'British, she's a Hunter 27.'

Tom swung round and grinned. 'You don't say – Dad Wilson's still got his – same boat he's sailed for fifteen years. He wouldn't change it for anything else.'

'Have you sailed in her?'

'You bet, me and a mate sailed over to Cherbourg last summer.'

'And your dad didn't mind?'

'No, he trusts me with anything to do with boats. Doesn't trust me with girls and money.'

'I thought he was rather sweet when I met him. I've never asked you what he thinks of me.'

'You really want to know?'

Tom delivered a rather bad imitation of the old sea captain's gruff voice. 'Lovely girl, you won't keep her – too good for you.'

Emily lay back and laughed. Tom leaned over and swung her legs into his lap. He began to rub the dirt from the soles of her feet and it felt nice. 'I've looked after my toenails,' she said. 'I want to wear my strappy heels to that ball Mum wants me to go to.'

'And who is taking you to that?' Tom had a sardonic grin.

'I rather hoped that you were, but since we've kinda' fallen out I did wonder.'

Tom looked her in the eyes. 'I'm sorry I cleared off like that. I will promise that nothing your father says and nothing that creep Hammersen hints at will push us apart – all right?' He lifted her until she sat astride him her face inches from his. 'How say we go on your boat over the bank holiday?'

'Oh, Tom, darling, I love you. That would be cool.' Emily felt excitement and inside her that familiar slow enveloping glow. 'Tom, make love to me.'

'Anytime you like, but not here. It's a bit too public and I can hear a whole gaggle of antiquated ramblers on the footpath over there,' he paused. 'Why don't you stay at my digs tonight?' He fumbled in his pocket and took a pen and a slip of paper.

'That's where I'm staying. So I suggest dinner in that restaurant in Lavant Street and then a bottle of wine and all the loving you want.'

'Can't we skip the dinner?'

CHAPTER 7

'Do you know who that was on the phone just now?' Kirsten stood in front of her disgruntled husband.

'Don't care.'

'I'm telling you anyway. That was Brian from Branham Sailability. We're taking you over there on Thursday.'

'Why?'

'They're putting your 2.4 in the water and you are sailing it.' Kirsten spoke with all the firmness at her command and she saw the flicker on interest on his face.

'Sailability on Thursday – you think I'm a cripple?'

'That's what you called yourself the other day. And don't you dare use that word at Branham, it's totally non-PC.'

She watched his face as a range of expressions showed. 'All right, I'll do it.'

She bent down and kissed him. 'Sailing, any sailing is what you need. Let's think of this as a turning point.'

Steve shook his head. 'I'll try it once, that's all I promise. Then on Monday I'm back to work.'

'Hello, Tom,' said Hammersen.

'What do you want?' Tom swung round to find the man standing beside the metal outside staircase that led to the bedsit.

'I've come to offer you good money. How would two K help you?'

'Coming from you I doubt it's clean.'

Hammersen was standing less than a foot away and his expression was not friendly. Tom clenched his fists. If this creep wanted violence he would have it returned with interest.

'You haven't taken my advice. My friend saw you with the Elgaad girl outside her house.'

'What friend? I would be surprised if you had any friends.' Tom was taunting the man now.

'I have plenty of friends, descendants of those who suffered in my country at the hands of Gerda Elgaad and her like.'

'Never heard of her.'

'My friend, as I call her, is another with grievance a bit nearer home. Her uncle died because of your girlfriend.'

'Emily never harmed anyone – she's suffered enough. Whose

uncle anyway?'

'My contact is Michelle Le Bois. Her uncle was a policeman. He died doing his duty.'

'Whatever he did, I've never heard of him either. I suggest that you sod off before I smack your ugly face.'

'I wouldn't do that, Tom if I was you. I wouldn't risk your employment potential.'

'Mind your own business.'

Hammersen smiled. 'My business is truth and justice. I don't want an evil line to be perpetuated. Believe me, I will go to any lengths to prevent that. So, what about that two thousand pounds?'

'Doing what?'

'Couldn't be more simple.' Hammersen held out a plastic tube. 'A DNA sample from Miss Elgaad. That should be easy.'

Tom hit him. He slammed his right fist into the man's face, following it with a straight left into the stomach below the rib cage. Hammersen seemed to fold in half as he slumped to the pavement. Tom ignored him and walked up the stairway to his temporary front door. Inside, he called Emily's mobile. She answered at once.

'Em, change of plan. I'll meet you in the town square and walk you to my place. Why? It's that man Hammersen he's been hanging around.'

Tom felt relieved that Emily did not ask questions. He determined not to reveal to her his recent violence.

'Right, Steve – today is the day, finish your breakfast and we'll go,' said Kirsten.

Steve grunted something before he replied. 'Where was Emily last night?'

'I think she's with some friends.'

'I want her here.'

'Never mind, you'll see her this morning at Branham – she's meeting us there. Now into the car with you – no arguing.'

Kirsten had a pretty good idea where Emily had been last night, but she wasn't telling Emily's overprotective father who had turned into a fractious child. Today was an important stage in Steve's recovery even if he didn't see it himself, and Kirsten was in a determined mood. She shoved the wheel chair down the little door ramp and across the gravel to the parked Volvo. 'Out of the chair and inside,' she ordered.

Steve grumbled but obeyed, sliding stiffly into the passenger side.

Kirsten fixed his seat belt and then folded the chair and put it in the back. Steve's bag of sailing gear and his buoyancy aid were already aboard. Kirsten drove the car through the gate and onto the road, heading north.

Emily had already arrived at Branham. This sailing club on a little lake was the place where she had honed her racing skills. Her name as Cadet World champion was on the honours board in the clubhouse.* But it had also been the place where she had encountered Grogan, the man who had abducted her and, with his mother and vile brother, had imprisoned her and threatened her with horrific death. She stood looking across the water. It had all happened just three miles away on the other side of that ridge. It didn't matter any more – she was at home here and it was a lovely day with sunshine and a gentle breeze from the northwest.

She wished Tom could be with her, but he and she had agreed this was not the time to confront Dad and declare the two of them to be an item. Their relationship had been welded in place last night, not just with great sex, there was so much more. The two of them seemed to have developed telepathy like an old married couple. Not that there was any talk of marriage; that was a long way off, if ever. Emily had ambitions to fulfil with her sailing team and her progress to barrister's chambers this autumn.

She walked back down the jetty and grinned as she saw the family's Volvo drive in through the gate and park in one of the disabled slots. Access Class dinghies and the big Challenger trimaran were being rigged by volunteer helpers. Already launched, and by the jetty, was a little 2.4 metre keelboat. Emily went and stood beside the boat. This was the Paralympic singlehander, a really competitive racing machine, actually a scale model of the 1970s America's Cup boats. Here came Mum and Dad. Dad in his sailing clothes was hobbling along supported by his crutches with Mum holding one arm. Behind him walked Brian, the guy who ran the Sailability arm of the club and with him a lady, who Emily remembered was Yvonne, the custodian of the hydraulic hoist.

Steve would not use the wheelchair. He would not be wheeled around like a baby in a place where he had taught his children to sail and had coached them and other youngsters to win races: he still retained some

---

* See *Emily's Hour* by James Morley.

pride. There was Emily standing beside a boat – his boat, the same that he had raced in Germany. He had good and bad memories from Kiel week. The medics had all insisted that sailing had not contrib.-uted to the stroke; that was down to inheritance, plus years of bad diet and careless lifestyle. It seemed he'd had it coming.

'Good morning, Steve – welcome home,' said Brian as he shook Steve's hand. 'Your boat's ready, we'll put you aboard and you can sail away.'

Steve's mood was lifting by the minute. Sailing was the one constant that had dominated his life. For weeks he had convinced himself he would never helm a boat again; his sailing had been lost forever. Now here he was back at Branham with a boat rigged and waiting for him. He felt something that he had thought he would never know again, the thrill of expectation before a race.

The cockpit floor looked a long way down from where he stood. 'Someone will have to help me in,' he said.

'No, said Kirsten. 'We will put you in the boat and when you finish we will lift you out.'

Yvonne held out a canvas with some straps and loops attached. 'This is your sling,' she said. 'We put it on you now and we'll lower you in. Just like your wife says; you sit in it and we lift you out again at the end.'

Steve had already noticed the hoist; a larger and more robust version of the one that Gwenda had lifted him in and out of bed with. He had bad memories of that one, but it looked as if he had no choice now if he wanted to try his boat.

'All right, just this once – but I'm not going to make it a habit.'

In the end the experience was not unpleasant and it certainly saved him the pain and struggle of finding his own way aboard. He settled in the cockpit and put his feet on the steering pedals. His left leg felt no different from last time although his right leg's response was slower. Kirsten and Brian were releasing the bow and stern lines and finally Emily, who had been watching him with a silly grin on her face, knelt down and gave the boat a mighty shove that took him past the end of the jetty and out into the lake beyond.

What followed became one of the most magical experiences of Steve's whole life. A gust of wind caught his sails. He adjusted the mainsheet and turned to run down the lake. He pulled the yellow line that poled out the jib and he was away. As he felt the wind on his face and the motion of the boat he was back in the world he knew. The sun was warm, and he could hear the ripple of the water past his hull and see the shoreline slipping by. Now a buoy, number six on the standard course lay ahead. He turned towards it, retrieved the poled out jib and rounded the mark to tack back up the lake. He could feel more wind on his cheek and see the tell-tale strings on his sails flutter and then straighten. As the boat heeled he tightened the jib and tweaked a tiny bit of tension on the backstay. Now they were really sailing. He and his boat were a single entity, as one with the wind and the water. What could compare with this? Nothing, not even sex – as if he'd had any of that for the last few months and he didn't care. He had a new love in this great little racing yacht. He was back where he belonged and nothing would ever change that.

That hour's sailing was better therapy than anything dished out by the medics. As he brought his boat gently alongside the jetty Steve was in as near a state of euphoria as he could remember. He knew his face had a stupid smirk as he was hoisted out of the cockpit and lowered into the wheelchair. 'Brian, that was brilliant,' he said. 'Can I join the race on Saturday?'

'Of course, we hoped you would, but don't beat the rest of us by too much.'

Steve laughed for the first time in three months. 'I doubt I'll beat anyone, not yet anyway.'

The drive home was a very different affair to this morning. Steve felt tired but he was relaxed and for the first time since his illness he felt happiness. At Firs Farm they found Emily and Christine preparing a late lunch, and for another first they allowed Steve to have a boiled egg. The day was hotter than ever and as he sat in the garden he saw Kirsten and the other two pull the cover off the pool.

'You coming for a swim Dad?' Emily asked. 'Elsa says that's one of the best things for you.'

'That woman is a bloody sadist,' he replied. 'But all the same, yes, I think I'll join you.'

He remained sitting in his chair and closed his eyes. A few minutes later he heard the patter of bare feet across the terrace and opened his eyes to see Kirsten and the two girls standing in front of him. Predictably all three were birthday-suit naked.

'You two dive in,' said Kirsten. 'I'll help the old prude into his trunks.'

Steve smiled inwardly. He'd had a good day. 'Forget the trunks – for the first time in my life the old prude will join you au naturel.'

Kirsten threw back her head in a gale of laughter. 'For an Englishman that is a life changing decision.'

CHAPTER 8

Emily was worried. Tom didn't pick up when she called his mobile and he wasn't answering her texts. She had wanted to tell him the whole story of Dad and his day's sailing. Yesterday Tom had suggested they eat a meal the following evening after he returned from work. She'd heard nothing from him since. Something had happened and she was worried. She had complete faith in Tom and felt secure in their reborn relationship. If she couldn't contact him it meant trouble. Had he crashed that unfamiliar car? Had he been in some other accident? She was apprehensive without any logic. She only knew something was wrong. The coming weekend was the holiday and she had staked so much on their clandestine sailing trip.

Ten minutes later her mobile rang. 'Miss Emily Simpson?' this very formal voice suggested trouble.

'Yes.'

'Miss Simpson, I am Paul Romero, I'm a Petersfield solicitor and I am acting for Mr Thomas Stoneman.'

'What's happened, has he been hurt?'

'No not hurt, Mr Stoneman has had a brush with the law. It seems he assaulted a man. The victim was treated in hospital and a complaint has been made. Mr Stoneman is in custody and will face magistrates in the morning. After that I am confident, at worst, he will be released on bail.'

Emily could not take this in. Magistrates courts and bail bonds were things she knew from her law degree but what on earth? 'Please, who is it Tom is supposed to have assaulted?'

'Yes, I can tell you that. It's one Karl Hammersen, he's a journalist and it seems he provoked the assault. But I'm afraid there are no witnesses. The thing is Mr Stoneman reacted to a mention of you, Miss Simpson. It seems Mr Hammersen asked him to obtain something from you and although I cannot condone Mr Stoneman's response I understand it.'

'Will he be out by the weekend?' Stupid question but that was all she could think to say.

'If we plead mitigating circumstances I am hopeful the bail option will not arise. I think it more likely he will receive a substantial fine.'

Emily felt that horrible sinking feeling. Tom would probably lose this new job and he hadn't money for a fine and certainly not for a substantial one. 'Would it help if I was a witness?'

‘Although you were not there at the time, as a character witness you might be able to smooth his path.’

‘Please, could you tell me what this is all about? What did this Hammersen want of mine?’

The solicitor coughed. ‘I will have to be absolutely frank with you, Miss Simpson. Mr Hammersen offered Mr Stoneman a considerable sum of money; two thousand pounds to be exact.’

‘Whatever for?’

‘Mr Hammersen suggested that in yours and Mr Stoneman’s intimate moments…’ The man paused and Emily sensed embarrassment. ‘Mr Hammersen wanted a sample of your DNA.’

Emily ran to find her mother. She felt confused, frightened, and like a child again. She couldn’t turn to her father so her instinct was to find her mother and pour out her troubles.

‘Why did Tom hit that man?’ Kirsten asked.

Emily could not tell her the truth. It was too humiliating. ‘Mum, Tom was defending me. That solicitor said the man made a dirty insinuation about me and Tom lost it.’

‘Oh, bloody stupid men, all of them,’ said Kirsten. ‘They never grow up.’

‘I don’t care what that man said about me. It’s Tom I’m worried about. He’s just got himself a job.’

‘Sweetheart, no recriminations; go to that court tomorrow and stand by him.’

‘That’s not like you, Mum. Where’s your feminism gone?’

‘No, remember we girls are stronger because we become mature. Men never stop being little boys.’

‘But we still need them.’

‘That is true.’

Steve had enjoyed his supper, even if consisted of boiled chicken and salad. Kirsten had opened a bottle of red wine and allowed him half a glass. Sailing at Branham had done more than restore his self-esteem; it had given him a new challenge. On Saturday he would sail his first race since Kiel. Already his head was buzzing with rig adjustments and tactics.

The swim had been a delight and the benefit had been instant. The water had been soothing and his leg and arm began to work in ways he remembered as normal. But swimming nude had been a revelation. He realised now what a hypocrite he’d been all these years. He had always loved seeing his wife naked in all her glory and the children had followed her habit from an early age. Kirsten was right and his squeamish English prudery was nonsense.

Emily had gone for a walk, something had upset her, but he knew better than to ask questions. Christine had vanished upstairs and he could hear the sounds of what he would not dignify as music. Not his cup of tea, but at least Emily was staying home tonight. Johnny was in the office with his homework: clever lad that one, and another good sailor in the making.

'Do you feel up to climbing stairs?' Kirsten interrupted his thoughts. 'We are fitting a stairlift tomorrow.'

'That's more expense. I'm sure I can get up our staircase without that. Why do you ask?'

'I sleep in a lonely empty bed and I haven't shared it with a man since we were in the hotel in Kiel. So how about it?'

'That's an offer worth struggling up a hundred stairs.'

'Come on then.'

'You have lost weight,' said Kirsten. 'We didn't realise how much until we saw you in the pool.'

'I've been ill and half-starved, so what's new.' Steve had enjoyed being stripped of his clothing, but this time it was in the security of the bedroom and a ritual they had performed a thousand times before. He lay on his back on the bed smiling up at his nude wife squatting astride his thighs.

'I also have been starved by your illness,' she said. 'Do we do this or do I have to hire a toy boy.'

'I'm up for it if you are.'

Kirsten bent forward and began to plant long smacking kisses into his groin while she soothed him with her hands. 'Up for it – what a true choice of words. The doctor tells me it is safe for us to make love, but she said we would probably need viagra to get you going.'

'It seems she's wrong about that.' He extended the fingers of his left hand between her legs. 'My little doorway to heaven.'

Kirsten did not reply. She slid forward and thrust him deep inside her.

The next morning Emily showered and dressed, choosing the dark outfit that she had worn beneath her academic gown at the degree ceremony. She recovered her car from the lean-to barn and drove the twenty-mile trip to the magistrate's court in Alton.

She hadn't slept too well last night, and when she had dozed off she had been inflicted with yet another visitation of her sun cult ordeal. Emily was destined for a legal career, but she wondered if any future court appearance would stress her as much as this one. She parked the Mini in the car park by the police station and walked the short distance to the court building. Mr Romero, the solicitor, met her inside and took her to an empty room. Despite his name the man did not look remotely Spanish. He was middle-aged with thinning hair. She suspected he'd been chosen for this job as the office Buggins' turn. But it was not routine for her.

'Can I see Tom?' she asked.

'Not until this case is heard. We're due in court at eleven but they're running a bit behind. The clerk isn't happy but Madam Chair is not in a mood to be hurried.'

This worried Emily. 'You mean she's in a bad mood?'

'No, I think she's very thorough, that's all.'

Romero looked at his watch. 'I've brought you in here to avoid Mr Hammersen. He's out there and looks a bit the worse for wear. I think it's better he doesn't see you until the actual session.'

'Do you know what's biting him?'

'Emily, may I call you Emily? To put it bluntly, Hammersen is a zealot, he's a genuine scholar but he's zealous in his pursuit of Nazis.'

'I gathered that, but there can't be too many of those around. It was all donkey's years ago.'

'That's not the point. Hammersen has got it in his head that you are descended from some war criminal whom he won't name.'

Emily understood now. For God's sake, was great Uncle Kaj a by-blow of Hitler? She wasn't an expert on World War Two, but received opinion seemed to think that Hitler was incapable of getting any woman up the duff. There was another more important fact that blew Hammersen into the water. 'My grandfather was Jewish, so he can't have been a Nazi. I know for a fact he only escaped death by the skin of his teeth.'

'It that so?' Romero looked smug. 'We'll save that for the court. I shall be asking you questions and we'll lead round to that. And you can testify that Mr Stoneman is normally all sweetness and light.'

Emily wasn't at all sure about that, but she knew an element of hypocrisy was common in court provided it stopped short of perjury. Romero excused himself and left to talk with his client.

She sat nervously for half an hour. If she had been a kid she'd be biting her nails. Distantly she could hear muffled voices within the courtroom and louder conversation in the corridors. At last a kindly looking lady in a black gown beckoned her to follow.

'I'll sit you in the witness seats,' she said. 'When you're called you'll take the oath and then answer any questions the court puts to you.'

Emily knew that in a few years it would be she who would be asking the questions but for now she was scared. The magistrates, two elderly males and the woman chair sat on a dais; all polished wood. Now she could see Tom. He'd been ushered into a glass-fronted cubicle accompanied by a policewoman.

The chair opened the proceedings. She called the solicitor for the crown to put his case. The man seemed bored but he described how Thomas Stoneman had assaulted Karl Hammersen resulting in Mr Hammersen being taken to hospital.

Hammersen was next. Emily had seen him before hanging around Firs Farm. The man walked steadily to the witness stand and didn't look particularly damaged. The prosecutor led Hammersen through his account of the assault.

Now it was Romero's turn. 'Mr Hammersen, there must have been some reason for you being attacked?'

'I made a reasonable request and the man reacted in a vicious and uncalled for assault.' Not a trace of a Norwegian accent.

'What was that request?'

'I am a historical researcher. I simply requested a DNA sample.'

The chair intervened. 'That's a rather personal request. Why did you want Mr Stoneman's DNA?'

'Not Stoneman's DNA, the woman's he's been seeing.'

'And Mr Stoneman didn't like that request?'

'He didn't need to turn violent, and I offered him money for it.'

'What is so special about this woman that you require DNA?'

'It's the last piece in the jigsaw. It will prove that she is of evil blood.'

The chair was clearly not impressed. 'What on earth do you mean by that?'

'I have evidence that this woman, who calls herself Emily Simpson, is descended in direct line from the leadership of the Nazi Party.' There was a timbre in Hammersen's voice that recalled something: a hell fire preacher perhaps.

'The facts please?' ordered the chair.

'Stoneman didn't give me a chance to explain – he attacked me. I wasn't prepared – it was uncalled for.'

'Mr Romero?'

'No more questions.'

'You may stand down.'

'Call Thomas Stoneman.'

Tom was released from the dock area and took the oath. Emily tried to catch his eye but he looked straight ahead. Emily knew from his voice that he was still angry. He was questioned by the prosecution and admitted the basic facts that Hammersen had claimed.

'And did that justify your vicious assault?' asked the prosecutor.

'He made a disgusting suggestion concerning my girlfriend. He gave me this.' Tom held up a tiny glass tube. 'He suggested I collect samples during our private moments. Then he offered money.'

'What private moments...?'

The chair intervened. 'I think we all know what Mr Stoneman means. Do you have any more questions?'

'No, your honour.'

'Mr Romero.'

'Mr Stoneman, you are fond of this young lady?'

'Of course.'

'Are you aware of the things about her ancestry that we have just heard?'

'They are fantasy.'

'Would you agree that your reactions were natural and driven by misguided chivalry?'

'That is fair comment.'

'Thank you, no more questions.'

'Mr Stoneman,' said the chair. 'I think we can trust you enough to let you sit in the court and not the dock.'

'Thank you,' said Tom.

'Mr Romero, have you any more witnesses?'

'Your Honour, I want to call Miss Emily Simpson.'

Emily walked down the steps from the witness seats and took the stand. She repeated the words of the oath and waited. Now a surprise; the chair addressed her.

'Miss Simpson, I see in the well of this court a lady and a gentleman of the press. I understand that you are the same Emily Simpson who was abducted seven years ago and was very much in the news...'

'Your honour, I must object,' said the prosecution. 'This has no relevance.'

'I think the newspapers will disagree about that, but carry on.'

Romero spoke. 'Miss Simpson, how well do you know Mr

Stoneman?'

'I've been going out with him for five months – we're friends.'

'Ask her about her grandfather?' Hammersen shouted.

'Silence,' the court clerk hissed.

Emily knew her part now. 'Which grandfather would that be? My grandfather on my father's side was a merchant navy officer and he was killed in the war.'

'The other one,' Hammersen snarled.

'Court officers, remove that man please,' called the chair.

Complaining loudly Hammersen was hustled from the room.

Emily saw her opening and she went for it. 'My mother's father was Jewish, so he couldn't have been a Nazi, could he?'

Suddenly there came a subdued rumble of supportive voices. Someone began to clap.

'Silence,' the clerk called.

'Mr Romero, have you any more questions for this witness?'

'No, your honour. I think the facts speak for themselves.'

She stared at the prosecutor. The man shook his head.

'Miss Simpson you may stand down.' said the chair. 'Mr Stoneman, please step forward.'

Emily walked back to her seat, while Tom was escorted to stand in front of the chair like a small boy facing his head teacher. The three magistrates conferred in a whispered conversation. The chair nodded and turned to face the court.

'Mr Stoneman,' the chair looked down with a severe expression. 'You have been extremely foolish and there is no doubt that you assaulted this man and caused some physical harm. However in mitigation it may be said that you were most sorely provoked and that you were defending the honour of your lady friend.' She paused. 'Don't let me ever see you in this court again. Case dismissed.'

'Thank you,' Tom replied.

Emily rushed forward and Tom caught her in his arms. Now all formality had gone. The spectators in the witness seats applauded and the Madam chair smiled down benevolently. Then Romero hustled the pair of them out into the foyer.

'Wait there a moment,' he said, and then slipped out into the street.

He returned a few minutes later. 'It's all clear; Mr Hammersen has vanished. I think it would be better to avoid any further confrontation with such a deluded individual.'

They both thanked the man. Emily knew that Tom could not qualify for legal aid. She asked how much his fees would be.

'Very modest in this case,' Romero smiled. 'After all I didn't have to do much work; the plaintiff sort of hoisted himself with his own petard. That's why the prosecution threw in the towel.'

'Send the bill to me,' said Emily.

'Oh, look here…' Tom started to protest.

'No!' Emily cut in. 'You're in enough shit anyway and I learned stuff today that will help me in my career.'

'She wants to be a barrister,' Tom explained.

'Judging by the way she spoke up today, I'd say she'll be a rather good one,' said the solicitor.

Tom could hardly believe his good fortune. He had been through this ordeal and come out unscathed, or at least he didn't have the stigma of a criminal record. He should be able to keep his job and face his mother and stepfather with a reasonable explanation. And he knew he owed it all to Emily. He put his arm around her waist and she snuggled her head against him.

'Let's get out of this town,' he said. 'Where can we get a bite of lunch a long way from here?'

'Come on,' said Emily. 'Let's get the car and I'll drive you.'

They left Alton and drove for half an hour past Petersfield and into the village of Buriton in the shadow of the Downs. Emily parked her Mini behind the pub and they stood breathing in the delicious warm air. The village was quiet but they could hear the drumming of combine harvesters somewhere not far away.

'Who was Master Robert?' asked Tom as he looked at the Inn sign.

'I'm not sure,' she said. 'I just thought this was a place we might find a quiet table for lunch. It's one of our favourite pubs and I'm hungry.'

It was only when they sat down at table that they realised just how hungry they were. Tom had had some meagre rations in the police cell but Emily had been too agitated to eat any breakfast. Both were overwhelmed with relief at the end of the ordeal. They were young, in love, and in need of a meal and a lot of talk.

'What will your father say, when he reads about today?' Tom asked.

'Why should he read about it? We don't take the local paper from that town.'

'Come on, Em; use some sense. Those journos won't leave it to the local rag, they'll sell the story on. Think, little Emily from the fire siege in court to defend her man. The London tabloids will love it.'

'Dad doesn't read the Sun and we wouldn't wipe our bottoms with the Daily Banner.'

'All right, but I wouldn't bet on the Times or the Telegraph not picking it up, and running with it and I know your dad always watches the local news on telly.'

'Tom, you are making me depressed again and I was on such a high. OK, what do I do?'

'There's only one thing you can do. Go home and tell him the truth, the whole truth…'

'And nothing like the truth,' Emily giggled. 'I say, do you know Dad swam nude in our pool yesterday – first time ever. He's all skin and bone now, but I can see why Mum fancied him.' She giggled again. 'He's amazingly well equipped.

Tom laughed. 'As well equipped as me?'

'If you're as big as that when you're pushing seventy, I won't be complaining.'

CHAPTER 9

'Steve, you will have to give way on this one,' said Kirsten. 'Tom is a good boy, I like him and I would have thought he was just your type.'

'I must say I like the way he stood up for Emily and I can't blame him for thumping that little turd of a reporter. I'm worried about how much that character really knows. I thought we'd buried Gerda's sins for all time.'

'He's certainly got hold of something but it could be the wrong end of the stick completely. Emily seems to have the idea that Kaj was Gerda's son by Hitler.'

'If this Hammersen thinks that he's wildly out. There's overwhelming evidence that Hitler was incapable of normal sex. It was one of the things that made him how he was.'

'I know,' said Kirsten. 'Not like Kaj's actual father. I would bet good money that Kaj wasn't the only love child of that philanderer.'

'I tell you something,' said Steve. 'There was nothing the least bit German about your Uncle Kaj. He was a Dane all right. His life story was almost a rerun of Hamlet.'

'Can we do anything legally to stop Hammersen from persecuting Emily?'

'Legal injunctions you mean?' said Steve. 'That's going a bit extreme and it would only make him worse. Let's leave it.'

In the meantime,' said Kirsten, 'is it OK for Emily and Tom to borrow *Puffin?'*

'I won't be needing her for a while. The boy can sail and Emily can navigate so I've no objection. They'll need the ship's papers in order if they cross the Channel.'

'They're not doing anything so ambitious; it's only a three-day holiday. They're talking of sailing the boat to Duddlestone where Tom's parents live. Tom says if the weather turns foul they'll leave the boat there and come back by train.'

'That sounds sensible.'

'Now,' said Kirsten, 'remember that tomorrow you will be sailing and you'll be racing your new boat.'

Having coached youth at Branham he knew many of these people already. There was little difference between the able-bodied and disabled competitors in sailing skills. The sit-down cockpits of the boats provided a level playing field, and Steve knew he would be up against some useful helms. The 2.4 race at Branham was a regular event on every Saturday of the year. To have an Olympic medallist, even a geriatric one, sailing was an event. The regular sailors were a mixed bunch of able bodied and disabled, some old, some young and all devoted to their miniature craft. Steve felt a bit of a fraud at the awe in which he was held.

Brian listed the helms and boats he would need to watch out for. 'Both the guys called Paul, Bruce, Phil, Richard, Myron, and Tim of course; I think you've already raced against him. The others aren't bad, except Jim – he's hopeless.'

'At least there's someone I'll beat,' Steve replied.

'More than one. You being here has raised a little flutter of anticipation.'

Sailability volunteers had already launched his boat and bent on the sails. The wind had picked up since Thursday's outing and sharp gusts were bouncing over the trees. Typical Branham weather and just the test he needed. This time he felt no indignity from being lowered aboard by hoist. It saved him from much pain and loss of concentration. Now for an hour's practice.

It was the same magic as ever, but even more so now as he got to grips with a fresh breeze. A strong wind at Branham was a different proposition to one on the open sea. It was one reason why so many top sailors, like his Emily, had been bred on this water. At sea a strong wind remained a steady and directional one. At Branham such a wind played tricks in the form of lulls followed by fierce gusts. And these gusts were anything but directional. Twenty-degree shifts were normal; to win a race a helm needed concentration allied to a complete understanding of his or her boat.

The start was not his best: Steve knew his hearing had been affected and he never heard the signal. As a result he found himself second from last at the first mark. He was angry now, not with the other helms, but with himself. He settled down to fight the windward leg of the course. Crouched in the cockpit he felt the wind slam into the rig, heeling the boat as water splashed onto the deck and the rigging began to vibrate. He tightened the backstay and steered gently into the gust. He hardly had to touch the pedals, so well was the boat set up and tuned. The gust passed and he released the backstay to increase sail power. Now he could see where he was. At least seven boats had taken a course near the north shore of the lake. He would pass clear ahead of all of them on the next tack. The windward mark was ahead now, closing fast. A foul shift forced him to bear away; he wouldn't make it on this tack. His racing brain was functioning as of old. No way would he short tack and lose ground. This was gambling time. He bore away some more to increase speed. The mark was five metres away to windward. Now, use that speed, harden up and shoot the distance straight into the wind if need be. Yes, his luck was in as the wind shifted again in his favour. The buoy slid safely by.

They were on a downwind leg now. Steve hauled on the line to pole out the jib and released the backstay to let the mast slope forward. His practice session had confirmed that the gusts were strongest in the centre of the lake but still shifting. The Steve Simpson of old had been one of the world's greatest downwind specialists. He set his sights on the two craft in front of him. He could feel the breeze in his hair and hear the stern wave bubbling behind. The wind was shifting – gybe over – reset the pole. Good, no reaction by the other two. Now steer up a couple of degrees, and yes, he felt the acceleration as the little digital readout said seven knots. The others were gybing but too late: Steve had the inside line as he rounded and went onto the next windward leg.

He was leading now, but he wasn't complacent. His opponents were all useful helms and had more experience in these boats than he. He blessed Dieter and old Wolfgang who had bequeathed him this beautiful state-of-the-art racer. He doubted if he had ever sailed a boat that had such a living personality. It was almost as if she was telling him to leave her alone to win the race. A dollop of spray smacked on the foredeck and into the cockpit. Water was slopping around the floor beneath his seat; must be a sign of his inexperience with this type of craft. He grabbed the pump handle with his right hand, the ill-functioning arm, but he didn't care. The pain meant nothing as, teeth gritted, he worked the handle until the pump sucked dry. His condition made it almost impossible to turn round and see his opponents. Maybe he should fit wing mirrors. Steve would take no more chances with the wind shifts. He tacked to gain windward position and then saw that the other boats were way behind and he had a perfect line to the mark. He almost punched the air. And this time he heard the sound signal and saw the number boards on the starter's hut. Finish from leeward mark.

Steve could hardly believe it. His racing sense was back, his coordination was good and he loved his boat. Ten minutes later it was all over. He crossed the line. He had won. He drifted back to the jetty, sails flapping and remembered to berth under the hoist. Now he felt very weary. He was intensely happy and in the grip of a pleasing languor and a sudden longing to lie down and sleep. Distantly he heard the finishing signals for the other competitors. He looked up and there stood Kirsten with a beatific grin all over her face. Beside her a volunteer helper was winding the hoist down to him. His sling was reattached to the rig and he was raised up onto the jetty. Kirsten pushed the wheelchair beneath him and he was gently lowered into it. A week ago he might have found this humiliating but now he didn't care.

Tom had confronted his problem head on. He wasn't going to let his new boss read a garbled account of the court case. He had dropped Emily at home and driven to his company's HQ in Southampton. There he was told he couldn't have an interview with the big-cheese without prior appointment. He explained the problem to the secretary and she told him to wait. Waiting meant kicking his heels for an hour.

The managing director was a cheerful technocrat in his early forties. Tom told him the whole story holding nothing back.

'OK, Tom, I'm not unsympathetic. Did you at any point give away who your employer is?'

'No! Absolutely not!'

'Is there any chance that this man you hit knows where you work?'

'Sir, I've only worked for you since last week. I can't see how he can know.'

'Well, that's good news. You've got excellent qualifications – very hard to find someone with as good as yours. But, Tom, this must be a one off. You will meet a few very irritating people in your line of work and I don't want more trouble.'

'I know, sir, but however irritating they won't insult my girlfriend.'

'Anyway, it seems you made a good impression on the court. You say the case was dismissed, and that means you have no stain on your character. We could be in trouble ourselves if we disciplined you.'

'Thank you.'

Tom's boss looked puzzled. 'This man you tangled with seems obsessed with heredity. My grandfather was an alcoholic – drank himself to death. I enjoy a glass of wine but in moderation.'

A very relieved Tom left the offices and called Emily from the car park. All he got was that maddening recorded voice telling him another caller was on line. He left a message asking her to ring back. At last all was clear for their sea trip to Duddlestone.

It was late afternoon when a call came on Emily's mobile.

'Hi, Emily, mate – it's me – Chloe.'

'I thought you were still in New Zealand,' said Emily. Chloe was the helm of their match racing team and the one who cornered all the glory. Emily didn't really mind too much as everyone in sailing knew that two thirds of the work was down to the middle and bow men, or girls in their case. Apart from that, Emily's duty was to look out and call the tactics and, without too much conceit, she knew she was good.

'Em, mate, you still there?' Chloe's voice was shrill and antipodean.

'Yeah, I'm here. Where are you speaking from?'

'Auckland, where else?'

'You sound like you're in the next room.'

Chloe cackled with laughter. 'Jeez, twelve thousand mile shout.'

'When are you back here?'

'Flying back next Friday. Tell you what: hear my news. We've had our funding renewed – what about that?'

'Chloe, that's fantastic.' Emily could have leapt with joy. Central funding was granted only to top-flight sailors.

'Guess what, mate. It's full steam ahead for Olifa.'

Emily knew practically nothing about this South American venue. 'Chloe, you ever sailed there? What's it like?'

'Good from all I've been told. Good facilities already and a swanky Yankee yacht club. Plenty of dosh – whole country's swimming in oil.'

The next Olympics were in four year's time and the South American Olympic Federation, had chosen the Republic of Olifa as their nominee location. All anyone knew was that this was a stable, if authoritarian, country with incredible wealth mixing with dire poverty. There had been rumbles of complaint from Mexico and the United States, but the rest of the world had endorsed the decision. Emily and her crewmates did not give a damn about the politics. They believed they were good at their sport and they wanted to prove it in the toughest competition the world could offer.

'When do we get together?' Emily asked.

'Erin's still in France. New boat should be ready in December. How about Christmas in NZ?'

Emily wasn't too happy about that. She wanted Christmas to be at home with her family and Tom. She had no idea what Erin, the third crew member, was planning. Olympic funding was all very well, but Emily had a career to follow. It was all right for Chloe the army officer. The MOD regarded such people as sporting role models and gave them lavish time off. Emily wanted to be a barrister and she wanted Olympic glory. Could she combine both? Time would tell.

She said goodbye to Chloe and then saw from her message box that Tom had tried to call. Momentarily she panicked and muttered an expletive. She had almost forgotten that Tom had this bloody interview with his boss. Fumbling with the mobile's buttons she called him back.

'Em,' Tom replied. 'It's all fine; I'm in the clear. Wait outside your gate and I'll be with you in twenty minutes.'

Emily laughed. 'Can't do that.'

'Why not?' he sounded suspicious.

'What do you think, I'm sunbathing by the pool. I'm not in a fit state to wander around on the roadside and you've been invited to supper. You are now accepted and respectable. Dad's OK, in fact he rather approves of what you did.'

'No longer persona non grata,' said Tom.

'Hey that's legal talk. Anyway, Tom?'

'Yes.'

'I love you.'

'Me too.'

'What, you love yourself. I know that – what's new?'

'No, you crazy girl, I love you.'

Steve woke slowly and drowsily. He looked at the bedside clock. It was seven o'clock and it was Sunday. Kirsten's side of the bed was empty, but the silly girl had this masochistic early rising habit. His mother had always called this: "the best part of the day". He tried to sit up but slumped back on the pillows. He'd forgotten his crippled state and he wasn't sufficiently recovered to leap out of bed and waltz around the bedroom. Things had improved the last few nights, ever since he had resumed his rightful place in his wife's bed. If he was careful and measured, he could swing his legs to the floor, grab a crutch and stagger the few yards to the toilet. Sarah had told him something about inflated prostates and the need to have the organ whipped out by surgery. For a disabled man who had rediscovered sex the prospect held no attraction. He would rather pay for his pleasure with three times a night struggles to the bathroom.

He was living, eating and dreaming sailing. His mind was buzzing with racing tactics. Ashore after yesterday's race he had been surrounded by his fellow competitors. He had demolished all of them in the race he had won but there was no jealousy; everyone had been genuinely pleased.

'You've got to sail in the Nationals,' someone had told him.

'Where's that?' he asked.

'This year, at Rutland.'

Steve knew Rutland: the huge inland sea, supplying water to Midland cities. 'I'm not up to driving yet, and there's no way I can get the boat there.'

'We'll get your boat there and your wife has told us she'll drive you.'

Steve was warming to this prospect. He knew he could use three racing weekends at Branham to sharpen his skills. But at the nationals he would be competing against the best helms in that class: all the heavy hitters. He would find out all he could about Rutland. But he had other things on his mind. Tomorrow was Monday, August bank holiday but Tuesday would be his first day back at work.

'Is that Hammersen still around?' Emily had to ask.

'No sign of him, thank God,' said Tom.

'But there's something still bugging you?'

'I've been wondering whether I should say something about it but now I don't know.'

Emily knew she shouldn't be exasperated, not on this lovely morning, but she needed to know. It was this telepathy between them or, more likely, she had developed a fine antenna for picking up Tom's inner thoughts. He was worried about something and it concerned her. And because it concerned her he didn't want to tell her.

She caught hold of his arm just below the elbow and squeezed. 'I would feel better if you didn't keep secrets. What is it you don't want me to know?'

'Bloody hell, Em – you're going to be a really intuitive lawyer one day. All right, it's not Hammersen; it's someone else he told me about. He said some girl called Michelle something, can't remember the surname. He said the woman's uncle had died because of you.'

'Because of me – how come?'

'Hammersen didn't say, but I think it was something to do with the fire cult.'

'Tom, for God's sake,' Emily was aware now. 'The two men in the cult were both bachelors and I'm sure neither had any kids. I would bet money they had no kids. That was the whole trouble; they were indoctrinated mummy's boys – sexually sterile.'

'Hammersen said the woman's uncle was a policeman.'

Now Emily understood and the revelation almost rooted her to the spot. ‘Oh Jesus. Tom, was the surname Le Bois? You know – French?’

Tom looked thoughtful. ‘Yes, that was it. Who is he, and why a French policeman?’

Emily didn’t know what to say. In her mind she had been lifted straight to that scene – the early morning – running for her life. ‘Le Bois came from the Channel Islands. I never heard that he had any family.’

‘Em, you’ve got to tell me now. Who is he?’

‘Philip Le Bois was a copper. He was mentally ill and delusional. He thought some friends of ours had done the murders and nothing would shift him from that. He was hanging around the scene at the end and that got him killed. It’s nothing to do with me. I never saw it. I was running and shit scared.’ Emily didn’t care to mention that she’d seen the man seconds before he’d been gunned down. She recalled the horrible whine of the bullets. Thank goodness she’d been too frightened to look back.

‘I must say,’ said Tom, ‘I can’t see why this Michelle should have a grievance against you.’

Emily wasn’t so sure but she did her best to be cheerful. ‘Come on, we can’t stand here; let’s get afloat.’

They launched their little inflatable and piled their sailing gear plus the food inside. Emily pull-started the little outboard motor and they headed away up the Chichester Channel to where their little ship awaited them.

CHAPTER 10

John-Kaj Simpson was awake. He glanced at his bedside clock. It read two in the morning: three hours until dawn. Normally he slept well but he couldn't tonight and for this he had no rational or medical answer. He rolled over and shut his eyes tight but it was hopeless. He turned on the light, slid off the bed and tiptoed across to his computer. Half an hour of solving mathematical puzzles should be just the catalyst to bring on sleep. His friend Pete used his computer to look at dirty pictures of girls. Johnny couldn't see what the interest was. Nakedness was no big deal. He saw it every day in hot summer weather, swimming or lounging around the pool with Mum, Emily and that Christine. Pretty clothed girls were another matter. Only yesterday Nikki had thrown her arms around his neck and kissed him before running away shrieking with laughter. He wondered if he dared ask Nikki for a date. Maybe, but she was just a kid, still a month away from her thirteenth birthday, while he was fourteen. And she was thick: couldn't recite her twelve times table without a calculator, let alone solve an equation. Pete said that didn't matter because thick girls made good wives and didn't want to rule the world. Johnny wasn't sure about that, but he knew better than to repeat this view in front of Mum and Emily.

That was odd, somebody was moving around downstairs. He had distinctly heard a sort of slapping thud – a book falling off a table he guessed. Emily was away sailing and Dad used the new stair lift. Anyway Mum and Dad were asleep. In that case, if one calculated the balance of probabilities, they had an intruder in the house. Dad wasn't in a fit state to tackle him. Mum would probably try but he didn't want to risk her being hurt. Emily's boyfriend, Tom, would flatten the intruder and then he, Johnny, could make a citizen's arrest. Well, Dad was ill, Mum was old and Tom was with Emily somewhere at sea. It was up to him to find out what was happening. As quietly as he could manage, Johnny slid open the drawer where he kept his little camera. He switched it on and checked the flash. His bedroom door was already open a fraction; probably that was the reason he had heard something.

He stood on the landing leaning over the banister. Now he felt nervous. He could see into the hallway and there it was: a flicker of torchlight from the open office door. Johnny tiptoed back along the passage and peered through the door of his parents' room. Moonlight was filtering through the open window. They were both there. Should he wake them? No way! Dad would want to do something stupid and Mum would go crazy, rush downstairs and get hurt. He'd do this on his own. No heroics – just gather the evidence.

He made no sound on the carpeted stairway and reached the hall in seconds. He made a calculation. Do not walk in a line of sight from the office door. He moved over and crept towards the opening. He could see the torch moving around, and he could hear the opening of drawers. He crouched on the left hand side of the doorframe, took a deep breath, stood up, and stepped into the doorway. He pointed the camera and pressed the button. The flash lit the room. Johnny found himself blinking but he had seen the intruder.

It was a slight figure bending over Dad's desk and clad from head to toe in black. The man turned sharply and Johnny pressed the button again and again and again. He could see now that this was no man; the face was that of a woman, not a lot older than his sister, but thinner and with a shock of short black hair. He prepared to run upstairs and take shelter in his parents' room. Instead of attacking him she vaulted through the open window. Johnny was relieved but he also wondered why Dad had been so careless as to leave a window unlocked and the burglar alarm unset. It was because of the heat wave of course but still careless. Now he was shaking. He felt cold and that was silly because the temperature must be at least eighteen centigrade. What would have happened had the woman not panicked but instead had done what she should have done and seized his camera?

'Have you any idea what this intruder was looking for?' asked the police officer.

'I have no idea. The drawers she opened only contain paperwork,' Steve replied. He was as mystified as the rest of them. 'We've a few nice pictures and vases in the sitting room and there's my Olympic medal in its case. Nothing valuable's been touched – we've looked.'

'Smart work that lad of yours did, but we don't recommend that sort of thing. He could have got himself hurt.' The policeman looked at them and his expression was unfriendly.

Steve was not pleased. Kirsten and he had given Johnny a mild ticking off but also a metaphorical pat on the back. 'What about the pictures? They look good enough to me. Will you identify this person?'

'They will be passed to experienced officers who will evaluate the evidence.'

Why the hell did coppers always talk in that sort of lingo? Steve gave up. In his office he could see a technician wearing white overalls busy dusting for fingerprints. As the intruder in Johnny's pictures was wearing black gloves Steve wondered how much good that would do. The pictures were a little lopsided but well defined and clear. Much better than any CCTV image. The police really shouldn't have too much trouble finding the girl. She was certainly a stranger to all of them. She stood, a thin dark-haired woman, maybe in her early thirties, with that short cropped hairstyle favoured by lesbians. Or so the popular media supposed.

Could there be a connection with Emily's troubles? 'Officer, there's a journalist called Hammersen who has been troubling my daughter, Emily. I'm wondering if there's a connection between that and this break in.'

'Could you clarify that, Mr Simpson? Does this trouble have sexual connotations – stalking is the term sometimes used.'

'No, we don't think it's that. The man's a journalist. He's trying to rake up something from my wife's family past.'

The policeman grunted and made no comment. Steve was not prepared see this incident buried in constabulary paper files, with no serious attempt to track down the culprit.

'Somebody must know that person,' he said. 'Somebody recognise her face.'

'Hurst Castle over there,' Tom pointed. 'Which way do we go – Needles or north Channel?'

'It's wind against tide,' said Emily. 'If we go Needles it'll be bumpy and sea sicky.'

'Girlie sailors – you like everything sunny and smooth.'

Emily laughed. 'Yes, while stupid macho guys fight wind and tide, and take twice as long to get to where they want to.'

'All right, good thinking – north we'll go.'

It had been a great sail and the two of them had bonded as a team. Emily knew every last metre of the Solent and had guided the ship on a leisurely cruise towards their planned destination, Old Duddlestone Marina on the Purbeck coast. They had anchored overnight in Newtown Creek and delighted in the peace of the place. Now they were on the second leg of their sail, and Tom felt anticipation at the thought of coming home. Not just coming home but arriving with this lovely girl in a fine sailing yacht. The emotion was pride, and he was confident that Mum and Dad Peter would approve of both choices.

Even the north side was not an easy ride in these conditions. The wind was rising as they sailed towards Poole, with the menacing South Shingles bank not far away. Emily clipped on her harness and shuffled forward to pull down a mainsail reef. Tom released the main halyard, while she pulled the sail down and hooked it in the new position. Tom wound the winch handle until the sail settled into its setting.

Emily was seated on the deck with an arm around the mast. She looked so beautiful in her red top and shorts with her suntanned legs. Spray had wetted her hair and face. He watched her wipe the lenses of her dark glasses and then slowly stand and make her way back to the security of the cockpit.

She looked at the GPS screen. 'You can keep on this tack for a while. That's Christchurch entrance and Hengistbury over there. Keep going and you'll see Bournemouth pier. After that we tack out into the bay toward Swanage.'

'We're in good time,' said Tom. 'I calculate ETA Duddlestone sixteen hundred.'

'Which I take it is macho man's speak, meaning we'll get there around four o'clock or tea time.'

'Seamanship is serious business and we conduct it in the correct form of language,' Said Tom.

'Pompous git,' replied Emily and then squealed as he made a playful slap at her behind.

The Southwesterly wind had slackened as they approached the shore at Studland. Ahead of them Tom could see the cliffs and the Old Harry rocks. It felt good to be on the lap to home. He had been born in Purbeck, the son of a schoolteacher and a rogue of a father whom he could barely remember. He had no feeling whatever for that man who had deserted his mother and him, fled to Australia, and then taken up with the very woman who had attempted to kill Tom. These were bad memories from fifteen years ago. He loved his mother and as far as he was concerned he only had one father in Dad Peter. He was fond of his stepsister, Emma, a fully qualified doctor now working in Canada with her doctor husband and their two children. He saw them maybe every eighteen months when they flew over for a visit home.

Tom looked up at the approaching land. 'I think we can tack now.' He swung the tiller over, the mainsail flapped and Emily winched in the jib. They were sailing again heading out into the Channel with the

Isle of Wight a distant blur on the horizon.

'Want to make a good offing,' he explained. 'There can be a bit of a tide race around Durlestone Head.'

'Hey,' said Emily, 'you were the one who tried to wind me up about seasickness and who's chickening out now.'

'Right, get it into your head, girl. I am on my home territory and I will pilot this ship into port in a good and seamanlike manner – got it.'

Emily sniggered. 'My mum says every man becomes a brute as soon as he boards a boat.'

Tom grinned back. *Puffin* was handling perfectly as they cleared the land and the wind increased. The land had been so near and he had smelt the scent of it. His birthplace and his home were very close now. He couldn't describe the depth of his feelings for Emily as she sat beside him. He adored this girl and her gibe was partially true. He was smitten with this lovely little seakindly yacht. He felt very near to Heaven, but he realised all too well that this bliss was short-term and soon they would be on land again, and on land usually meant troubles.

'I wasn't much impressed with those police,' said Kirsten. 'It's a pity Emily wasn't here. They must know who she is and what a cockup they made of finding her.'

'Do you think this has something to do with this Hammersen?' Steve asked the question that had exercised him all morning. 'Why was that woman so keen to look at my paper work?'

'Could be a druggie looking for cash, you know – anything – small change even.'

'Why here?'

'This appears a big house if you see it from the road, much grander than it is for real.'

'If that's all it is they should track down the woman and deal with her.'

Kirsten was staring at the sky. 'Is this weather going to hold?'

'Should do for the rest of the week. There's a big high-pressure system pushed up from the Azores. That means a long dry spell. I bet the farmers are pleased with the harvest flat out.'

'We haven't heard a thing from Emily.'

'Yes we have. She called us last night. They were anchored in Newtown, remember. They can't have reached Old Duddlestone yet.'

'I know,' she said, 'but I worry.'

'I worry too. I worry about a lot of things but not that. Those two are experienced sailors in a good boat in quiet weather.'

‘And they’ve got each other,’ Kirsten had a dreamy look. ‘So romantic – I feel jealous.’

‘Well, you can’t have a toyboy like Tom so you’ll have to stick with me.’

Kirsten looked her husband up and down. ‘You’ll do.’

‘Thank you for that. Tuesday it’s back to work.’

‘Steve, in three weeks’ time we go to the meeting at Rutland. Have you thought about the Paralympics? You’re eligible you know.’

‘At my age?’ Steve was startled. It was a thought that hadn’t entered his head.

‘*Age shall not wither them nor the years condemn*,’ Kirsten quoted.

‘It’s *weary them*,’ Steve corrected.

‘All right. Brian mentioned the Paralympics to me, and some of the others thought it was a great idea.’

‘I suppose so, but what would people think if I said openly that I wanted that. You know the words of the Olympic ideal. They invite “the youth of the world to gather” etc. And that means youth, not crotchety old men of seventy, and seventy is what I’ll be for the Olifa games.’

‘OK, but just think about it. It would give you something to aim for and you’ll have to keep fit and mind your health, so double incentive.’

‘I’ll think about it, if you will also get back on your windsurfer.’

‘They don’t allow windsurfers at Branham.’

‘That’s a cop-out,’ said Steve. ‘Anyway, let’s wait until the race next Saturday. The others know me now. I’ll probably be thrashed.’

‘There it is – the day mark – see on the cliff up there,’ Tom was pointing at the cliff tops to starboard.

Emily could see it now – a metal triangular structure silhouetted against the sky.

‘We put that up to mark the harbour entrance. It’s not that easy to see otherwise.’

She sensed a change in Tom. He had become quieter, almost introverted. She knew this was an emotional moment, the mariner returning home by sea. But she suspected something else was troubling him. She wished that he would tell her.

‘Em, see that cliff top a bit to the right of the mark?’

She followed the direction of his hand. The cliff was less white than a sort of off grey and it was sheer and high.

‘That was the place that Jolene tried to jump over and take me with her.' Tom lapsed into silence. 'Another thing I need to tell you. My real father, Stoneman, was killed just inside the entrance here. He was with a gang trying to abscond with a cargo of loot. They hit the rocks, boat exploded and they all died.'

'Oh, Tom,' she hesitated. 'We've got an awful lot in common. I think you should talk about it: tell me the whole story. Not now, only when you're ready.'

'I know. We've both been through hell. OK, I'll not only tell you all; we'll walk to that cliff top.' Now he smiled at her. 'Right, stir yourself, you raggedly crew. Prepare to square up and enter port.'

Emily glared at him. 'You sound like a recycled Johnny Depp.'

She could see the need for the day mark. A safe harbour lay somewhere in that land among the cliffs but its position was not obvious. Tom lined up *Puffin* pointing her straight into the coastline. 'See those two leading beacons,' he said, 'line them up and in we go.'

Emily could make sense of it now. To port stood a long quay with a brick building on the end. Lining the adjacent shoreline was a little village of stone cottages and a modern glass fronted clubhouse with a dinghy park. Along the quay lay yachts moored to floating pontoons. She could see the need for the leading marks. On the starboard side were jagged looking rocks, dark and slimy, but beyond lay a perfect ttle cove of smooth sheltered water with the high ground looming above. Emily had met Tom's parents just the once, at the graduation, and she had liked them. Now she was about to meet them officially as Tom's girlfriend, and it was important that she made the right impression.

'Darling, what a fantastic place; if I lived here I'd never want to leave.'

'Forced by necessity in my case,' replied Tom. 'I wanted to go to uni and then make some money.'

'But this is where you grew up?'

'I wasn't born here in this village. It was still deserted and MOD property, but I went to the village primary in New Duddlestone, just over the hill there, and then as a boarder at Clayesmore, north of here near Blandford. After that, Bristol, where I met you. Story of my life.'

'Not over yet for either of us.'

'That's true. After what we both went through I guess we'd settle for something less exciting.' He reached forward and started the diesel. 'OK, let's get the lines ready, and we'll berth alongside that empty space over there. Then I can show off the yacht and her beautiful crew to the harbour master.'

Emily snorted. 'I see your order of priority.'

'Just grab that centre line and standby port side.'

They lowered sail and Tom motored slowly toward the vacant pontoon. 'Hello,' he said. 'We've some help.'

Emily saw a formidable looking woman of late middle age standing hands on hips. Her pose was observant and critical.

'Tom, who is that, she's not your mum?'

'Christ no way! That's my Aunt Laura: supreme queen bee and tyrant.' He laughed. 'She and Dad Wilson had a bit of a fling years ago. Mum still gives him a bad time about it. You'll never believe it but Mum and Laura are sisters.'

Tom gently eased *Puffin* towards the berth as the woman on the pontoon waved hand signals in an imperious fashion. Of these Tom took not the slightest notice as he put the engine in neutral, letting the yacht glide to a full stop a few inches from the dock. Emily jumped onto the pontoon and fixed a lightweight centre line to a cleat.

'Tom, you're early,' said Aunt Laura. 'Your mother and Peter have gone to Swanage, but they should be back within the hour.'

'We made a good passage,' Tom replied.

'And you are?' Laura had switched her gaze to Emily who stared in return. This Aunt was a still a good-looking woman with a well-preserved figure. Her hair was styled and dyed a sensible shade of brown, and she wore gold earrings. She was dressed in a white top, stylish blue slacks and white deck shoes. Emily was conscious of her own shabby waterproof, dinghy shorts and bare feet. Her hair and face were wet and salt encrusted.

'I'm Emily. I'm a friend of Tom's and I'm his crew.' That was as neutral a reply as she could conjure out of nothing.

Now the woman smiled and held out her hand. 'Emily, welcome to Duddlestone.'

CHAPTER 11

Steve returned to work on the Tuesday following the August holiday. He had been away from the office for nine weeks and nobody seemed to have noticed. That was both satisfactory and highly irritating. Easterbroke Marine's UK workshop was beside Chichester Marina and had been sited there for twenty-five years. Steve had managed the operation for all of that time, before and after the business was acquired by Kirsten with her inherited Danish fortune. No one cared to mention the origin of that fortune salted away by Kirsten's tragic uncle.

Not for the first time economic recession was hurting the business. Orders for new sails had halved, although the high-tech racing-sail sector was still buoyant. Steve had filled the gap with a sail repair service, a downmarket enterprise that he wouldn't have touched ten years ago. Within the building was Easterbroke Europe's main office where Kirsten presided as company chairman. Here she maintained the records of all the ten overseas branches, now reduced to seven.

Kirsten parked the Volvo and then she helped him out of his seat and handed him the crutches. He most definitely was not going to enter his work place in a wheelchair. In his briefcase he carried an A4 notebook with a series of plans and sketches. Kirsten had preceded him into the office and reappeared grinning.

'I've rung the harbour office,' she said, 'and they say *Puffin* is safe back on her mooring.'

'Why didn't Emily come home then?'

'She's twenty-one, for God's sake. She doesn't have to clock in at home.'

'I like to know what she's up to with that young man.'

'I don't need three guesses about that, Steve. Emily is a responsible adult, she won't take stupid chances.'

'It's just the times we live in. Standards…' Steve caught sight of Kirsten's expression both mocking and reproving.

'Don't do as I did, do as I tell you. That's about it.' She held his gaze and winked.

Steve sighed and went in search of the chief sail cutter. He found the man and produced his notebook. 'I've started racing a 2.4 metre. The sails I'm using are tacky Swedish rags. I've worked out something better. Two versions: lightweight and heavy weather. See what you can do within the rules.'

'All right, Steve, we'll have a go, we're not exactly run off our feet. You know have you thought about the Paralympics – make it a double?'

'You're the second person to suggest that. I said before; I'll be seventy by the time the games get to Olifa.'

'So what? Anyone can race one of those little boats. Doesn't matter if you're nine years old or ninety.'

'Winning though, that's another matter.'

'I'm not going any further down here,' said Tom. 'This is a company car and I don't need it scratched.'

Emily agreed. The track that she remembered had almost gone; disappeared beneath overhanging branches and gorse bushes. She was surprised that she felt not a pang of nervousness, the reverse if anything. She wanted to show Tom the scene of her own ordeal. Three days ago at Duddlestone they had walked to the cliff top and Tom had pointed to the spot where the crazed Joline had tried to leap and take Tom with her. She knew it had been a difficult decision for him to go there with her and he'd declined to walk to the cliff edge. Now it was her turn to take him to the site of the cottage in Branham Forest.

They left the car and Emily led the way dodging the undergrowth and trying to make out the proper path. Now they were in the open. Emily knew they were in the right place but nothing looked the same as she remembered. The cottage, of course, was demolished and buried but the woodlands looked different. She could place things now and she almost felt a resentment to see that the trees that had been her refuge were felled and the trunks lying in neat triangular stacks. Even as they watched a heavy tractor with a grab was building a further stack and she could hear the buzz of chain saws.

'It's all different,' she muttered. 'Let's go over there.'

They walked across the sandy waste, Emily searching the ground for any disturbance that might place the ruin for her. She could see nothing. Was she relieved as she should be? Or was she annoyed that she couldn't prove to Tom that she was stronger than him and didn't shy away from the exact spot of her ordeal.

'Oi,' shouted a voice. They looked up to see a little man strutting towards them.

'You people is off the footpath. This is private Forestry Commission land.'

He approached them, tubby and truculent beneath his hard hat. 'We is doing a felling operation and it's not safe for members of the general public to be arsing around. Got it?'

'Do you have to use that language in front of a lady?' Tom's tone was biting.

Emily was worried. She didn't want Tom in another violent clash.

'Mate, I'm only telling you for your own safety. No more back chat – sling yer 'ook.'

'Come on, Tom. Let's go – there's nothing to see here.'

She turned and Tom followed with obvious reluctance. 'Rude little shit. Who does he think he is?'

Emily giggled. 'If anyone's descended from Hitler it's that guy. He even looks a bit like him. Perhaps we'd better tell Hammersen.'

'Why didn't you say who you were?'

'What's the difference? Sod it, the thing happened eight years ago nearly. It's over and done with.' She paused, put her arms around his neck. 'Come on, let's go to the sailing club and look at Dad's new boat.'

'That's the one, it must be. Look there's a name, Bartels, stencilled on the cover and that is old Wolfgang's surname.' Emily touched the boat's hull. Tom was a dinghy racing sailor with his Laser. These boats must be new to him.

'It looks like a toy,' he said.

'They're sort of model yachts. Based on the America's Cup Twelves from the 1970s. The 2.4 bit is only a metre formula. They must be at least thirteen feet long.'

'I must say she looks nice. I can see the Twelve-metre connection. Apart from cruising boats like your *Puffin*, I've never done much with keelboats.'

'Chloe rang me from New Zealand the other day. She wants to get the team together for practise.'

Tom made no response apart from a grunt.

'What is it about Chloe that winds you up?'

'Nothing really – she's your friend.'

'No, Tom. We'll have this out. I can't force you to like my friends. I doubt I'll like all of your mates. But Chloe's important; she's the helm of our boat. She's good and I want to stick with her.'

'She's a noisy Kiwi and she's a lesbian.'

'So that's it. Are you thinking I might want to share her bed and not ours?'

'No I don't think that, of course I don't.'

'Prove you're not a racist homophobe.'

Tom glared at her. 'No way. The Maoris are great people: great fighters and rugby players. I don't really mind gays. I just wish they'd keep it among themselves.'

'Chloe used to play in a women's rugby team. That was before she got hooked on boats. The Maoris are fine seamen. You know to get to New Zealand in the first place they crossed the Pacific in canoes. Chloe has lots of songs and legends about it.'

'Do you know,' said Tom, 'people still talk about your Dad. That last lap of the race he won gold. He was the only one who didn't capsize. I've seen the old film of it, the seas were horrendous.'

'You don't need to tell me. I've seen that film a hundred times. We've had it put on DVD along with the medal ceremony and we've another one of Mum when she got her bronze with the windsurfer. But the Danes got the credit for that one.'

'Well, she was in their team.'

'Brian, at this club, wants Dad to think about the Paralympics. Dad's a bit dubious but I think it's a great idea.'

'He's left it too late for the next ones. He'll be with you sailing in Olifa.'

'Not the same week he won't. Paralympics are later.'

Tom looked across the lake. 'What happened to your brother while we were away?'

'The silly kid heard a burglar in our house, and instead of ringing the police he takes his little camera and snaps the intruder. Intruder runs and we're all none the wiser.'

'Anything stolen?'

'No, she was ransacking the drawers in the office. Mum thinks it was a druggie looking for cash.' Emily fumbled in her handbag and produced a copy of the photograph. 'That's her.'

'Scrawny looking bird,' said Tom as he handed it back. 'I suspect Hammersen.'

'But that's a woman.'

'Hammersen could have put her up to it.'

'Tom, I'm puzzled myself about all this, and Mum still won't tell me the family secret. Only that Gerda had a child that wasn't her husband's and it can't have been Hitler what done it. So, where's the big deal and why is Hammersen so obsessed with me?'

'Because he's unbalanced. Maybe there's something in his family's past that's bugging him. We'll probably never know.'

Emily looked at her watch. 'I feel hungry. Let's walk down the road and have dinner at the Lakeview.'

'Girl, am I paying?'

'I think we share. Start as we mean to go on.'

'Your mum's lovely,' said Emily.

'I agree, but what's brought this on?'

They were sitting in the Lakeview dining room, sipping their post-lunch coffee while watching the waters of Branham Lake.

'She's nothing like your auntie,' said Emily. 'Are they really sisters?'

'Yes, Laura's the elder. She's not as bad as she pretends.'

'She strikes me as the sort of bossy business type. I would guess tunnel vision and no love life.'

'Oh, God,' Tom laughed. 'Laura's a divorcee with a most lurid sex life. Anyway why all this about my family?'

'It's only that you asked me to spend Christmas with you, but something's come up.'

'Tell all.'

'It's Chloe.'

'Oh, not her again,' Tom grumbled.

'No I'm not spending Christmas with her, God forbid. No, it's just that there's a match racing indicator meeting in Auckland.'

'Not during the Christmas holiday.'

'No, Chloe said it's late January.'

Tom looked relieved. 'Well, have Christmas and then fly out.'

'That's what I'd like to do, but I don't want to seem rude if I push off the day after Boxing Day.'

'What about your other crew?'

'I don't know what Erin's planned. She's doing an au pair stint in France at the moment.'

'Well, some of us have to work our way in life.'

Emily felt a spark of anger. 'That's not fair. Dad won't give me a job in his office; says I'll crash all his poxy computers.'

Emily had a bad conscience on this subject. Some of her university friends were doing voluntary work in gap years and others were trying to pay off loans with mundane jobs. Everyone thought that because she had a wealthy mother it gave her a license to skive. It wasn't true. She still had a trickle of money from that writer: royalties on the fire siege book, but that was all, apart from a few pounds saved from the previous Olympic funding. No, she would spend Christmas at Duddlestone with Tom and his family. If Chloe wanted to work up the Auckland boat she could do it on her own.

‘It’s that bloody red Audi again. I’m sure it’s the same one,’ said Tom.

‘What are you on about?’ replied Emily.

Tom was driving through the village of Greatham on his way to Petersfield. ‘I’ve twice been followed by that car, and twice some little runt has taken a photo of me.’

‘When was this?’

‘First time it happened I was on the bike.’

‘Were you dressed in those leathers?’

‘Yes, so he couldn’t have identified me. I thought he was just a Ducati fan like me. Second time I was in this car. I was standing beside it on the roadside and along he comes, slows, and takes a snap. Same car both times.’

‘That was cheek, I agree. It wasn’t Hammersen was it?’

‘No, the man looked older and greyer. He wasn’t the one driving. I didn’t see who that was.’

He gave a quick glance to Emily. She looked troubled. ‘Em, sweetheart, what’s up?’

‘Nothing really. No that’s not true. It’s Hammersen and all this business. I feel I’d like to give him my DNA. That should stop all this shit.’

Tom wished he could believe that. He didn’t care a jot about Emily’s ancestry. Emily was Emily, and he loved her more each day. But he couldn’t help but wonder why Kirsten kept refusing to discuss the matter. ‘No,’ he said, ‘we don’t give him the satisfaction.’

The Audi was still behind and Tom was becoming annoyed. A traffic-calming bollard was coming up ahead leaving a lane for just one vehicle. Tom looked ahead. No oncoming traffic. Without warning Emily, he swung the wheel to the left and hauled on the hand brake. Emily squealed as the car skidded round, blocking the road. The follower had already slowed and came to a stop. Tom had released his belt and was out of the car storming towards the Audi.

‘What the hell is going on?’ he shouted as he leaned towards the open passenger side window. As he had expected, the startled occupant still held his camera. A rather nice professional-style Olympus, Tom noted. Now he saw her; the driver was a girl, woman rather, and she was remarkably like the one Emily had shown in her brother Johnny’s photo.

‘You dropped anchor a bit quick didn’t you, Mister,’ the girl had an irritating sneer and that was all that Tom needed. He walked round to the driver’s door and wrenched it open.

'I wouldn't do that, mate,' the passenger had a squeaky voice with a touch of a London accent. Tom saw the camera pointed at him and had the sense to draw back. Something about this passenger was familiar. Tom had seen that face before but in not real life. She could be the one in that picture but he wasn't sure.

'You're Tom Stoneman?' asked the man.

'I think you fucking know that,' Tom replied.

'And the young lady with you,' sneered the woman, 'is the famous Emily; little Emily the nation's darling from the sun siege.'

'Come to the point,' said Tom.

'I'll come to the point all right,' said the girl. 'I'm Michelle Le Bois and that little bitch got my uncle shot.'

'Here's my card, mate,' said the man.

Tom took the square and threw it on the ground.

'Please yourself. All we're doing is getting a hero his due respect.'

A horn blast brought Tom back to reality. A white transit van with an impatient driver had stopped unable to progress further. Tom returned to his seat and extracted his car from the roadblock. The Audi overtook them and sped away. The van driver passed them and mouthed an expletive. Tom opened his door, left the car and picked up the card. He glanced at it and passed it to Emily. The effect on her was immediate and disturbing. She read the card and at once broke down in tears. Tom put his arm around her as she shook.

'Em, darling, whatever's wrong?'

She didn't answer, only cried some more and handed him the card. He read: *Sidney Everett –writer and investigative journalist.*

'Tom, take me home please.'

Tom scanned the laptop screen, working through all four of John-Kaj's pictures.

He shook his head. 'It's not the same woman although there's a bit of a resemblance. This one's younger and her hair's cropped. Even if that Michelle whatsit had shaved her hair it wouldn't be her.'

Emily had calmed herself but she was still shaken. 'Le Bois, was that the name again?'

'Yep, that's it, Michelle Le Bois. She said you got her uncle shot.'

Steve was standing behind them. 'I don't like any of this. Le Bois was shot because he was indistinguishable from the cult people. If his relations have a grievance it's with the Army, not Emily.'

Emily sniffed, her tears were welling up again. 'They're employing that little rat Everett. Tom, what did he say?'

‘Oh, something about restoring the honour of a hero.’

‘But the man was mental. He should never have been there.’

‘Have the police come up with anything?’ Tom asked. ‘I mean has anyone recognised this girl?’

‘If they have we’ve not been told,’ Steve replied. ‘I think the time has come to take some legal advice. Tom, who was that solicitor you used?’

‘Romero, but he’s a partner in Giggs and Stent.’

‘I’ll give him a call. Do you know their phone number.’

‘I do,’ John-Kaj spoke. None of them had heard him enter the room. ‘It’s local code, then 772 007: ask for James Bond – he’ll sort it for you.’

CHAPTER 12

Chloe Te Kooti-Stamford, cleared customs at Heathrow; this was always an irritating ritual. She had a UK passport and held the rank of Captain in the British Army, but that did not exclude her from the narrowed eyes of immigration officers and the odd sotto voce comment. Sod them; racist whinging Poms. Not that all Poms whinged, most weren't too bad. Anyway she couldn't talk. Since she'd attained joint citizenship she'd been instantly labelled a Pom herself every time she returned on a visit home. Chloe was a delightful mix that she was rather proud of.

A Pakeha Maori was the term used. She was the product of a grandmother's mixed marriage to the younger son of an English aristocratic family.

Careerwise she'd had a few battles to fight. Her sexuality had been fixed in her early days, and concealing that from her relatives was a strain. It had been uncomfortable, and in spite of few desultory relationships at university, it hadn't brought happiness. Sport was Chloe's escape, and in New Zealand culture it was a release that brought her respect from her peers. She loved rugby and could have aspired to a place in the women's All Black forward line. Then, one day, at eighteen, she had been taken by a friend to the yacht club in Auckland. They had sailed around the harbour in a dinghy and from that moment Chloe was hooked.

With an engineering diploma in her luggage she'd made her way to England. Sandhurst had followed. She had loved the physical challenge but still had to conceal her gay inclination. Since then a more civilised army had relaxed their prejudices, and Chloe had found her niche as an officer in R.E.M.E. Her prowess as a racing helm had won her time off work to pursue an Olympic career. This had brought her together with Erin and Emily. They had proved a good team, but in spite of winning the European women's match racing trophy they'd been pipped for Olympic selection by a rival crew. Chloe couldn't honestly disagree with the selection although Emily had taken it badly. The rivals had been a threesome all in their mid thirties, and it was certain that they would not be around in four years' time.

Emily and Erin were great company but they were pretty girls and definitely ones for the boys. But the three of them had formed a different bond. An instinctive racing team who not only worked as a team: it was almost as if they functioned as a single racing brain.

Chloe's leave was up so first duty was to report to her unit. Second priority was to find her way to Cowes and see the building of the boats for the European legs of the match racing circuit.

She pulled out her mobile and called the number. 'Em, I'm back home. How's things?'

'Hi, Chloe, oh, it's great to hear your voice. I need cheering up.'

'What's the problem, Em? No, don't bother, it's love life, isn't it.'

She heard Emily laugh. 'No, that's going rather well, so far. It's other problems. Tell you when I see you.'

'OK, I've gotta report for work but then I'm going to have a look at our new boats. Can you come with me?'

'Yeah, when's this?'

'Can't be this week, but there won't be much to see until next month anyway.'

'All right, Chlo' – give me a call when you're ready.'

'I want to talk tactics with your dad. How is he?'

'He's a lot better and he's sailing again and he's winning.' Chloe heard Emily laugh. 'Dad asked his people to make some sails for his 2.4 and he got the measurements wrong – only a few millimetres. You'll never guess how we found out. It was my little brother recalculated on his computer and it turns out he was right.'

'That's a boat with metre rules: bloody complicated,' said Chloe.' She paused. 'You still got the same boyfriend?'

'Tom, yes. He's introduced me to his mum and dad.'

'Oh, mate, that means he's serious so watch out.'

'We're in no hurry, and I've got to go to law chambers in September.'

Chloe was worried on both counts. She found Tom moody and stiffed-arsed and she needed Emily sailing. 'Does that affect you for Auckland at Christmas?'

'No, luckily the head of chambers is a yachtie. He says go ahead as there's not much happening in January.'

Chloe said goodbye and stood for a moment. Chloe's employers, the British MOD, had no problems with her sailing, but Emily was fixed on her career. Erin was due to take up a teaching post, but long holidays went with that as a matter of course. Olympic selection would depend on Chloe keeping her team together. Even one new unfamiliar crew could lose places on the racecourse.

Kirsten helped Steve up the three steps into the solicitor's offices. Romero greeted the pair and ushered them into the waiting room.

‘I’ll be with you in a tick,’ he said. ‘We’re a bit short handed at the moment.’

They sat in comfortable armchairs surrounded by shelves of leather bound legal tomes. Outside in the passage they could see passing figures carrying files.

At last Romero reappeared and they followed him to a lift. ‘We won’t use the stairs,’ he remarked. It was tactfully said and the only sign that he recognised Steve’s illness.

They reached an office and Romero ushered them in and waved them to more armchairs. ‘I’ll call for coffee,’ he said, ‘but it may take a few minutes.’ The man looked uneasy, no, more like diffidence, thought Steve.

‘There is something I would like to suggest,’ said Romero. ‘My wife Anna, our regular receptionist, has just had a baby and she’s going to be away until late autumn. I understand your daughter Emily has an honours degree in law and wants to be a barrister.’

‘She’s been accepted by a law firm starting in October,’ Steve replied.

‘I thought it might be good experience for her to man our front desk, at least part time. You see, I saw her on the witness stand. It was her interventions that destroyed the prosecution. I would say she’s got a bright future at the bar. She’s a natural.’

‘I’ll put it to her,’ said Kirsten. ‘She’s been tied up helping while her father’s been ill, but she’s at a bit of a loose end now. We feel she should be earning her keep.’

‘It’s up to her. Ask her to get in touch if she likes the idea. Now, about this harassment. How can we help?’

Steve, with additional comments from Kirsten told the whole story. ‘This man Sid Everett worked for the Daily Banner, and even at the time he was building up Le Bois as an unsung hero. But it’s not so. Le Bois was in a deranged state. He tried to grab Emily as she was running for her life. Emily says he called her Rachel. You see in his mental condition we think he had confused her with another little girl who’d been dead for years.

‘I’m sorry for Le Bois’ family, but their facts are just wrong and Everett is exploiting them.’

‘This is not easy,’ said Romero. ‘If Mr Everett or one of these Le Bois people had actually threatened Emily, then we could ask for an injunction. The same thing applies with Mr Hammersen who seems to have vanished. I think our best course might be to find these Le Bois’s and convince them that they have no grievance with Emily. If

Mr Everett starts to intrude on your privacy you must let me know.'

'What about telling the police?' asked Kirsten.

'That's a very fine line. Yes, if any of these people call at your house and offer physical threats or abuse, then the police are the ones to contact.'

'Did you know that we caught an intruder in our house a few days ago?' said Steve. 'It was a woman and she was riffling through my desk. Our young lad Johnny snapped her with his camera and we got a near perfect mug shot.'

'Then the police will catch her. Put the picture on television. It usually works. Sometimes the culprits hand themselves in.'

Kirsten was studying the pictures on the solicitor's desk of his wife and children. She could see another photograph, much older and faded, of a man dressed in some sort of drab military fatigues.

Romero followed her gaze and touched this second photograph with his forefinger.

'He's my late grandfather, he was Spanish, hence my family name. He was a refugee from the Spanish war of the 1930s. I had relations murdered by the subsequent regime. So I understand Mr Hammersen, even though I agree that he is wrong.'

Sid Everett was having reservations, and for Sid that was an alien sensation. Since his retirement from the Banner he had set up his successful publicity agency and investigation business. It had worked well at first; still worked well as a money-spinner, but he missed the old job. Now he had got himself enmeshed with these odd Le Bois people, while there was a brilliant news story growing in front of him. He was buggered if he would tip off his replacement at the *Banner*. He hadn't made the connection until yesterday when that young lad Stoneman had blocked the road and confronted him. He had been watching Stoneman only because he was friendly with Emily Simpson. Sid had sized up the lad as a possible source of information in the Le Bois investigation. He had dropped that idea when he heard of the court case. Stoneman would more likely give Sid a bloody nose. But Sid had recalled an old news story of fifteen years ago. It was that name, Thomas Stoneman, that was ringing a hundred bells.

Sid had driven to Alton and taken the short walk to the police station. Sid did not on principle have dealings with bent coppers, but he had no compunction in calling in favours. Hadn't they recently charged one Thomas Stoneman? Yes, but the case had failed. Was this Stoneman a local man? No, he had given a temporary address in

Petersfield. The police had wanted to check him further and Mr Stoneman had given them a home address in Dorset. What part of Dorset? The man checked. Somewhere called Duddlestone near Swanage.

Sid left the building with that smug sensation he knew so well. He had no intention of alerting the *Banner* or any other tabloid. Instead he called the local newspaper in Bournemouth. The senior reporter clearly knew Sid by reputation and was less than co-operative. Yes, Tom Stoneman would now be twenty-five. No, they did not know where he was at present. The man was a liar of course; it took one to know one, but Sid had heard enough. Tom Stoneman and Emily Simpson were an item: two well-remembered victims of violent abduction. In Stoneman's case the whole episode had been filmed from a police helicopter. Sid began to whistle happily as he walked to recover his car. He would keep his mouth shut and continue to watch this happy young couple. For Sid, the Emily Simpson story had been one the highlights of a long journalistic career, and it seemed it still had some mileage yet.

Steve's new success with sailing had not proved to be a one off. He had sailed three weekend races at Branham with two further wins and a third place on a light weather day. He was now preparing to travel to the national championships on Rutland Water. Steve had sailed on this location a few times in the past. This inland sea of three thousand acres, visible from space, was a vastly different proposition to a tiny stretch of water like Branham. Steve had supervised the loading of his boat on a double trailer with another 2.4. A Sailability helper with a four-by-four had hooked on the boats and driven away. Steve had always towed his own dinghies to past events and was not too happy to have to delegate this task to a stranger.

The next day, Kirsten and he had set out for the Midlands. Steve had hoped that Emily might come with them but she had arranged to meet Chloe at the ferry terminal for the Isle of Wight. The two girls were keen to see the building of the boats they would be sailing at Hyeres. Steve could not argue with that. Emily's Tom had not chosen to go with her but had managed to borrow a very ancient Land Rover on top of which he had lashed a Laser dinghy. He had entered for another open event on the same water. John-Kaj had gone to stay with the family's close friends, Harry and Liz, and would be sailing his Cadet dinghy at Branham.

Steve was as excited as he had ever felt in the past when attending a major sailing event. His recovery was close to complete even if he would always walk with a stick and would never run again. His speech was still contaminated with this odd West Country intonation. Emily's Tom, who spoke with a similar but refined burr, had told him it was music.

Kirsten drove on the way north while Steve kept his eye on the satnav. Kirsten had a style of driving that could be defined as Copenhagen, a technique derived from fierce acceleration, hard braking, dodging hordes of cyclists and tending to take the wrong exits from roundabouts. True to form, his wife had given him a white-knuckle ride around the M25 and nearly missed the exit for the A1. There followed a reasonably peaceful run with a stop for lunch in St Neots, where Steve was thankful to find a men's toilet. Finally they had completed the trip, reported in at the sailing club and checked the safe arrival of Steve's boat. For the duration of the meeting Kirsten had booked them into the old-world comforts of the Barnsdale Hall Hotel, a stone's throw from the big lake. Steve was uneasy with all this luxury: it conflicted with how a race meeting should be experienced. In days gone by Steve would have camped on site or found a friendly floor to doss down on. He had to admit those days were done with: he was a disabled man with a wife who could afford the cost, so why not enjoy it. They were joined at dinner by friends from Branham and a few from the wider world of Paralympic sailing, including a rather pretty girl called Megan who had already won the big event at Kiel and was due to represent Great Britain in a few weeks time.

The next morning, Steve was out of bed at six am. He limped to the window studying the sky before accessing local weather reports on his laptop. He began to go through his old remembered big-race preparations; a ritual he hadn't thought he would ever use again. An easterly breeze was increasing across the flat landscape. The temperature was forecast to be warm, but that might not apply on the water. So it would be drysuit wear.

'Why are you putting on all that gear?' Kirsten sounded sleepily.

'Because in a few hours I shall be competing in a major event.' He knew he sounded tetchy. 'Preparation is everything.'

'It's only a yacht race – it's not war.'

'Oh, come on.' He recalled Kirsten's own race winning rituals. 'I remember when you won bronze medal. All that transcendental meditation and mumbo jumbo you went through for hours.'

'Yes, and it worked. But you English; all these superstitions like putting on your under vest back to front. I bet you've already done that.'

Steve had done exactly that but he wouldn't admit it. 'Why do you Scandinavians and Krauts all wish each other broken masts? If that's not superstition what is?'

'Superstition no. Viking lore yes.'

Steve didn't see the difference but left it there. He lay back on the bed again and circled an arm around his wife's naked shoulder.

'Stop it,' she squeaked. 'That suit is like sandpaper. Why are you up now anyway? It's not breakfast for another two hours.'

By the time they did reach the sailing club conditions had worsened. A force seven wind was strumming across the unobstructed landscape and waves were breaking and white crested. Most of the 2.4s had been launched and were bumping alongside the pontoons. Steve retrieved an extra rubber fender from the boot of his car. With support from his stick he limped along the pontoon. A Sailability helper snatched the fender and bent down to fix it between the boat and the pontoon woodwork. Steve thanked the poor man, although he had been prepared to struggle with the task himself. It seemed that this was to be the story of his life from now on and he'd better get used to it. He returned to the car once more and took out the two covers with his new heavy weather sails, Easterbroke's finest. These had been tried the previous weekend, and Steve had been pleased with them. They were his design, with a little bit of help from Johnny, and he felt they had given him a degree or two higher pointing and maybe one tenth of a knot downwind.

'Steve, sorry, but first race is postponed an hour.' He looked up to see a fellow Branham sailor.

'Sod,' he replied. 'I was going to enjoy this.'

'I know, the light weather guys aren't grumbling, but we thought you might not be overwhelmed. Megan didn't say much but I guess she'd rather get out there and get on with it as well.'

Steve retired to the clubhouse for another cup of coffee and watched the scene from the windows. A rigid inflatable launch, a RIB, was quartering the racecourse bumping and banging through the waves.

'Give it an hour or two and it should moderate.' A man Steve didn't know had walked up to stand beside him. The stranger's English was faultless but Steve caught a trace of an accent and come to think of it he'd seen this character before.

'I'm not sure I want it to moderate that much,' he replied. 'I need to give my boat a heavy weather workout.'

'Great stuff,' replied the man. 'May I introduce myself? Primo Garcia.'

'Oh, you're the guy who won the Star class worlds and you were in the Olympics for Argentina.'

'Not quite correct. I sailed for my home country. I am an Olifarian. We are a small nation and sometimes we are confused with our larger neighbours.

'And in four years' time you'll be hosting the whole shebang.'

'Quite right,' said Garcia. 'We hope we are already ahead of the game. Olifa Angelo, our top football side, has a magnificent stadium already: only needs a little bit of work. I suspect our South American Federation united behind Olifa for that reason.'

'My daughter's in a women's match racing team. They didn't make it for next month's games but they stand a better than evens chance of getting the UK slot for your games.'

'And you too, Mr Simpson. Rumour has it you could make an impact in our Paralympics.'

'Hey, wait a minute,' Steve laughed. 'There's two or three others in the running including young Megan and she's already selected for these games.'

Steve wasn't sure what to make of Garcia. The man certainly had a proven record but he was just a bit too well-dressed for Steve's taste. White trousers, blazer and cravat were a bit too stereotypical Riviera yachtie. The man's looks certainly fitted the image. He reminded Steve of the late David Niven.

Ten minutes later the race was declared to be on. Steve shambled down to the jetty carrying his sling for the hoist. Finding the device was busy he persuaded two helpers to sit him on the jetty and then slide his legs into the cockpit. The effort of lowering himself the last two feet left him sore and breathing heavily. Now at last he was out on the lake and sailing fast. Suddenly, he rather fancied his chances of winning this one. Rutland Water was a different proposition from Branham. Sitting low down one had a definite illusion of being at sea in a bigger yacht with the horizon a distant blur. The wind was still strong but it was steady. A few competitors had decided to exercise discretion and sit this one out, but Steve could still count sixteen entrants. He had learned a lot about this class of boat, and he felt comfortable racing one against any company.

Steve saw the gust coming and he was ready for it. It came screaming through the packed start line, and for forty seconds all was a mayhem of flogging sails and a few collisions. Steve could ignore it as he made as good a start as he'd ever achieved in his life. Could it be possible he had this race already won? He had twenty metres on the whole fleet and was to windward of all of them.

The other boat caught him on the third tack he made. A beautifully handled yacht, with the union flag of the Olympic squad on the mainsail, crossed him on starboard tack. Where the hell had that one come from? He resolved to fight this other boat tack for tack. He was Steve Simpson, and he was not to be carved up like that. The wind was increasing again, the rigging was humming musically as his boat slammed and bumped through the short breaking waves. Spray was flying everywhere, splatting on his decks and filtering into the cockpit. His new electric pump had failed, of course. Steve never had had much faith in it. He was pushing his own boat as hard as he could in the conditions, riding the gusts, freeing off a little when the wind relaxed. But it was no good; the other 2.4 had reached the weather mark and was running down towards him, surfing a wave with the jib poled out. As they passed, the other helm glanced across and flashed a smile. She was Megan, the Paralympic star. Steve suddenly realised he had lot to learn and a long way to go if he was to master this boat and reclaim his old status. Mentally, he gave himself a kick in the backside. All this talk of him and the Paralympics in Olifa: rubbish. If one little girl could sail a ring round him on an English lake what chance would he have at the age of seventy in an international fleet on a seaway?

Steve finished second, half a leg behind the first boat. Behind them was a scattered bunch of surviving craft. There was nothing for it but to sail back to the pontoon and berth alongside as gently as one could manage in the conditions. Kirsten was waiting for him at the hoist point, and this time Steve was grateful to be wound skywards and dropped into the wheelchair.

'You were fantastic,' Kirsten shouted against the wind and the sound of flapping sails.

'Not good enough,' Steve grunted. 'That Megan, I couldn't get near her.'

'What are you talking about?' Kirsten pulled his wet hair. 'You can't always win. You know only eight finished. Three boats swamped.'

Steve grimaced at her. 'You know, if I was forty-five years younger, I would fall deeply in love with that girl.'

'You can indulge in any fantasy you please. You are old and lame and I am watching you.'

'Dad's finished joint second at Rutland,' Emily pushed the laptop across the table to Chloe.

'Good for him,' said Chloe. 'If I can sail like that when I'm old I won't complain.'

They were sitting over drinks in the Island Sailing Club bar. Emily was not sure if she was pleased or miffed that the barman had demanded she prove she was over eighteen. Chloe had giggled uncontrolled for a minute and muttered something about "Po-face Poobah Poms".

They had spent the morning in Cowes inspecting the new match racing boats. Not that there was much to see. The hulls were moulded but only in their crude and basic form. The concentration of chemicals had reminded Emily of that awful occasion at primary school when the village copper had caught six kids, herself included, sniffing glue outside his house. Emily had pushed the glue pot into the hands of the dimmest and slowest of the group, a small boy, while she and the others had fled. This crafty ruse had availed them nothing. The PC had noted all their names and informed the parents.

'All the boats allotted for Auckland are standard, so we'll be on level terms with Sammy,' said Chloe. 'Of course this is a Kiwi design. They build them under licence here now.'

Emily resolved not to react to the naming of her most hated rival. 'You'll be on your home ground, Chlo. We'll stuff them wherever the boat's been built.'

'Should do.' Chloe was staring at her. 'Come on, Em. What's the big bug that's biting you? You've been as miserable as a castrated crocodile all this trip. You sure it's not that Tom?'

'No, it's not Tom. He and I are just fine. It's something else and it goes back eight years.'

'Is it something to do with your troubles then?' Chloe's abrasive tone had gone. Emily could see that her friend was concerned.

'Sort of, but nothing to do with the nightmares. I thought I'd put it all behind me and then these newspaper men start crawling out of the woodwork.'

'Shit to those assholes. What are they saying?'

'Only that the copper who was shot at the scene was a hero and … and,' Emily wiped a tear away, 'they're trying to make out that my Mum's family are descended from Hitler.'

'Hitler! For crying out loud, Em, that's crazy.'

'I know. You see my great grandma had a child out of wedlock…'

'Yeah, a bastard…'

'Illegitimate, yes, Chlo', but he wasn't a bastard in the sense most people think of the word. He was a nice gentle guy by all accounts.'

'How come Hitler for Chrissake?'

'Great grandma Gerda was a nutter and she was close to the Nazis – worshipped them so Mum says.'

'I thought your mum's Danish.'

'Yes, she is, but Gerda was a collaborator. She was mad and died insane before she could be tried. But she had a daughter as well. That was my grandmother, and she married a German who was my grandfather but they were both long dead before I was born and granddad Schmitt was Jewish, and it was Gerda saved his life.' Emily was gabbling all this long-dead family history to a blank faced Chloe. But it felt good to share it with a friend. 'Oh Chloe, what if some evil Nazi fathered both Gerda's kids. What does that make me?'

'It makes you Emily. Everyone loves Emily. Christ, my great-great-great four time granddad was Chief Te –Kooti Rikirangi. He killed Brit settlers in cold blood. To my people he's a hero; to the Pakeha he's a terrorist – take your choice. But I'm just Chloe and I've never killed anyone, although a few flipping Afghans tried to kill me. Anyway, what's that other bit about a policeman?'

Emily explained about the Le Bois family and about the break in at Firs Farm.

'You see, Chlo', the man thought I was another girl called Rachel, and he tried to grab me, so the Army shot him, and I didn't see it but I heard the bullets, and those people died within yards of me but I was so scared – it was horrible.' Emily buried her face in her handkerchief. She didn't want the other drinkers to see her in this distraught state.

'Come on, mate, it's over. If people try to stir things you've got the truth on your side.'

'I know that, but you've been in a war zone – been shot at. It much easier for you.'

'Oh, Em, don't you believe that. I saw things out there that I ain't going to forget as long as I live. Cheer up, mate – let's talk sailing. After all, it's what we came here for.'

Sid Everett stood on the sidewalk staring at the Daily Banner Building. It was an impressive structure but had none of the atmosphere of the cramped old Fleet Street offices. This place was a squeaky clean geekland: all computers and not a piece of paper in sight. He had fond memories: the shouting, the chaos, scraps of paper littering the floors and the roar and clatter of the antique printing machinery. That was journalism as he remembered it should be. Excitement, alcohol-fuelled achievement, great internal feuds: it was his world. Here he was on Canary Wharf, what a bloody silly name that was.

'Have you an appointment, Mr er…'

Sid bit his tongue. Here he was now in the offices of *The Banner* and this silly little floosie didn't even know his name. He was Sid Everett for Christ's sake: the greatest investigative reporter of the old Street.

'Yeah, I have an appointment with Andy, photo editor.'

'I think Mr Ikes is in a meeting, Mr Everard.'

'Everett's the name and Andy's not in any bloody meeting. He's expecting me.'

The girl tapped away at her computer keyboard.

'How the hell can you type with finger nails that long?' Sid glared at her.

The floosie scowled back. 'It seems Mr Ikes is expecting someone of your name. He is on his way down now.'

'Thanks sweetheart.' Sid found a comfortable chair and waited. Andy had been the young up-and-coming photographer who had worked with Sid on the fire siege story. Now Sid had a spin-off from that time; a story he was not prepared to share with these computer-ised cretins.

'Hi Sid.' It was Andy smartly suited and grinning. 'You'll have to put this on if we're to go further than this lobby.' Andy held an identity square attached to a piece of narrow ribbon.

'What the hell's that?'

'Electronic ID – guard against terrorists.'

'Your photography's not the sharpest, Sid, but yeah, we could use these. But I don't know whether it's much of a story now. I mean we've a government minister on the fiddle and that footballer with three girls in his bed. All stories our public has a right to know.'

'Sure, but this is a nice story for once. Sort of romantic – don't you need to keep your female readers sweet?'

'I dunno, the couple could say we were invading their privacy.'

'Come off it, Andy. Since when has that stopped us.'

'All right, Sid. We'd better have a word with Cliff.'

Cliff was the young home editor. Sid had heard he was ambitious and ruthless.

'These are interesting, Mr Everett.' The young editor looked up from the pictures. 'But I'm sorry to tell you someone has got in ahead of you.'

'What – I mean who?'

'It's all right – not one of us. We had a man called Hammersen, an agency journo in here yesterday. If he's right then that little girl, Emily, has a very interesting ancestor.'

'Who's that?'

'We were given a name but we need to do more checking. However, Mr Everett I'll buy your pictures for five hundred pounds. We'll use them, face pixeled at first, then much more money if we identify the girl.'

'What's that police car doing?' Kirsten was surprised and now increasingly worried. They had arrived home in South Marshall to see a police panda car parked in their drive. 'Oh no, has something happened to Emily?'

A policewoman was standing by her motor speaking into a radio. She at once put the instrument away and ran across to them. 'You are Mr and Mrs Simpson?'

'Yes,' Steve answered. 'What's happened?'

'Your neighbours saw intruders and as they knew you were away they phoned us.'

Kirsten's relief was rapidly replaced with anger. 'What did they take?'

'We need you to check your house and see what's gone; you know you shouldn't have gone away without leaving a contact number.'

Kirsten accepted the reprimand; she could easily have driven home even if it would have taken an outbreak of war to separate Steve from a racing regatta.

'Come on,' she replied. 'Let's go and see.'

'Thank God for that – they've not touched our medals,' Steve was standing in front of the sitting room's glass case with all their Olympic memorabilia.

'They'd have been hard put to find a buyer for those. They'd be hot property,' Kirsten looked at the WPC for confirmation.

'You know this is the second break in we've suffered in a fortnight?' said Steve. 'It's got to be that woman come back while she knew we were away.' Kirsten watched him turn and walk briskly into his office cum study. 'Can't see anything different.'

Something was wrong. Kirsten could sense it and then she saw. 'Emily's photograph has gone. The one you took when she was four.'

'There's a file box missing,' said Steve. 'Oh, shit; they've taken your nationality papers and the kids' birth certificates. This settles it. It's Hammersen's – work got to be.'

The WPC was busy writing notes. 'Please, could you explain?'

'Right,' Said Chloe, 'this is the racing programme, but the Olympic indicators are the ones in bold.' Emily studied the list. The indicator events were the ones they needed to do well in if they were to be selected for Olifa. There were a dozen spread over the next three years. Of course if they had runaway wins they could well be selected much earlier.

'These are the ones we need to work on right now,' Chloe continued. 'Most of 'em we've done before, but this one's new on the schedule: Israel in July, straight after Hyeres and Lake Garda.'

'Isn't that a dodgy place to go these days?' said Emily. 'You know, bombs going off all over the place?'

'Yeah, but the organisers say they'll have massive protection during the week and there's been soccer matches there in the last year and no problems.'

'So it's Auckland, Hyeres, Lake Garda, and Israel. That's going to cost a bomb without letting one off.'

Chloe laughed. 'Don't worry. We've our funding and our sponsor's paying all the transport.'

'Erin will be working by the summer,' said Emily. 'She's not a student any more.'

'I think your schools finish in July. I want her in the team – you too. How are you placed?'

'Tony Travis is going out for Hyeres. He says he'll stand us dinner.'

'You sure he doesn't want you to bunk with him?'

'Chloe, for your information, Travis is one of our top QCs. I'm sure he could find a better bed partner than me, and he's married.'

'Men ain't my bag. How did your Tom do at Rutland with his Laser?'

Emily had received a disconsolate call from Tom. 'He scored a fifth but messed up on the other three races.'

'Poor Tom. He's a bit in your shadow isn't he?'

'I don't know what it is. He's fit enough, but maybe his coordination isn't quite right. If he was racing big boats I think he'd do better.'

'Is he thinking of that?'

'No, I doubt it. He's a good seaman though. He handled *Puffin* OK.'

'Do you think he would work with our campaign on shoreside?'

'Team manager, you mean?'

'Yeah, something like that. Keep the boat in shape, see we girls get fed,' Chloe sniggered. 'See we go to bed on time.'

'Tom's just got a new job. He won't have time off at the moment, but he'd do the job well once we qualified for Olifa.'

'You can put it to him and see what he says.'

'You can't place charges? What do you mean – that's crazy!' Steve was clearly angry. 'What difference does that make?' Kirsten watched as Steve listened to the reply. She was concerned now as her husband's face reddened and his neck muscles tensed. Whatever this was about it was not a healthy conversation for a man recovering from a stroke. 'I suppose I'll have to accept this, but it doesn't mean that the same person stole those papers. That photograph of my daughter was the only copy we had and it is irreplaceable... Yes, and you're not half as sorry as I am.' Steve slammed down the phone and turned to Kirsten. He was still breathing heavily.

'What's happened?' she asked.

'The idiots have identified the woman in Johnny's photo. They say she's got diplomatic immunity, for God's sake. Since when have a lot of bloody foreigners got the right to break into decent English homes and run off with our most personal things?'

'What embassy does she come from?'

'They won't say.'

Kirsten needed to stay calm on behalf of both of them. 'The girl in the picture didn't look particularly Danish. Could be Italian.'

'What would any bloody Eytie mafia wops want with our papers?'

Kirsten put her arms around her aggrieved husband and laughed. 'All this racist stuff. You sound as if you're in a football crowd.'

Steve flopped down on the sofa. 'The only thing they could say was that the embassy would be asked to send her home.'

'At least she can't be anything to do with the Le Bois girl that Tom spoke to.'

'No, it's got to be something to do with that Hammersen.' He paused, and Kirsten sensed, as she always did, that he wanted to tell her something that was troubling him.

'Isn't it time we told everyone – cleared this up once and for all?'

She was angry in her turn. 'I am not besmirching the memory of Uncle Kaj. He couldn't help his birth.'

Steve's expression was troubled and his voice nervous. 'Darling are you sure in your own heart that Erik Elgaad was your grandfather…'

Kirsten felt her cheeks burn as her old temper exploded. 'You disbelieving old sod! My poor mother was born in 1933 in Copenhagen. Listen. Erik and Gerda didn't go to Munich until 1935, and she met that evil man there on his bloody film set. I know she'd never set eyes on him until then, and when that picture with Hitler was taken she was already pregnant with Kaj.'

'All right, love I believe you. No need to shout. You've upset the cat.'

Kirsten swung round to watch Gerry, Emily's ageing cat, fix them both with a steely gaze before exiting the room. She relaxed and smiled. 'Cat shows a proper contempt for you. I can always tell.'

CHAPTER 13

Emily stood on the landing looking down the stairs. She had just emerged from her bedroom dressed in all her finery including these ridiculous high heels into which she had struggled. Tottering down those stairs was not an option. She had two choices, lose all her dignity and take Dad's stair lift or pull the bloody things off again. She listened intently, but the others were all watching the Olympics on the sitting room television. Sod it; she would try the lift. She dropped the seat, slid aboard and pressed the descent button. Very slowly the contraption lowered her towards the hallway. She reached the end exactly at the moment when Chloe, Erin and Tom emerged from the sitting room, the three of them witnessing her humiliation with grins all over their stupid faces.

'Strewth, mates, look at Cinders in her chariot – ha ha – ti hi hi hi.' Chloe was pointing at Emily and doing a sort of Maori dance.

Emily extracted herself from the seat with as much savoir-faire as she could manage for the moment. 'You lot try walking downstairs in these things.'

'Not really my style of shoe,' Tom spluttered.

Dad had appeared and was eyeing her up and down. 'What the hell do you call that dress?'

'Don't you like it?'

'I would if you could raise the neckline by about a foot and add some secure straps. If you do as much as sneeze you'll fall out of it.'

'No I won't, it's held in place, underpinned so I can hardly breathe, but my tits are taped to it.'

'I don't know – your generation…'

'We know all about your generation,' said Kirsten who had followed the others. 'All boring grunge, denim and unisex in your day. These young ones are glamorous and tasteful with it. Emily, take no notice of your father: he is fast becoming the new Victor Meldrew. I think you look lovely and I'm very proud of you.'

'So am I,' said Steve. 'You look gorgeous.'

'What's happening in the Olympics?' Emily asked.

'We, NZ that is,' said Chloe, 'have got gold in the women's heavy lift and you Poms have done bugger all.'

'Wait until the sailing gets going, and the bikes and the rowers – you won't get near us.'

'That's true. Sammy and her girls sounded confident,' said Erin.

‘We saw them interviewed just now.’

‘It’s easy to talk big,’ Emily grunted.

‘Put a sock in it, Em,’ said Chloe. ‘Sammy and that crew deserve a go. Four years on they’ll be over the hill.’

‘They’re not the best; we are. They’ve just sweet-talked the selectors.’

‘Emily that is not true.’ Steve was reproving. ‘I was privy to the selection and it was results-based. If you girls had won that final indicator you’d be there now, but you didn’t – did you?’

‘C’mon boys and girls,’ said Chloe, ‘time we’re off and away.’

‘Mike’s already out by the car,’ said Erin. ‘He’s a bit shy.’

Emily winked at Tom. Mike was Erin’s latest: a quiet but likeable young man and another dinghy sailor. Tonight was the big charity ball at one of the posher South Coast yacht clubs. It wasn’t normally the sort of function where Emily felt at ease, but her parents were members and had told Emily that she and her team could meet some influential backers for their Olympic project. The boys had full evening wear and Emily couldn’t fault their appearance. Her mother wore a demure black halter-top gown, Erin had an ensemble only slightly less revealing than Emily’s, and Chloe had upstaged them all with her formal Army evening mess kit and medals ribbons. Only the lack of a dress sword spoilt the effect.

‘Where’s Johnny?’ asked Emily.

‘He’s gone to Midhurst with Christine,’ said Kirsten. ‘He’s staying the night with some of his school friends.’

The two cars arrived at the Royal King Henry Yacht Club to find the place alive and floodlit with an illuminated path to the front entrance. Kirsten thought the whole thing a bit pretentious and over the top, considering the straitened economic times. Bar staff flitted around a crowded foyer with trays of champagne glasses. Kirsten sipped one but did not finish it. She, as usual, had been volunteered for the drive home, as had poor Tom with his car. She walked out through the open glass doors by the harbourside. More chains of coloured lights lit the balconies and made pretty reflections over the water and the lines of moored boats, while sedate ballroom music filtered out from within the main building. She wondered how her youngsters were taking this, to her mind, boring English middle class ritual.

A man was walking towards her. He was immaculately attired in eveningwear and had a smug self-confident air. Here was no Englishman; the man was familiar from nearly twenty years ago: that week when Kirsten won Olympic bronze for Denmark with her wind surfer. The man had helmed in the Star class, as she remembered, representing some tinpot South American country. He had received a medal of some colour; she couldn't remember what, at the same medal ceremony as hers. At the time she remembered him to be brusque and too pleased with himself.

'Miss Kirsten Elgaad, I believe,' the man held out his hand, accompanied with a formal bow. 'I remember you so well. Skill and beauty combined.'

'Thank you, Mr…'

'Primo Garcia. I met your husband again a few weeks ago at Rutland Water. A fine sailor who is still achieving great things.'

'That's interesting,' she replied. 'He never mentioned you.'

'I'm sure he had other things on his mind. He was well back to winning ways. Perhaps we shall see him for the Paralympics in my country.'

'Your country?'

'Indeed, my country. I am an Olifarian.'

'It's a bit early to talk of Paralympics. My husband is still recovering from a serious illness. Who can say what he will be doing in four years' time? Do you realise he will be age seventy?'

'Will he really. That is most interesting.'

Kirsten was not pleased. 'Why is that so interesting?'

'If he won a medal that would make history, would it not?'

Emily was puzzled and not really enjoying herself. She had already downed three glasses of champagne but found the yacht club members and guests a bit off-putting. The place seemed to be crammed with superior gushing ladies, while their elderly husbands and escorts were all too keen to stare down Emily's cleavage. Some of them must be almost as old as her dad. It seemed peculiar to her that no one seemed to be talking about sailing or even motor boating for that matter. She had tried in politeness to initiate talk on sailing and the Olympics but had been met by blank looks. All the talk, around and about and over her for that matter, seemed to be about business, the stockmarket, or even worse, politics. On the walls were framed photographs of ancient yachts and gloomy looking old men in funny Victorian gear and yachting caps. In Emily's imagination they were all glaring at her strapless frock with disapproval.

'Can't we go for a walk?' she asked Tom.

'No, I've been told that you and the other two are up for a

presentation and Chloe's got to make a speech.'

'That'll be water off a duck's back for Chlo', as long as she doesn't use any Kiwi expletives.'

Tom squeezed her hand. 'Once that's done we can go to the marquee.'

'Where?'

'Outside, there's a DJ and a disco laid on for us riffraff, while the oldies do their strictly dancing.'

Emily put an arm around him. 'Mum and Dad used to be rather good at that lark, but with Dad's leg I doubt they'll do much tonight.'

Chloe was signalling from the far side of the room. 'You'd better go,' said Tom. 'Your captain commands.'

Emily reached Chloe through a crowd of people all heading for the ballroom; a space into which one could have fitted the Branham Lake clubhouse four times. The band had stopped playing and its personnel departed for a break, an alcoholic one Emily guessed. The commodore of the Royal King Henry was beaming at the assembly, hand mike at the ready. He was a hearty old buffer, one of Dad's former sailing set. It was his pleasure, he said, to welcome their distinguished yachting guest, Signor Primo Garcia, a vice-president of the South American Olympic Federation. Signor Garcia was already an Olympic silver medallist representing his nation of Olifa. As they all knew, Olifa was staging the next games in four years' time.

'Get on with it, man,' Tom muttered in Emily's ear.

'Now for the awards,' said the Commodore. 'These annual awards have been voted for by members of the South Coast Union of Yacht and Sailing clubs.'

'Christ,' muttered Tom. 'Wouldn't have thought these capitalist, toffee-nosed buggers would like the word union.'

'Shuddup, Tom,' she whispered as she stifled a giggle.

'For the outstanding local team, I am delighted to say we have European and United Kingdom Women's match racing champions: Chloe Stamford, Emily Simpson and Erin Walsh.' Emily bit her lip. She wasn't nervous, but she hadn't reckoned on having to climb four wooden steps in these heels. No handrail was provided and the other two wore flat shoes. Erin gave her a helping pull up the last two steps. The South American guy handed each of them a tiny silver trophy and a certificate. While doing so the man had a good look down both girls' dresses. Emily supposed she should take that as a Latino compliment. The guy seemed slightly nervous of Chloe: maybe military uniforms were a bit of a turn off for someone reared in a dictatorship.

‘Ladies and gents all,’ Chloe began. ‘You’re not quite accurate, Mr Commodore. My full family name is Te-Kooti-Stamford, but that’s a mouthful, so I’m just Chloe. I’m a Kiwi by birth, but I’m proud to serve in Her Majesty’s forces, and I’m just as proud to sail for Britain, the nation that supplied one half of my ancestors.’

A warm applause greeted this. Emily knew that Chloe was popular with the sailing community as a good helm and a colourful character.

‘Many thanks for this award. We will all try to live up to it in the future. To one and all, good sailing and kiaora as we say where I come from, and that means good health.’ More prolonged applause.

They could now escape. Tom helped Emily down the last steps while she handed him the silver trophy. ‘Come on, we’ll put this in the car for safekeeping and then hit the dance floor.’

They strolled arm in arm down the illuminated path to the car park. Small knots of smokers had gathered. These people seemed so consumed by their addiction as to be unaware of passers by. Emily winced as she flicked hot ash off her bare shoulder. Tom had stopped abruptly and was staring at one group of three. Two girls and a man slightly obscured by a bush. Tom released Emily and strode up to these people.

‘Excuse me, I think I know you but can’t place you at the moment.’

‘I am sorry, but I don’t know you – but I think your friend is Emily Simpson. Am I right?’

Tom replied. ‘Didn’t you see her just now, in there?’

‘No.’

‘Well, as it happens you are right. But I still think I’ve seen you around. Are you Mary?’

‘No, I’m Leila.’

‘Sorry, perhaps I’m mistaken.’

Tom rejoined Emily. ‘Come away from here,’ he whispered. ‘Let’s find your parents.’

‘Tom, what was all that about?’

‘I’m right, I’m bloody sure I’m right. That girl is the same one as in your Johnny’s pictures. She’s the one who broke into your place.’ He pointed towards the clubhouse. ‘I’ve seen her in there and out here. She’s been watching you.’

‘Paul, I’ve a research job for you.’ Steve had rung Paul Matheson, head of his family’s investigative firm. ‘It’s a bit of a long shot, but can you check on the employees of foreign embassies in London?’

‘I’m not sure about that, Mr Simpson.’

‘I don’t mean hang about outside. They must have to publish lists of their staff. I want to find any female employees – first name Leila. I’ll explain why.’ Steve did just that, telling Paul the whole story of the break in the photographs and Tom’s sighting at the Royal King Henry.

‘All right, Mr Simpson. I’ll have a go but it may take a few days.’

Steve had been sceptical when Tom had hauled him away from the party inside the Royal King Henry. With Emily, the two men had scoured the surrounds and had been about to give up when Steve had spotted the group of three under the floodlights in the car park. Tom was right; the resemblance was too alike for it to be a mistake.

‘I tried to catch her out,’ said Tom. ‘I asked her name and she said Leila, or that’s what it sounded like and I don’t think she was lying. It was too spontaneous and a serious gaffe on her part.’

‘I wasn’t happy about going out and leaving this house unattended,’ said Steve. ‘but I was committed to that do at the King Henry.’

‘Em was the belle of the ball,’ said Tom. ‘She stole the show with that dress.’

‘You mean she was flaunting herself,’ Steve grunted. ‘I saw her posing for that camera.’

‘It was the Yachts and Yachting guy. He’s putting her in the next edition. They’re doing a piece on the three girls. Anyway they all looked great. That’s more than you can say about Sammy and her macho two. Are they really girls?’

‘At least they’re winning at the moment.’

The Olympic sailing had commenced and true to form, Emily’s rivals had chalked up two wins in the group stages and were looking good for a medal in the finals. Other British competitors were doing well, boosting sailing in the public imagination while the athletes were busy coming fifth.

Emily was not sorry to ditch the glamorous dress. It had been nice to be the centre of male admiration for a few hours, but the thing had felt horribly constricting and the high heels’ strapping had bruised her feet. It had been a relief to run downstairs nude for her early morning swim, but today the weather was gloomy and damp. She was happy to pull on her patched jeans and a T-shirt.

She had agreed to drive her father over to Branham so that he could take part in another race. He was leading the second summer series even though he had joined it late. It was great to see his new enthusiasm as he rediscovered the sailing skills that had made his name. Today was going to be a bit of fun as Chloe, Erin and Emily had been invited to take part in the 2.4 race in club owned boats. Steve was still frustrated that the doctors had not cleared him to drive. His car already had automatic gearing from the time before his hip operation. He grumbled that his right leg was a lot more mobile than it had been then. The grumbling gradually subsided as they passed Petersfield and headed north up the A3. Emily was enjoying driving the Volvo and could cheerfully ignore the muttered comments on her driving. She was looking forward to being in a boat again. Later she would be going out with Tom and then back to his bedsit. It was going to be a good day. They reached Branham and Emily parked in a disabled slot.

'Your not disabled and you're the driver,' Steve grumbled.

'Dad, stop whinging, you're the disabled one and I've got you right next to your boat.' She opened the boot door and lifted out the wheelchair.

'I don't want that bloody thing,' said Steve.

'Yes you do, you need to conserve energy. I'll wheel you down to where the helpers are and they'll get the boat ready.'

'What are you going to do?'

Emily settled her father in the chair and pushed her towards the group of supporters. 'I'm going to the clubhouse to get us both a cup of coffee. Be back in a minute.'

Emily knew they were early. She looked around, but there was no sign of the other girls. Chloe had a full weekend's leave and Erin was still at a loose end. On Monday, Emily was due for her first stint up front in the solicitor's office. She would be gainfully employed as Dad put it. The clubhouse was crowded with cadet kids and the queue for the kitchen was almost out to the front door. Emily shrugged and took a seat at a table. She yawned and picked up an abandoned newspaper – yesterday's *Daily Banner.*

Not much news and rather more trivia. She turned to the sport to see a photo of Sammy and her crew smirking out of their boat's cockpit. Emily muttered a single expletive and turned to the inside pages. Now her mouth fell open as she stiffened in shock to the point where she felt sick.

SPAWN OF EVIL.

A young girl living in the heart of the English countryside. Does she have a story to tell?

The piece had two pictures. One was of a tall blonde-haired woman staring with a rapturous expression at a uniformed man. The man was Adolf Hitler. Beside the woman was another uniformed man with thin-faced features. The second picture was recent and it made Emily gasp. A boy and girl holding hands but with both faces electronically blurred out. The disguise didn't count. The boy was Tom and the girl was herself.

CHAPTER 14

Steve had been preparing his boat when he saw the distraught Emily running the length of the car park. She was crying, brushing the tears away with a rumpled newspaper. What the hell was going on? Trailing in Emily's wake were Chloe and Erin who had just arrived. It was Erin who caught Emily and put her arms around her friend.

'Emily what is it?'

'I can't tell you. They're out to get me and I haven't done anything.'

'Steve had reached her. What is it?'

Emily was shaking. He had not seen her in this state since the aftermath of the fire siege.

She pushed the newspaper into his hands and subsided in a burst of sobbing. Steve saw it for himself now and he too was appalled. He hadn't known that there were copies of the picture of Gerda Elgaad with Hitler and Goebbels and he was hard put to contain his cold fury at the obscured picture of Emily and Tom.

'Emily, forget about the boats, come for a walk.'

They walked along by the Lake View Hotel and round towards the hill overlooking the western end of the lake. Steve needed the support of a stick for every inch of the way, but the further they walked the easier the task became. Every time Steve suspected his daughter was about to speak, he would squeeze her arm and shake his head. Very slowly, with Emily supporting him, they climbed to the top of the hill. Here they found a park bench and sat down.

'All right, sweetheart, let me read this rubbish.'

Exhaustive research may prove that a young twenty one-year old Sussex girl is the only living descendant of the most evil man to have lived in our times...

'Rather windy language for the Banner,' said Steve. He was battling his own emotions now but trying to appear controlled. 'This nonsense will have to stop.'

'Does Mum know the truth?' Emily turned a wan face to him. 'Am I going to be evil?'

'Look, your mother loved and revered her Uncle Kaj. She kept house for him when his marriage broke down. And his marriage broke down when his wife discovered the same skeleton in the cupboard.' He put his arm around Emily's shoulders. It seemed as if the girl had shrunk back in time and size. 'First, don't worry. You are descended from your great grandmother Gerda but your mother has no connection with the father of her Uncle Kaj. For your mother this is a very sensitive matter and I will leave it to her to tell you the true facts when she feels ready.'

'What do I do though, Dad? They must know my name. If it's blasted all over the tabloids I could lose my place in law chambers and be thrown out of sailing.'

'No you won't and I'm going to take steps to see this persecution stops. Just remember it all happened years ago. I can only tell you this: if the true facts come out I doubt anyone will hold it against you. It's nothing like such an interesting story as these newspaper creeps are making out.'

'I've always known there was some secret about Uncle Kaj, but you've never told me, and mum bit my head off when I asked her, and I never asked her until a few weeks ago when that man Hammersen turned up.'

Steve kissed her cheek. 'Try not to worry. First thing on Monday I'll come with you to the solicitor and we'll start proceedings.'

Emily turned sharply and her mouth dropped open. 'No, Dad! Don't come with me like I'm a little girl on first day at school. Come in later and I'll show you into the boss man.'

The return walk downhill was a more painful experience for Steve, but he made it back to the sailing club in time to take part in his race. Emily was still sunk inside herself and Steve didn't pressure her to sail. The other two girls were concerned for Emily, but Steve told them it was better they take part themselves as arranged and let Emily find some solitude.

It was a damp grey early autumn day with little tangible wind and some nasty shifts. Steve's performance by his standards was poor, and his thoughts were elsewhere. He made tactical errors, failed to read the wind patterns and finished a lowly sixth out eleven. Chloe and Erin had a fierce battle for last place but seemingly enjoyed the experience.

'Cripes, these little boats are a bit of a learning curve, I guess,' said Chloe.

'You haven't got a crew to shout orders at,' said Emily who had strolled down the jetty when the race ended. 'You've got to do everything yourself.'

Steve was relieved to see that the girl was smiling again.

'Come on,' he said, 'let's pack these boats up and go home.'

The return drive was in silence, and Emily made no reference to her troubles. On reaching home Steve delegated her to put the car away while he limped indoors with the offending newspaper.

'We are going to have to do something about this,' Steve addressed his wife. 'I won't let Emily suffer. She's already been through hell once. I think we should tell her the truth.'

'Only if she swears on her life to tell no one else.'

'Darling, I know how you feel…'

'No, you don't – you never can!'

'Listen, please. If Emily is sworn to silence it won't stop this persecution. These newspaper people will believe what they want to believe because it seems sensational, when in truth they haven't got a story.'

'So, you think I'm deaf?' Emily was standing in the doorway her face twisted in an anger that neither of them had witnessed before. 'You've got to tell me the truth now and what I do afterwards is down to me – it's my life!'

'All right, Em,' said Kirsten. 'Uncle Kaj's real father was Josef Goebbels.'

Emily's mobile face had relaxed in puzzlement. 'I've never heard of him.'

CHAPTER 15

Emily arrived on time for her first morning in the solicitor's office. She had to admit to herself that she was a victim of her own over-indulgence. She was required to present herself at nine o'clock, a time when hitherto she would have barely been awake. Added to that was the glorious night she had shared with Tom in his bed. If she was tired it was good form of tiredness: a pleasing post orgasmic languor and full of memories.

Mr Richard Giggs, the senior partner who had interviewed her last week, greeted her with a friendly smile and gave a briefing of her duties. This involved little more than minding the front of the shop and answering the phone. It didn't look as if her law degree would be much use, but she was grateful for the chance to watch her profession at its grass roots.

Last night in the midst of their lovemaking she had poured out her troubles to Tom. 'I've never heard of this Gobbler or whatever, but just mentioning him really screws Mum up.'

Tom had both his arms around her as he pulled their naked bodies tight. 'Em, sweetheart, I suppose it's better than being descended from Hitler but not much. Who taught you your history?'

'I don't know anything about that war except old Gerry and the Battle of Britain, and we had a DVD of Auschwitz that Mum and Dad made me watch.'

'All right. Hitler was a man with an evil warped vision. Josef Goebbels was Hitler's propagandist – spin-doctor we'd say these days. Hitler was mad and bad, but it was Goebbels that conned the German people into following Hitler.'

'Mum told me that Gerda was an actress and that this Gobbles, whatever, fell for her 'cos he saw her on a film set.'

'Yes, that follows. Goebbels made clever feature films: sort of epics with a message.'

'Tom, how do you know all this?'

'How? Girl, I went to a rated public school, not a rowdy comprehensive dump. They taught us history … and … ow stop that!'

Emily had retaliated the insult by squeezing her lover's most delicate parts. 'Tom, darling,' she whispered, 'if we were to have a baby that would stop a lot of this shit; like Hammersen saying I never should.'

She could sense the alarm in him. 'Em, for Christ's sake, not yet.

You've got your career to follow, and so have I, and there's your sailing. It would be great if we had kids one day. We will, we must, but only when we can afford to and not just to spite a moron like Hammersen.' He began to run his fingers over her back and bottom. 'Come on, my love, I'm ready again.' He began to roll her over so gently as she released her hands. 'You have taken that pill, haven't you?'

'Yes, I've told you twice already. And even if I hadn't it's a bit late now.' She lay back and subsided into a long gurgle of laughter.

Emily sat at her desk and tried to pull her mind back into the real world. It had been such a wonderful night, but one thing troubled her. Tom was a mature man of twenty-five. If he knew how to please a girl in bed as perfectly as he did, then someone must have shown him, and that would be another woman wouldn't it?

A very tall lady had entered the room and was staring down at Emily. 'I want to see Dick Giggs.' Her voice was English county, secure upper class; different from the pretentious city wives the other night at the yacht club.

'I'll tell him.' Emily pressed the intercom switch. 'Is it Mrs…'

The woman drew herself up to full height. 'Lady Anthia Harmon-Hackett. Tell him I want a bloody divorce: ASAP – got that?'

'Yes, er, lady… Would you care to take a seat in the waiting room? I'm sure Mr Giggs will be down in a minute as soon as I tell him.'

'Quicker than last time, I hope.' Lady Anthia, stared at Emily. 'You're new. Not seen you before.'

Emily showed her client to the waiting room and returned to her station.

'Let her stew for a bit,' said Giggs's voice on the intercom.

'What do I tell her?'

'Nothing, just sit tight and I'll come down. Sorry, Emily, not a good one to have on your first day.'

Kirsten parked the car and the two of them walked the few yards to the solicitors. Emily seated at her desk had greeted them with a happy smile.

'Where did you get to last night?' Steve asked.

'I told you, I was staying overnight with friends.'

'Doing what?'

'Nothing.'

Kirsten intervened. 'That will do. This is not what we came for.'

'Mr Romero is free to see you,' said Emily. She dropped her voice to a whisper. 'There's a ghastly woman in with Mr Giggs. He's fixing her divorce.'

'If she's that ghastly, I'm not surprised,' said Steve.

'I want to reassure you that everything you've told me is confidential. We are bound by client and legal advisor's rules.' Romero was serious but not shocked by the revelations. 'Can you tell me – how many people know this secret?'

Steve thought for a moment. 'My eldest daughter Sarah, and her old school friend, Francine: Kirsten, of course and myself: also Frank Matheson.'

'I know him, if you mean the investigator,' said Romero. 'If he's agreed to keep confidence he will do so.'

'That's it and I'm one hundred percent certain none of those others would talk to the press. The two girls are loyal to each other and both nearly died because they knew too much.'

'If Mr Hammersen is Scandinavian, it follows that the source of this information is in Denmark. And logically there must be some record in Germany as well.'

'Please,' said Kirsten. 'What do we do about the *Daily Banner?*'

'This is the tricky bit. If the newspaper were to say your daughter was a descendant of Hitler that would be so preposterous that they would be liable for substantial defamation damages. Likewise with Goebbels. Now, DNA is not going to be a lot of help as no one is going to dig up Goebbels, and no trace of Hitler is supposed to exist.'

'We may have some things of Kaj's,' said Kirsten.

'If you found anything usable for DNA it would only prove that Emily is not descended from the late Mr Kaj Elgaad.'

'Is there anything we can do?' Steve felt desperate. 'Look, it won't be good for you if the *Banner* say your receptionist is Hitler's descendant.'

'Emily, I've great news. I've got my posting.' Chloe was shouting down Emily's mobile.

'Hang on Chloe.' Emily looked at the door but could see no sign of any more clients. 'OK, what's happened?'

'I've a posting to Bovington, next month.'

'Oh yeah – where's that?'

'It's the Royal Armoured Corps top base, but from our point of view it's just up the road from Portland.'

Now Emily understood. Portland was the National Sailing Academy and the main base for Olympic training. They had been planning to berth a boat there for practise.

'That's fantastic, Chlo'.' Emily wished she could sound more enthusiastic. She had so much going for her at home and her London appointment was vital to her future. The girls' previous attempt had been based at Hayling near Portsmouth while they had shared a flat in Havant. It hadn't been the ideal base but it was a handy location. Emily lived not far away in Sussex and Erin came from Portsmouth.

'Tell you something else, mate,' continued Chloe. 'We won't be far from Old Duddlestone Marina and your Tom.'

'He doesn't live there any more,' Emily murmured almost to herself.

Kirsten had no compunction in digging into her family's financial reserves. The high court injunction served on the *Daily Banner* seemed to have frightened that publication and all mention of Emily had ceased. As the solicitor told them, the *Banner* had already paid more than two million pounds in damages this year and their board-room was not inclined to risk more. Emily had settled into her part-time job and was enjoying being useful. She obviously missed Tom when he spent days away fixing computers the length of Southern England. These young ones' relationship seemed almost too perfect for Kirsten. She detected none of the fireworks that enlivened her own life with Emily's father. But Kirsten knew that Emily was strong-willed and had much of her mother's emotional and tempest-uous nature.

It was autumn now, and the colder winds were breezing across the lake at Branham. Kirsten was pleased that Steve had been cleared to drive his car. He could walk short distances without support, although his speech still had that odd West Country intonation that surprised old friends. Steve's rediscovery of small boat racing had been the best therapy. He had an obsessive love of his new little boat and was winning his races more often than not. Her husband was now very near the top of the ratings for disabled sailors. The Paralympics in Olifa might not be a dream after all.

Steve's rediscovery of his old self had been complete with his return to full work at Easterbroke Sails. Kirsten, as company chair-man, had kept the ship afloat but Steve was the technical expert who talked the talk with a whole raft of customers, from parents with children's Cadet and Mirror dinghies, to the heads of World girdling race teams. The international financial crisis had done massive damage to the sailing industry everywhere. Easterbroke had closed branches including the engine maintenance shop at Birdham. This had been an easier decision, as all remembered the first man to manage it and the grief he had caused.

'What do you think, Mum?' Emily had come into the room wearing the dark suit ensemble she had chosen for her stint in the barrister's chambers.

'Stand up straight and let's look at you then.' Kirsten passed her gaze over this new outfit. The girl certainly looked professional. 'You only need the wig to make you look the part.'

'Won't get that for a year or two,' said Emily.

'It's kind of Mr Travis to let you go off to the other side of the world.'

'Tony Travis is boat crazy. He says he might fly out himself and he's going to arrange for me to sit in a few New Zealand court hearings. Their judicial system is pretty much like ours.'

'Chloe will be on her home turf. I expect she's looking forward to that.'

'That's right. It's not Auckland so much, but her Maori relations come from the King Country. Her Uncle's got a big dairy farm and he supplies that butter-making firm.'

Kirsten smiled. 'I know the one. We've got some in the fridge.' She was happy to keep her daughter distracted.

Steve and Tom were in the sitting room in front of the television. They were watching the triumphant return of the Great Britain team, and the sight of Sam and her crew waving their medals had been too much for Emily who had stalked angrily from the room. Her father had shouted something about her lacking sportsmanship and being un-British. Kirsten was British by adoption but at heart she remained the Danish child she had been born. A creature of deep loves and fierce hates, and in this respect Emily was very like her.

'Are you going to wear that outfit in New Zealand courts?' Kirsten asked.

'I 'spect so.'

'It'll be very hot out there – it's summer.'

'You've got a point. Chloe says we're a bit restricted on personal luggage because our sailing gear weighs loads. We're sending the dry suits, buoyancy aids and tools by airfreight. As for personal things, clothes and stuff; Chloe wants me to take my strapless dress. She says they have a posh ball out there. Didn't think Kiwis went for that sort of thing.'

'Don't see why they shouldn't – where's the function being held?'

'The Royal New Zealand Yacht Squadron. Christ, Mum, I'd never get inside the one at Cowes. No women or dogs is their rule.'

'Not nowadays, I gather. This is the twenty-first century, they've moved on. Although your dress might wake some of the old farts up a bit.'

Steve took the call on Friday morning.

'Mr Simpson, it's Paul Matheson. We've tracked down the woman in your picture.'

'Well done, Paul, who is she then?'

'I'm afraid it's a bit late to do anything. Her embassy sent her home as you heard.'

'But Paul, we saw her at the yacht club a week later in September.'

'I gather the embassy gave her a few days to get her things together.'

Steve realised that they were getting away from the point. 'Who is she?'

'We found seven women called Leila in various London embassies, but the only one leaving under a cloud is a Leila Lissmann. She worked as a clerical officer in the Middle East department of the United States Embassy. We showed your picture in confidence and she was positively identified as your intruder.'

'Why should she be interested in us?'

'I'm sorry, Mr Simpson, but we could find nothing positive about the woman. No friends or interests. We can delve a bit more if you think it's worth it.'

Steve knew that he had probably already incurred a hefty fee for this search. 'No thanks, Paul. If she's gone she's gone. I only wish she hadn't taken that framed picture of Emily when she was young. It meant so much to us. Who would want it – what would be the point?'

Tom was relaxing in the bar restaurant of his favourite Winchester pub. His mobile phone was ringing as he yawned and withdrew it from his jacket pocket. He assumed this was another redirection from head office but he was wrong.

'Hi, Alix, how's things?'

'Hi, Tommy, what are you at these days, and how is the new little girl?'

'I love her.'

'Ooo, I'm so consumed with jealousy.' Alix's well-remembered laugh echoed down the line.

'I thought you were fixed up with that old horse trainer bloke.'

'Ray? He's fantastic – my dream guy.'

'Is he G.I.B?'

'That as well – unbelievable.' He heard a shriek of delight.

Alix was Tom's first love and childhood playmate. They had shared an exciting adventure together a few days before Tom's abduction by the crazy Jolene. They had maintained a close platonic friendship, a brother-sister relationship, between two only children of single mothers. Apart from that they occupied very different worlds. Alix was the daughter of a Holywood male heartthrob, and she was also cutting a career on the stage at the moment in a supporting role in the TV soap Gravesenders. Emily enjoyed watching this, but Tom always found it too depressing and unreal to bother with. Never once had he revealed to Emily that the girl playing the unhappy and put upon Charlene was in real life someone to whom he, Tom, told his troubles. Alix would never be a rival to Emily but he wanted to keep their closeness a secret, or at least until the wedding. Now what the hell was he thinking about weddings for?

'Hi, Tommy – you still there?'

'Yeah of course – what's the news?'

'I'm killing off Charlene.'

'Really – why?'

'Because, darling, she is driving me insane. The silly little bimbo has to cry in every fucking scene I play, either that or scream and rant.'

Tom was concerned. He only knew that acting was the most insecure profession, and being in a TV soap was a steady earner. 'Will you find something else?'

'Yeah, you bet. That's why I rang. I'm going to play Aladdin's girl in panto in Southampton. It's an all-star cast. You've gotta come and bring the little girl with you. After that I may get to be Doctor Who's new assistant.'

All this was beginning to be a bit complicated for Tom. 'I'm sure we'd love to come but not meet backstage or anything. Alix, you see … Em doesn't know you exist.'

A gust of laughter came back down the line. Tom held the phone away from his ear and glanced nervously around, but no one was bothering to look at him.

'I exist all right,' Alix shouted. 'Wow! The seductive other woman. That's a role I haven't played yet.'

Tom couldn't help but laugh himself; Alix had that effect. 'Well, you are not playing it with us. Em loves watching Charlene by the way. She shouts at Big Max when he's being mean to her. I keep saying, "He can't hear you".'

'Oh, Tommy, that is just so wicked. We pre-record weeks before anyway.'

Tom finished his lunch and left the pub. In the car park he took out the phone again and rang Emily. He didn't exactly have a guilty conscience but he wasn't sure that Emily would understand his friendship with Alix or the fact that it was no threat to her real relationship with him. In his short life Tom had already learned that women were not rational beings in their understanding of men.

It was an unexpected warm autumn day and Emily was chewing her sandwiches in the little garden behind the office.

'Hi, Tom,' she replied. 'Where are you?'

'In Winchester. I've one more job in Basingstoke then that's it for today. How's the training going?'

'Hard work, I can tell you. We've scrounged a boat to practise with and the rest is all running and gym work.'

'You're well on your way for Auckland then.'

'Yeah, but we don't know what boat we'll get until we're there. All the boats in the competition are standard designs built as a batch. Tell you something else. Chloe's got an army posting to somewhere called Bovington. She says it's near Portland and your Duddlestone.'

'That's right. I know it. I've been round the tank museum enough times. But Em, I've just thought. Are you looking for a flat for the three of you?'

'Well, yes. Erin's made a few enquiries but Portland is bloody expensive even to rent, and Weymouth's worse.'

'Easy solution. Dad Wilson says they've just renovated the last of the Old Duddlestone cottages. He and Mum have always said I can have it as my weekend hideaway. I'm sure they won't mind letting it to future Olympic stars. If I lean on them you'll only pay peppercorn.'

'It sounds great, but how far is it from Portland?'

'Twenty minutes to half an hour trip if the road's clear.'

'What if it's not clear?'

'Then it will take you a few minutes longer. Anyway, we've got haul out facilities at Duddlestone; you can keep your boat there and sail across the bay.'

'OK, I'll put it to the others – but it sounds good.'

Steve was in an especially grumpy mood. He was stuck in the office at Chichester when he would far rather have been in the workshop. But with a dodgy leg and a lack of coordination he no longer had the satisfaction of a hands-on role. He could supervise all he liked and generally get in the way but that was the limit. It was Kirsten who presided over the Europe-wide operation with Steve's technical expertise. It had taken all the combined skills of both of them to keep the business turning over at somewhere near its pre-recession figures. There was less money in the world and less to be spent on sailing boats. That was the hard reality.

'Steve?' It was Sue, his PA. She stood just inside the closed office door and pulled a face. 'Unscheduled visitor,' she whispered. 'Shall I tell him to piss off?'

'Is he going to buy sails?'

'I would say not.' She handed him a card.

Steve looked at it and exploded. 'That little turd – he's got a bloody cheek coming in here.'

Sue grinned. 'I guess you're in a meeting.'

'Wait a minute. I think this is a case of damage limitation. All right I'll see him. Just stay in reach and if I buzz you can invent an important phone call, and then show the little bastard out.'

Steve was angry, worried and interested: all mixed emotion. Sid Everett was easily recognisable as he breezed into the office. The man was older and greyer but he still retained that ferret-like manner that Steve had good reason to remember.

'We will keep this brief, Mr Everett. Why are you harassing my daughter?'

'Here, come off it. You make me sound like a dirty old pervert.'

'Mr Everett, if you were that, Emily would deal with you herself. She has survived homicidal maniacs already. Why are you here, if not to bring her unhappiness?'

'No, Mr Simpson, I'm the one with a grievance. Who was it gave you the Leigh Park tip off in '89? Your other little girl's got good reason to thank me for that.'

'That was over twenty years ago, and I seem to remember it gave you a few column inches at the time.' Steve was not going to give ground. 'Get on with it. Why this visit?'

'I want a trade off. All right, all right – just listen please. I think your Emily could be in danger again. I can't give you details yet. Now the nice story. Your little girl's taken up with young Stoneman and that's an amazing coincidence, isn't it?'

'Never mind that – what danger?'

'Tell me first. Is it true that she's descended from Hitler?'

'For God's sake man. This is rubbish. Yes, her great grandmother was unhinged and she did meet Hitler, but for heaven's sake it's almost a matter of record that Hitler was incapable of normal sex. This is a stupid rumour being put around by that man Hammersen. You've heard of him I would guess.'

'Sure, Norwegian Nazi hunter, but I agree with you – the Hitler thing is balls.'

'Of which Hitler is reputed to have had only one,' Steve couldn't help the smile.

'What worries me,' Everett continued, 'is what the *Daily Banner's* yachting correspondent told me…'

Now Steve laughed. 'Oh come on, Mr Everett. Yachting correspondent – *the Banner* – pull the other one.'

'Not so, Mr Simpson. Your yachting isn't all posh, not no more. There's young working class boys and girls, *Banner* readers – like Samantha Robstron and her twins with their Olympic medal.'

'Don't mention them to Emily,' Steve muttered. 'OK, I accept I was wrong. I'm delighted the *Banner* is interested in sailing. So what did your correspondent say about Emily?'

'Only that she's in a yacht crew and they are going to some dodgy places. Not healthy, if you know what I mean.'

'No, Mr Everett. I do not know what you mean.'

'Mr Simpson. You spent a lot of dosh with that injunction. Bit of a waste of money wasn't it?'

'It seems to have worked.'

'I don't write for the *Banner* these days but I keep in touch. I happen to know that they won't deal with Karl Hammersen.'

'I suppose they know he'll only cost them another million in damages.'

'Yeah, well that's part of it. Look, Mr Simpson. We, the press that is, are going to cover your daughter's yachting. We'll do more than that. We'll watch out for her. She's little Emily of the fire siege for God's sake. Someone's got to take care of her.'

Steve was losing patience now. 'What are you going on about? Why should my daughter be in any danger at a yacht regatta? She's been to dozens of them.'

Sid stood up. 'All right, squire. The press won't run with the Hitler thing – it's too hot, but you can't stop them linking little Emily with young Stoneman. That's sort of romantic isn't it?'

Steve pulled himself upright with the help of the desk. 'Everett – out!'

Tom was fumbling in the dark for his dressing gown. It had to be somewhere, he was certain he'd left it dangling over the back of that chair.

'What are you up to?' Emily's voice came sleepily from their bed.

'I want to go to the toilet and I can't find my dressing gown.'

Emily was laughing. 'Tom, you don't want it just to go out of the room and back.'

'Yes I do. I don't go for all this nudity stuff. It's all right for you, your mother's brainwashed you, but I'm sticking to the decencies.'

'Tom, darling, I have already explored every inch of your lovely body. You don't have to hide from me.'

'I'm not hiding anything, I'm just doing the right thing.'

'You are just being bloody English. I think we should introduce you to that bloke on the telly who thinks he can cure the Brits of body shame.'

'Lost cause there I'd say.' He slipped the comfy white robe over his shoulders. 'That's better.'

Tom knew he was being an idiot, but much as he loved Emily he couldn't face standing in front of her stark naked. In the cosy security of their duvet it was different. Emily had vented her disappointment volubly when he had declined to stand naked under the shower with her and wash her back. He only hoped that his girl would not disclose his phobia to her mother. He didn't care to think of that lady's laughter and scorn.

He had been invited to dinner with the family that evening at Firs Farm. Kirsten had come up with a delicious lamb stew, but the conversation had been desultory and Tom had suspected that all was not harmony in the Simpson house. Emily's father seemed preoccupied and kept looking at Tom. Tom was unaware of having offended Steve; in fact the man had thawed in his attitude to Emily and him and had of late been warm and friendly. In the middle of the meal Chloe had called Emily. Emily had handed her mobile to Tom who had told the caller of his plan to offer them the Duddlestone cottage. Chloe had accepted the offer with thanks and a loud cheerful shriek. At the end of the evening Steve had made no comment about Tom taking Emily away for the night. Whatever was wrong it was not opposition to their relationship.

Tom returned from the bathroom and snuggled back under the duvet once more minus the dressing gown. Emily was still awake and propped herself up on one elbow as she watched him.

'What's biting your Dad this evening? I don't think it was me but something's wrong.'

'So, you picked up the vibes.' Emily wrapped her arms around him. 'I honestly don't know. He was fine in the morning when I went to work. It was when he came home from the sail loft that I noticed.'

'Is it a business problem?'

'No, I'm sure that's under control now. But something happened today while he was at work and I know it was something to do with me.'

Alix rang while Emily was in the shower. It was eight o'clock and outside the sun was shining on the wet street. 'Could you wait a second? Emily's with me, I'll talk to you outside.' Tom slipped through his front door onto the metal balcony that topped the entry steps.

'Tom, I've been reading today's *Daily Banner*.'

Tom was instantly on his guard. He sensed trouble and he was right. 'What does it say?'

'You'd better hold on to your cool, Tommy. There's a picture of you with the little girl and a piece about you two love birds both being famous abduction victims…'

'Oh, shit – is that all it says?'

'More or less. You'd better both keep your heads down because the paper are making it a great romantic slop story.'

'We can't vanish. We've both got jobs in sensitive professions. This could be a bloody disaster.' Tom was beginning to panic. That poxy little shit Everett; didn't dare use his Hitler story, so he was working off his spite for Emily with this garbage.

'Tommy, you're fond of your little girl. You've nothing to hide – just tough it out. I had to when they found out about me and that scumbag rat Nico. Give it a few days and it'll go away.'

Tom was aware that Emily had appeared in the doorway towelling her naked body. Now horrified, Tom glanced down at the narrow street but it was empty of vehicles and people and, fortunately, the opposite wall was blank with no windows. He gestured and glared at the girl, but she only grinned while she wrapped the towel around herself in at least a semblance of decency.

'Got to go now,' he said. 'Thanks for the info.'

'I sense the little girl is near,' he heard Alix's sultry laugh. 'Bye, Tommy.'

'Who was that?' asked Emily.

'A colleague who has just read an article in the bloody *Daily Banner*. For heaven's sake get indoors and be decent.'

'What article?' Emily looked worried.

'Get inside and I'll tell you.'

CHAPTER 16

Autumn passed seamlessly into winter. Emily lamented the draining and covering of the pool, while her father grumbled at the cost of heating the house. The furore over the article in the *Banner* died within days. Nobody locally had seemed too bothered, and Emily's friends had been supportive. Emily had joined her barrister's chambers in London. This had been a wrench as it meant separation from both her family and Tom for five days of the week. She couldn't afford the commuter rail fare and had to settle for a bedsit share in Earl's Court, with two other trainees. Tom had settled in well with his new company and had even had a good pay rise: enough for him to rent a flat in Alresford near Winchester. Emily stayed there most weekends.

Steve had settled into his sailing with a new determination. He was winning races again each weekend while he and Kirsten had driven over to Branham on spare afternoons for his practise sessions. Kirsten was relieved to see Steve sticking rigidly to his special diet and medications. The doctors were satisfied that a second stroke was unlikely while the patient continued this life style. Steve seemed to have accepted Emily and Tom as an item. Kirsten was more amused than annoyed by her husband's double thinking. One moment he would grumble about his daughter not being married to her man, while almost in the same breath complaining at the potential cost to himself of a wedding. For the moment at least they had heard no more of either Hammersen or Sid Everett.

Sid was in the unusual position of a man on the defensive. He, the professional news hound, was the one who did the pestering and felt no conscience about it. Now it was Sid who was being pestered and he didn't like it.

'Michelle Le Bois here, Mr Everett. You haven't been back to me when you promised that you would.' The girl had an irritating whining voice emphasised by the telephone.

'Michelle, love, I am doing my best but the facts are not quite panning out as you would like…'

'What facts – who have you been talking to?'

'I have talked to police who were there on the day. I've talked to an ex-SAS guy. Your uncle was killed by accident. It was unfortunate but that that's how it was.'

'He was trying to rescue that silly little bitch – can't think why.'

Sid took a deep breath. He knew that he had dropped himself into this one. After the fire siege he had deliberately run the story of the heroic police inspector shot down while doing his duty. He had almost believed it to be the truth at the time.

'Mr Everett, I'm told that Emily is German and her people were Nazis. Uncle Phil came from Guernsey – he hated all Germans.'

'I must correct you there. Emily's mother is born Danish, but her father, Kirsten Simpson's that is, was German, certainly; but he was Jewish – was lucky to survive by all accounts.'

'If you're not going to help me I'll have to go elsewhere,' the voice whined again. 'I know people who are going to fix that little bitch. And, thanks to your *Banner,* I know who her boyfriend is.'

'Michelle, you'd better think twice about who you get involved with. And if you step outside the law you'll be in deep shit. Now your uncle was a dedicated copper. Would he like that?'

The petulant Michelle had rung off at that point. Sid hoped that this was the end of it. He was not used to being emotionally caught up in a story or to have any kind feelings towards the subjects of his reporting. But little Emily was an engaging girl: feisty and pretty and hadn't she suffered enough? Sid was also worried about something that Karl Hammersen had told him. That guy was charging into battle on his own hobbyhorse, but he had dropped enough for Sid to piece together yet another story and this one he really didn't want to report.

'I don't think much of that,' said Emily. She was standing on a pontoon at Portland looking at their practise boat, a decrepit over-worked Yngling class.

'It's the best I can scrounge for now,' replied Chloe.

It was a cold December morning. A chill east wind funnelled across the harbour and short wavelets slapped against the dock. It was not an inviting prospect but that didn't matter. All three girls knew that they needed time on the water sailing something, anything with mast and sails and a crew of three. Runs on the road and workouts in the gym were fine but it was on the water that mattered.

'I wish we could have a boat of our own,' said Emily.

'No way, Em. Match racing has to be a level playing field. The organisers supply the boats and that's the way it is,' Chloe was firm. 'Come on, let's get out there. We want smooth tacking and slick kite hoisting. I don't know about you guys, but I feel a bit rusty.'

The Yngling had been an official Olympic women's class in the early years two thousand. Now outdated and replaced she could still provide a good sailing test as the girls discovered. Although clad in drysuits, it took time for them to warm up, and cold hands, even gloved, led to slow winch work and some fumbling spinnaker drill. The harbour was nearly deserted apart from one or two dinghies under instruction. Emily's skills as crew tactician were not needed on this trip so she concentrated on her mainsheet trimming. In the end each girl took a turn on the helm. It was cold; all three were splashed by flying spray and ended with wetted hair but it didn't matter. There was joy in being afloat and together once more.

They docked and watched the boat hoisted ashore. 'We'll have our coach watching us next time,' said Chloe. 'Here, Em, when can we see this cottage of yours?'

'It's not mine, but I'm staying with Tom's parents over Christmas, so you can come over and look any time.' Emily had worked a compromise: Christmas Day with Tom at Duddlestone and then return to Firs Farm for New Year's Eve, followed by her first trip to New Zealand. A week to acclimatise, and then serious competition.

Tom collected Emily from the Portland centre and drove her the short distance to the Duddlestones. New Duddlestone was the main community and it was not new in any way. It lay in the shadow of the Downs; a Purbeck stone tourist village not far from the more famous Corfe Castle. Emily was intrigued by the countryside and by the sight of the heritage steam railway that ran to nearby Swanage. Tom did not enter the main village but took a left turn into a side lane. The sign read *Old Duddlestone Marine Village.*

Emily had already visited that place by sea, and was excited at the prospect of living there in hers and the girls' own cottage. The only disadvantage would be living within a stone's-throw of Tom's parents. She had met them twice now and liked them and was reasonably sure that they approved of her. Tom's mother, Carol, was nice and had made Emily feel part of the family. Tom's stepfather, Peter, was the harbour manager and ran the marina and boatyard facility. He had spent much of his previous life as a ship's master and he looked the part. Carol's sister, Laura, ran the business side of the marina. She was the oldest of three children of a local farmer but had advanced herself from humble beginnings to a Cambridge honours degree. But a disastrous and short-lived marriage to a lazy philanderer had hardened her as a personality. Emily rather liked Laura, seeing certain of her traits in herself. Tom's parents lived in a cottage near the water and

Laura lived in an identical one two doors up the street.

'This is the new road,' said Tom. 'When the marina started we had to drive in over military land and that caused nothing but trouble. This road is ours, although the surface belongs to my Uncle Ian; he's the farmer at Honeycritch, the place we've just passed.'

'Oh!' exclaimed Emily. 'There's the sea.' The road had turned to the right and was running parallel with the cliff top.

'We're nearly there,' said Tom. The car was driving down a steepish, incline and Emily could see the whole village laid out below them with the harbour and the dock wall.

This mid-winter scene was so different to last time. The boatyard was filled with laid up yachts, with a few still in the water alongside the marina pontoons. The new sailing club building looked deserted, but the dinghy park was still full with racing craft. They drove into the top of the village street. Emily noticed the cliff face had a steel framed extension butted into its base.

'That's the old workshops from World War Two,' said Tom. 'It's a museum in summer season but the far end is sealed.'

'Why?'

'That's the entrance to the Duddlestone wartime research centre.'

'I think I read something about that.'

'A lot of people died in there. It's still argued as to whether it was murder or accident. It was a little bit of both I guess.'

'Tom, it's got to be one or the other – can't be both.'

'There speaks the lawyer. Don't mention it to Mum – it's still a bit sensitive, but Peter will explain.'

Tom's mother, Carol, greeted them, hugged her son and gave Emily a welcoming kiss. 'So nice to have you with us, Emily. This will be a real family Christmas. Have you met Ian and Tricia?'

'Not yet.' Emily knew that the family dinner on Christmas Day would be in the Honeycritch farmhouse with Tom's aunt and uncle. She was both nervous and interested at the prospect. Best behaviour would be called for, although she understood from Tom that the couple were laidback and welcoming.

Carol was a cheerful middle-aged lady, dark haired with flecks of grey. Emily knew that Carol still worked part time as a teacher in the local primary school. She spoke with a soft Dorset accent and seemed a complete contrast to her sister, Tom's aunt Laura. Tom finally extracted them from his mum's chatter and they went in search of his stepfather, Peter Wilson.

Peter was in the harbour office, a squat brick building on the end of the harbour wall. Laura greeted them in the outer reception room. It was a cheerful place with paintings of sea views and a book display of work by local writers. Emily could hear the sound of the sea washing on the quayside and the chatter of the VHF radio; big ships talking this time with yachts all safe in port.

'Hi, you love birds,' said Laura as she grinned at Tom and gave Emily a kiss. 'Looking forward to Christmas?'

'Of course,' said Emily.

'Not sure I am,' said Laura. 'I like sunshine and warmth.'

'I would never have guessed,' Tom grinned.

Peter came into the room and the greetings were repeated. 'Hello, Emily. So it's Duddlestone by road this time, a bit different from August.' Peter was a middle-height, greying-haired man in his early sixties who had obviously taken care with his appearance and fitness. He wore blue jeans that didn't quite work with his harbour master's formal jacket and the cap hanging on a hook on the wall. His face was still tanned and weathered, with the same neat beard that Emily remembered from the summer. 'I expect you'd like to look at your cottage?' he said.

Emily was surprised because Peter addressed the question to her and not to Tom. She wasn't certain how to respond when Tom spoke. 'Peter says you girls can have the place rent-free for six months. Only conditions, no crazy parties breaking up the place and you pay the electric and council tax.'

'Oh, thank you – that's fantastic,' said Emily. 'That's generous and it'll solve so many problems.' She couldn't think of anything more appropriate to say. This was so unexpected and it solved the team's accommodation problem. The extra mileage to Portland was nothing compared with the money they would save.

'It will mostly be Erin and me when we can get away from work,' said Emily. 'Chloe's in the army not far from here but she'll be with us for weekends.'

Peter nodded and stared at Tom. 'And where will you be at week-ends, young man?'

'Where do you think?' Tom smiled.

'I know where I'd be at your age,' Peter laughed.

'He's not bad old stick,' Tom remarked as they walked back up the village street.

'I like him,' said Emily, 'and he was wrong about me.'

'How so?'

'Remember, you said he told you I was too good for you.'

Tom recalled that moment. 'Yes, he did. I think he had a bit of a tangled love life.'

'I bet the girls went for him when he was your age.'

'I suspect from what I've heard that he was sailor with a girl in every port. He's been married before but it went sour – his first wife left him for another bloke. He's got a daughter who is my step-sister but she's overseas.'

'He should write his memoirs,' said Emily.

'I think his mum should. I never told you that Peter's father was a bit of a war hero. He won the VC.'

'The what?'

'VC – Victoria Cross of course.'

'What's that?'

Tom groaned both out loud and inwardly. Emily's complete blank with any knowledge of history was one thing about her that he couldn't grapple with. 'Em, the Victoria Cross is the highest honour for bravery in battle. Peter's dad won it in 1944 just before D-Day and don't go telling me you've never heard of D-Day.'

'Sorry no. I don't know much about that war. I told you, I only know about Auschwitz and the big battle that Gerry fought in. It's all right for you; all that stuff about you learning history at school. We didn't do history. Our teacher said all wars were caused by men because men are violent and like killing. I must say after last week I'm beginning to see that.'

'Why last week?'

'Don't you read the papers or look at the news?'

'Yes, sometimes.'

'The Kessel trial.'

'You mean that murdering little bastard. People like that should hang.'

'No, we don't want to go back to those days, but Tom, last week I sat in that court watching. Travis was prosecuting: I was just running messages…' Emily had gone very quiet. Tom knew her well enough to say nothing.

She continued. 'They showed the jury the photographs of the little girl; she was only six. He slashed her stomach and the bowels were hanging out; some of the women cried. I felt sick. Kessel didn't bat an eyelid. He just sat there. After the verdict, Tony Travis was so blasé: said that was an easy case to prosecute. Tom, I began to wonder if I've the bottle to be a barrister.'

Tom wasn't certain how to react. 'You've gone too far to turn back now. You're good at it. You got me off that time.'

'I know,' she smiled him with that wan look he couldn't resist. 'Anyway even if I make QC, I wouldn't have more than a handful of those sorts of trials in a working life.'

'Come on; let's have a look at our new house.'

'Our new house?' Emily laughed. 'Chloe will be here some of the time.'

'Let's have a look anyway.' Tom pulled out two keys and gave one to Emily. 'This is yours – don't lose it.'

Tom entered the house and Emily followed. He hadn't been here for some months and was pleasantly surprised. It was larger than the cottages nearer the water and the marina company had built an extension over much of what once had been a garden. It had been hoped to rent out the place as a holiday let, but with economic times being bad there had been no takers. 'If Chloe's in camp,' said Tom, 'it will only be you me and, Erin.' He pointed to the stairs. 'That'll be our room up there. If you want to you can sleep up there when I'm not here, or you can share with the girls downstairs. If Erin wants to bring a friend she can have the spare room next to the kitchen.'

'What if Chloe wants to bring a girlfriend?'

Tom snorted. 'I suspect she won't try that while I'm here.'

The mobile phone in his pocket was sounding. He looked at the screen – dammit the caller was Alix.

'Aren't you going to answer?' said Emily.

Tom answered. 'Hello.'

'Tom darling, are you going to see me in my panto?'

'Yes, I got the message, and I'll see if I can do the job one day next week,' he tried to sound neutral.

'Aha, you're with the little girl, I guess. Don't want her to suspect the seductive other woman.'

'Well, yeah – something like that, but I expect I can fix it.'

There came a splutter of laughter. 'I'm sure you can do that – bye Tommy.'

Emily was looking at him in an odd way. 'What was all that?'

'Work,' he lied.

'That was a woman's voice.'

'So what – we're all supposed to be equal. There's plenty of women giving orders to poor downtrodden men.' He looked at Emily. Her face had an expression that signalled disbelief.

CHAPTER 17

Chloe rang Emily's mobile that evening. 'You all set for Auckland?'

'Have you got our tickets?'

'Yeah, Heathrow. Five days time.'

'Chloe, it's all right for you, but I've done nothing about a visa. We've never needed one before because all our meets have been in the E C.'

'Don't worry about it. For some warped reason, we actually let Poms and dumb Aussies, into our country without one – can't think why. But you've gotta clear out after six months. The only rule is you bring enough dosh to pay your way.'

'I don't want to stay for six months, Chlo' – we'd be back in winter again. I like it sunny.'

'Yeah, me too. What've you been up to, Em? How's Tom?'

'Tom's fine and I like his people. Bit of a bore, but we're off to a panto in Southampton tomorrow afternoon. They're all keen to go – like a lot of kids.'

Chloe released her most raucous chuckle. 'Oh no there isn't – he's behin –d'yah!'

'That's it, but how do you know?'

'It's a Brit custom that we've imported, but mostly amateur theatricals that do it.'

'They tell me this is an all-star cast,' said Emily. 'Lots of people off the telly from soaps like Gravesenders.'

'That follows. Erin told me your Tom knows someone who acts in that one.'

'Who is that? He's never told me.'

'Dunno, she never said.'

Chloe said goodbye. Emily felt the anticipation. New Zealand beckoned and with it sailing in warm sunny seas. Not all play though; she remembered that Tony Travis had recommended her to his associated law firm in Auckland. He had given her the phone number to ring on arrival. She only hoped nothing in New Zealand would rival the gruesome Kessel trial.

'Kirsten, telephone,' Steve called.

Kirsten was puzzled – who on earth? She wiped her hands on the kitchen towel and went to the office room.

Steve handed her the phone. 'Danish Embassy,' he whispered.

‘Mrs Kirsten Simpson?’

‘That’s me.’

‘Anna Olerstrom, press officer.’ The voice the other end paused for a few seconds. Kirsten racked her brains to think of any reason for this call. ‘Mrs Simpson, we can speak in English, but I would suggest for security that we talk in our native tongue.’

Kirsten made the mental switch to her own language. ‘If you say so, of course.’ She still couldn’t make this out. Speaking Danish within their London embassy was pretty useless for keeping secrets.

‘That’s better,’ was the reply. Middle-age female with Jutland East coast accent, surmised Kirsten. ‘Mrs Simpson, I have with me a gentleman name of Aaron Sikorskie who tells me he’s from the Israeli Yachting Association. I am a bit baffled by what he tells me.’

‘No more baffled than I am right now.’ Kirsten was not in the best of moods without being waylaid by diplomatic bureaucrats. ‘What does he want with me?’

‘The point is that Israel has very strict entry qualifications for non-Jewish visitors. Mr Sikorskie tells me that your daughter is due to take part in a yachting event next June and that there is a move to prohibit her entry.’

It was all becoming horribly clear now. Hammersen again. ‘May I know the reason? And before you answer that, let me tell you right now that my father was Jewish. He was lucky to have survived the war. I would have thought there was enough Jewish in my girl to let her into their stupid little country.’

‘Please, Mrs Simpson. Mr Sikorskie is fully prepared to welcome your daughter. He says she is a good sailor and of course we all know of your deeds and your husband’s…’

Sweet-talking me won’t help you or anyone, Kirsten muttered inwardly. ‘So why are the Israelis taking against my Emily?’

‘I’m not sure, and my visitor is a bit vague, but it’s not the safest country in the world right now. As I say, you and your daughter are both highly thought of back home…’ Another pause. ‘Mrs Simpson, I’m a press officer and a journalist. Off the record, I have a bad feeling about this.’

‘Ms Olerstrom, I think I know where you are coming from. Can you ask this Israeli man to be more precise? Also, the allegations against my daughter are pure fiction.’

Kirsten could hear a muttering in the background. Then the other speaker came back. ‘Mr Sikorskie says he knows the Israelis can’t keep your daughter out but he feels she may be the subject of opposition or even of demonstrations.'

'All right, I'll talk to Emily when I next see her.' Kirsten put the phone back and sat head in hands.

'I was listening to that,' said Steve. 'My Danish isn't brilliant but I could make out some of it.'

'I only hope to God that we will have stopped this nonsense by the time Emily goes to Israel. Steve, what have you got there?'

Steve had been staring at a letter that had come in that morning's post. 'This is from the British Olympic Association. They've asked if I can head a delegation to go to Olifa.'

'When, and whatever for?'

'In March. I had some inkling of this when I spoke to that guy from Olifa at the King Henry. They want us to inspect and advise on the sailing facilities.'

'What about your walking?'

'I'm much better now, but you can come along as well. They say so.'

'*South America take it away*,' Kirsten sang. 'Why not? It's time we took a real break.'

'C'est la vie,' said Chloe as she sipped her wine. 'Guys, this is a bit of all right.'

Emily poured more wine. 'I've got to hand it to you Chlo', this town is great – it's got the lot.'

'Yeah, Auckland grabs you that way. Not the biggest city in the world and that ain't its real name.'

'I know', said Erin. 'Your people call it the "virgin with one hundred lovers". They call Pompey back home something like that but much ruder,'

'Tamaki Makau Rua,' said Chloe. 'We also called the place: "Te Herega Waka" which translated means: "a good place to park your canoe". Bit more prosaic.'

The girls were relaxing, sitting outside a waterfront restaurant, a peaceful spot redolent with the scent of fine seafood and freshly ground coffee. Their first day had been spent recovering from the long flight. On the second day they had examined their allotted boat and helped set up the mast and adjust the rig. The competition was based on Waitamata Harbour and the Royal New Zealand Yacht Squadron, a magnificent modern building. Chloe had already told them about the strong tides in this area. They had spent a happy afternoon, including a visit to the Maritime Museum to look at the

America's Cup boats.

Emily stiffened before dropping forward with her head on the table. 'Oh holy shit,' she exclaimed. 'Look who's coming – I thought this might be too good to last.' She pulled a face at the others who appeared not to notice.

'Hiya, Sammy,' called Chloe. 'How ya' doin'?'

'Do you have to?' Emily hissed.

'Yes we do,' said Erin. 'Emily, you're being daft. This feuding has to stop.'

'Hello, there – you been hiding?' Samantha Robstron was not always the most tactful person. She was followed by her crewmates: the twin sisters, Tracie and Tanya. Both were sluts in Emily's opinion.

All last year their teams had fought for the coveted Olympic spot and Sammy and her crew had narrowly won the day. Emily had to admit that it wasn't only jealousy that had turned her against Samantha and the girls. Sammy was older than Emily, although she was one of the helms that Emily had beaten fair and square when she was a teenager. If not close friends they had got on well enough then. Emily had tried to tell herself that Sammy couldn't help that raucous Brummie accent, any more than she could help her offensively large bottom.

'You girls ready for it?' said Sammy. 'It's not fair is it? You a Kiwi on your home ground.'

'Waitemata Harbour is where I learned to sail,' Chloe grinned. 'But it's a level playing field. We should have a good old battle.'

'Tell you why I've been looking for you,' said Sammy. 'There's a creepy little woman asking about you, Emily. She latched on to Tracie, here, thought she was you.'

'Who is this?' Emily forced herself to show interest and to be outwardly polite.

'I wrote her name down,' said Sammy. 'She gave me a contact number. Then she started to tell me the story of her life – Oh, Jesus what a bore. Said she's a Kiwi now by second marriage, but she was a copper's wife in the UK, but she left him for the bloke she's married to now. Anyway, Emily, she says you got her first husband killed.'

Emily despite her hostility was worried. She guessed what was coming. 'What's her name?'

'Miranda O'Phelan, but her first husband had a sort of Frenchie name…'

'Not Le Bois?'

'Yeah, that's it.'

'Sam, I'm being hounded by that lot. This Le Bois was a copper who'd lost it, gone mad. The Army shot him because he was in the way when they got me out of the fire.'

'Oh, yeah, little Emily's moment of glory,' Samantha's expression was one of deep malice. 'And how you've milked it: basked in it. But who was it got an Olympic silver medal?'

Emily consumed, by the metaphorical red mist, kicked back her chair and sprang at her enemy, scratching at the jeering face. Now strong arms had caught her around the waist lifting her off the ground. 'Em, you stupid bitch.' It was Chloe. Emily tried to struggle, but she reckoned without the upper body strength of her friend. 'Come on, you sit back down.'

Samantha was breathing heavily while fingering her right cheek. 'She's crazy, a real nutter. Chloe, you should drop that one from your crew right now – she's all twisted. Come on, girls.' She turned and walked away before briefly looking round. 'We'll settle this one out on the water.'

Emily watched them go. She was breathing heavily and on the edge of tears. How she wished that Tom was here.

'Em, for Chrissake,' said Chloe. 'I hope nobody saw us. This isn't a pub in bloody Oz – we don't tolerate that sort of thing here. 'Bloody hell, girl. You want headlines? "Brilliant young lawyer in bar brawl".'

'You heard her,' said Emily. 'Settle it on the water. I'm up for that.'

Chloe was looking towards the far end of the bar. A young man was watching them. 'Dave, come here,' she commanded. Her call was ignored as the man slipped away into the night.

'Who was that?' asked Erin.

'Dave Manning. He's a Kiwi, thinks he know everything about sailing. Fucking journalist. Let's hope he didn't see what happened.'

The next morning Emily had reported to the offices of the law firm linked to the Travis chambers in London. She found a very different ambience: shirtsleeves and other casual wear and a friendly if curious welcome. Emily knew from long experience that she was being gossiped about behind her back. Her temporary colleagues were coming to terms with her notoriety. Little Emily, the girl from the fire siege, was to work with them part time for ten days. Otherwise, much was the same as the London chambers. Here she was once more in a familiar world of solicitors and clerks, barristers and high court judges. Although no one spoke with the standard English diction Emily was becoming used to the Kiwi accent, finding it no longer crude, but interesting.

She sat in on parts of four court cases. The civil case, a land dispute, was boring. The criminal case was in its second day and involved a drugs related brawl in dockland. Emily asked her barrister about murders.

'Murders! Emily, this is New Zealand, we don't do murders, well, maybe two a year. This isn't the UK.'

The man seemed almost envious when she told him about the Kessel trial.

Next, a civil court hearing: a bad tempered money-disputing divorce case. Then a criminal trial ending with the jailing of a Vietnamese carjacker. Emily went back to the bedsit and wrote up her notes. She wondered if she could have worked a better deal for the wronged wife, but guessed that this was still a male-dominated world.

The evenings were long and light, and the three girls were able to have a first workout in Waitemata Harbour. Back ashore they hosed down the boat and went back to the waterfront for an evening meal. They had struck lucky as this was the middle of the city's annual seafood festival and the fare on offer was varied and mouth-watering. They kept a wary eye out for Sammy and crew but saw nothing of them. Chloe had ascertained that their rivals were based at a campsite outside the city.

Tom rang with the news as they were eating. 'Em, what have you been up to. You've really got to cool it with Sammy Robstron.'

'Tom, what are you talking about?'

'It's in today's *Daily Banner,* I'll read it to you.

Sailor Girl's Cat Fight
Daily Banner yachting correspondent Dave Manning reports.

Angry words were exchanged between British Olympic silver medallist, Samantha Robstron and her rival crew led by Kiwi helm, Chloe Te-Koote. The girls confronted each other on Auckland's picturesque Vulcan Lane, favourite spot for UK tourists. Sammy and her crew girls, sisters Tracie and Tanya, approached the others who were dining at an outdoor restaurant.
Harsh words were exchanged, especially from Emily Simpson, the

daughter of two sailing Olympic medallists. Chloe and her crew accepted a challenge to settle their differences in competition. News of this has caused a flurry of interest among the betting fraternity.

Emily for once in her life was unable to speak.

'Em, darling, are you there?'

'Yes.'

'What happened?'

'It was Sammy who started it, not me. She wound me up; made a stupid joke about the fire siege. Then she waved her medal at us.'

'And let me guess, you lost that temper.'

'Maybe I did, but Tom, please don't tell Mum and Dad and don't let them see that newspaper.'

Emily wanted to ask Tom about home – wanted to hear his voice but she was too worried by what she had just heard. 'Chloe, who is Dave Manning?'

'He's a journo. Classic example: if you can't do it, write about it.'

'Tom says he works for the *Daily Banner*. They've printed something about me and Sammy the other night.'

Chloe looked worried. 'I didn't think he saw that much. Did Tom tell you what he's written?'

'It could be worse – more like just a slanging match.'

'OK, it takes a day or so before any of your UK papers get here. In the meantime we've the regatta ball at the Royal NZ.'

'Shit, Chlo', will Sammy be there?'

'Probably, they want the girls to show off their medals. So, Em, you will keep your cool.'

'I'll try.'

'Anyway, none of those three can carry off a dress like yours. Most of our blokes'll be more interested in you than in Sammy's medal.'

Steve climbed painfully from his bed and limped to the window. The lawn was white and the trees glittered with frost in the morning light. The house was warm, but the outside world was gripped by the coldest spell for many years: so much for the doom warnings of the sun cult. Non-violent and lawful since the fire siege, the cult was still out there predicting global disaster. This cold weather was doing nothing for his recovery. His right leg hurt, as did his shoulder. Kirsten had been up for two hours. She had already told him that Branham Lake was reported frozen; a skater's fun park but no sailing that day, nor in the foreseeable future.

Steve dressed slowly. He pulled on full thermals and thick socks. He had no intention of staying indoors. He would work off his gloomy mood with some walking around the garden or maybe beyond. He stopped on the landing looking down the stairs. He could climb them unaided but going down was another matter. Today he would swallow his pride and use the stair lift. On the ground floor he limped to the kitchen and slumped into his chair by the Aga range. Johnny was sitting at the table, breakfast complete, with his head bent over an open book. Kirsten sat opposite reading the daily paper. It was Saturday, the sailing day at Branham, summer or winter, until all was stopped by the weather: gales more often, or in this case, ice.

'Emily emailed earlier,' said Kirsten. 'They've sailed the boat and the weather is thirty centigrade.'

'It's minus seven outside here,' Steve replied.

'And they're forecasting heavy snow for tomorrow night.'

Johnny looked up. 'How am I going to get to school?'

Kirsten laughed. 'A kid who wants to go to school.'

'Of course I do,' said Johnny. 'I'm being moved up a set for maths. The others in my lot are so thick, you wouldn't believe.'

Johnny's school was ten miles away in Midhurst, and Midhurst was where Sarah lived. 'Would you like to stay with Sarah and Chris?' Steve asked. An idea was germinating, a most attractive idea.

'Dad, that would be fantastic!' Johnny stood up face alight with a broad smile.

'All right, son. Don't overdo it. I'll ring Sarah and see what she has to say.'

'Are you thinking what I'm thinking?' said Kirsten.

'Yeah,' said Johnny. 'With me away you can fly to New Zealand; cheer on Emily, Erin and big Chloe.'

'You've got intuition,' said Kirsten. 'That's the first thing I thought of when I went outside.'

'Will they be that pleased to see us?' asked Steve.

'I would guess they will have mixed feelings, but from what Chloe was saying on the phone, they could do with your help.'

'I know, it's the light weather trim she's worried about.'

'At least that sneaky little thief never took our passports.'

'Right,' said Kirsten. 'Ring Sarah, then see what flights are available.'

The girls had a successful practise sail in the harbour. By now eight other crews in their competition were trying their boats, with more due to arrive. They saw Sammy and crew sailing in the distance, but both rivals seemed content to keep away from each other.

The regatta eve was to be the night of the grand ball. Once more Emily had gritted her teeth, sucked in her breath and struggled into the constricting glamour dress. It was a warm humid evening, with thunderstorms forecast, and she wished she could have put on something looser and lighter. Erin had dressed in a similar rig and Chloe had emerged in a sleeveless gown that displayed to the full her muscular biceps.

'You ancestors would be proud of you,' Erin grinned.

'Give her a long spear and she'd be just the part,' Emily agreed.

'Piss off you stupid Poms,' replied Chloe. 'Right, girls, are we all set?'

Emily had been apprehensive about the yacht club but she was soon relieved. The Royal New Zealand Yacht Squadron was a modern structure near the foot of the Auckland Bridge. It was designed to give stunning views of the surrounding waters. Apart from the shared name there was no similarity with its counterpart in Cowes and even less with the Royal King Henry. Members and guests alike were relaxed, laid back, and determined on a good time. The conversation was all sailing, yacht racing, and more sailing. Emily forced herself to show restraint as Sammy and her girls appeared with silver medals dangling. A master of ceremonies introduced them to loud cheers. Emily nearly choked to see that Tanya, Sammy's bow girl wore a yellow halter dress made with hardly any material above the waist. It was vulgar, tasteless and no more than she would have expected. Her sister Tracie had a phoney Polynesian dress with too much midriff on show – typical. The two teams had exchanged glances, and after that kept out of each other's way.

Chloe had a hero's welcome as the MC announced her. No one seemed put out that their local girl was sailing for another country, and worse than that, for Great Britain. A club member explained to Emily that Chloe's ancestor had been the Maori Lord, a Robin Hood figure, who had fought the occupying colonial forces to the bitter end and was the last to accept peace terms. Ethnic bitterness had declined over the century and both the incoming European and indigenous peoples had absorbed elements of culture from each other. The member explained that she herself was part Maori and that widespread intermarriage meant that pure native New Zealanders were becoming a rarity. Chloe's family had a legendary status. Chloe had alluded to this that time in Cowes but had not mentioned it since.

In the end it was a memorable night. Beer flowed, wine corks popped, a local choir sang and the dance floor was a scene of wild abandon. All three girls were swept up in the party fun. Emily enjoyed basking in the gaze of the young men present even though she felt a bit guilty when several of them pulled her unceremoniously onto the dance floor. She couldn't help wondering what Tom would say. Too bad, she knew what he would be up to if their roles were exchanged: two-faced men, all of them. Emily knew she had eaten too much and worse, drunk too much and in less than twenty-four hours time they would be competing in the first rounds of their event.

The shock moment came out of the blue. It was nearly midnight when the MC took up his microphone and announced. 'Folks, here's a real treat. Straight off a plane from the UK, I invite a warm welcome for former sailing stars: Steve and Kirsten Simpson.'

For Emily it was one of those moments, similar to a TV drama, when all sound seemed to cease for her and she stood transfixed staring into the far corner of the room. And, yes, there was Chloe greeting Dad with a handshake and Mum with a kiss.

CHAPTER 18

'Oh, Mum, Dad, how come? I didn't know.' Emily flung her arms around each of them in turn.

'Didn't you get our message?' asked Steve.

Chloe and Erin were both smirking. 'We got it,' said Chloe, 'but we thought we'd make it a surprise.'

Emily eyes moistened as simultaneously she laughed. 'You rats – I'd no idea.'

'First race of your competition tomorrow afternoon,' said Kirsten, 'and we find you girls living the high life.'

'Up early tomorrow,' said Steve. 'Boat in the water and go for it.'

The party was winding down, with little groups of people gathering beside the glass viewing windows. The sounds of thunder were loud, and the lightning flashes were coming nearer by the minute. Now it was raining in torrents with a force that Emily had never seen in her life. They had walked to the yacht club, but she had no enthusiasm for a return trip through the downpour wearing a fashion gown with bare shoulders.

Her father intervened. 'I think two taxis are called for. I will do the honours.'

They reached the security of their bed and breakfast lodgings and fled the last few yards through the deluge.

'I knew it was going to piss down this evening and I never thought to take waterproofs.' Chloe was apologetic.

Emily was watching the television in a corner of the lounge. It was showing a month-old episode of Gravesenders. Big Max was shouting at his mother who crouched tearfully against a garishly papered wall.

'Hi, Erin. Is it true my Tom knows someone who acts in this?'

'Yeah, I thought you would know that. Alexia Ford-Watts, the one who plays Charlene. It seems they were very close in childhood in Dorset.'

'When did he tell you this?'

'At Hayling last year. He was there with his Laser for their nationals. Gravesenders was playing in the bar and he told everyone. It seems he still keeps in touch with her.'

'And he's never told me – I wonder why?'

'Well, you'd better ask him,' said Chloe.

‘I bloody will – right now.’

Emily fumbled in her handbag for her mobile phone. She was annoyed that her two companions were grinning at each other.

‘He’s turned his bloody phone off – why?’ She glared at them.

‘Don’t blame us when there’s simple explanation,’ Chloe replied although by now she and Erin were spluttering with laughter.

‘What explanation? It’s morning over there.’

‘Maybe he doesn’t want to be pestered by any of his women.’

‘Sod it, I’m going to bed and one of you can help me out of this stupid dress.’

The thunderstorms had died in the night but left behind a morning outlook that was murky and windless. The entry had increased to sixteen boats from ten nations.

‘Right, usual format,’ said Chloe. ‘Two round-robin series to start with, so if we do things properly we’ll be up against Sammy and her girls at the knockout stage.’

‘They haven’t forecast any more wind,’ said Emily. ‘I’d rather fight them now. We’re stones lighter than them.’

‘Emily,’ said Erin, ‘we are not fighting, we are competing.’

‘You may be.’ Emily walked away and stared across the water.

‘Briefing in ten minutes, Em,’ Chloe shouted.

The briefing took half an hour while the race officer and umpires went through the intricate rules that they all knew anyway. The draw for their first round-robin races was against a cheerful trio of Belgian girls, a new team that they hadn’t met before. Chloe had also drawn yellow flag, which meant they must approach the start zone from starboard. Following this they were paired in turn against each of the other entrants. A race would normally take twenty minutes for the two windward-leeward legs, but in these wind conditions it was difficult to put a time. The race officials were clearly hedging their bets.

The crews emerged from the briefing. The boats were already launched and the girls found Steve and Kirsten busy adjusting the sail setting. ‘She’s all ready,’ said Steve. ‘Off you go and enjoy.’

They were away from the dockside, released from the tow launches, following the fleet and the umpires’ boats out to sea and the start line. Such wind as there was came from onshore over the roofs of the city far behind them. The three of them had now fallen into the routine they all knew from long experience. Already double champions, they had a reputation to defend and also, as they were aware, a reputation that made their initial opponents nervous. The pre-start drill was crucial. This was the time to push your opponent away from the line, but aware that the umpires watched, ready to flag an infringement and award a penalty turn.

Chloe helmed, ready to take quick action. Emily controlled the mainsheet while watching the other boat and feeding information and advice to Chloe. It was almost as if they had ceased to be individuals and had become one finely-tuned racing brain. Erin in the bow was ready to watch the tactics after the start and to call wind shifts. After that sail handling and spinnaker drill were vital. A race could be lost and won by sail handling.

'I'm going to track them. Put the wind up,' said Chloe quietly. She steered a course behind the other boat and began to follow them move for move. In every case Chloe's team was just that little bit slicker and quicker. The signal sounded and they won the start. Upwind they blocked the other boat tack for tack. Downwind, spinnaker set and with Erin calling the shots they pulled away. By the time they came to the second windward leg they were fifty metres clear. They only had to stay out of trouble to win. Experience counted: coordination, tactics, sail handling and mark rounding favoured them to the end.

'One point in the bag,' Chloe smiled.

The first round-robin series was completed that day in mediocre windless weather. So with days in hand, and more wind forecast, the race officers decreed a second series.

Steve and Kirsten had watched the racing from an escorting launch.

'I can see trouble ahead,' said Kirsten. 'I can see how the final is going to work out.'

Steve could only agree. Chloe and crew were dominating their series and likewise Samantha and her team in theirs. A confrontation in the final stages was inevitable.

'Can't be helped,' said Steve. 'Our daughter has got to learn.'

'I hope so, but this is not just about boats. That Sammy jeered about the fire siege in Emily's face.'

'She's still got to learn to treat that sort of thing with the contempt it deserves. The Robstron girl is a slob and those twins are what we used to call scrubbers. Emily is a better person and she shouldn't be riled by people like that.'

'Steve, we still want our girls to win?'

'Of course we do, and I think they will. I believe they want it more than the others.'

Emily had avoided her enemies while keeping a wary eye on them. She had hoped in vain that Sammy might overdo the alcohol, while the oversexed twins be tempted by the dozens of hunky males on show. It didn't happen. Her rivals remained disciplined and intent on winning. Chloe and crew won the second series, twelve wins to three losses, despite being handed two penalties. Sammy and crew came through to qualify with three penalties, and four losses. They were now into the quarter-finals. Tomorrow would be the showdown.

'Is there anything more you want me to do regarding your boat?' Steve addressed the girls.

The three looked at each other. 'What do you think?' asked Chloe.

'I would say we're about as quick as we're going to get,' said Emily 'I don't think we should tinker. The rules limit us anyway.'

'OK, have lunch on us and then, Chloe, could you show us the sights?'

Steve and Kirsten bought the girls lunch at an upmarket restaurant not far from the waterfront. They all lingered over the meal, though they avoided alcohol. The fun and games of the pre-race week were in the past now that they were in serious competition. The next day's forecast was already talking of twenty knots blowing in from the Pacific. They said goodbye to Emily's parents and walked slowly back to the Westhaven Marina. They reached the dock and Emily halted so abruptly that Erin bumped into her.

'Right, I'm not stopping.' Emily pointed. Sammy and the twins were standing twenty yards away talking to a policeman in uniform.

'Too late, Em – they've seen you,' said Chloe.

'Keep your cool – don't start anything,' Erin had caught hold of Emily's arm.

'Hi, Sammy,' Chloe called. 'What's up. Someone try to knobble your boat?'

'Why,' said Sammy. 'Were you thinking about doing that, Emily?'

Emily was thinking of a robust reply but Erin only tightened her grip and Chloe glared at her.

The policeman had walked across to them. Emily felt no apprehension but there was something vaguely familiar, and for that matter, disconcerting about the man.

'Are you Miss Emily Simpson?'

'Yes.'

'May I have a word in private?'

'Why – what've those bitches been saying?'

'All right, Miss – you've done nothing that would interest us, but I saw you in court the other day. Do you remember?'

'Of course. You're the inspector who gave evidence in the car-jacking.'

Emily gave her friends a wan glance and followed the policeman for a short walk along the marina.

'Now Miss. Those young ladies may have done you a good turn. I've been trying to track you down for two days but you always seem to be out there.' He grinned and pointed at the sea.

'Please tell me what I've done.'

'You've done nothing against New Zealand law. My mother read that you were coming here and she asked me to find out more. I think you may have guessed who my mother is and who my father was.'

'You're something to do with Inspector Le Bois?'

'He was my father.' He held up a hand. 'No, Miss Simpson. I have no grudge against you nor has my mother. I understand my father's mental condition and I remember his treatment of us when I was young. We ran away, both of us, and ended here. I joined the police because that's what all our family do.'

'I didn't want him to die – I'm sorry.'

'I know that. Now my warning. Do you know Dave Manning?'

'The journalist. He wrote something vile about me.'

'He came to us yesterday. He says he's had a message from a workmate in London. They think you are under some sort of threat and we've been asked to look out for you.'

Emily did not know what to think. 'A threat?'

'The newsmen said it's something to do with your granddad. Can't tell you more.'

Emily understood now. Surely – twelve thousand miles away…

'Another thing,' the man continued. 'You know sailing's big in this country. So men here bet on results. You've a popular Kiwi skipper, there's a lot of money riding on you, and Mr Manning says you don't get on with those other three UK beauts.'

'Well, yes, but we try to keep it on the water.'

'I think you should do just that. We'll be watching you for your own health – so don't spoil things. No more cat fights – OK?'

Emily looked at the man. He seemed a nice guy, and yes, he did have a slight resemblance to Le Bois. She could see it now. Much younger, but similar features, and he was gazing at her with steady but friendly eyes. The idea that Hammersen might have found his way to New Zealand frightened her. If only Tom was with her.

'What's she been up to?' Sammy addressed Le Bois. Emily hadn't noticed the woman.

'Do you mind,' Emily snapped. 'This conversation is private.'

'She must have done something,' said Sammy, 'or you wouldn't be looking for her.'

Le Bois smiled. 'I had some classified information for this delightful young lady and I think we'll leave it at that.'

Sammy snorted.

'Remember what I said, Miss Simpson. I don't want to arrest any of you girls for murder. Keep it to the open sea.'

Le Bois left, walking briskly toward a police car that had stopped nearby.

'That was a private matter,' said Emily. 'Why can't you keep your nose out?'

The other four had joined the fray and were staring at each other only a few feet away, rather like boxers pre-fight.

Emily knew that it was for her to cool things, but at this juncture she just couldn't.

'Say, Sammy, you've got dark hair and the twins are blonde. Remember when they used to talk about three blondes in a boat? Well, they've long gone, and now it's one fatso and two slappers in a boat.'

'Emily…' Erin glared at her.

'No, let her have her say,' said Tracie. 'And Chloe, how come you sail for GB?'

'Yeah,' said twin Tanya. 'It's supposed to be ladies match racing but that one looks more like a bloke.'

'Maori,' said Tracie. 'That's just another sort of Paki if you ask me.'

'How dare you address our friend with that racist crap?' Emily shouted. 'Apart from which you two have shagged with enough nationalities to form the United Nations.'

'Emily, leave it!' said Erin.

'Yes, Emily,' said Chloe. 'We'll leave this sad bunch to their stupid insults and settle it on the water.'

They knew they were heading towards the inevitable. Race by race the field was whittled down, and the two rivals still remained apart.

Chloe's team defeated the Americans in the quarterfinal. Sammy beat the Spanish. Only the semifinals separated them. Emily was amazed at the interest in the event shown, not just by the sailing fraternity but by the sporting public. Live TV covered the penultimate races, with some amused comment by the presenters about the cutthroat nature of the competition. The semi-final drew Chloe against a local New Zealand crew and Sammy against a glamorous trio from Argentina. The sun shone, the wind blew twenty knots from the west over a short breaking swell. Athleticism was on the side of Chloe's crew, body weight favoured Sammy's girls.

Just two more contests for each team to win and then face each other. A match-racing semi-final is a best of five races. All the crews knew that the umpire boats would be especially vigilant. Any rule infringement would be punished. Penalty turns lost time, but no one could afford to back off at the start, or be less than resolute tactically on the course. In the end it went well. Chloe's crew won two races but lost the third following two penalties. The conditions were now on the limits for handling these lightweight boats. Their teamwork saw them through with a decisive win. They were in the final, and predictably, the final was to be against Sammy and her team.

It all went so well at the start. Chloe crossed the line ahead and covered tack for tack. The girls were hiking, hanging their full body-weights over the weather rail. Sailing flat, keeping the boat upright was vital. Sammy's crew weighed many kilos more, so in that respect Emily's derision about fat was backfiring. The wind was rising by the minute. Spray flying, they were all temporarily blinded by it or had dark glasses fogged. It was hard, they were stretched but they won the first round. In the excitement even Emily forgot the deeper rivalry.

Race two was disaster. Within seconds of the start signal, a coming together of the two boats earned Chloe a penalty. 'It wasn't us,' Emily screamed towards the umpire boat. 'That was fucking deliberate – are you blind?'

'Shut up,' yelled Chloe. 'We were windward boat.'

'They steered into us,' shouted Erin.

'Stand by for the penalty,' called Chloe.

They took the penalty turn at the first opportunity and watched as their rivals rounded the upwind buoy. With spinnakers hoisted the two boats sped towards the downwind mark. Chloe fought to cover and take the other's wind but Sammy was too far ahead. They closed the gap on the next windward leg but it was not enough. One race each and three more to go.

'Em, watch them, tell me second by second what they're doing,' said Chloe.

Emily relayed everything she could see. Every tweak of helm from the other boat she registered and fed back to her own skipper. At the same time she called the count down of the start. 'Three – two – one…'

'Tacking,' shouted Chloe. 'That's it – we've got 'em.'

It was their best result of the week with a clear win by over twenty metres.

Euphoria was short lived. They lost the fourth race by almost the same distance. Even Emily couldn't fault Sammy's crew. What had gone wrong? Was it overconfidence? They would have to get it right next time. As they manoeuvred for the final start Emily had a quick glance around. She was shocked, alarmed almost, by the number of escorting and spectator craft, the nearest mounting television cameras. This interest in sailing was something they had met before, but always outside Britain and rarely on this scale.

Emily exchanged quick glances with her crewmates. Concentrate, stay calm, think straight, we've got to do this, we've got to – got to! 'Three – two – one…'

'Hold on this tack,' shouted Chloe.

The start could not be closer. The boats exchanged tack for tack. It was spitting distance as several journalists reported next day. Chloe just secured the inside line at the windward mark. Spinnakers filled and powered. Both boats surfed. The wind had increased by a further five knots, but neither crew was fazed. The next windward leg saw the boats separate on diverging tacks. They came together near the windward mark but Chloe held the starboard advantage, forcing Sammy to tack. Chloe narrowly took the inside line but it was now too close to call. One leg of the course to go, with two boats speeding side-by-side; this was a moment they would never forget. Nothing mattered in the world, nothing at all, except to balance their boat and keep that spinnaker drawing. They must concentrate and keep the power on. It was a test of seamanship and skill that would decide the winner.

The finish line lay ahead. Emily looked across at the other boat. They ran level, ten metres, apart as they crossed the finish. If there was a finish gun they never heard it above the cacophony of cheering and air horns. Emily felt too shattered to wonder about anything. Some of her hate had gone as she glanced across at Sammy and the twins. She raised a hand waved and grinned, and amazingly, they smiled back. The two boats closed to within a few feet.

'Chloe,' Sammy called. 'Fantastic – who won?'

Chloe released a gale of laughter. 'How about a dead heat?'

A press boat approached them. 'Yellow flag,' called a loud hailer.' That was their start colour. 'No winner declared yet. We reckon you got it, but it's a photo finish.'

Erin looked at Emily. 'Do we have photo finishes?'

'Don't think so,' said Chloe. 'If they say it's a dead heat we'll have to sail a repechage and I don't fancy that – I'm knackered.'

'They'll be even more so,' said Emily, although truly she didn't want to go again.

The committee boat had upped anchor and was heading for shore as were the umpires and the spectator craft, and yes, the boat was flying the yellow flag.

'Looks like it's us that won,' said Chloe. 'We won't know by how much until we get ashore.'

They picked up the tow launches and came into the marina. The docks were crowded with people, but Emily only had eyes for her parents. They stood on a pontoon and were waving and grinning.

'Well, done – I'm so proud of you,' called Kirsten. 'You won. It was millimetres. We saw it on the telly. They used a computer magic line to separate you, like in rugby or tennis and the race committee have just confirmed it.'

They wondered if Sammy would dispute the result, but it seemed she too was satisfied with her day. Both teams had proved themselves. The animosity had diminished, and in reality Emily was glad of that. Shortly afterwards they stood on the top of the podium and received their medals. Emily was surprised to see that the man presenting them was the Olifarian, Primo Garcia; the same man they had met at the Royal King Henry. Emily still wore her drysuit so this time there was no deep cleavage for the man to ogle.

They stood there while the cameras clicked plus the TV and video. They left the podium and made there way into the clubhouse.

'Jesus, could I do with a cuppa,' said Chloe. 'What a day, I can't begin to think straight.'

Emily saw Sammy and the twins waiting for them. Now what would happen?

'Hey, you guys,' said Chloe. 'Bygones be bygones, eh?'

'Yeah,' said Sammy. 'That was a great final, folks – let's not spoil it.'

‘What about you, Em?’ asked Chloe.

Emily felt tired but happy. She was gripped by a similar languid glow to the one she felt after a great night’s sex: a different kind of orgasm, but a mighty good one.

‘OK,’ she said. ‘Let’s call a truce – end the war.’

‘Sammy,’ said Chloe, ‘what are you guys doing next?’

‘We’re staying on here for a few days. The twins fancy some blokes.’

Surprise – surprise, thought Emily.

CHAPTER 19

'Dad, can you get me a ticket on your plane?' Emily asked.

'We can try, but I can't promise. Why in such a hurry? You don't have to be back with your lawyers until next week. I'd stay on and have a good time.'

'She's missing her Tom,' Kirsten winked.

'I do miss him and I'm worried. Chloe and Erin think he's got another girl.'

Steve looked at Kirsten. This kind of thing was beyond him.

Kirsten shook her head. 'I think your friends are winding you up. You are a lucky young lady. Tom is besotted with you. Who is this other girl?'

'She's an actress in a TV soap. She's Alexia Ford-Watts. I've seen her in Gravesenders and she doesn't look much.'

'Then what are you worrying about?'

'Tom met Erin at Hayling for the Laser nationals, and he told her he played with this Alexia in Dorset as a child.'

'Oh yes, what about Jamie and half a dozen other young lads you played with. You start getting jealous like this and you will lose him. I had a nice Norwegian boy once called Sven and I was jealous.'

'What happened?'

'I was jealous, so I gave him a bad time and he ran away to America. Then I met your father.'

'I don't know – you two are different.'

Steve intervened. 'Never mind, if we can get you on our flight we will. What about the other girls?'

'They want to stay on. Neither of them are due back at work until next week.' She smiled. 'Erin wants to do a bungee jump off the bridge, and Chloe's going water skiing.'

The girls' trophy win was writ large in the sailing press but failed to register with the mainstream sporting media, apart from a few lines in the *Daily Telegraph.* Tom noted that the *Daily Banner* had run a story, but it was another raking over of "little Emily the brave teenager and survivor of the fire siege…" There was a further piece of bullshit about some other competitor from Britain and it was hinted the two crews were on bad terms. Tom assumed these to be Sammy Robstron and her two. He knew that Emily had an irrational dislike of this trio.

Tom and Emily had kept in touch by phone and email throughout the ten days. Emily's calls had been muted, but Tom assumed she had her mind on the competition – quite right too. He was ashamed to say that he hadn't felt much sorrow at his girlfriend's absence. He had been able to throw his energies into his job and was pleased to have already earned a commendation from the top. One Saturday he had taken part in a Laser training session at Portland, and for the first time began to discover and correct some of the faults that had spoiled his racing. It had been a lovely still winter's day the following Sunday morning, so he had sailed his Laser home across Weymouth Bay to Duddlestone. This had resulted in a furious ticking off from Mum, for taking such a risk.

Then Emily had called. 'I'm at Heathrow with Mum and Dad.'

'You're early. We weren't expecting you until next week.'

'I know, but I wanted to come home. Now I'm not so sure – it's cold here.'

'It's cold everywhere – it's winter.' Tom stated the obvious.

'Well, it's all right for you. I've been in summer.'

'When can we meet?'

'I'll be at home and Dad says you can come to dinner tonight. I can tell you all about Auckland.'

They exchanged endearments and rang off. It was good to hear her voice again.

'Back to work on Monday,' said Steve. 'Ten days to catch up and then we're off again.'

'To Olifa, you mean,' said Emily.

'Why's this?' asked Tom.

'There's a delegation from the British Olympic Committee. We're going to inspect the plans for the facilities and all that. But I'm going to the coast to look at the sailing side.'

'Emily should be there in four years,' Tom grinned.

'There's no sign that Sammy's giving up,' said Emily.

'Well, you got your own back in Auckland,' said Kirsten.

'Too close to call though,' said Steve. 'However from what I saw I'd say you have a better than even chance.'

'A lot of people are saying you'll be there as well,' said Emily. 'They've heard about you and your new boat.'

Steve had no reply to this. He made a disclaiming gesture but he did wonder. He had rarely felt so in tune with a new boat. Every time he sat in her the years seemed to fall away until he felt little different from the thirty-year-old one time champion of long ago. Paralympics at seventy? Hell, why not!

'Has there been any more trouble?' Emily asked.

They all knew what she meant.

'Sarah house sat for us,' said Steve. 'The local police promised to keep an eye out and I suppose they did.'

'What about Hammersen?' asked Tom.

'As far as we know he's vanished.'

'I told you we met Le Bois's son in Auckland?' said Emily.

'I didn't know that,' said Tom.

'He was fine, no hard feelings. He hinted that he knew his dad was manic. He said he and his mum were frightened of him. But that's not why he wanted to talk to me. You see, Tom, the man's a policeman like his dad and he'd had a report that I was under threat.'

'Oh, Em,' said Tom clearly distressed. 'Who would want to hurt you?'

'You know who, Hammersen. Le Bois said it was to do with my grandfather but that was a bit vague.'

'So Hammersen's still out there pushing the Hitler thing. The man's not a historian he's a head case.'

'Emily,' said Steve, 'does Mr Travis know anything about all this?'

'I nearly told him, but it sounded so weird and we've Jewish people in the chambers. I was worried that they might believe all this rubbish.'

Steve sipped his drink. He felt disturbed, but surely, there was nothing Hammersen could do to Emily apart from spreading filthy rumours. No smoke without fire; a cliché of course, but all too true with people like readers of the *Daily Banner.*

'Come on,' said Kirsten. 'No more gloom. Let's eat.'

A week later Emily met Chloe and Erin at Heathrow and drove them to her Earl's Court lodgings. Emily was back working with her law firm and her two-year pupillage, before her call to the bar. She had settled into the office round, shadowing the Clerk, and generally being useful. Tony Travis QC, the head of chambers, had been delighted with the girl's match racing success. He invited the three to have dinner with him at his yacht club.

'Did you have a good time?' Emily asked.

'I'll say,' Chloe laughed. 'I kept falling off the water skis but Erin was good. And, believe it or not, we both did the bungee.'

'What was that like?'

'I can tell you, I left my tummy behind and I'm not sure it's caught up yet.'

'Are Sammy and the twins on your plane?'

'No,' said Erin. 'The twins are playing the field with the Kiwi hunks.'

Emily smirked. 'Surprise, surprise. What about Sammy?'

'No chance. Her husband flew in just after the racing. She's on best behaviour.'

It was good to see the others again. They were soon engaged in sail talk; thinking ahead to the next competition in Hyeres. This Mediterranean resort was hosting a major regatta in late April, and all three knew this would be as stiff a test as Auckland had been. There would only be a narrow window between their arrival home and the start of a gruelling run of events. Hyeres in April would be followed by a regatta on Lake Garda in Italy, followed by Israel in early June. It was a good thing that they had renewed Olympic funding as Erin had taken unpaid leave from her job. Travis had given Emily time off, but she would have to fly home immediately each series was complete.

The weekend couldn't come quickly enough for Emily. She had spent Friday sitting in on an insufferably boring court hearing: a civil case about a supply of faulty building materials. She was glad to escape straight to Waterloo station and the home train to Petersfield. Mum and Dad gave her a royal welcome and together they sat down and watched the DVD of the Auckland series. For the first time she was able to have a relaxed look at the desperate final leg and the decisive finish. Only yards from the line they had been behind Sammy's boat, no more than an inch or so, but that final surge had done the business and as the computer line showed they had scored the win and the trophy by the tightest of margins.

'We're off to Olifa in ten days time,' said Dad.

Emily recalled the ultra-feminist geography teacher from her school days. 'Dad, Ms Flotton was always banging on about Olifa, something about a people's revolution.'

'That was nearly one hundred years ago,' her mother replied. 'It was partly British led.'

'How come?'

'Olifa was a rich country, still is. Copper mines in those days but even more oil now. The revolution was a movement for the native people to take back their country from the companies exploiting them.'

'That's good – why not?'

'Of course, but it didn't last. You recall Signor Garcia who presented your medals?'

'I had my sailing gear on last time so he wasn't able to stare at my boobs.'

'Emily,' intervened her father. 'Less of that sort of talk…'

'Shut up, Steve,' said Kirsten. 'When we were at the King Henry the man had a lecherous look at me too. I was flattered. Anyway, Garcia's grandfather fought on the rebel side, the liberators. Now our Garcia is an oil baron and the poor people are as exploited as ever they were.'

Emily was puzzled. 'He must have been pretty good at sailing to have won a silver in the Star class.'

'Try telling that to the poor down-trodden miners.'

Emily took her car and drove over to meet Tom. Tom rented a flat over a shop in Alresford's Broad Street, a few doors away from a tasty fare Indian restaurant where they were due to eat later. Tom made them both cups of coffee; they sat arms around each other on the settee.

'How's the legal stuff going?' Tom asked.

Suddenly Emily saw an opening. 'Mr Travis suggests I put in some practise at home. Are you up for some cross examination?'

Tom grinned. 'I guess so,'

'Have you got a bible?'

'Of course I haven't'

'All right, you can swear on that copy of *Nuts* that you've been hiding from me.'

Tom picked up the glossy magazine from under the pile of papers. He looked suitably sheepish.

'All right,' she said. 'Never mind the swearing – we'll take it as done. Stand there and don't move.' Emily walked to face Tom. 'Mr Stoneman, tell me. Do you know Miss Alexia Ford-Watts?'

'Eh?'

'No, Mr Stoneman. I asked you a question. Please reply yes, or no.'

'Well, yes, sort of.'

'We will take that as an affirmative. Mr Stoneman, will you tell the court how long you have known this lady?'

'Wait a minute. What is this?'

‘Mr Stoneman, this is a court of law and you must answer truthfully.’

‘I’m being strung up.’

‘No, Mr Stoneman. One hundred years ago you might have been. Now will you please answer my question?’

‘I played with her when we were kids.’

‘And now you have ceased to be kids, as you put it. Have you seen the lady recently? A straight answer please.’

‘How recently is recently?’

‘Mr Stoneman, you are anticipating my next question. Please answer the one I put to you.’

‘Well … last Wednesday if you must know.’

‘And what, Mr Stoneman, was the purpose of this meeting with Miss Ford-Watts?’

‘Oh, Em,’ Tom put his hands to his face. ‘You’ve got this all wrong. Oh, Jesus Christ, I feel sorry for any poor bloody criminal who has to face you in few years’ time. Look, I don’t know how you found out about Alix, but she and I played as kids, and we’ve stayed friends, but that’s all. Oh, Em, I love you. Alix is a mate, but you’re my girl, my Emily.’

Emily laughed with relief. The wretched man was telling the truth. ‘No further questions, my Lord.’ She flung her arms around him.

CHAPTER 20

Both Steve and Kirsten were well into the throes of jetlag even as Olifa City hove into sight beneath the wings of the British Airways 747. Tired and twitchy after the fourteen-hour flight, Steve was none the less impressed. Half an hour ago they had crossed the Andes and then the region Gran Seco, where so much of the Olifarian wealth was produced.

The wide Pacific was as blue as the brochures, and miles of smooth beaches followed the shoreline dotted with tiny human figures. The distant city shone in the sunlight: a spectacle of high-rise glass and wide freeways. First impressions of course, but he felt this to be a place they might enjoy. For the benefit of the Olympic delegation the captain pointed out the huge stadium, home at present to *Olifa Angelo Football Club*, champions of South America. In three and a half years' time this would be the central venue for the Olifa Games.

Next came the final approach to the airport south of the city, or *el Liberator Enrique Castor* airport. Steve and Kirsten emerged onto the hard standing, rubbing their eyes, not only from sleep, but from the blinding light and the heat: oven-like heat, far hotter than Auckland a few weeks ago and a complete contrast to wet and windy March back home. As Olifa lay near the equator this allegedly autumn day felt like the interior of a blast furnace.

They were raced through customs with little formality to be met by the welcoming party and a string of limousines. Steve saw Primo Garcia standing among the official delegation. As ever the man looked lean and fit, and the more so compared with his fellow ex-athletes and administrators.

Steve, submitted to being hugged and kissed on both cheeks and was amused to see Kirsten positively glowing from the same greeting. This Garcia certainly had a way with the ladies, even if he had, that time, made too close an inspection of Emily's breasts. Anyway that was the stupid girl's own fault for wearing that provoking dress.

'Steve, welcome to Olifa and welcome too, Signora Simpson, you grace our country with your loveliness.' Garcia bowed gracefully and then raised Kirsten's right hand and kissed it. And the silly woman was lapping it up. The fellow might have once been a great sailor but he was all Latino conman right now.

Thank goodness the limos were air conditioned as they motored down the five kilometre freeway into Olifa City. The closely packed skyscrapers were coming closer, standing bold against the skyline, but looking to left and right the view was a contrast. Here were shanty-towns; multiple structures of corrugated iron and rough timber covered with tarpaulins. Steve noted that these communities were held back from the freeway by eight-foot fences topped with razor wire. Not all that secure, it seemed, as Steve spotted five ragged youths and a scrawny dog scavenging by the roadside. Garcia muttered some imprecation in Spanish as an escorting military Humvee overtook them. Steve just had time to see armed soldiers jump down and surround the youths.

'What's going on?' asked Kirsten.

'It seems those vagrants are trespassing on government property,' said Garcia.

'What will happen?'

'A short period of re-education and public work.' Garcia seemed surprised at Kirsten's obvious indignation.

Steve remembered everything he had been told about South America. Olympics or no, it seemed Olifa was a more attractive country when viewed from the air. Ten minutes on they were entering the city along a way lined by opulent villas and impressive public buildings.

'This is our Avenida de la Paz,' said Garcia proudly. 'All this part of the city is one hundred and fifty old years old. There ahead is our parliament. We are so proud of our liberal democracy. Over there you will see the basilica of San Francisco and that is three hundred years old.'

Steve was looking at an even larger structure, a tall building in classical style, fronted with Doric columns and a broad flight of white steps.

'Ah, La Administracion de Gran Seco,' said Garcia following Steve's gaze. 'Once it was a bad place, a centre of the people's exploitation. My grandfather fought in our 1927 revolution to bring democracy, and now that building is our commercial centre, our stock exchange.'

The Avenida seemed endless and lined with affluence. Steve could see docks ahead and berthed in them ships: the same container carriers and unloading systems that he had seen in Southampton.

'A little further and we will come to the Club Nautica da Olifa,' said Garcia. 'Once there was a fishing port but now we have the finest yacht harbour in all South America. Steve, we offer it for your inspection and that of your colleagues, then tomorrow we will show you the Olympic village. It is not far from the Angelo Stadium so our sailing competitors can share it with all the sportsmen and women present.'

Their limousine was alone now, the others having branched off, taking the road to the proposed athletics stadium. Steve did wonder why, if Olifa was such a stable democracy, they needed another Humvee escort.

The Club Nautica was as a grand a yacht club as any Steve had visited. It was tall, seemingly all glass fronted with a wide terrace overlooking the water. On this terrace were tables and white-coated waiters scurrying to and fro with most tempting food. At the sight of this his spirits began to rise, and he realised he was hungry. The airline food had been adequate, but the sight of these gourmet menus was another matter. In front of the club lay the harbour and the marina. It was extensive, of course, and full of the usual gin palace motor yachts, mostly with American flags, but also a variety of sailing craft and an antique full-rigged ship.

'I will show you where we are building the Olympic facility,' said Garcia. 'It is only a short walk from here.'

'Is it fairly level ground?' asked Kirsten. 'My husband's walking is still not one hundred percent.'

'I can manage if we don't have to run,' Steve felt a bit testy. His walking was so much improved. 'It's not a problem.'

Personally he was annoyed with Garcia and the Olifarians for not realising how tired they were after the flight across God knew how many time zones.

'Not a problem, I hope,' said Garcia. 'We are making smooth paths and wheelchair access for the Paralympics.'

In fact there was very little to see. A level site had been cleared and Garcia showed them plans for a boat park, workshops and floating pontoons as well as launching ramps for the dinghies and haulout facilities for the keelboats. Steve felt he could give a satisfactory report. The arrangements were as good as any previous Olympics, provided the Olifarians got off their backsides and completed on time.

Kirsten was impatient. 'Signor Garcia, can you tell us what's happened to our luggage? I lost touch with it at the airport.'

'You must not worry Signora. It has already been delivered to the Hotel de la Constitution and that is a stone's throw as you English say. We will take you there now and give you a chance to rest after your journey. Then tomorrow we will discuss our plans.'

'We would certainly appreciate a rest,' said Kirsten. 'It's been a long trip and we're both pretty jetlagged.'

'I understand. Tomorrow we will have a formal conference and go into the sailing facilities in more detail.'

They returned to their limousine after passing through the club dining area. Steve hoped the fare in the hotel would match the food on show in the yacht club. Both of them were feeling increasingly shattered and Steve had to make a real effort of will not to close his eyes and fall into oblivion.

The hotel was on a promontory not far from the yacht harbour at the end of a broad tree-lined street.

'This is Calle Roylance,' said Garcia. 'It is named in honour of an Englishman, a brave pilot, who led the revolutionary air service during our fight for freedom.'

At last they had reached the hotel. It was a magnificent nineteenth century building, old world and grandiose both inside and without.

'I will pass you to the good hands of the management,' said Garcia. 'Then tomorrow we will take you to the Olympic village, and after that you may like to talk to our architects and engineers who have been detailed to build the sailing facility.'

'Thank you,' replied Kirsten. 'We really are very tired.'

'Dear lady, may you rest well and lighten our day with your grace and beauty tomorrow.' He bowed again and was gone.

'Bloody Dago,' Steve muttered. 'Lecherous sod.'

Kirsten put her arm around him. 'Steve, you are skating on the edge of political incorrectness – even racism. That man is what he is and he was a useful racing helm in his day.'

'And he stared down Emily's dress that time in the King Henry.'

'Who can blame him? She looked lovely that night.'

They were shown their room, an ornate high-ceilinged apartment with a fine view over the harbour and the Pacific beyond.

'God, I need a shower,' said Kirsten. 'Are you going to be prudish?'

'Why?'

'Good, they've left some writing paper.' Kirsten seized a writing pad from the little art deco bureau and began to scribble. She handed him the result.

Wouldn't be at all surprised if they haven't bugged this room. Forget your blushes, strip and come in the shower with me. They won't hear a thing and I want to talk.

Steve took the pad and wrote. *You could be right. OK.*

They both undressed and went into the en-suite shower cubicle. Steve was happy to comply and looked forward to his wife soaping his body and he hers. The water streamed down under power.

They adjusted the heat to suit and then Kirsten spoke her thoughts. 'Look, you're not as dense as Emily about history, but you're still English and detached from it.'

'What are you on about?'

'Only that I'm Danish and half-Jewish, so I sense things. Garcia's been banging on about their glorious revolution of 1927, right?'

'Yes, I heard him.'

'It was a wonderful thing. A group of British and American adventurers mobilised the native people to take back their country from the copper mining company that was running the whole show, and brutally at that. Millions of dollars earned by the rich while the poor worked and starved.'

'That happens.'

'Then the people rose in rebellion. They were led by a man called Castor...'

'Castro, couldn't be. He was hardly more than a baby.'

'No!' Kirsten slapped her husband's bottom. 'Castor. Although there's some evidence that at first he was co-opted against his will, and it was only later that he converted to the rebellion. Garcia's grandfather fought for the liberators in the great battle up in the mountains. The rebellion was on the defensive and then their army caught the government forces in a mountain pass and annihilated them.'

Steve listened although he was more interested in soaping her erect nipples and breasts. 'Sounds like justice prevailed,' he said.

'Everyone thought so, and then Castor was assassinated and gradually things went downhill. In the 1940s they found oil on the coastal plain. The Yanks arrived of course, and then the copper companies reverted to the bad old ways. Now Olifa is run exactly as it was before the revolution – nothing's changed.'

Steve turned his wife around and began to happily soap her spine and buttocks. He could do without this history lesson and couldn't exactly see its relevance. 'How come you know all this?'

'I've been reading in the library and on the internet. I had vaguely heard about it, but I thought I would get my facts straight.'

‘But we’re part of an official Olympic delegation. I’ve been to worse places than this. Christ, in Beijing the secret police were breathing down our necks from day one.’

‘You are going to be locked in committee and location visits. While you are doing that I want to have a look at this country and make up my own mind. Garcia is the man who could help me if I want to get further than the usual tourist spots.’

‘All right flatter him, flirt with him, anything short of going to bed with him. It could help my work here as well.’

She laughed as she put her arms around him and their lips came together under the torrent of water. ‘I suspect he’s got a harem of maidens for his bed already, much tastier than a middle-aged mum – so don’t worry.’

‘Well, I will settle for the middle-aged mum, every time.’

They left the shower and towelled each other’s bodies and then not bothering with the sheets or covers they fell on the bed and together, naked in each other’s arms, they slept.

CHAPTER 21

'Hi, Em. I've news,' Chloe's voice blasted down the phone line.

Emily winced and held the phone away from her right ear. 'What's happened?'

'Oh, Em, I just do not believe it and it's so sad in a way.'

'For God's sake, Chloe. What is it?'

'Sammy and her girls have split up.'

'Never!'

'No it's true and official. I caught it on the *Yachts and Yachting* website and there's a piece in the poncy *Daily Telegraph* and another bit in the scumbag *Daily Banner.'*

'Do we know why?'

'No, the *Banner* has a whole lot of stuff, but it's all hints about jealousy.'

'I don't believe that.' Emily was puzzled. She had never liked their rival trio but they were a cast iron team, she had to give them that.

Chloe's laugh shrieked. 'You're not going to jump ship and go with Sammy, I hope.'

'Bloody hell, that'd be like signing up with Captain Bligh. No thanks.'

'That's not fair. In New Zealand we reckon Bligh was a good guy; must've been. He navigated an open boat for a thousand miles. We Maoris really rate him for that. Later he was governor of Oz.'

'Serve them bloody well right. Does this mean Sammy won't be in Hyeres?'

'Unless she can cobble together a new crew in three weeks, I doubt it. We'll wait and see.'

'In the meantime we'd better practise while we can,' said Emily.

'Too right, mate. We've another week before we have to pack for Hyeres. If there's no Sammy, we'll be expected to win that one.'

Emily was baffled by this news. She ought to be pleased because she couldn't see Sammy recruiting another crew half as good as the twins. But the news only made her feel guilty. She couldn't honestly say she liked any of them, but the hate had gone. The final in Auckland had been a great healer and she was prepared to live and let live.

Emily put her phone away and looked at her watch. She had just eaten lunch in a little self-service café not far from the Inns of Court. In twenty minutes time she was due back in the chambers to answer the phone and relay anything important to the clerk. Travis QC was away at the Old Bailey, taking two of the juniors with him. She hadn't much taste for this case and had not asked to go along with them. Travis was defending an alleged rapist. Frankly Emily would have made the man defend himself and then she would wish him a twenty-year jail term. Travis had gently reminded her that it was possible the man really was innocent. Well, not this time he wasn't. She'd read the case notes and wanted nothing to do with it. She wondered how Mum and Dad were getting on in Olifa. Her mum had phoned her, woken her up actually, and told her that dad would be tied up in committee meetings and that she was taking a tour of the countryside.

Emily yawned, paid her bill and took a leisurely walk back to the chambers through the early March sunshine. In the office was William the clerk. Everyone called him William, although he must have a surname. William ran the whole show. William had no formal law degree, only forty years in the business. He remembered men being sentenced to death, and, much more amusingly, anecdotes from the Lady Chatterley trial. William was genial and gruff at the same time, and Emily loved him. Travis had already told her that William was a better tutor for her than anyone else in the firm.

'Hello, young Emily. Thought I'd let you know that the jury's out – Mr Travis rang just now. He thinks we might have just got this one. Judge seemed to be on our side.'

'He bloody would be of course. It should have been a woman judge,' said Emily.

'Well, you've got to be neutral in this game, Emily, and it could be the girl was lying. Don't tell me you ladies are always that truthful.'

'But you don't believe that, do you? Hell, the girl ran down the street crying with her knickers down round her ankles.'

William stared at her with that sardonic expression she was beginning to know so well. 'I've told you before, Emily, and so has Mr Travis. When you prosecute you play fair with the facts. You present the jury with the facts and no more. If the police and the CPS have done their job, and that's often a pretty big if – anyway if the facts stand up you get a guilty verdict. We're defending today, but we have to portray the facts reasonably and in favour of our client.'

'What about Evans, who they hanged? What about Stefan Kisko, what about those poor girls who were supposed to have killed their babies?'

'Now, Emily, you are getting emotional and that won't do. Evans was before even my time and the police should have realised what kind of man Christie was. Kisko was a flawed police investigation combined with a poor defence. With the baby trials, we can all learn. Never, Emily, and I emphasise never! Never regard a so-called expert witness as God, because he ain't. When it's your turn to question one, you make him reveal his facts and his thinking. Don't ever let a pompous bastard blind you with his superior knowledge, and then make sure the jury don't get conned by him. In those cases it always seems to be him and if it's like those women's baby trials, he's usually a raving misogynist.'

Now Emily smiled and leaned across to give the old man a kiss on his cheek. 'Thanks, Mr Travis is right – you are the best teacher around here.'

William laughed. 'You haven't left any lipstick on my face I hope. My missus will get out her rolling pin if you have.'

'I've finally persuaded Garcia to let me go up country,' said Kirsten. 'He's been hedging up till now. I've seen enough old churches and castles and God knows how many luscious vineyards. I want to have a look at this Gran Seco. It's not on the tourist route but that's where they mine the copper. I've seen the oil wells but when you've seen one you've seen the lot.'

'How are you going to get there?'

'I'm going to the airport tomorrow morning and they'll fly me. Garcia's persuaded the copper company as a great favour. Anything's possible if you mention the Olympics.'

'Wait a minute,' said Steve. 'I don't want you flying over desert in some clapped out Cessna.'

'I'm not, I asked that myself. It's an American crew and the plane's an Islander, British built. Old, but well maintained for the copper company's execs.'

'I've flown in one of those,' said Steve. 'They built them on the Isle of Wight and they're safe enough I suppose. Two engines anyway.'

'How did the meetings go today?' Kirsten asked.

'We were shown the Olympic village. It looks like a bombsite at the moment. They've cleared a square mile of old buildings and levelled the place. The city mayor swears it'll all be ready on time.'

'I wonder what happened to all the poor people who lost their homes?'

'I don't know, we didn't ask. But you're right I'm afraid. It looks like Beijing all over again.'

'Anyway, I'm going to the Gran Seco, but I've got to take some bloke from the British embassy with me.'

'All right, but don't forget we've both got to be at that formal reception in three days time.'

The Islander aircraft was an improved version with a soundproofed cabin. Kirsten had joined it at the main airport in company with the young press officer from the British Embassy, and an American copper company executive. Gareth Day, the press officer, was nothing like Kirsten's stereotypical idea of a British diplomat. He was cheerful, mid-thirties, with a slight north-country accent. Gareth admitted that this was only his second trip to the Gran Seco. 'Bit of a wild and dusty place,' he said. 'The name means "Great Thirst" and that follows. Most of the rainfall is on the coastal plain before it gets into the mountains.'

The American was a pleasant enough guy, thought Kirsten. He was a company geologist who hailed from Seattle and was of Norwegian descent. Kirsten was rather pleased to find that they could speak in a sort of crossover Scandinavian language and still understand each other. The geologist explained that as well as his Norwegian background, his mother's family name was Douglas and she came from Scotland. Kirsten was even more delighted to find that he remembered her sailing achievements.

An hour into their journey and they had left the last of the green countryside far behind. The land below was brown with scrub and outcrops of rock. The flight was also becoming increasingly bumpy. Below them, clearly visible, was a substantial railway network. Kirsten could see a long train of empty bulk wagons drawn by two diesel locomotives.

'Gradient's steep,' said the American, noticing her interest. 'They need two engines for the return trip through the passes.'

'The railway is still the only way they can get the copper ore out of the Seco,' said Gareth.

Kirsten's eye was drawn to an object on the first mountain ridge. It was clearly a mighty obelisk of gleaming white stone with sunlight reflecting on some metal at the top. 'What's that?' she asked.

'It's the memorial to the Battle of Santa Ana,' said Gareth. 'It's the place where the revolutionary forces defeated the Government army in 1927. It was a big battle. The rebel forces were commanded by General Peters: the main Government army was smashed and a few days later the remnants under their C in C, General Olivarez surrendered and the war was over. The man who took the surrender was an English lord called Clanroyden.'

'No he wasn't,' replied the American. 'He was a Scot.'

'Yes,' said Kirsten. 'I've read about the liberation, and yet I still saw shanty towns and armed soldiers.'

'What goes around comes around,' said the American, 'and this is South America. But things are not as bad as they were before the revolution. Then the workers were virtually slaves. Conditions are not good today, but they do get a regular wage.'

'But trade unions are banned.'

'I guess so.'

'I can tell you something else about the pre-revolution,' added Gareth. 'The copper company execs were all cocaine addicts – that is the junior and middle management, not the top men of course.'

'How did that happen?' she asked.

'They were all introduced to the stuff as a company policy. Do what we say or we'll cut off your dope supply was their line.'

'All this oil and the copper, why can't they treat the people better?' Kirsten was becoming angry. 'I'm told this is the wealthiest country in all Spanish America. Frankly that's why they got the Olympics.'

Gareth and the geologist glanced at each other. 'There's a third line of wealth and it's maybe just as lucrative,' Said Gareth.

'You mean Castinnio.com.'

'Worldwide internet gambling system,' said Gareth. 'Perfectly legit, not a scam.'

'I've heard of it,' said Kirsten. 'There's a little man in our Chichester office who uses it. You can bet on everything from the local dog track to the next American president. He says it's good. You pay online and they pay you back by return every time you win.'

'How often does your guy win?' asked Gareth.

'Rarely, I would guess.'

'Like everyone else. And we all know who wins. You should see the new mansion the Garcias have built on their estancia.'

'Not Primo Garcia?'

'That's the bloke,' said Gareth. 'Off the record, the biggest villain in this God- forsaken country and that is saying something.'

'He was a great racing sailor and his grandfather…'

'National hero.'

'And I rather liked him,' Kirsten mused. 'The present day one that is.'

'He has that effect on the ladies,' the American laughed.

Steve was relieved to see his wife return unscathed. He collected her from the airport in the limousine by courtesy of Garcia.

'Well, how was your little jaunt up country?' he asked.

'Interesting,'

'I wouldn't find a lot of copper workings interesting myself.'

'Oh they showed me a few of those. All hot and dusty and the wretched workers, no more than I expected.'

'How so?'

'They're kept in camps and have to buy everything from the company stores.'

Steve looked at his watch. 'We've got an hour and a half, then the British delegation, us included, are invited to this reception. The President, or el Presidente I should say, will be there.'

'Will Garcia be there?'

'Of course.'

Kirsten made that facial expression that Steve knew so well. Something in her attitude to Garcia had changed.

Steve felt tired and was not sure he was really up for a formal event. Having endorsed the plans for the sailing facilities, he had limped along with the main British delegation on a final tour. They had sat in the presidential box at the Angelo stadium, a bowl that would dwarf even Wembley or Twickenham. They had travelled by coach out of the city to watch as excavators dug a channel to divert a river into the long rowing lake, and then travelled a short way into the hills to see a cascade that would feed the canoeing white water course. However, the equestrian and shooting facilities were still under army control and off limits even to their delegation. The day had been hot, and Steve was tired and sweaty before finally they had viewed the nearly completed velodrome. They all knew that that place, along with the sailing, rowing, and swimming complexes would be the source of most of the British medals.

Returning to the hotel they took another shower together and Kirsten told him of Garcia's alleged gambling empire. Steve by now was inclined to agree that their room could be bugged by whatever secret police operated in this town. Perhaps he was becoming paranoid, but places like this had that effect. Reluctantly Steve unpacked his formal dinner suit. Kirsten was busy sliding into her expensive Paris halter-top black gown. He had to admit that she looked graceful. Her bare back he had moisturised for her, to the point where even her tanned and weathered skin could have passed for a twenty-year old. Thinking of twenty-year olds reminded him of Emily. They must buy both her, Johnny, Sarah and Christine, some suitable gifts before they departed for home. They inspected each other in the full-length mirror, embraced, and Steve picked up his walking sticks. They were ready, willingly or not, to party.

In less than five minutes their limousine arrived at the Club de Residentes Extranjeros. This building lay in a tree-lined square to the north of the Avenida. The place was clear proof of Olifa's material wealth. This was the centre of the nation's cosmopolitan community and it was impressive. Lines of limos were unloading passengers onto the forecourt where a large floodlit fountain was the centrepiece. The flowers and shrubs wafted a delicious scent on the warm evening.

The whole scene put Kirsten in mind of an Oscar award ceremony. They stepped from their car onto a broad red carpet. She put her arm through her husband's, partly because it seemed the right form but mainly to give him extra support. Two other Olympic delegations, French and Russian, were also gathering: the men elegant and the ladies competing in over-flamboyant finery. Kirsten was pleased to note that she and Steve had at least got their own restrained attire about right.

The building's interior was brightly lit but cooled by large diameter overhead fans. The whole place had an old-fashioned colonial aura that reminded Kirsten of the Royal King Henry Yacht Club back home. Suave waiters and pretty dark haired serving girls offered glasses of local sparkling wine. Kirsten sipped hers and was pleased to discover it was good and far better than the cheap Champagne on offer at the King Henry. She noted that she must keep an eye on her husband who was already drinking his second glass.

The reception lounge was a long room in Italianate style. Pictures on the walls looked to be genuine eighteenth century paintings of ships. But one wall was blank apart from a single portrait flanked by the Olifarian national flag. Kirsten could not help but be drawn to the subject of this portrait. She saw a man whose features commanded. He was dressed in an early twentieth century high collared dark suit and the painter had caught to perfection the man's eyes. Even on canvas these eyes dominated the room seemingly following each individual with an interrogative stare. The high forehead, slightly curled dark hair and pointed beard gave the face a faintly nautical air.

'That's him, El Liberator.'

Kirsten turned to see Gareth Day studying the portrait.

'That's Castor is it?' she asked.

'He never lived to preside over his revolution. Things might have been different if he had.'

At that moment came a diversion. Trumpets blared in uncertain unison as a group of uniformed soldiers slipped through the main door. They were followed by a second group of dark-faced men dressed in garish Conquistador costumes. Following them came a tall balding man wearing a dark suit with a coloured sash.

'El Presidente,' announced the MC.

Following the great man came a baffling all male entourage: soberly dressed ministers, four gladiatorial looking wrestlers with rippling muscles and a Roman Catholic Cardinal in robes and a red hat. Kirsten could hardly take this in before the string orchestra struck up the Olifarian anthem. This put Kirsten in mind of the saying, "the smaller the country the longer the national anthem." No sooner was the tune completed, before the band struck up the Russian anthem, followed by the French and ending with a high-pitched rendering of God Save the Queen.

The atmosphere was now much more relaxed. El Presidente circulated amicably. Gareth Day ushered the man across to meet them. 'El Presidente sailed boats as a young man,' he said.

The President replied surprisingly in perfect Home-Counties English. 'Come now, Mr Day, am I really that old? Mr and Mrs Simpson, I am not so old but I remember your achievements both of you. Is it true that your young daughter is following in your foot-steps?'

'Yes Sir,' Steve replied. 'She is a keen sailor and would like to be here for your games.'

'Indeed I saw a picture of her in our own yachting press. A beautiful lady, as you are also, Mrs Simpson. As for your daughter, please accept that we followed the news of her tribulations seven years ago, and all Olifa rejoiced at her escape.'

'Thank you,' said Kirsten. 'I will tell her that when we return home.'

The President bowed and moved on.

'He's nice,' said Kirsten.

Steve laughed and looked at Gareth. 'My wife is a sucker for Latin flattery.'

'Fancy him knowing about the sun cult,' said Kirsten.

'After your daughter's troubles,' said Gareth, 'the government here suppressed the sun cult and none too gently. At least two were executed. As for the President, he's a good friend of Britain. He's smoothed the way for us with oil concessions. Speaks good English as you notice, but as he's Eton and Oxford I suppose that follows.'

'Must be a good bloke then,' said Steve.

'And he's el Liberator's great nephew,' said Gareth.

Kirsten caught the eye of a familiar figure. The man was Dimitri Panov, the head of the Russian delegation and the Finn class bronze medallist who had finished third behind Steve. Dimitri's English was sketchy at the best, and Kirsten was relieved to find that the man had an interpreter at his elbow.

'Please, Mr Simpson,' said the interpreter. 'Mr Panov is wondering if you would care to join him on the water tomorrow?'

'What, sailing?'

'That is so. Mr Panov has been loaned the use of a yacht of six metres.'

'That sounds good, but I would like my wife to be invited.'

The interpreter mumbled in Russian to Panov who waved him aside and spoke directly to Steve. 'Stefan, yes your wife also. It would be like times that are old. We try out the sea course here – OK?'

'We haven't got our sailing clothes.'

'Mr Panov says that matters not,' replied the interpreter. 'He will provide aids for the floating of life.'

Kirsten thought that the interpreter's English was only marginally better than his boss man. Presumably he meant they should wear their casuals and that he would find them buoyancy aids.

Panov plus interpreter moved off. The gathering was drifting as one towards the dining hall while in the background the string orchestra played Strauss waltzes.

Steve touched her arm. 'I think we've struck lucky. We're due to inspect the sailing conditions out there tomorrow and I'd rather do it in a genuine sailing boat than in Garcia's gin palace.'

'Won't Garcia be offended?'

'The sailing delegations are only a small section of the whole. Garcia's been a racing helmsman. He ought to understand. I'll tell him I haven't seen Dimitri for a year or two and we want to reminisce. That's true.'

Kirsten could see Garcia coming closer. She wasn't sure that she wanted any more of his flowery compliments. She had her own questions that she would like to put to the man.

'Ah, Signora, and how was your visit to our Gran Seco?' Garcia looked even more elegant, although Kirsten was not much taken with the scent of perfume.

'It was most interesting, Mr Garcia.'

'Hardly a tourist trap. It lives up to its name.'

'I must say, Mr Garcia, I would not care to be a copper miner.'

'Nor would I, Signora Simpson. But they are a tough breed and proud.'

'Why cannot they form unions?'

'That is a strange question for someone from England. I was living in your country when it was almost destroyed by trade unions. There is no appetite in this country for self-destruction.'

Kirsten realised she would get nowhere on worker's rights with this man. She hoped he would walk away but instead he leaned forward and spoke quietly. 'Would it not be rather exciting if both your husband and daughter were to sail for gold in our games?'

'We have hopes for our daughter but Stephen is still recovering from illness.' Kirsten was not sure where this was leading.

'From all reports I have heard, your husband would be no mean competitor in the 2.4 Paralympic class.'

'Mr Garcia, you will have to ask him yourself.'

'This yacht is a beauty – a classic,' said Steve.

They were sailing close-hauled, miles offshore with Olifa city just a smudge on the horizon. Steve was trimming the mainsheet although this was somewhat of a challenge to his weakened arm. Fortunately the line was a multiblock tackle. Kirsten was manning the jib, and before that the spinnaker, with one of the UK delegation. Dimitri, the Russian, took the helm in turn with an American member of the yacht club. The boat was a vintage Six Metre, a classic wooden build in an incredible state of preservation. The yacht club member had told them she was over eighty years old and had once been forfeited after the revolution by her owner, a copper mining profiteer.

'What happened to him?' asked Kirsten.

'Ran away to Chile,' was the reply.

Steve was watching the receding shoreline. 'Have you noticed that wind shift? Every time we cross that line around 95 degrees there's a bad shift around ten degrees. That's worth noting.'

'Sure,' said the American. 'I race out here – it's always that way when there's an offshore breeze – can't say why, don't think anyone's quantified it.'

'We'll note it for Emily,' said Kirsten.

'I've read about your girl,' replied the American.

Oh, no, thought Steve. Not the fire siege again. He was wrong.

'Ladies' match racing. I'm told her crew have just been rated World Number One.'

'Really, I didn't know that.'

'Yeah we saw it on the internet yesterday.'

'That's good, 'said Kirsten. 'Maybe you, Steve, will be competing here as well.'

'2.4 class in the Paralympics?' said the American.

'Wait a minute,' Steve had to intervene. 'All of you are jumping the gun on that one.'

The American was silent. He glanced at Dimitri.

The Russian was staring at the masthead windvane. He adjusted the tiller to meet another shift. 'Garcia,' he said.

'That's it, Steve. Seems you've interested our gambling king.'

'Why?'

'Oldest man to win a gold, and a double if his daughter gets one as well,' Kirsten was grinning. 'Potential bookies clean out, or potential disaster.'

CHAPTER 22

'Hi Dad, Hi Mum.' Emily had spotted her parents amidst the crowds at Heathrow and ran to them. It was strange, but she had actually missed them while they were away and had worried herself about Dad's illness. She hugged them both and then stood back. Both looked amazingly well although they must be in the throes of some reverse jetlag.

'And what have you been up to?' Dad asked. 'Shouldn't you be at work?'

'Mr Travis has given me the rest of the day off. He's pleased with me. He thinks I'll sail through the dine tests.'

'The what?'

'The practical tests – gotta do those before I'm called.'

'Talk about sailing through tests – congratulations,' said Mum.

'Thanks, but why?'

'We heard that Chloe you and Erin are World number one.'

'Oh yes, but do you know why? No, of course you don't.' Emily was laughing, she couldn't help herself. 'We beat Sammy in Auckland, but that's not the half of it. She's spilt up with the twins. You see,' Emily spluttered, 'the twins stayed on in Auckland afterwards and they've both got themselves pregnant – up the duff.'

'That was careless,' said Steve. He looked at her mother. 'I can hardly understand a word this budding lawyer is saying through the hysterics. Shall I slap her on the back?'

Emily fought to control the giggles. 'Slap's the right word. Sammy told me about it. 'Cos those twins are identical they share everything. Sammy says they're both preggers by the same bloke. He's a water ski instructor…' she was laughing tears now. 'He's known as Dud the Stud…'

'Emily,' Kirsten looked severe. 'I know you don't get on with those two but that's no reason to gloat over anyone's misfortune.'

'Yeah, I know.' Emily dabbed her eyes with a handkerchief. 'Because Anna from Estonia fouled up in Auckland, it leaves us at number one.' Again she laughed. 'I asked William at work about; maintenance payments. To give them credit the twins are both going through with the babies even if it does put them out of sailing for a year. William says that Dud the Stud had better not come to the UK anytime soon or he'll have a nasty hole in his pocket courtesy of the CSA.'

'Knowing those two girls by reputation I would say he's not wholly to blame,' said Steve.

'Typical man's reaction,' said Mum.

'If you say so. Anyway, Emily, we've presents for you and Johnny in our luggage, assuming this place hasn't lost it.'

Sid Everett had kicked off his shoes and was dozing in the lounge of his Guildford flat. Sounds in the kitchen reminded him that girlfriend Shirley was trying to cook some sort of meal. He would far sooner the silly old bat went out and bought a takeaway. Now the telephone was ringing and the ex-directory phone too; so who the hell?

'Everett here.'

'Good evening, Mr Everett, it's Karl Hammersen.'

'Oh, yeah, how come you knew this number?'

'Anything is available at the right price. As a fellow journalist you should know that.'

'Come to the point, Hammersen, are you still persecuting that poor girl?'

'Mr Everett, you should know me better…'

'That's good, because I don't know you at all, mate.'

'I would like to discuss the matter with you face to face. I have news that might interest you.'

Sid did not reply at once. He wanted nothing to do with this creep, but at the same time he might be on to something that would become a story. But he would have nothing to do with any plot to hurt little Emily. For the first time since his young days he had an uneasy conscience. It was an alien sensation and unsettling.

'You still there, Mr Everett?'

'Yeah, say what you have in mind.'

'Meet me at Halcyons tomorrow evening eight o'clock sharp.'

'You mean that bloody strip joint?'

'There's only one Halcyons. I didn't know you were so squeamish, but we have been allocated a private room.'

'All right, I will listen but don't expect favours.'

'Look what Mum and Dad bought for me in Olifa.' Emily pointed to the coloured bead necklace.

'That looks nice,' said Tom. 'Did they enjoy Olifa?'

Emily wasn't certain herself. 'I think Dad had a good time. His walking is better, he's picked up a bit of a tan. He did some sailing and he met a lot of old blokes from his time.'

'What about your mother?'

'I think she enjoyed the break, but she wasn't too impressed with the country. I always know when she's a bit wary or uncertain about people or places.'

It was Friday evening and it was good to see Tom again. All week she had been so involved with the Travis chambers. Tom had been neglected but never pushed to the back of her mind. She felt almost torn in two. She was committed to her future career. No one in chambers went in for extravagant praise, but both Travis and William had hinted that she was a star pupil who could go to the very top. She wasn't so conceited as to imagine herself as a judge but she secretly saw herself as QC or even head of chambers. Her squeamishness in court was being replaced by the necessary professional hardness. She would never forget the Kessel trial and that sense of being in the presence of evil, but subsequent criminal trials had been routine. Most of the defendants had been pathetic damaged individuals: backward and ill educated. Many had spent most of their lives in jail. But did Tom expect her to lay ambition aside to devote her life to him? He had vehemently denied this, but he was a man with an authoritarian and traditional stepfather.

Tom held her in his arms, and once again she felt that slow burning glow inside her.

'So, it's Hyeres next week,' said Tom.

Emily sensed that he was unhappy. 'Oh, darling, I wish you could come with us.'

'So do I, but work calls.'

Emily made up her mind. 'Tom, if we get to Olifa in three years time … would you be our team manager?'

His mouth opened. 'What would that entail?'

She laughed. 'You look taken aback, which is a good sailing term.'

'But what would I have to do?'

'Keep an eye on the boat and sails. See we girls get fed properly and go to bed on time.'

'What would Chloe think of all this?'

'We did discuss the idea and she was fine. If we made it that far we really would need someone in our team to do all that, and you're the right man.' But only if we are still together she might have added.

He tightened his hold of her and slowly rocked her like a child. And now she was losing it, humiliating for a professional modern woman, but she was in thrall to a man and wanted nothing more than that they should lie down and make long slow delicious love.

He spoke again. ‘Where do you go after Hyeres?’

She rubbed her face on his chest. ‘The following month it’s Lake Garda, then in July we go to Israel.’

‘All right, if the others agree, I’ll arrange my holiday to come with you to Israel. It’s a contentious country and I’d rather like to see it.’

Sid Everett had years ago lost his taste for places like Halcyons. In earlier days he worked on a well-known Sunday sheet and it had been a pleasure as well as a duty to visit such places. He had enjoyed watching the stripper girls perform and had come to know several of them in different venues. A few pounds in hand and they would feed him useful information. On receiving such tip-offs he could come to the club and see for himself who went up the secluded back stairs to the alleged massage parlour: politicians of course, some showbiz types and even members of the clergy. Those were happy days and his editor had rewarded him well.

He entered Halcyons at the arranged hour and glanced around with distaste. This place on the fringes of Soho was seedier than ever, although the absence of tobacco smoke was a relief. A barman was serving the usual overpriced alcohol while a skinny little girl with fake blonde hair cavorted around a pole. It was all so predictable and boring.

‘Oi, fellah, it’s members only – you paid yet?’ A fat sweaty bouncer was standing in his path.

‘I’m due for a private meeting with a Mr Hammersen. He told me he’s already paid.’

The man lost his hostility and became almost obsequious. ‘You are Mr Everett? This way please,’

The bouncer led Sid through an opening covered by red curtains. Beyond was a small space with four round restaurant tables. Hammersen was sitting at one and with him was Michelle Le Bois. Sid looked at this pair hoping the dislike he felt for both was evident in his expression.

‘Mr Everett,’ said Hammersen. ‘So pleased you could make it. What’ll you drink?’

Sid almost refused the offer, but if this man was paying the stupid prices that was fine by Sid. ‘Double Scotch with a bit of ice.’

A girl in a phoney French maid outfit, with her tits almost hanging out, served them drinks. Sid was becoming impatient and Hammersen was keeping his mouth shut. Sid wanted to know the form and get out, but Hammersen insisted they must wait for another guest.

Sid tried a fresh tack. 'Why are you here, Michelle?'
'Why d'you think?' she was surly.
'If you want me to slag off Emily Simpson in print forget it.'
'It's gone past that now.'
The bouncer drew back the curtains and another man entered. He was tall, dark haired, casually dressed and, despite the heat of the room he wore a woolly cap pulled over his ears. This he removed and Sid recognised him. He had met the man once covertly in New York and had seen his police photograph a dozen times. Sid wasn't sure of the man's true name, but he knew that this was a character wanted by the police in every continent and major city in the world.

'I've got the new car – come and look,' said Chloe.
She led the way into the street at Old Duddlestone and there was the new Subaru standing with their sponsor's garish bow and arrow crest. 'Girls, it's ours for France and Italy, then we gotta return it in good nick.'
'Emily,' said Erin, 'you've got the tickets?'
'I told you I had. It's Cherbourg tomorrow and then full speed for Hyeres. Got your bikini packed?'
'Yes, but I didn't think you bothered with one from what Tom said.'
'All right,' Chloe laughed. 'Let's not go over that ground again.'
'There's a proper nude beach there,' said Emily.
'No way!' said both her friends together.
Emily knew that they would have little time for relaxation on beaches. Hyeres was a big multi-class regatta, and they had to sail well to build on their Auckland success. They had had a good practice workout all the preceding weekend and were feeling confident. It was odd that she was feeling sad that Sammy and the twins would not be there. They had run into Tracie at Portland. The girl was not as downcast as they had expected and seemed to be looking forward to becoming a single mum. Tracie was quieter than at any time that Emily could remember and she found herself almost liking her. She wondered what it would be like to have a little baby. Would she ever know? She would have to juggle children with her ambition and she would have to persuade Tom into marriage. She felt cold at the thought of her child being fathered by anyone else.

Sid Everett had gone to the top: Scotland Yard. He was pleased to find the senior commander he knew well was still in place and was willing to talk to him.

'I'm sure it was that Joel,' said Sid. 'He's shaved his head and had some sort of facelift but it's him all right. I'd know that voice again.'[*]

'All right, Mr Everett I hear what you say and you've been right in the past, but tell me, why should an international terrorist reveal himself to you in the middle of London?'

'He wants publicity and he thinks I'll give it to him but there's no way I'm going to condone what he intends.'

'Yes, Mr Everett, you've said all that, but, why should that man want to harm a young woman? This Joel and his Redemptionists kill old Nazis, not young girls. And they haven't been active in the UK since that incident in Hampshire years ago. '

'Not many old Nazis left these days. The man Hammersen has got it into his head that young Emily is directly descended from Hitler.' Sid was worried now that time was slipping away. 'Both Hammersen and this Joel are flaky. They both think that the girl might give birth to another Hitler. Hammersen's got this stuff in his head about wiping out an evil line.'

'I'm not sure that I can buy any of this, Mr Everett but I tell you what I'll do. If you'll wait there for a minute I'll arrange for a patrol on the ground to pay a visit to Halcyons. It's probably overdue anyway.'

The commander returned. 'We've pulled up the suspect's face picture as last seen and we've emailed it to the station involved. They have agreed to send officers there in the next twenty minutes.'

'By which time Joel will have long gone.'

'More than likely, but Halcyons are vulnerable, we suspect there may be things going on upstairs that our city magistrates are not keen on.'

'Maybe, unless they use the services themselves.'

'Mr Everett, you are a cynic.'

'Gotta be in my business.'

---

[*] See *Magdalena's Redemption* by James Morley.

CHAPTER 23

May in Hyeres was well before the height of the tourist season, but this week the fun capital of Provence was awash with competitive sailing crews and their supporters. The three girls had enjoyed the drive south in their new transport. They had made good time in spite of a stopover in Paris. Emily had visited Paris before and Erin had worked there, but for Chloe the city was an exciting first and something to talk about back in New Zealand.

Emily had been home to Sussex the week before and had been puzzled. Both of her parents had been secretive, uncommunicative and absorbed in work at the sail loft. Dad said there had been an important order and he needed to see it was dispatched on time. Emily was disappointed that her Dad had not gone to Branham to sail. She had driven over to the lake with Tom and there she had a shock. Her father's boat was not in her berth. One of the club members had told her that it had been loaded on a road trailer a few days earlier. Dad was devoted to his new sailing, but he had given no indication that he might move to a new venue. He and Mum had agreed to fly down to Hyeres for a couple of days, and Dad had agreed to keep an eye on their boat.

The girls had included a good-sized tent with their other gear. Hyeres was part of the millionaire Riviera playground, a place where one saw pop stars, Hollywood personalities or perhaps James Bond. It was too expensive for three cash-strapped sporty girls, so a tented stay it was to be. This time they were committed to competitive sailing all the way. Apart from a dinner invitation from Emily's boss, they would avoid glamour-dressing parties. This suited Emily even if the other two were a tiny bit regretful.

Every Olympic racing class was included and Emily had a happy time exploring the boat park and meeting old friends, some from her World Championship time seven years ago. The shock came as she walked in the sunshine towards the end of the boat park and the water's edge. It was moment that brought Emily to a standstill and then sent her running.

'Chloe, Erin – Dad's here. I've seen his boat.' Emily staggered the last few yards, tripped on a sail cover and sprawled at the feet of her crewmates. She sat up gasping and retrieved her left flipflop.

'Take it easy, Em',' said Chloe, 'we want you in shape not in hospital.'

'I didn't know Dad was sailing or – at least his boat's here – I've just seen it in the Paralympic section.'

'Didn't he tell you? Haven't you read the entry list?'

'He never said a thing, but I saw his boat had left Branham. I should have guessed.'

'Emily,' said Erin, 'you realise what this means? I know it's three years to go, but this is an Olympic indicator regatta.'

'But why didn't they tell me?'

'I can only guess that he was coming here anyway so he thought he might just as well compete. For God's sake, Em, your dad's a top sailor. If he comes to a bash like this he'll want to take part, not hang around on shore.'

It had taken some hard persuading from Kirsten and some prompting from the British Paralympic organisers. Finally, with a few days to the entry deadline, Steve had agreed and as a finite decision had resigned from the British Olympic committee. He found inner excitement building and the old competitive juices flowing. As Kirsten said, it would be nice for the family to be racing together in the same event. Steve felt guilty for not telling Emily he would be sailing as well as advising her crew. In the end he felt it better that she concentrate on her competition and not worry about him. They all felt sorry for Johnny who had to return to school and stay with Sarah. The boy's Cadet sailing was improving by the month and one day it would be his turn.

Then Tony Travis had announced that he would be attending Hyeres and had obtained the loan from a client of a private Learjet. He had invited Steve and Kirsten to come with him. This was opulence beyond their imagination, although Emily had told them that Travis had been involved in two lengthy showbiz libel and defamation hearings, and that these were a lawyer's invitation to print money.

Kirsten was not wholly easy with this jaunt: the chauffeur-driven trip to Southampton Airport, and the private jet, all in a time when the nation was barely recovering from recession. Kirsten found these things hard to enjoy. It seemed that Emily's choice of career might be a sound one if she was as good a prospect as Travis seemed to think.

It did ease the travel burden for Steve. He still limped but now only with the help of one stick and, although he never complained, she knew his arm troubled him. His speech was clearer but still with that odd West Country intonation that reminded Kirsten of some of the rural provinces back home in Denmark.

The smooth journey in an almost empty aircraft was a strange experience. A light lunch and drinks were served and then the pilot announced that they were about to make the approach to Nice Airport. To Kirsten it felt as if she was a character in some film epic, or maybe this was a dream from which she would awake at home in rainy Sussex.

They declined politely Travis's offer of a room in a five star establishment as they had already booked in the smaller Hotel du Parc in Hyeres town. This friendly family-run place was more their style. They checked into their room, unpacked, and then walked to the regatta centre. It was late afternoon, and they learned that the girls were afloat on a practise session.

Steve left Kirsten to watch out for them while he found his own boat. He undid the cover and began to check everything point by point. The mast had been stepped, but the shroud pins were in the wrong slots. He would have to ask someone to help him put this right. He didn't feel up to scaling the trailer frame and then climbing into the cockpit. He replaced the cover and walked to the yacht club to confirm that his two suits of sails were safe. His event didn't start for another three days, but the girls would be in action tomorrow.

'You are Monsieur Stephen Simpson?'

Steve looked up to see a younger man in chinos and T-shirt. He held an identity badge from his right hand. 'Yes.'

'I am Inspector Mathieu, Bureau Securite d'Etat.'

Steve was at a loss but tried to make the mental adjustment. 'What are you, police?'

The man smiled. 'I work for state security.' The man's English was good.

'Why do you want me?'

'Mr Simpson, I understand your daughter is taking part in the yachting here.'

'Well, yes...'

'Do not worry we have only her best interests in mind.'

'What's this about, and please may I have a closer look at your ID?'

'Of course,' the man handed Steve his badge. It certainly looked real. 'Monsieur Simpson, we have detained a man in Toulon whom we have reason to believe may wish your daughter harm.'

'Who on earth...?'

'The man is a journalist and his name is Hammersen.'

Now Steve understood. 'I know of him, he's a man with a crack-pot theory about my wife's ancestors.'

'Indeed, we do not think that this man is so insane as to hurt your daughter but there is another man and his followers who may be dangerous.'

'What do you want me to do? I doubt I can persuade Emily to go home. She's got a lot at stake with her sailing.'

'No, Mr Simpson, there is no need to be so precipitate. It is much better that your little girl carries on with her yachting while we watch.'

'I don't like this,' said Steve. 'She's only just recovered from something bad that happened in her childhood.'

'I understand that Miss Emily is the same Emily Simpson who was vilely abducted by mad people. Am I correct?'

'Yes, the fire siege – it's no secret.' Steve was surprised.

The man held out his hand. 'Mr Simpson, I remember when your daughter's picture was in all our newspapers and on the television. My wife wept with joy when she was saved as did so many in this country.'

'Thank you.' Steve shook the man's hand.

'Mr Simpson, we will watch over your Emily. We will not compromise the honour of France by letting any harm come to her.'

Steve wasn't sure that this was much comfort. 'Should I warn her?'

'I would prefer that you did not. But it would be better that she did not stray too far from Hyeres.'

Steve went in search of Kirsten and found her seated on the waterfront still waiting for the girls to return. He told her what he had just heard.

'That Hammersen,' Kirsten almost spat the name. 'What do we do?'

'The girls are camping outside the town. I don't like it. I think we should ask the hotel if Emily can stay with us.'

'You'll have to explain to her why, and to Chloe and Erin as well.' Kirsten stood up and faced him. 'We've got to do something to kill these rumours.'

'Darling, you've always been against that. But what can we do?'

'I've an idea but I'll need you're help. Just now I saw Dimitri Panov, the guy we met in Olifa. I'm going to talk to him. Did you know that he's a surgeon and a medical historian?'

'I only know him as an Olympic sailor. How do you know about his other life?'

'Steve, there is something called the internet.'

The three girls were not wholly satisfied with their practise session as they picked up a tow launch and came back to the slipways. Emily called out to her parents on the dockside and waved. As they drew closer she became uneasy. She knew their expressions and body language of old.

'There's your mum and dad,' said Chloe.

'Something's wrong,' said Emily.

Emily was ashore and she ran to greet them. 'What's wrong?'

'Nothing,' said Kirsten, 'but we need to talk to the three of you in private.'

They waited as the boat was recovered while the girls went into the yacht club and showered and changed. The Riviera weather was not behaving to script. It had started to rain, a warm penetrating downpour.

Emily reappeared and ran to them. 'Something's happened,' she said. 'I know you too well.'

'Very perceptive,' said Steve. 'I want you and the other two to come to our hotel for a talk.'

'Why, has something happened? Is Johnny all right? Is it Tom?'

'Calm down,' said Kirsten, 'we're not sure ourselves what's going on. Come to the hotel and we'll explain.'

'That's it,' said Steve. 'The policeman said not to tell you but that wouldn't be fair.'

'I wish Tom was here,' said Emily. 'Do you think he'd come over if I phoned him.'

'Not a good idea,' said Steve, 'he'd only try and flatten Hammersen and get himself into more trouble.'

'Do we know where Hammersen is?'

'The man told me that they'd picked him up over the way in Toulon. I guess they must have had intelligence from the UK police so we take this very seriously. We don't want you on that campsite. You will move in here with us – no argument.'

'But Dad, I've got to be with the others. It's all part of being a team.'

'No problem. It's out of season here and the hotel are happy to offer you a three-bed room.'

‘We can’t afford that.’

‘That’ll be down to your mother and me. The important thing is to have you where we can see you. The police are watching around the harbour but I’ve a nasty feeling they take you to be the bait in their trap.’

That was all Steve was prepared to say. He suspected that the police needed Emily as bait to tempt some bigger fish than Hammersen. It was not unknown for a shark to take the bait and escape the fisherman.

The next three days were difficult for everyone. The girls moved into the Hotel du Parc. They seemed relaxed enough although Emily was quieter than usual. At least the tension ashore did not affect their performance on the water. They reached the match racing semi-finals with only two lost rounds. Steve and Kirsten had patrolled the waterfront and the nearby streets looking – for what? Steve had no idea. He kept seeing shifty looking men, stereotype villains, round every corner. He began to wonder if he should withdraw from his own series. Kirsten had been firm about that. He would be on the water racing not far away from where the girls were competing. She would stay ashore and watch.

He had spoken once more to the security policeman, Mathieu. He had already noticed Steve’s patrolling antics and had assured him that trained men were watching the whole area. He hinted that the man they were looking for had probably noticed the security cover and thought better of any action. He had given Steve a contact, not the usual emergency service number. Call that and a rapid response was promised.

In the end it was a relief for Steve to be on the water. It was not the season for a Mistral wind but with the overnight rain gone, a sharp breeze was blowing off the land. Two miles offshore it developed into sharp gusts and breaking waves. Steve sorted out the committee boat and the start line and began his count down. He knew hardly anything about his fellow competitors except that he counted fifty of them and was aware that he was competing against the cream of Europe, able bodied or disabled, it didn’t matter. Out here everything was a level playing field.

The start line was too short. He wasn’t going in there mixing it in close contact. He turned and lay back from the line spilling wind. Thirty seconds to go. He pulled in both sheets and set course for a narrow gap in the line close to the committee boat. He would be to windward of the pack and faster, so it wouldn't do to touch another boat. He was moving now and pointing well. The watch said eight seconds. He was gambling that he'd estimated the distance correctly. Five-four-three-two-one-start! A quick glance at the committee boat only yards away and yes, he was clear, close to the line but safe.

Increase backstay tension – concentrate – get away from the pack – find clear air. A short breaking wave slammed over the bows, and water poured into the cockpit. Now he blessed the electric pump in the keel hollow. These seas were on the limits for a little 2.4 keelboat. A quick glance to leeward. Several boats were spilling wind and floating sluggishly. Concentrate, steer clever, try and ride these seas and not smash through them. He could see the windward mark, a bulbous inflatable orange blob bending with the force of the wind. He was on starboard tack but could see no one on port to trouble him. Squeezed in this cramped cockpit he had no view astern. He thought he could hear another boat. He half turned and felt a shimmer of pain. It was all right; the noise was only his quarter wave. He'd better watch out – never have another stroke – die. He could almost hear some idiot saying he'd died doing what he loved. Bugger that; he wanted to win this one first.

The windward mark was well placed and he would need at least one more tack. Decision time: hold on this course or tack early? He would hold on and see. He was much closer to the coast now and the wind was heading him. Was it temporary? No, here was another shift. Time to tack. The breaking waves were delivering him no favours. Another dollop of water slapped the foredeck. He was on port tack now and yes, he was the lead boat. Port tack or not he would cross every starboard tacker with time to spare. Here came the windward mark. He mustn't foul up the turn. He rounded and poled out the jib. The next mark of the course was a dead run. Nothing mattered now except boat speed. He would throw caution away. He let the mast forward to its maximum and concentrated on watching the waves, anticipating angles and riding these short seas. This course was very different from Branham lake or even Rutland.

It didn't affect his confidence. The Steve of old had been one of the finest heavy weather sailors of his generation. It was a euphoric moment to discover that the Steve of today might have lost his athleticism, but he still had his sailing sense. He rounded the mark and now he was on a reaching leg. The ultimate thrill experience for a planing dinghy was the least desirable point of sailing for a small keelboat. He had to concentrate now to stop his craft yawing and dipping her boom in the water. He let some line off the kicking strap and this released some excess power. Now he heard a sound signal. Turning his head, he saw the shorten course flag and a board with a number 4. He realised now that the wind had risen by several knots since the start. A quick look around showed several competitors had swamped and were lying immobile with rescue launches standing by. Ten minutes later he crossed the finish line. Steve had won the first race of the series against all comers and he was first disabled competitor. He still had five races to go, but for now he was as happy as he'd ever remembered. Far away, he could see the boats in the women's match racing but they were too distant to read the sail numbers.

Steve's delight was enough to make him careless. He came onto the pontoon too fast and bumped the rope fender. Kirsten, who had seen his approach, caught hold of a shroud and was nearly dragged into the sea. Steve braced himself for a tirade but this time his wife was smiling. 'Darling you were wonderful,' she shouted above the noise of wind and flapping sails.

'Now that's what a chap likes to hear.' He grinned back.

'You did it! We said you could and it gets better. The girls are in the final. They're still out there, but they've taken three races to one so the last is a formality.'

'Great day for the family,' he replied. 'Come on, I don't need a hoist. Can you give me a pull up?'

Slowly and painfully he climbed onto the jetty and rolled over on his side to recover his breath.

'Hello there, Mr Simpson. Can I give you a hand up?'

Steve knew that voice. It was Tony Travis QC, Emily's legal mentor.

'Thank you, I think my wife is a bit fed up with hauling me upright.'

Travis was a strong man for one with such a sedentary profession. He pulled Steve to his feet as if he was a child. Steve thanked him.

'Mr Travis,' Kirsten asked, 'do you know anything about French law?'

'I've a vague knowledge, but it's different to law in the English-speaking world. Why do you ask?'

'Come into the club house and I'll tell you,' said Steve.

'I see your difficulty,' said Travis. 'I would trust the French, no reservations. I would be sorry for any miscreant who falls into their hands.'

Kirsten had reluctantly told the lawyer the whole story. She worried about the number of people who were familiar with her family's disgrace. Travis had not seemed particularly shocked, but she supposed that very little shocked him. She had only just finished her story when into the room rushed Emily and the other two. All three girls were flush faced and bubbling with excitement.

Emily had raced up to them and hugged each of her parents and then Travis. 'Mum, we're in the final and we're top British boat by a mile. We race off against the Germans tomorrow.'

'That's great news and you deserve it. Now, do you know that your father won his first race?'

Emily hugged Steve again. She was trembling in a mixture of celebration and at times tears. Erin seemed to be in a similar state but Chloe only laughed.

Travis smiled and looked at his watch. 'I must go. Now, when your competition is over I want you to have dinner with my wife and me. We are staying in a villa near San Tropez.'

'Oh, yes, Mr Travis, we'd love to – but should we dress up?'

'Well it would be better not to come in dry suits or tacky jeans.'

'Don't worry,' said Kirsten, 'we'll kit you all out before we go.'

Emily couldn't sleep. She should be sleeping. She would need a good night's rest before tomorrow's final. She felt this growing apprehension. That horrible creep Hammersen was looking for her. Why wasn't Tom here to protect her? This should be one of the best moments of her life, and yet she had this corroding fear. She was a member of a world beating sports team, she was shining in her chosen profession, but there were mysterious people who hated her. It wasn't fair. Just because a great-uncle she'd never met was the bastard son of a man she'd never heard of.

'Holy shit!' Chloe sat up and turned her bedside light on.

'What's the matter, Chlo'?' Erin sounded sleepy.

'I don't think I put the blocks under the cradle wheels. If the wind gets up in the night she could roll away.'

'Are you sure?'

'No I am not sure, but I've gotta check.'

'OK,' said Emily. 'Let's go, all of us. I can't sleep anyway.'

Chloe was already pulling on jeans and a sweater. Erin had swung her legs out of bed and was rubbing her eyes. 'You two don't need to come with me,' said Chloe.

Emily wanted to do something. Doing something, anything, would help her eventually to sleep. She didn't really think there was much likelihood of their boat blowing away, but a walk in the night could be the right therapy. She pulled on her clothes and remembered to drop her mobile phone into her pocket. If in trouble, the policeman Mathieu should come running.

'Don't they lock the gate at night?' Emily asked. They were in sight of the boat park.

'There's another way round,' said Chloe. 'Security's not that tight, and who's going to launch a boat with no sails and run away with it?'

Chloe led them around the side of the yacht club and over a low wooden rail fence. Two minutes later they were in sight of their boat. 'Stop,' Chloe whispered and pointed. In the moonlight they could see a small dark figure crouching by the stern of the boat. Then they heard it; the whirr of an electric drill.

Chloe released a shout that developed into a war whoop as she charged. Emily and Erin ran after her. The shadowy figure was standing now and, turning away, began to run. It was no match for Chloe who pursued and felled it with a crunching rugby tackle. 'Who the hell are you,' she rasped, 'and what were you doing to our boat?'

This was enough for Emily. She clasped the mobile phone. French area code then 5550555.

'Securite,' came the reply.

'Do you speak English?'

'Of course. Emily is it?'

'Yes, we've caught someone damaging our boat – not sure who.'

'Is this person still there?'

Emily glanced across. 'Yes, it's a girl. Chloe my friend has her held.'

'Wait, we shall be with you.'

Three cars arrived together on the yacht club precinct, and six men and one woman came running as Chloe called to them. The sight of these people made Emily feel cold. As a collection they were the most evil looking bunch she had ever seen.

A man dressed in casual clothes caught hold of the intruder by her arms and a second thug pulled her head back by her hair.

'Votre nomme?' demanded the woman.

'Let me go you fucking gorillas,' the girl screeched.

'You are English?'

No reply.

‘What were you doing with that boat?’

‘She was drilling a hole,’ said Chloe. She held a cordless electric drill.

‘Sabotage, huh – why?’

Still no reply. The second man threw a punch into the captive’s stomach. The girl collapsed.

Emily was horrified. Her legal training was affronted. Any British cop who behaved in that way in front of witnesses would be out on his ear.

The woman interrogator looked up. ‘Is there considerable damage?’

‘No,’ said Chloe, ‘bit of a hole on the port quarter but we can plug it in the morning.’

‘Very well, we will remove this malefacteur to custody.’

The captive had recovered enough to speak between gasps of breath. ‘Emily Simpson, you’re a dead ’un.’

CHAPTER 24

The regatta was over and as triumphant returns go this was a special one. For the girls, a trophy won; and for Steve, a silver medal. Chloe, Emily and Erin had cemented their position as World number one. Steve was now number one for UK Paralympic single-handed sailing. The only cloud was the damage to the girl's boat. Steve could extract no detailed information from the French police. That man Mathieu was unavailable, it was almost as if he did not exist. Steve could only sense that the police were disappointed in catching one insignificant saboteur when they had hoped to land a very big catch.

'The only thing I was told, and that's sort of off the record, was that the girl was English but she has a French name.'

'Michelle Le Bois!' said Emily. 'Of course – it's got to be.' She looked worried. 'So, it's nothing to do with Hammersen after all. It's just that warped little idiot.'

'They're holding her in custody and charging her with criminal damage. So she'll be out of your hair for a bit.'

'Maybe,' said Emily. 'But she'll be ten times more vindictive when she gets out of jail.'

Hammersen still cast a shadow over the family, but Steve was determined that this would not spoil their celebrations. He hardly dared to hope, but it seemed that Kirsten might have found a way out of their trouble.

'I've told Dimitri Panov the whole story,' she said. 'You know both Hitler and Goebells were cremated, but there were samples of tissue retained by the Russians and Dimitri thinks he can get at them.'

'I'd heard that the KGB had all that sort of stuff,' said Steve.

'I know, but things have relaxed a bit since Soviet times and Dimitri's got a lot of pull. I told him he could reveal the truth. It'll become public anyway if we get Emily and me cleared of contamination.'

Steve wondered if they could really hope. Dimitri was a world authority on DNA. It seemed their luck might be changing. He strolled to his boat and was pleased to see that the local staff had taken down the mast and secured the under-cover. The sun was shining and it was hot; warm enough for him to revert to T-shirt wear. Someone else it seemed appreciated the warmth. A young woman was walking towards him clad in nothing but the stringiest bikini he'd ever seen.

He knew that an elderly gentleman like him was not supposed to ogle. In England he would be required to look at anything or anywhere but the lovely vision that had stopped beside him.

'Hi there, you are Steve Simpson?' The girl smiled and held out a hand.

Permission to stare. Steve shook the hand. It was tiny but had the hard palm of a dinghy sailor. She was truly beautiful. Her little elfin face was crowned with a black bob-styled hair. Her arms strong, her slim body lightly tanned. He could remember when he'd last seen such physical perfection. Nineteen years ago he had encountered Kirsten on her windsurfer and fallen in love.

'Steve, may I call you Steve? I am Maria,' the voice was sweet, good English but with a familiar lilt to the accent. 'I have always wanted to meet you, then I saw you in the distance in Olifa, but never close enough to speak.'

'You're an Olifarian?' He really must stop staring at that lovely flat tanned stomach and the bejewelled belly button.

'Oh yes, but I love sailing. I was in the ladies' Laser class this week but I did not emulate your success.' The little temptress had tilted her head on one side as she smiled.

'How can I help you, Maria?'

'You could teach me lots of things about sailing, but I only wanted to say I had met you.'

With massive self-control Steve took a hold on his scattered thoughts. 'I am very happy to meet you, Maria. I hope we shall see you sailing in Olifa in three years time.'

'Thank you, Steve. I hope I shall see you again before then – adios.' She smiled, turned and walked away showing a breathtaking view of a lovely muscular back.

'Why are you staring at that woman?' Kirsten's voice grated.

'She's a pretty girl.'

'It seems she and you had a lot to talk about.'

'She sails a Laser. She was asking about sailing. She comes from Olifa – saw us there last month.'

'Huh, I turn my back for five minutes and I find you chatting up a woman half your age.'

'Now – now: who was it that was going all drippy with those Olifarian men?'

'I've seen her around at big events,' said Emily. 'She's Maria Olivarez. I don't think she was in Auckland, but we've seen her in other places. Does Mum really think she's trying to run off with you, Dad – cos' you should be so lucky.'

'I think your mother likes to be protective.'

'I don't know Maria well, but she's a useful helm and I don't expect there's too many as good in Olifa.'

'I gather she came fourth in this one,' said Steve.

'I know,' said Emily. 'With her other results she's probably reached Olympic qualifying already. If so she'll be on her home water.'

That evening Kirsten had taken a saliva sample and tiny cuttings of her own and Emily's hair. She placed these in the containers that Dimitri Panov had given her and sealed them. She had passed them to Dimitri the next morning. He had assured her in his fractured English that he would make the test a priority. He was confident that the World War Two material stored in Moscow came from the two men responsible for so much evil. Now they must all wait and hope the results would give Emily and Kirsten the peace they deserved.

Kirsten and Steve were not happy when Emily had insisted she travel home by road with her friends. They would not linger, Emily promised, as all three were due back at work that next Monday. Travis was due to prosecute in a high-profile trial and he wanted Emily in court with his team. Travis had insisted that Kirsten and Steve travel home with him in the private jet and for that they were grateful.

They picked up their own car at Southampton airport and drove home. Sarah had driven over from Midhurst with Johnny and had aired the house and turned on the heating. The May evenings were chilly and Sarah had guessed that this would be a shock after the Riviera temperatures.

Steve had limped into the house with his medal still around his neck. Sarah, who had followed his and Emily's progress all week, gave him a huge celebratory hug. Johnny seemed largely unfazed. After all – winning sailing races? Wasn't that was what Dad and big sister did?

Sarah cooked a meal for all of them, and they had relaxed in the satisfaction of being in their own home again. The telephone rang at ten o'clock. Kirsten stood up and went into the office to answer.

'It's Sid Everett here. No missus; don't hang up. I've information that affects your Emily and it won't wait.

CHAPTER 25

'Do you think he was telling you the truth?' asked Steve.

'I'm sceptical, but I would say yes,' said Kirsten. 'It all fits with what happened in France. The police there were obviously fed intelligence.'

'But nothing happened except that silly little Le Bois girl,' said Emily. 'Did she really think Chloe wouldn't notice a hole in her boat?'

'Emily,' said Steve, 'there are more important things than sport and sailing. I don't think you should go to Italy.'

Emily gaped at him before reacting. 'But I've got to go. The others need me. Why should I be more at risk there than here?'

'We would feel safer if you were in England.'

'Oh Dad, that's silly. Think about it. In Italy I'll be with the whole sailing crowd, not just the match-racers – the whole international circus. Chloe and Erin will keep an eye on me.'

'If you insist on going then we'll have to go as well.'

'No, Dad, you're talking daft. What'll happen to the sail making business? Does Mr Everett know if the Italian police have been told? I don't like the way the French beat up suspects, but they were right on the ball when we needed them.'

Steve sighed. The problem with Emily was her self-confidence. She assumed that that having survived violent death once had somehow made her safe for all time. She was right about the sail loft. He could not afford to go away from work indefinitely. His own Paralympic campaign was digging deep into the family's reserve funds. 'All right, Emily, go to Italy but I will have a word with the police and you will agree to protection – no arguments.'

'I'm more worried about the trip to Israel. One whiff of this Hitler story there and we could be in real trouble,' said Emily.

'All right,' Kirsten replied. 'Stay away from that one.'

'No! I won't – it's the meeting that could see us qualify.'

'I know, sweetheart. One thing I will do is search out documentary proof of your Jewishness. Not everyone knows about that.'

'At school they knew. They said it made me stingy, tight-fisted, and I'm not.'

'Those kids should have been taught better manners.'

Emily laughed. 'They didn't mean it and I gave better than I got.'

Steve looked at his daughter. 'I can believe that.'

Tom had dropped Emily at the gym and then driven on to the nearby pub. He knew that he had better be careful and restrict himself to one beer. Emily wanted him to accompany her at the gym. She had told him that his failure to win sailing races was down to unfitness. If this was partly true he wasn't sure the hours on a bloody treadmill, plus lifting weights, would make much difference. For Emily, her gym sessions were almost a religious observance and she was welcome to them. If he couldn't cut it on the racecourse he would be a great team manager. The butch Chloe was a natural leader, he had to give her that, but she was short on detail, while Emily and Erin relied too much on Chloe doing the thinking for them. He, Tom, had the logical mind of a well-educated man, and as onshore manager he was exactly what these scatterbrain girlies needed to launch them to success.

Tom collected his beer and a packet of crisps and found a table. The television in a corner was relaying news of South Coast sport, or in this case Pompey Football Club's losing woes. Then, without warning, a fresh clip appeared and astonishingly it showed old Steve in his 2.4 surging along downwind, surfing on a broken sea. The sound was down so Tom didn't know the context, but he was surprised. Sailing was not a spectator sport, although it had tens of thousands of adherents. No doubt having an old guy taking on the world was encouraging to fellow pensioners.

When Emily reappeared he told her about the TV shots he had seen. She was pleased but seemed to have other things on her mind. Tom did not pressure her and drove her back to her home in untypical silence. He wondered if tonight's dinner was on her mind. 'You're very quiet, Em. Are you still not sure about this evening?'

'Oh yeah,' she replied. 'Me meeting face to face with the other woman – I think I can manage that.'

'You'll like Alix. She's funny and full of acting stories.'

'I still think of her as Charlene in Gravesenders. I thought she was backing out of it, but she was on again last night.'

'They pre-record weeks in advance. She meets a miserable end next month.'

'That'll be fun.'

Tom groaned. 'Nothing about that show is fun.'

'Some people think it's true to life.'

Tom was nervous about this evening. He believed he had reassured Emily about his friendship with the extrovert Alix. He would not quickly forget that savage cross- examination at the hands of his future QC girlfriend. He had pre-warned Alix to behave and not to put on a theatrical flirting act.

They reached Alresford at seven o'clock, and having parked the car in Broad Street they walked the few yards around the corner to the Bell Inn. Tom could see Alix sitting at a table with a male companion. Good, this must be Ray the racehorse trainer and Alix's sugar daddy. Having him present should defuse the last of Emily's suspicion.

'She doesn't look anything like Charlene,' Emily whispered. 'Who's that with her?'

'Boyfriend,' he whispered back. Certainly, without the dishevelled hair and tear-stained make-up, Alix bore no resemblance to Charlene. Her hair was styled and she wore figure-hugging jeans and a white poloneck jumper.

'Hi, Alix. You look every inch the country lady,' Tom called.

Alix stood up and advanced to meet them. Tom and she exchanged a chaste kiss. 'This is Ray,' she said.

The boyfriend was more than a few years older but looked lean and fit with handsome features and greying-haired. 'Good to meet you both,' said Ray. He had a deep voice with traces of Irish. 'You're the great yachting folk. I'm a horseman myself but I don't suppose you bet on yachting.'

Emily laughed. 'They do in New Zealand. They were betting on our crew a few weeks ago.'

'And did you save the bookies money?'

'As we won by the thickness of a piece of paper I would think we were bad news for them.'

'I'll have another gin,' said Alix. 'What about you, Emily?'

'I can't stay here tonight. I've got to be in London tomorrow morning.' Emily looked at Tom. 'Who's driving me home?'

'Tom is,' said Alix. 'Don't let him con you so that he can get rat-arsed.'

'It's the only car we've got tonight anyway, and I've got to get back here again,' said Tom. 'So teetotal it is for me.'

'That's a first.' Alix caught Emily's eye and winked.

Tom was relieved to see Emily responding to Alix's personality. The two girls were not dissimilar and could and should be friends. Both were bubbly, as current description put it, and if Alix were the actress, then Emily as a barrister would be in a not dissimilar profession. Racehorse Ray, as Tom secretly named him, was an amusing character and contributed anecdotes from his own world, a world that Alix seemed to have adopted as her own.

'We've a horse running at Plumpton, *Dingledell*. Two-thirty next Saturday.' Ray lowered his voice that had now become distinctly Irish. 'It's one of ours. If you want to put a bet on he would be a good'un.'

'What do you know about Castinnio.com?' Emily asked.

'Not a lot,' Ray replied. 'But they're straight – always pay up. Bit impersonal though isn't it – internet and all that? I think they're based overseas, but as I say, they're honest. Put our big bookies' noses out of joint. They're starting to lose out.'

'Castinnio are based in Olifa. Mum and Dad have just come back from there and they were talking about it. They said there's a man called Garcia who runs it. I met him once – he's got a wandering eye and it went right down the front of my frock.' She giggled.

'That's true,' said Tom. 'I witnessed it.'

'And you weren't offended?'

'No, Emily has that effect on men and so does her mother.'

'Mum's getting on a bit now, Dad more so,' said Emily, 'but she still watches him. You know, after the regatta in Hyeres, Dad was chatting with one of the Laser girls. Mum saw him and went ballistic. It was funny.'

'Who was the girl?' asked Tom.

'Maria Olivarez. She said she'd seen Dad in Olifa and hadn't been able to speak to him.'

'What's she like?'

'Femme fatale, turns male heads and you are not getting anywhere near her.'

The others, Tom included, laughed. 'This Maria must be quite something to get both you and your mother so uptight,' said Alix.

'It's not that I'm the jealous type,' Emily replied, 'but if both Tom and this Maria are at the Israel regatta…'

'You will be watching,' said Alix.

'Too right I will.'

Emily would far rather have stopped the night with Tom, but duty called. She was due in London to report in chambers. Tony Travis had got together with William, and both had agreed that Emily should be present during this court hearing. Travis had been firm with her. She was his star pupil. The last graduate with anything like her ability was now a practising QC. But Emily must learn to be dispassionate:

to build a mental carapace and never become emotionally involved. Emily knew they were right, but she still dreaded this hearing.

Courtroom One at the Old Bailey was smaller than it appeared on film or television but it still remained an intimidating place. Travis had spent several days conferring with the Crown prosecution and the police. A woman and her male partner were facing a murder charge and it was the nature of the charge that disgusted Emily. A two-year old child of the accused mother had died malnourished and with broken bones. Emily could not help but look at this dysfunctional couple as they sat blank-faced in the dock; incredibly the woman kept chewing gum. Emily could only deduce extreme stupidity linked with mental backwardness. Of course she mustn't think this way – she was not a reporter for the *Daily Banner*. However sick these people were she did not have that sense of pure evil that she had felt in the Kessel trial.

Travis had led the prosecution with no problems: the facts were overwhelmingly on his side. The defence had responded mainly with attacks on the inefficiency of social services and the laxity of the police. Personally Emily felt, however repugnant the facts, that she could have done a better defence herself and mentally prepared her notes for later.

The whole sordid business dragged on for five days. The judge summed up and the jury went out. Six hours later came the guilty verdict and sentence: life with minimum tariff of ten years. Emily returned to chambers with Travis and promptly sat down at the computer and typed up her impressions of the trial and her criticism of the defence. It was not Travis's custom, or William's, to lavish praise, but she knew that she had struck the right note and that they were both pleased. And yes, she had become that little bit harder.

CHAPTER 26

The weeks had passed quickly for the girls and once more they were together preparing for competition.

'I find it kinda' frustrating,' said Chloe. 'They send us around the world to all these places and we can't enjoy.' She was looking across the water at Lake Garda, Italy's largest and most beautiful inland sea.

'What's the problem?' said Erin.

'Smell it, mate. All that great cooking, all that real pizza, those chocolates, and we can't even have a nibble.'

Emily knew what her friend meant. The lake and surrounds were seductive, and their pre-ordained diet must be especially hard on the well-built Chloe. But they all knew that the eating and partying they had enjoyed in Auckland was over. They had set a standard, and only a total focus from now on would do. They might indulge a happy hour once the regatta was over, but until then discipline counted.

Apart from that there were the security men. These two were hardly covert; they clumped around behind the girls staring suspiciously at passers-by. It would have helped if the men had not looked so blindingly obvious, dressed in elegant white, with huge dark glasses. The men were employees of a firm linked to the Matheson agency in Portsmouth. Emily's parents had arranged for their services. The French police had released Hammersen, but Michelle Le Bois was languishing in a French women's jail. Emily was not overly worried, so long as she was with her friends and part of this huge gathering of sailors, she felt safe. She was confident but she wished Tom were here with her.

'They've done a good repair on that drill hole,' said Chloe. 'Can't see a mark.' They had walked around their boat and were happy it had travelled the road to Italy unscathed. Tomorrow they must start all over again and with the next round of racing.

The weather ashore was warm and they awoke each morning to a windless expanse of water. Then at midday, as if by some magic intervention, the wind began blowing down the water from the mountains. The lake offered a whole set of new challenges. For Emily it seemed like a gigantic replica of Branham with directional shifts combined with dead spots. The trio raced, they worked together, they fought as hard as ever, but on the fifth day the quarter-final was their downfall. They lost a disastrous three races only to pull one back and to lose the last. Emily knew that their aspirations had been so high, and yet they were in competition with the best women sailors in the world. They had been overconfident and had paid. True, they had emerged fourth in the regatta and no rival British boat could touch them. They were on the verge of qualifying for Olifa. Bring on Israel, thought Emily, at least they'd be on the open sea.

'So, Dad's little girl came third.' Emily was studying the results in the other classes on her laptop.

'You mean Maria from Olifa?' said Erin.

'That's her. Women's Laser. There's no one else from Olifa so I guess she's qualifying standard already.'

'I can see why she makes wives jealous,' said Erin. 'I saw her in Hyeres in that bikini, wobbling her butt and flashing her tits. I thought South American girls were supposed to be demure.'

'I expect she'll be at the party tonight,' said Emily. 'See who she flirts with there.'

'You two got your glam rags?' asked Chloe.

'I've got a pair of style jeans and a top,' said Emily. 'I'm not getting into that Auckland frock again in a hurry. It's like a strait-jacket.'

That evening was the farewell party and formal reception at the largest yacht club. With the week's racing completed, it was a chance for the few hundred competitors to let their hair down. In the event the party was more formalised than at Hyeres and wholly lacking the laidback atmosphere of Auckland. The food was amazing, the wine flowed and a tenor sang arias. It was all very Italian. Emily thought the young competitors were enjoying the occasion rather less than the officials. She recognised a couple of bigwigs from their own RYA and then she saw, moving towards her, the elegant Primo Garcia and with him a girl; she was Maria Olivarez.

Garcia seemed to be looking around for something. Emily had no idea what her friends thought but she felt tempted to hide behind some nearby curtains. Too late, Garcia had seen them and was moving, or possibly simpering, toward her. The man was wearing spotless white trousers and a blazer with an odd badge that looked like an insect. He wore a cravat and under his arm was an ornate yachting cap.

Maria had changed into a stunning blue patterned mini dress that showed off her long brown legs. This gown, thought Emily, must be Prada or similar quality. Her dark hair still showed signs of wind and sun. She wore diamond earrings and a gold neckband, while her pedicure was complemented by a gold ring on one toe of each foot in her jewelled sandals. The whole outfit must have cost all of two thousand pounds, more maybe.

'What a trollop,' Chloe whispered.

'Who pays her sailing funding?' added Erin.

'There's some bloke paying for that gear she's got on,' whispered Emily.

'Senoritas,' said Garcia, 'I am so pleased to see you again. Maria here, I think you already know.'

Emily was surprised to see Maria's reaction. The woman was standing slightly behind Garcia. She smiled at Emily and then pulled a face in the direction of Garcia.

These two were not an item – that was certain. Emily began to look at Maria in a new light. Maria was beautiful, no one could deny that, and she was stylish. No wonder she turned men's heads, including Emily's own father. Was that why she, Emily, felt this prejudice?

'Senorita Emily?' Garcia was looking at her. Emily turned to him and just saw Maria pull another face. Emily flashed a quick smile.

'Mr Garcia, what can we do for you?'

'I wanted to know how your father is, Senorita. We all remember him winning gold. Would he be about to achieve a similar feat?'

'You mean the Paralympics? It's really too early to say. Why do you ask?'

Garcia leaned forward. 'He is a great person in our sport and many people are asking about him. I too have followed his progress, and I have seen him race at Kiel then at Rutland and at Hyeres, and I could not help but be impressed.'

Emily had a nasty feeling that this time she was the one on the end of a cross-examination. She saw Maria make another grimace. 'Mr Garcia, we are really not sure what my father intends, but he is enjoying his sailing and that is enough for our family.'

Garcia nodded and gave that irritating little bow. 'Come on, Maria we must not delay these young sailors further.'

Maria stood back and looked her fellow countryman in the eye. 'I want to have a private word with Emily and her friends, so go Primee, please leave us.'

Garcia was not pleased. 'Very well, but do not be long. Our ambassador is arriving shortly.' He walked away.

Emily looked at Maria. 'What did you call him?'

'I called him Primee, his name is Primo after another famous

Garcia. He hates people to use his nickname but Primee is what they call him when his back is turned.'

'Is it true he won an Olympic silver in the Star class?' Emily asked.

'Oh yes, it was in the same games where your mother won her medal. He was a fine sailor, no one can dispute that.'

Chloe snorted. 'He looks a right ponce to me.'

Maria shook her head. 'If you mean a gay man you are wrong. He pursues the women and many fall for him.'

'How come both of you speak perfect English?' asked Chloe. 'I've got a second language in my country, but I don't speak it that well.'

'Tradition,' answered Maria. 'Our great Olifa families have a tradition of sending children to your English public schools. I spent four years at St Winifred's; that's a convent school in Yorkshire. I was asked to leave though.'

'Why?' asked Chloe.

'I was too friendly with a nice boy from the Catholic boarding school…'

'How friendly is friendly?'

Emily squirmed. 'Chloe, I thought I was the lawyer around here. You're cross- examining Maria and it's not fair.'

Maria laughed. She really looked stunning and she was clearly having an effect on Chloe. 'I was friendly enough for the nuns to call me Satan's daughter. But Emily?'

'What?'

'The Garcia family and the Olivarez family, are like the Montagues and the Capulets, you follow me? The feud runs deep and I have no intention of playing his Juliet.'

CHAPTER 27

'Did anything happen while you were in Italy?' Steve asked.

'We think we could have done better,' Emily replied.

'No, I'm not talking about the sailing. You know what I mean. Any unpleasantness?'

'We met that Olifa bloke, Garcia. We all think he's a bit creepy.'

Steve felt relieved. If Hammersen had showed his face the girls would have noticed. Presumable the expensive protection must have worked.

'We met your girlfriend Maria as well. She's not only a good helm she's actually rather nice. Chloe fancies her I reckon, but Maria's definitely one for the boys, or actually for older men so the gossip goes. Garcia made a play for her and she told him to get stuffed.'

Steve relaxed. He would never admit it to Emily and certainly not to Kirsten, but Maria had caused him to fantasise. A stunning girl at the helm of a dinghy was always a turn on for-him.

'Tom sailed in the Laser open at Stokes Bay,' said Steve. 'You must be having an effect because he came second.'

'I know,' said Emily. 'He's coming to Israel with us. We're trying him out as team manager.'

'That's six weeks' time,' said Steve. 'Where's your boat?'

'They're shipping it straight to Israel. We'll have to practise in something else. Anyway it's back to work for all three of us tomorrow.'

At five o'clock Chloe escaped from the office and drove out through the gates of the camp. She was at a loose end but decided to go to Portland sailing centre. Afterwards she could catch up on shopping in Weymouth. She was missing her crewmates. They were great company ashore and a magic combination on the water. Never would she regret teaming up with them. Both the other girls were heavily involved with boy friends and that suited Chloe. To have an intimate relationship with a team member would never work. Chloe had disciplined herself to be hard and to suppress her lesbian instincts. True, it was not something that she had to hide any more, but her career and her sailing were paramount and she would let nothing disturb either. She had no desire or expectation of children, so relationships could wait.

She had not been at the Sailing Academy for ten minutes before she spotted a married woman she knew well: Samantha Robstron. ‘Hi there Sammy, mate, how yer doin’?’

‘Hi, Chlo, I wondered if you’d be around. How are your other two girlies?’

‘We’re all fine. We missed you in Hyeres and Italy. How are the twins?’

‘Looking forward to having their two babes. That means a year out of sailing but I doubt we’d have been together for the Olifa games anyway. The writing was on the wall when we couldn’t match you guys in Auckland. I think that’s why the twins decided to go out and have a good time. My hubby was getting pissed off as well. I was never around to cook his dinner or fetch the kids from school. That’s men for you, but then you wouldn’t know.’

‘Have you any plans, Sammy?’

‘I’m switching to the two-person boat, that’s still the 470. But I need to find a crew.’

‘Shouldn’t be hard.’

‘Chlo’, is it true someone tried to nobble your boat?’

‘How did you hear about that?’ Chloe was surprised.

‘It’s common knowledge. Tell me, was it a silly little girl called Michelle?’

‘Yes, I didn’t think anyone knew that. But it was Emily she was out to get. It is so pathetic. This Michelle’s uncle was shot by accident during the fire siege and the girl blames Emily – can’t understand the logic of that. Then Steve Simpson hires a couple of comic Eytie heavies to follow us around at Lake Garda.’

‘I think you ought to know that this Michelle approached us with a bloke and they suggested we damage your boat. That was before we went to Auckland. You understand we told them to eff themselves – no way!’

‘Thanks Sam, I know you wouldn’t do that.’

‘Tell you what, Chlo’. Peace offering. Our boat is here collecting dust and gull shit. Would you like her for practise?’

‘Sammy, you’re an angel! Too right we would like her. Our boat’s in a container for Israel.’

‘You’re welcome. Come with me and I’ll show you the sails.’

I’m more and more worried about this trip to Israel,’ said Steve.

‘I’m not happy about it,’ said Kirsten, ‘but the Israelis can’t play the Nazi card to keep Emily out. I know my Dad was Jewish and I can prove it.’

‘Why on earth have they moved a major event to a trouble spot like that?’

‘There’s a huge new sailing complex just opening in Haifa and the Israelis want to show it off. The country is still tense, but it’s been quieter since the international conference.’

‘I suppose so,’ Steve sighed. ‘You’ve already sailed there. That time you went and left me here to guard the house. Emily really missed you.’

‘1996 World Windsurfing championships,’ Kirsten replied. ‘Wasn’t one of my best performances. But it seemed a nice venue. Lots of whispers about terrorists, bumps in the night and all that, but we never saw or heard a thing. Nice climate in summer but one huge drawback that I’ll warn Emily about.’

‘How come?’

‘Whole place grinds to a standstill on Saturdays. It’s the religious day for Jews. So no sailing and no celebrating. ’

‘I did notice the regatta runs from Monday to Friday.’

‘Do we let Emily go there?’ she asked.

‘We won’t be able to stop her, but I’m going as well and so is young Tom. Paul Matheson says he can get an alert through to the local police and security.’

Kirsten was looking at the office computer screen. ‘Hi, this could be helpful. It’s from old Dimitri. He never wrote it himself. The English is too good.’

Steve looked over her shoulder and read.

D. Panov

Medical examination.

My friends.

I have accessed the archive in Moscow and located the items we are interested in.

I have been allowed small samples and will take these to my own laboratory in St Petersburg.

With my sincere felicitations

Dimitri Panov.

‘No, Emily, you must not fumble. If you’re going to throw chapter and verse case law at the judge you’ve got to have the reference marked and ready.’ Tony Travis looked severe. ‘Preparation is all.’

‘Sorry,’ said Emily. She was turning the pages of the heavy leather-bound volume and still couldn’t find the item she had in her head.

'It's better to have all these texts worked out in advance and typed in hard copy,' Travis continued. 'It may look dramatic to read straight from that tome but it probably won't impress. Leave it to Perry Mason.'

Emily didn't understand.

'Never mind, I suppose he was before your time. Ask William, he was a great fan.'

It was a slack afternoon in chambers and Travis was putting Emily through a practical exercise, the sort of thing she must master before she qualified to practice at the bar.

'Right, let's try again,' said Travis. 'You are prosecuting this man who has been selling dodgy re-stitched transit vans. Convince the jury it's fraud and a danger to whoever drives the vans and all the others on the road. Go for it.'

Following an hour of this Travis at last seemed satisfied. 'All right Emily, we are getting there.'

'Thank you.'

'Don't look so woebegone. I'd put good money on you being Emily barrister-at- law in three years, and Emily QC in ten. And let's hope it's Emily Olympic gold before then.'

Emily was still uncertain about her performance in Travis's test session, but it had been useful. She mused over the day, it was something to take her mind off the cross-London journey to her shared flat in Earl's Court. The District Line train was crammed with fellow sufferers as it rattled and banged through dark tunnels and then into daylight and drab surroundings that would make anyone depressed. How she wished she could be at sea in pure air, riding the waves and feeling the wind and spray.

No time for daydreaming as the train stopped and the doors slid open. This was her get-off station, thank God; she joined the stream of people leaving the train and flooding to the exits. Ten minutes' walk and she was at the little block of seedy apartments and bedsits that was her London home. She fumbled for her latchkey, opened the door and sank into a battered armchair. She really wanted a stiff drink, but no, that would breach her fitness rules. Later, when things were quieter, she would join one of the other girls in a jog around the block. London being what it was these days she couldn't go far or do the run on her own.

No strong drink; a cup of tea would have to do. Emily yawned and retrieved the mobile phone from her bag. A text from Tom. The thought of him cheered her – two more days and they would be together again.

ringme tom
xxxxxxxxx

That was cryptic enough. No room for a please, of course. She glanced at the clock. Just coming up to six, news time on the telly. Half seven was Gravesenders and Alix, or Charlene's, last appearance – her suicide so she understood. Should she call Tom on his mobile, or the Alresford flat? She would wait ten minutes and try the landline.

'Hi beautiful – great news, I think.' Tom sounded upbeat about something. 'I asked my boss man about time off to go with you to Israel. Then he gets all excited and says he needs someone to go there anyway, but nobody wants to because of the passport thing.'

'Hey, darling, cool it, what about passports?'

'We do a lot of business with Saudi and you can't get in there if you've an Israeli visa stamp on your passport, but you see mine's only got six months to run anyway and then I get a new one.'

'OK, I think I follow. It doesn't affect me or the girls as we're not going anywhere in the Arab world anyway.'

'The big thing is that my boss wants me in Tel Aviv the week before you lot go out there. Once I've done his business I can hop up the coast to Haifa, unpack the boat and get everything hunky-dory ready for you.'

Emily giggled. 'Hunky-dory, that term sounds ever so public school.'

'Well you're starting to speak quite posh yourself now.'

'That's my courtroom diction.'

'Don't I know it. I was on the end of it that time.'

Emily smiled. It was so good to hear his banter. 'Don't forget to watch the last of Charlene. Do we know what happens?'

'She's going to be fished out of the Thames, but Alix is not allowed to say if it's suicide or whether Max has topped her.'

Sid Everett was allergic to boats large or small. He had never learned to swim, and even the Isle of Wight Ferry made him feel queasy. Flying was a much better way to travel, particularly First Class with girl stewards serving double gins. Dave, the *Banner's* alleged yachting correspondent, was in London and had been giving Sid a crash course in this weird sport. Sid wanted to immerse himself in the world of Emily Simpson, hoping it would bring him closer to a story he knew was waiting there for him to clean up. If he could help to protect the girl on the way to that story then he would be doubly satisfied.

Sid had been surprised a few weeks ago to see Emily in the Old Bailey as part of Travis QC's prosecution team in the child abuse case. He had checked with sources in Lincoln's Inn and had learned that Emily was Travis's pupil, and that Travis reckoned he'd discovered a star who might just be the one to take over from him on his retirement. For Sid that was all the more reason to keep in touch with young Emily and see that nothing unpleasant befell her. But it had been a shock to be told that the silly girl was determined to go to a regatta in Israel: the one place where Joel could stalk her with impunity.

Sid had outlined his potential story, or as much as he dared, to the *Banner's* foreign affairs editor. The stupid woman had been sceptical but mention of "little Emily from the fire Cult" had had an electric effect. Sid had been readmitted to the fold on a special commission.

'You'd better see if the FO will give you a second passport. If you have an Israeli visa in your proper one you'll be banned from anywhere in the Islamic world. The Israelis are a bit picky as well as to who they let in.'

'I'd better get my granddad's birth certificate,' said Sid. 'He was a Yid – family name was Levi. He was an East End guy when Mosley's thugs were breaking up the place, so he changed to Everett by deed poll.'

'You mean he disowned his heritage for expediency. Your family doesn't change much, Sid.'

'The boat's set up almost the same as ours but different sails,' said Chloe.

It was the weekend now and the three girls were back at Portland and examining Sammy Robstron's former boat.

'These sails are OK,' said Chloe, 'but I'd rather stick to the official brand we know.'

'Longest day tomorrow,' said Erin, 'but it's not much like summer.'

Emily had to agree with that. A persistent drizzle fell from a grey low cloud base. Not a zephyr of wind touched the water of the harbour or in Weymouth Bay beyond. The three looked at the scene knowing all of them shared the same despondency.

'Tom's arrived in Israel,' said Emily. 'He rang last night. He says it's hot and there's a good onshore breeze.'

'Our proper boat's got there OK,' said Chloe, 'I rang the yacht club in Haifa just before I started for here.' She laughed. 'Overseas call at the Army's expense.'

'Isn't that irregular,' asked Erin. 'I couldn't do that from the school.'

'No, they don't mind, as long as we keep winning.'

'Did you get someone who spoke English?' Emily asked. 'Tom told me his firm there had to give him an interpreter.'

'No problem. The guy I spoke to was English – spoke upper class Pom speech.'

Sid watched as a new man entered the room. He seemed friendly enough but Sid was wary. This scenario had happened at least twice before when he had visited an embassy and applied for a visa for some controversial destination. Now he needed to visit Israel and remembering the *Banner's* pro-Palestinian stand he had half-expected trouble and he was prepared.

'Mr Everett, we are not refusing you an entry but I have some questions for you.'

'Fire ahead.'

'Mr Everett, it seems from our researches that trouble follows you wherever you are.'

Sid had not expected this line. 'I'm a journalist. I'm the channel that informs my public of what is happening, but facts only.'

'Well we could argue about that, but we have no interest in what you write about Britain. You claim that your visit to our country is for family reasons. Would you care to clarify that?'

Sid opened the envelope and slid out the photocopies. He had no intention of mentioning either Joel or Emily Simpson. 'This is the birth certificate of my great grandfather, Rabbi Ephraim Goldstone. His daughter married Elias Levi: they were my grandparents. But they've nothing to do with my visit to Haifa.'

'Enlighten me.'

'Elias Levi had three sisters all living in Poland. Adolf Hitler did for two of them but the third, my Great Auntie, the baby of the family, made it to the US but she died in your country.' Sid dropped his voice. 'I think I've located her grave and I know my old mamma would wish me to make the trek – you know, pay homage.'

'That is most commendable, Mr Everett,' the man frowned. 'You seem to have acquired a new name. May I ask if you attend synagogue?'

'Sorry, I don't believe in God.'

'At least you are honest about that.' The man stood up and offered his hand. A shrewd guy, thought Sid. And, rightly, he doesn't believe a word of what I've told him.

CHAPTER 28

Tom had only just arrived at the new marina complex in Haifa. He stood on a pontoon, and for the first time in three days he relaxed. He looked around and took in the scene. It could have been any Mediterranean yacht harbour, although this one seemed strangely empty. A handful of modest local boats, both power and sail were moored, but little else. This was a port of call that only a few brave or very curious yacht crews would visit. Anyway, why bother when Greece, Turkey, Cyprus and historic Alexandria were so close? Even wartorn and divided Lebanon was a bigger draw.

Tom felt a self-congratulatory glow. His first overseas mission for his firm had been a success. He had programmed three new and sophisticated systems and the delighted company had wined and dined him into the early hours. This was an odd country but he couldn't fault the hospitality. This morning they had helped him find a taxi with an English-speaking driver, and he had sped up the coast road from Tel Aviv to Haifa. The sun was shining on blue water, he could have been anywhere in the Mediterranean region were it not for the tension and suspicion he felt all around him. He detected no hostility to himself, but everyone he came across or worked with wanted to justify themselves and their country's actions. It was the stifling politicised atmosphere that got to him. Even a student visit to Libya had not been as claustrophobic as this. He remembered his step-grandmother describing her life in South Africa during the apartheid years; there was the same self-justifying nervousness here.

He was pleased to find Emily's boat already removed from the container and sitting in the parking area with other boats assembling for the regatta. He took the checklist that she had given him and went over the boat from end to end. He removed the sails and tools stored in the cockpit. The mast was lying on a rack nearby. He checked the rigging and was satisfied that all was well.

'That's the English boat isn't it?'

Tom swung round to find a man standing behind him. This person had approached so quietly that he hadn't noticed him. 'It's one of the British boats,' he replied. 'But there'll be more coming.'

'This would be for the women's competition, I understand.'

'Women's match racing. This team are world number one – they're good.'

'I understand they are Te-Koote, Walsh and Simpson.'

'That's right – it's their first time sailing here.' Tom studied this character. He spoke the English of an educated Englishman. That did not surprise Tom as he knew Israel had a sizeable population of UK birth. 'Are you from these parts?' he asked.

The man held out a hand. 'Simon Richards. I'm British by birth, Jewish by heritage and a citizen of the world.'

Tom shook hands. The man was early middle age, tall, with thinning black hair. There was something about him, something that would mark him out from a crowd, but Tom couldn't put a finger on precisely what.

'Do you sail?' he asked.

'No, I don't, but I follow all sport.' Richards nodded cheerfully and walked away. Tom thought he detected smugness in the man's body language and couldn't think why.

Emily and her friends arrived in Tel Aviv four days later. A bus was waiting for them outside the airport complex and, having cleared customs, a mixed group of sailors from a dozen nations boarded and headed north for the regatta centre. The entry formalities went smoothly and Emily didn't need the envelope of documents proving her family's remote connection to Judaism. The country through which their transport passed was flat and covered by drab suburbia. The sea on their left appeared empty apart from an occasional grey warship. They passed an unusual number of army vehicles and soldiers by the roadside. At one point they saw a military airfield. The English language guide explained that Israel was a peaceable society that was constantly under threat but only used force in self-defence. Emily didn't have an opinion – she only wanted to see Tom again and sail her boat.

Eventually they were in the approaches to a big city. Now Emily could view the sea again, and ahead of them were docks with ships. Shortly afterwards they were parking in a marina with a fine yacht club building. The coach stopped and the passengers descended blinking in the bright sunlight. Emily looked across the boat park and there stood Tom. She ran and flung her arms around him and smothered his face with kisses.

'Oh, Tom, it's so nice…'

He laughed and stroked her hair. 'I'm sure it's nice but remember we are British.'

'What's that supposed to mean?'

He gently released her grip. 'This is a bit public and I don't know what the locals think.'

'Come on, you two,' said Chloe. 'Break it up, and Tom – show us our boat.'

Tom threaded his way through a now crowded boat park; the others followed.

'We'll need help to step the mast,' said Chloe.

'I can do that,' said Tom, 'if you'll give me a hand to lift it in.'

Emily left the two of them to sort out the problem while she and Erin walked over to the launching slips. The usual groups of on-lookers had gathered, young and smartly dressed. Emily would not normally have given them a second glance had not she been drawn to a girl standing slightly apart from a group of five. Was she a competitor that they had come across at some other event? There was something so teasingly familiar about the woman but Emily couldn't place her. She searched her mind for some detail, some cross-reference, but gave up. It really didn't matter.

Chloe and Tom had managed to step the mast while Chloe at ground level was sorting out the rigging. 'We've beds in the club-house,' said Chloe. 'First come, first served, but that RYA bloke's fixed it.'

Emily knew this was inevitable but she was still disappointed. 'Where are you sleeping, Tom?'

'Elsewhere,' said Chloe. 'He's our team manager and we've all got a job to do – so it's strict self-control. Less booze and no sex.'

'I've got to share a hotel room with that British Embassy trouble-shooter. He's here to keep an eye on all the Brits and smooth our path,' said Tom.

Emily hardly heard him. The cross-reference that she had been searching for hit her mind like an electric shock. Photographs and the Royal King Henry, of course: that girl over there was Leila – the same one that had broken into Firs Farm and been caught by Johnny's camera. What the hell was she doing in this place? Emily's first instinct was to tell Tom, but she thought better of it. Her quick-tempered boyfriend would be up for a noisy confrontation and that was the last thing they needed in a strange city in an insecure country. Emily would take her time and try and find out more about this mysterious person.

Steve Simpson arrived in Tel Aviv two flights later than Emily and her friends. Obtaining his visa had taken longer, but at last he was here. He found a taxi willing to take him to Haifa. He had no idea of the current rate of exchange and suspected he was being ripped off as he parted with a wad of the local currency. He took out his mobile and called the yacht club. Eventually an English speaker was found and she reported that Chloe and her crew had arrived and would be staying in the club building. Steve felt relieved. So far all was well. After several wrong turns the taxi driver arrived at the yacht club, and standing in the front entrance was Emily.

'Dad, fantastic, so you got here.'

'It wasn't easy but I've done it. Now, has anything odd happened?'

Emily glanced around towards the yacht club. 'Dad, there's something you should know. I saw that woman called Leila, the one who broke into our house that night.'

Steve couldn't take this in at first but he knew from Emily's face that she was worried. 'Are you certain it's the same one?'

'Yes.'

'I take your word for it.' Steve knew his daughter was observant and not given to fantasy. 'I can't do a thing legally, but I will confront her. I want to know what was so interesting about our house. No sign of Hammersen I suppose?'

'No.'

'Thank God for that.'

This was nasty, and just the kind of thing that had given Steve sleepless nights. Leila, he couldn't remember her other name, was technically a United States diplomatic employee. She had been sent home in disgrace but maybe had earned another deployment.

'All right, Emily. Tom is here and so am I. We're both going to keep an eye out for trouble. Don't go anywhere on your own; stick with the other two and keep your eyes open.'

'Yes, Dad,' she sounded subdued.

'Remember, you are in foreign country where crazy theorists like Hammersen probably have some pull with the authorities. By that I mean that Gerda Elgaad and her like arouse pretty strong feelings even now.'

Steve left it at that. He was worried but didn't want to frighten Emily. Once the girls were out at sea racing he would feel more secure, but they still had five days to go before the start of the regatta.

Emily was just beginning to enjoy herself. The new yacht club facilities included a magnificent restaurant and plush lounge and bar. This room was crammed with competitors for the forthcoming regatta. Emily and her two were soon in happy reunion with dozens of old friends from other yacht classes and rivals from their own.

'We could get lucky,' said Chloe. 'The Indonesian girls are not sailing and I rated them among the best.'

'Why aren't they here?' asked Emily.

'Oh, politics again. Their government stopped them travelling. Same with the girls from Goa.'

'I don't understand that.'

'I think I can,' said Chloe, 'I'm from a racial minority; I have a sort of radar for these things and this country is beginning to get to me.'

'I'd rather be in your country,' said Emily. 'There's a sort of atmosphere here that I don't get and I'm part Jewish.'

'I'm a bloody half-breed in the British Army so I know a bit about prejudice, but there is a mindset in this place that worries me.'

'In what way?'

'They say, "We're surrounded by enemies and we live in a world where everyone hates us. So we will defend ourselves in any way that suits and to hell with international opinion".'

This was all a bit too deep for Emily. She made her way to the bar. She fancied another glass of that red wine. Whatever was right or wrong about the Israelis they certainly knew how to make wine.

'Excuse me, but I think you are one of the British team.' A very English voice spoke, and Emily turned to see a man standing beside her. He was tall, oldish, but still athletic looking and rather handsome. She glanced around trying to see where Tom was. Yes she could see him, chatting to Maria Olivarez of course. Maria was standing in her usual coquettish pose with glass in hand. Well sod it; that gave her a license to chat to this amazingly sexy bloke.

'Yes, I'm Emily. I'm part of a match racing team.'

'The top team, so I understand,' he held out a hand. 'I'm Simon Richards.'

'You're not a journalist are you?'

'Oh no, don't get that idea. I'm just a sports nut. I like meeting top sports people. You have an ethos that is a whole lot healthier than mine.' He smiled at her, a most compelling smile that made her relax. 'Come, on Emily, may I call you Emily? What will you drink?'

'I'd love another glass of that local red wine.'

Steve was also enjoying himself. This was the kind of social gathering that he could relate to. These were his kind of people, a few old fogies from his generation of course but, more significant, a hundred younger, fitter and ambitious boys and girls. Even if they all regarded him as yesterday's man they were the future of his sport.

He had caught an occasional glimpse of Emily, Tom and the other two girls. All seemed to be immersed in gossip with their opposite numbers. A familiar person was heading towards him: Maria Olivarez with a sweet smile on her face.

'Steve, we meet again.' She reached up and laid her hands on his shoulders and kissed each cheek.

'Maria,' he smiled back. 'You're sailing this week?'

'Indeed I am. I need to improve. I want to be some competition for Andrea from your country. I have just been speaking with her over there and she says you could give me tips.'

'I can try, but I haven't raced dinghies for years.'

This girl was stunning. She wore a tiny mini dress that revealed her long suntanned legs. Steve wished he was fitter and younger and was glad his wife was safe home in England. He chatted with the girl for a few minutes, answered her questions as best he could and hoped he wasn't being a conventional boring old fart. Maria smiled again and tripped away towards another group of younger sailors. Ten minutes later he caught a glimpse of her in earnest conversation with Emily's Tom. Emily couldn't be too worried as there was no sign of her anywhere near.

'Erin, where's Emily got to? It's past nine o'clock. We need to get some sleep.' Chloe was looking around the crowded bar. She couldn't see Emily; she presumed she was with Tom. Tom was a guy Chloe was never entirely at ease with. She found him stiff-arsed, a typical public school Pom.

'There's Tom,' said Erin. She waved to him. 'Tom, it's time for Emily to catch some sleep. Is she with you?'

'I'm looking for her too,' he said. 'She was around here about twenty minutes ago; she was with Maria and Andrea, the Laser girls.'

Chloe could see Maria talking to some men. 'Hi, Maria,' she called. 'A minute please.'

'What is it?' Maria asked.

'Have you seen our Emily?'

'Yes, I think she's outside. She didn't look well just now. There was some guy helping her walk. Looked like she's about to be sick.'

'Oh, that's all we need,' Chloe felt exasperated. 'Silly girl's had one glass too many and I thought we agreed…'

Chloe led the way outside into the night air. Erin and Maria followed. Small knots of people were smoking and talking. 'Anyone speak English,' Chloe called. Several people replied or held up their hands.

'Have you seen a dark haired English girl looking as if she wasn't too well?'

'Is it Emily Simpson you're talking about?' An American male voice answered.

'You know her?'

'Sure, seen her around the sailing scene. Just now she looked spaced out bad: some guy helped her into a car over there.'

'What kind of car? What did he look like?' It was Tom speaking.

'Didn't really see. Does it matter?'

'Yes, it bloody well does. She's been threatened.'

'What's all this? What's going on?' Steve had arrived now and his voice was tense.

'Steve, I don't like it,' said Tom. 'Emily's got into a car with a stranger and it sounds like she's drunk, only I know she's not drunk; she stuck to just two glasses of red wine.'

'Oh my God, not again – surely not again,' Steve cried.

'I'm going in there to call the police,' said Tom.

'Already been done, squire.'

Chloe swung round to see a small grizzled looking man of late middle age wearing a leather jacket.

'Everett,' Steve snarled. 'What the hell are you doing here?'

'Don't rubbish me, mate. I'm going to save your girl. I know who's taken her and I've a good idea where.'

Chloe was alarmed to see Steve stagger to this new arrival and seize him by the throat. 'Where is Emily, what have you done to her?'

Tom grabbed Steve by the shoulders and seizing his wrists forced him to release his grip. 'Steve, cool it for Christ's sake.'

Sid Everett was red faced and breathing heavily. 'Leave it out. I'm on your side, that's why I'm here.'

'Quiet Steve,' said Tom. 'I'll deal with this.' He stared at Sid. 'You're that little rat of a reporter. Is this something to do with that Michelle?'

'Nothing to do with her, or not directly, but she gave me a lead on this.'

'Not good enough. Tell me what you know.'

'Back in London I met that man Hammersen, the bloke you nutted…'

'That bastard. Is it him that's taken her?'

'No it isn't. Hammersen's all wind and piss. It's another guy.'

Tom took a step forward. 'Tall man, lean build, thinning hair, calls himself Richard something?'

'Sounds like him. He's not called that though. His name's Joel and half the world's police are looking for him.'

Steve intervened. 'You say you've called the police?'

'Yeah, and they were expecting a call from me. I went to the police station this morning and briefed them. Wasn't sure if they'd be that friendly, but seems they want to catch Joel as well. He brings the world Jews into disrepute with his redemptions.'

'What the hell are you talking about?' Tom's fury was mixing with clear panic.

'The Redemptionists. They hunt down ex-Nazis and kill 'em. They've done fifty or more since the war.'

'Kill them!' Tom shouted. Several heads were turning towards them. Chloe was catching the fear in his voice. Erin looked white-faced and puzzled.

'No,' said Sid. 'Joel's not going to kill Emily. He'll return her to you in one piece but she won't be in a fit state to sail in your little boat.'

Emily knew she was half awake but she couldn't slip back into sleep again. She couldn't remember where she was or what day it was. Memories were emerging – fearful ones. Waking up in a damp cellar and not knowing her name or the where and why of anything. Oh, no, not again, surely not again. She was still drowsy but her memory was coming back by the second. She was Emily and she was going sailing.

She could open her eyes now, and could see and feel that she was lying on a clean surface, not like last time. Her hands felt cloth. She wore some sort of cotton gown – why? This was crazy. She tried to sit up but she couldn't, she was fixed to the bed by straps around her legs, her middle and her upper body. Oh, God help me. It was happening all over again, but why, why? Someone was nearby. Emily could hear footsteps. She opened her eyes again to see a face peering at her. It was a woman's face and Emily knew her, or she had seen her before, but where, when?

'Emily,' the woman spoke. 'You are in hospital. You are in safe hands but you need an urgent operation.' The accent was American.

Emily tried to croak a question but the words wouldn't come.

'Lie still, the doctor wishes to give you a pre-med. Then you can relax and forget your troubles.' More words now but in a foreign language.

A man was standing next to her, masked and gowned and he held a syringe. He probed her arm and emptied the contents. The effects were slow but remorseless. She felt light headed and relaxed, although she could still feel, hear, and smell that distinctive tang of hospital. She tried to think back. What had happened so bad that it required her to have surgery? She knew she was in Israel for a sailing regatta but where were Chloe and Erin? Oh Dad, where are you? What's happened? Why have they tied me to this bed? She could see now that it was a hospital trolley; the wheeled device that Americans called a gurney.

'Come along Emily, the surgeon is ready,' said the same voice. The face was peering at her again and now Emily knew her. It was Leila again: the woman who had broken into Firs Farm and had been here in the yacht club only hours earlier. Her face filled Emily with cold fright.

The trolley began to move. Emily looked up at the ceiling of a long corridor flitting by above her. She could lift her head and see open doors ahead and the bright lights of an operating theatre. She was confused. Everything was hazy and surreal. She gave herself up to whatever was about to happen.

She could hear shouting, men's voices, harsh and guttural. Gunshots, one, two, three! Oh no, it was all happening again and this time she couldn't run away. She was tied to this trolley and helpless. Footsteps were thundering down the corridor, not footsteps but heavy boots. Emily heard a shrill scream. A large man had caught Leila, who was struggling and spitting. The man was a soldier or a policeman dressed in black with body armour and a peaked cap. Dare she hope? It had been this way last time, but why, why?

Another uniformed man was by her and releasing the straps. 'You are Emmy Simps?' His accent was thick and laboured.

'Yes,' she replied. 'Or I think I am.' With difficulty she sat up. The brightly lit theatre was there in front of her; Leila and two gowned doctors were lying flat on the floor. A man holding a handgun was standing over them.

'Mr Everett, I owe you the most profound apology.' Steve held out his hand.

'That's all right, Mr Simpson.' Sid shook hands with Steve. 'I've been following this story for a few months, but I wasn't going to be a part of anything harming your Emily.'

‘What happened?’ Steve asked. ‘The police spoke to me just now but they are being really close with information.’

‘They want to catch that Joel. It seems he hired a private clinic outside Tel Aviv. They’ve got his sidekick woman but no sign of Joel.’

‘Have you any idea of what they wanted Emily for?’

‘Yes, Mr Simpson. Hammersen let that slip in London. That’s why I’m out here. He and Joel have got it into their heads that Emily is a direct descendant of Adolf. I guess that’s a lot of crap?’

Steve took a deep breath. ‘Well the truth is going to out anyway. Emily had a great uncle who was illegitimate. The father was Josef Goebbels but there’s no blood line to either my wife or to Emily.’

Sid nodded. ‘I guessed it was something like that, but there’s no shifting fanatics like Joel.’

‘Mr Everett. Were they going to kill her?’

‘No, as I said, she would have come back to you in one piece, but she’d never have kids. They were going to perform a hysterectomy.’

‘Good God, but why?’

‘Look, Mr Simpson. I’ve seen things in my job. I’ve known the kids of the vilest serial killer who are decent citizens and kind parents. I don’t know what it is that makes psychos how they are but their traits don’t get inherited. That I’m sure of.’

Emily trembled and sobbed as she clung to both Tom and her father. She felt physically sick as her mind twisted through the after-effects just as it had eight years ago.

‘Oh why is it always me?’ she cried. ‘What have I done for it to be always me?’

‘Sweetheart, you’ve done nothing wrong,’ her father gently rocked her in his arms. ‘It’s not your fault – it’s a crazy world.’

They were all in a comfortable office in the Haifa police headquarters. A woman officer with faultless English had asked the questions but there was nothing Emily could tell her. It was only as an afterthought that Emily mentioned the last person she could remember at the yacht club: the Englishman, Richards. That had produced a reaction all right. Emily had been whisked into a small room with a projector. The screen had filled with a series of photographs and photo fits. The fourth one had been Richards, no doubt about it. The interviewing lady had not tried to conceal her excitement and had instantly called to someone on a pocket radio, gabbling in a language that Emily assumed was Hebrew. After this,

Emily had been taken to the other room and there, waiting for her, were Tom and Dad.

Dad looked severe. 'Emily, I'm sorry but you and I are flying home – no arguments.'

Emily's mouth fell open and for a few seconds she forgot her troubles. 'But what about Chloe and Erin? They can't sail without me.'

'Yes they can,' said Tom. 'Maria Olivarez has been kind enough to fill the gap for this week only. She's already qualified for the Olympics in her boat so she's a free agent.'

Emily found a little of her old spirit coming back. She glared at Tom. 'You like that Maria – admit it.'

'Not in the way you are suggesting. She's giving up a chance to win a trophy in her Laser, so don't be mean. You take your father home. That'll please your mother.'

'Why?'

'Going home will protect you from harm and him from Maria.'

Tom laughed, and her father did too in a shamefaced manner. Emily couldn't help it as she began to laugh and laugh until, unable to stop, her body convulsed and then she sobbed without restraint.

Steve felt a mix of emotions that he knew he could never come to terms with. Poor Tom looked ghastly, and Steve began to realise just how much his little girl meant to both of them. It blew away his last doubts. Tom Stoneman could have his daughter's hand in marriage whenever it pleased him to ask.

The Israeli police inspector broke into his reverie. 'Mr Simpson, we think it best that Emily stay here in our building tonight, and we will arrange for you both to fly out from Tel Aviv in the morning. You see we have yet to catch the perpetrator of this outrage.'

'You mean the man called Joel.'

'That is right. In the past there has been an inclination by many in this country to ignore his activities, but there are few Nazi criminals now still alive. We will not allow this man to besmirch the name of the Jewish nation by this madness.'

'Please,' said Steve, 'can you tell me how he came to abduct Emily?'

'Oh that is simple. Joel is an attractive man and your Emily was unwise enough to accept a drink from him at the yacht club. Unwise, because that drink was laced with the substance that is called the date rape drug. Of course the man was not interested in rape, only in his own madness. Please believe me Mr Simpson we in Israel will pursue every last Nazi to the grave but we will never take our spite out on the innocent.'

'Sid,' said Steve, 'we seem fated to cross paths, and we owe you for Emily and I guess you played a part in destroying Lindgrune all those years ago.'

'Too right,' Mr Simpson, 'but that was a good story. Only wish we could have got the bastard in court.'

'Next point. What are you going to write about Emily? She's going through mental torture right now.'

Sid didn't answer. His mobile phone was ringing with an irritating jingle. 'S'cuse me,' he said.

'He has … where? … Istanbul? … Yeah, Mr Simpson is here now, I'll tell him.' Sid put his phone away. 'Joel has been arrested in Turkey. The police were suspicious of a name on a flight out yesterday and it seems they've hit gold.'

Steve was far from happy. 'Does that mean he'll be charged with Emily's kidnap?'

Sid grinned. 'Half the police of the world will be after him, but I guess our own Home Office will come in with an extradition. Joel killed three men in Hampshire ten years ago. They were ex-Nazis, really nasty Nazis, but the law is the law.'

'It's just that I don't want you dragging Emily's name through the mud. She's never recovered from the fire cult and I dread to think what this will do to her. You know this Joel was trying to sterilise her. How evil is that?'

'That's what got me onto this story,' said Sid. 'Hammersen was such an idiot he spat out the whole plot: sort of gloried in it. Well, I wasn't having that. When I heard that your Emily was coming here, well…'

'And we are eternally grateful to you, Sid, and I didn't think I'd ever say that.' Steve paused. 'Did you believe the Hitler connection?'

'No, but Hammersen does. Look, Mr Simpson, my granddad and grandma were Jewish. What if old Adolf and his army had come to Britain? He'd've killed them both and my mum and dad, and me too although I was only a baby. I said before, even if Adolf was capable of having kids they wouldn't necessarily have been carbon copies. You say the connection was Goebbels? God, he was an evil bastard too, but what a great-media man – what a spinner.' Sid's expression was almost dreamy.

‘But,’ said Steve, ‘believe me there is no bloodline connection to my wife and none to Emily. We should have DNA proof within a week or so.’

Sid looked alert. ‘How’re you going to do that? You’d need bits of Adolf and old Gobbles.’

‘You don’t give up do you? Never mind, we know a man who can. Would DNA proof shut Hammersen up?’

‘Dunno’, but they can’t charge him with complicity without they involve Emily.’

‘That’s what worries me,’ said Steve. ‘I doubt we’ll ever be free of all this.’

PART 2

Three years forward.

CHAPTER 29

Emily always enjoyed being the centre of attention even if this time she felt a trifle odd dressed in this black gown and white bands. Her calling party was in full swing above a pub a few strides from the Travis chambers in Lincoln's Inn. The wine was flowing and the table could almost be said to groan under the weight of party food. Tony Travis was there and old William had come out of retirement. Both had been fierce taskmasters but today they only wanted to honour their star pupil.

Mum and Dad were chatting to Tony and Angela, Tony's wife. Tom was in a corner with a glass of beer. He kept fumbling in his jacket pocket. Emily knew he was psyching himself up for his part in the afternoon: the not-so-big surprise. Chloe and Erin were in deep conversation with Maria Olivarez and with Nick, Erin's boyfriend. John-Kaj now aged seventeen was sipping wine and looking rather shy in this company.

Apart from Tom's surprise, Emily and the other three had something extra to celebrate. Two weeks ago she'd had another call – Chloe and her crew had been selected to represent Great Britain in the Olifa games in just six weeks time. Maria was already Olifa's single-handed Laser girl. And then there was Dad. The silly old man couldn't make his mind up, but he too had been invited to be Britain's Paralympic single-hander. His nearest rival had moved to another class of boat, yet Dad was still dithering.

Tony Travis called for quiet. 'This is a special day for so many reasons. I have made a few good decisions in my time and a few mistakes, but it was a great day when a beautiful young law graduate applied to these chambers to train for the bar. Emily has progressed through her training faster and better than I ever did in my time. She is a star who will grace the courts of justice long after I've gone. May I give you a toast: Emily, barrister at law.' Emily knew she was blushing as the whole company raised their glasses smiling in her direction.

'Thank you so much, Mr Travis. Without you I would have got nowhere. You taught me my new profession and I will do my best to live up to the standards you and William set for me. Thank you, all of you: my family, Mum and Dad and all my friends and my partner Tom. Without the support and love of all of you I might not be here today.'

Her speech of reply was met with warm applause. Emily wiped a tear from her eye. She could see Tom walking slowly towards her with a cryptic expression on his face. On cue he dropped on one knee and stared up at her. He looked more like an errant small boy than a devoted lover. He groped in his jacket pocket and produced the ring.

'*Can I compare thee to a summer's day…*' he began and faltered. 'Oh shit I can't remember the rest. Emily, I love you, will you marry me?'

'Get up you clown,' she laughed. 'Yes, you know I will.'

Kirsten didn't know why she was worried but worried she was. Her innate Scandinavian pessimism was seeping through her consciousness. Things were too perfect and everyone was too happy for this euphoria to last. Somewhere around the corner was fresh trouble.

Emily was on the road to a successful career in her chosen vocation. More important, she and Tom had finally agreed to tie the knot. Emily would be going to the Olympics and so would her Steve if she gave him a good push. Everyone at this party was so happy and fulfilled. Kirsten even tolerated the girl Maria in spite of Steve's ridiculous fascination for the silly temptress. Three years ago Maria had doubled for Emily in the disastrous Israel regatta. With no Emily in the boat the team had not worked. The fourth place was not what the girls had hoped for but was still far and away the best British result. Instead of being annoyed with Maria the girls now included her in their friendship. The Olympic selectors had accepted Maria's presence in the boat as she had a residential qualification on top of her Oxbridge education.

'What do you think?' Kirsten asked Steve, indicating Tom and Emily. 'Those two after all these years; still in love and with the future in front of them.'

'I can't help wondering what it's going to cost me,' said Steve. 'Church wedding, full-blown reception at the Lakeview Hotel and the rest.'

Her husband's grumpiness was just the tonic that Kirsten needed. 'It's once in a lifetime, and with those two I think it will last, which is more than you can say for most couples these days. And after all your grumbling about them living together, well, you can't have it both ways.'

With Emily back in the crew again the results had been good. All in international sailing agreed that few teams in the world could challenge Chloe, Emily and Erin. Maria would be sailing on her home water in her Laser. Whether Kirsten liked it or not Maria was one of the girls, part of a tight little clique. She only wished that Maria would settle down with some nice convivial millionaire and stop provoking Chloe's and Steve's fantasies.

'When is the big day?' asked Tony Travis.

'Got to be after the Olifa games,' Emily replied.

'Assuming she doesn't come last,' Tom grinned.

'That'd be your fault as much as ours – team manager.'

Travis laughed. 'Have you made up your mind where you'll live?'

That was certainly to the point. Tom didn't want to live in London. His company had promoted him, and his work ranged over the whole of Southern England from Kent to Cornwall with the Scillies and the Channel Islands thrown in. Discreetly, the couple had been looking at houses near Alresford. Both Emily and Tom were bored with the restriction of his bachelor pad.

'We need to live near Tom's work, but I can still commute to London.'

Travis smiled. 'How would it be if you were to double for me on the Winchester circuit? There's Dorchester and Portsmouth Crown Courts as well. We've some interesting cases coming up in all those courts, and one or two you could cut your teeth on. Some big ones, of course, where you'll have to junior for me. How about it?'

'Mr Travis, you are the best boss in the world. I won't let you down – promise.'

'And less of the Mr Travis. You are a professional equal now, so it's Tony and Emily unless we're in court and then it's…'

'My learned friend,' Emily giggled.

'That's when we're on opposite sides,' said Travis, 'and for all my years I'm not so certain you wouldn't pull a trick or two when we are.'

'I would try my best but I don't think I could outsmart you yet.'

Travis indicated Johnny. 'Your brother seems a really bright lad. Would he make a lawyer?'

'Johnny's a scientist, a real whiz at maths and chemistry. At the moment he's all set to study medicine.'

Emily saw Chloe grimacing in her direction. 'Excuse me … er … Tony.'

'Hi Em,' said Chloe. 'Did you know that Maria isn't going back to Olifa until a month before the games?'

'I know,' Emily half whispered. 'Don't tell my mum yet but

Maria's got a spare Laser and she's basing it at Branham. She says it'll let her have a chance to practice with Andrea, the Brit selection.'

'Maria says that Garcia bloke's in London. She says he keeps asking about your dad.'

'What about my dad?'

'Garcia's something to do with gambling isn't he?' asked Chloe.

'Internet gambling so I'm told,' said Emily. 'Hi Maria, are your ears burning?'

Maria had sidled up to them glass in hand. Her hair was immaculate, her jewellery expensive, her perfume was a mite powerful, but the little black cocktail dress she wore was stylish. 'Should they be burning?'

'Why is Garcia asking questions about Dad?'

'That is easy. He doesn't want your father to compete in Olifa.'

'Whyever not?'

'That is your fault. They are betting already on you girls to win gold. Two weeks later your father wins Paralympic gold. Father daughter double and father's second gold at age … I don't know?'

'For your information Maria, he will be seventy.'

'Ah,' Maria sighed. 'That surprises me and still such a handsome man and so sexy.'

'Well, my mum is watching you,' Emily laughed. 'OK, we all win medals so what's it to Garcia?'

'That's easy. Unique double, very long odds, worldwide betting, huge sums on the double. Then you both do it, win the gold. Garcia is seriously out of pocket, has to pay out millions, and he is a greedy man.'

Chloe shrieked with laughter turning some heads in the room. 'Strewth mate, me the centre of an international gambling scam. That'll shake up the folks back home.'

'Do not laugh too much, Chloe.' Maria had a serious expression. 'Primee is not a very nice man and would be vindictive if his pocket is touched.'

'It seems you don't like him,' said Tom who had joined them.

Maria had changed before their eyes into the haughty Conquistador lady aristocrat. 'Garcias are nothing. They are half Italian; not true Spanish blood and all they do is make money.'

Tom drove Emily from London to their temporary home in the Alresford flat. She was happy and she felt she deserved to be happy. She had learned her profession, and she had reached the top in her sport. She had survived a terrifying childhood experience, and a second one in her adulthood. She wore Tom's ring on her finger and she knew Tom would be loyal to her, or as loyal as one could expect any man to be. To her knowledge he hadn't faltered yet, even with Maria around. It had all been a long haul and she had won in the end.

An awkward moment had emerged when Tony Travis had been called by the Crown Prosecutors to act for them in the trial of Joel Simons, the British-born terrorist who had wanted to mutilate her during the Israel visit. She still felt a cold sickness when she thought about that. The man had so very nearly succeeded. Had the Israeli police arrived only minutes later Emily would have been denied the chance to have her own children. It was this that gave her nightmares now that memories of the fire cult were fading. Joel Simons was serving life for the murder of two ex-Nazis in Hampshire. He and his followers had sealed the men in an old home guard bunker and gassed them with carbon monoxide. Maybe the Nazis had earned their fate, but it was still murder in the eyes of the law. Travis had sent Emily home for the duration of the trial in order to avoid claims of prosecution bias; although no one apart from Simons himself knew Emily's story and Leila, his accomplice, had committed suicide in an Israeli jail. Sid Everett, now retired, had passed Emily's DNA profile to the Nazi hunter Hammersen. This result proved that no link existed between either Kirsten or Emily and the human remains held by the former KGB. Everett was not certain that Hammersen accepted this evidence. Surely the Russians, of all people, would have no inclination to protect descendants of the Nazi leadership.

At home, Emily had seen the pictures on television shot outside the court of the pro-Simons demonstrators and their violent clashes with Islamic counter-protestors. Simons had made no attempt to defend himself and had gloried in his day in court, listing as he did some scores of other murders. Travis had got his verdict of course, but he had been worried.* The Crown Prosecution, plus the political establishment, had not given him the full facts. A third man had died in that bunker, someone prominent in British life and they had been barred from mentioning him. A leading politician who still clung to Nazi sympathies would be an anomaly that the establishment would rather bury. Simons had threatened to shout the name in court and the judge had ordered a session in camera, which drove the press into a fury.

---

* See *Magdalena's Redemption* by James Morley

‘At least the last eighteen months has restored you to what you should be, but it’s still a complete waste.’ Kirsten saw her sarcasm hit home.

‘Why the waste?’ Steve asked.

‘We have spent a bloody fortune sending you and your little boat to Hyeres, Miami, Kiel again and Greece, all so you can prove yourself to those selectors, and now you’re going to throw it all away.’

‘I’m not throwing anything away. I’m happy that I can still cut it at that level but as for the Olympics or even Paralympics, well, that’s for young people.

‘Oh dear,’ she jeered. ‘You poor decrepit old thing. It’s decision time; you’ve only got two more days to agree. Are you going to represent your nation in the Paralympic Games in Olifa?’

‘Probably no.’

‘I think it should be certainly yes. Will I tell them or will you.’

Steve groaned and threw the newspaper he’d been reading on the floor. ‘Leave it off, love. I’ll think about it. Let’s leave it until tomorrow when I’ve been to Branham.’

The bedside telephone was ringing. Emily rolled over and took in the time: nine thirty. The space beside her was empty. Tom had departed for work an hour ago. She reached, picked up the handset and answered.

‘Emily Simpson?’

‘Yes,’ she yawned, ‘that’s me.’

‘You may remember me. I’m Paul Romero, partner in Giggs and Stent of Petersfield.’

Emily was awake now as memories of the courtroom in Alton four years ago returned. ‘Of course, Mr Romero. I worked in your front office and you acted for my parents.’

‘I well remember all of your family and, of course, your friend Mr Stoneman. Are you still in contact with him?’ That at least was tactful.

‘Actually we’re engaged to be married.’

‘Excellent – my congratulations.’

‘Thank you.’ Emily had a sneaking suspicion that she knew why a solicitor was calling her. ‘How can I help you, Mr Romero?’

‘We’ve a client in need of a defence barrister. We’ve spoken to Travis and Partners and you have been recommended.’

‘Of course, Mr Travis is passing me cases on the Winchester circuit but, Mr Romero, I haven’t long been called.’

‘Mr Travis was very enthusiastic about your abilities and thinks this would be an ideal opportunity for you, but I have to say the defence may be a lost cause.'

'What's the charge?'

'Our client is a Mr Doyle. He is charged with theft of a boat, I think it is what you would call a rib…'

'Yes, that's RIB – stands for rigid inflatable boat.'

'This boat went missing from private premises near Hamble along with four outboard engines. The owner of the rib directed the police to the suspect's house and the stolen property was discovered there.'

'Crikey, that's pretty conclusive.'

'So it seems, but our client claims he was hired to maintain the engines and only took the rib and motors so he could more conveniently work on them.'

'That's a new one.'

'I know, we hear some amazing excuses in this office. So, Miss Simpson, we would like you to represent Mr Doyle in court in Winchester on next Monday week.'

'Is this Doyle being held in custody?' Emily was up and standing, grabbing for a note pad.

'He's still being held in Winchester police station, there's no room in the prison remand wing. I can give you the details and make an appointment with the police for you to speak with him. I'll email your brief today.'

Andy Doyle was a small man with dark curly hair, still dressed in his mechanic's overalls. He was escorted into the police interview room by a PC and given a seat opposite Emily.

'We'll be posted outside the door, Miss Simpson. Please press that buzzer if you need assistance.'

'What do they think I'm going to do?' Doyle muttered. His accent was Irish and Emily guessed that had prejudiced the police from the start. 'I wanted a brief for court,' Doyle continued.

'Well, that's me – I'm here.'

'But you're a woman.'

'I'm aware of that. Why should you be bothered?'

'Well I'm being stitched up and, it's all about a boat and well, you're a woman. Do you know a thing about boats?'

'I know some things, Mr Doyle, like I've sailed boats all my life and I've twice navigated a boat from Chichester to Duddlestone.'

'You did?' The astonishment on the man's face was almost comic.

Emily was brusque. 'Come on, Mr Doyle, let's get on with this.

First, I don't want to know whether you are guilty or not. Give me your side of the story and as many provable facts with it.'

'I'm being stitched up by that bastard Smidgin…'

Emily couldn't help herself. 'Not Walter Smidgin from Warsash?'

'Yeah, that's him.'

Emily remembered her Cadet dinghy days and the dour offensive man who had sworn at Johnny and her with a stream of foul language. All they had done was to pull their capsized dinghy onto a private slipway to bale her out. This screaming maniac had run down and let loose his filthy tirade and both she and Johnny had been reduced to tears. Dad had gone round immediately to remonstrate and the man, name of Walter Smidgin, had threatened to punch Dad. As Dad would have given better than he got in those days maybe Smidgin had been let off lightly.

'Right, Mr Doyle, the story in your own time.'

'Smidgin booked me to service his rib engine. It's a big one – hundred horse four- stroke, too heavy to remove off the boat.'

'I know, we've got one at Branham Lake, they service it on the boat.'

Doyle nodded and sat silently for some seconds. 'Smidgin was away from home, but his little wife, Lucy was there, poor bitch. I had the wrong set of plug spanners so I asked if I could borrow Walter's tools. Judy, she went white in the face and I know why. Walter would beat the last bit of shit out of her given the chance. So I tell her what I was going to do. I hitch the rib behind my Land Rover and take it home. My workshop's up the Meon Valley: too far to be going back and forth for odd tools.'

Emily fixed him with her best eye contact. 'The prosecution say you helped yourself to four smaller motors.'

'Sure, they were the little dinghy outboards. I was taking them to my shop anyway. Smidgin wanted 'em serviced.'

'Mr Doyle, if you are telling the truth we can call Mrs Smidgin to give evidence in your defence.'

'Jesus' sake, Miss, she be a dead 'un.'

'All right, if you service Mr Smidgin's equipment why is he so anxious to land you in this trouble?'

'That, Miss, I can guess, but it's between him and me.'

Emily gave up and called the PC from the passage. Doyle was led away meekly and Emily was left with a feeling of puzzlement. This was to be her first appearance in court, and it was not going to be the straightforward failure that she had anticipated. Smidgin was a vile individual, but Tony Travis would say that was irrelevant, as were her personal feelings. Only the facts counted.

Well she, Emily, was at a loose end for the rest of the day and she knew the Hamble. No harm in going there and maybe picking up a bit of background.

'Irishman there give you a load of the blarney did he?' said the PC: the man hardly tried to conceal his sneer.

Emily did not reply.

She left the station, recovered her car and took the M3 heading south for Hamble. The river had three sailing clubs where she was known and could ask a few discreet questions. But first she would drive to Warsash on the east bank of the river where she knew a pub that served a satisfactory bar lunch. Emily might be the qualified professional woman and anything but a shrinking violet, but she knew when it paid to play the ingenuous and silly dumb girl. She emerged from the pub an hour later whistling quietly to herself with a stupid smirk on her face. The sailing clubs could wait for tomorrow, today she had a call to make at an unobtrusive address in the village of Wickham.

Saturday at Branham was the open event for the 2.4 class. Steve drove the car there, and Kirsten sat in the passenger seat. Ever since Steve's arthritis problems they had used an automatic version Volvo and today the fact made them both feel safer. Steve was still a very competent driver, but his slow acting right leg was the brake operator and he had to keep a watchful eye and think ahead.

Kirsten counted twenty-six entries gathered for the meeting, and this alone would give Steve a good workout before his boat was shipped to Olifa. It was a glorious hot summer's day with only a light breeze ruffling the lake surface. The water had been reserved for the 2.4 boats but Kirsten could see two reduced rig Lasers in a fierce roll-tacking duel. Kirsten noted that one of the boats was Maria's.

She sat next to her husband for the pre-race briefing. Graham, the race officer, introduced Steve as: "Great Britain's choice for the forthcoming Paralympics..." Kirsten sensed that Steve wanted to intervene and gripped his arm sinking her nails into the bare flesh below his elbow. Steve visibly winced but stayed silent. Good, it meant she was in control of the situation and he knew it.

The boats were rigged and made a pretty sight as they made their slow way down the lake to the committee boat.

'Hi, Kirsten, how are things?' It was Maria. The woman was

wearing a pair of shorts and that same, far too tiny bikini top that just covered the nipples and not much else. Kirsten, as one grounded in nudist culture, knew that this attire was far more provocative and exciting to the male species.

'Hello, Maria, how is the Laser going?'

'It is going well, but your Andrea is still quicker than me.'

Kirsten fixed Maria with an inquisitive glare. 'Maria, what is it that pulls you towards older men? Sorry to be rude, but at your age I just do not understand it.'

Maria was not offended; it was almost as if she wanted to share her secret. 'Kirsten, you have a lovely older man. You must know that older men have years of experience of life. They know well how to please a girl and in bed they are gentle and considerate, they take much longer to come, and that is great.'

Kirsten could not help but laugh. Once she had been a bit that way herself. 'You've got most of it right, but you go and overdo the bed part and you'll end up a merry widow.'

Kirsten left Maria to recover her Laser while she took her binoculars and went to watch the race. It was light weather, not really Steve's forte, but who knew what the wind strength would be in Olifa.

Steve was happy. Every time that he sailed his boat he felt the years fall away; he might be seventy but out here he was thirty five again. His boat was perfectly tuned: the lightweight sails that he had designed himself were hoisted and drawing. His mind was concentrated on the job in hand and everything felt good. He watched the committee boat and heard the start count down. One minute left and, stupidly, while he had been dreaming, the wind had died and he was too far from the line. Change of tactics required. Everyone else was crowding to the biased starboard end so he would take port. He was drifting toward the line as the start signal went. There was the usual close-quarter shouting to windward but he would ignore that. He needed to sit still, still as if frozen. Bodily movement would kill what little speed he had conserved.

The sun was beating down and he began to sweat, but he still wasn't going to move even to wipe his forehead or clear his eyes. He could sense a change; a wisp of movement on the water away to the left. He could just detect the beginnings of a breeze on his cheek. Yes, it was a shift and for once a good one. He could point high if he wanted but he wouldn't, it was speed that counted now. Speed and concentration were his weapons and he could see now that he would pass the upwind mark in third place. He remembered another sailor, the most famous in Olympic history telling him: "Think of those boats in front of you as obstacles in your way". Steve settled down to close the gap on those obstacles.

'Hi, Mum, how's it going.'

Kirsten had been concentrating on the race and hadn't heard Emily walk up behind her. 'Hello,' she replied. 'You look like a black cat with a tub of cream. I didn't know you were coming here today.'

'I've driven up from Hamble.'

'You been sailing there?'

'No, Mum. I've been sleuthing.'

'I don't understand – explain.'

'Tony Travis has given me a defence brief at Winchester on Monday week. I thought it looked a no hoper but now I don't think so. I'm going to stop a gross miscarriage of justice and get a big slice of own-back.'

'Emily,' Kirsten sighed, 'I do not understand a word of this. I hope you aren't being too clever for your own good.'

Emily shook her head and laughed. 'Dad always tells me I'm a bad listener, but this morning I've done nothing but listen and keep my mouth shut. Anyway, how is Dad getting on?'

'Third at the first mark and now he's second. Em, something's got to be done to commit him to Olifa. We're loading the boat for the transit tomorrow.'

'Mum, leave it to me. I have a cunning plan.'

Steve was feeling much happier. The wind had increased for the third and last race and it was the opportunity he had waited for. He settled down to dominate the field. By the time the fleet had completed the third lap of the course he had built up a lead that he never lost. He felt nothing but a complete fusion with his boat, the wind and the water. He forgot about the pain in leg and arm, he forgot everything except the job in hand. He wanted to win this race and he would do so.

Steve crossed the finish line the winner not only of race three, but the Branham Cup. Now he felt both happy and very tired as he sailed back to the landing jetty and parked his boat under the hoist. He connected the harness loops to the metal crane and submitted to being raised back to terra firma. He no longer needed the wheelchair; he could stand and release the sling himself. Kirsten greeted him cheerfully and, to his surprise, Emily was with her. His daughter was up to something. She had that self-satisfied smirk that didn't fool him.

'Steve, we were so looking forward to seeing you in Olifa and now Emily says you may not go.' Steve put down his teacup and turned stiffly in his seat. He was relaxing on the terrace area overlooking the water and he had not heard Maria's near silent barefooted approach. She looked down on him with a sweet smile. He took in her sun-tanned arms and shoulders that blended seamlessly with the white sun frock into which she had changed.

His thoughts were in a whirl while he groped for a reply. 'Maria, I liked your country and would love to see it again, but I always think the Olympics and the Paralympics are for the young.'

'You are not so old, Steve. You are a great man and a fine sailor. I have watched you today and I do not see many who could take you on.'

'I don't know, Maria, I really do not know. I could be set to make a fool of myself.'

Her expression changed. 'Steve you make me feel angry when you say these things. I had so hoped that you would go to the games. I promised my father I would take you to see our family estancia. I hoped you would talk to my sailing friends – you are a legend. Did you know that?'

'Legend is a term in our sailing that means geriatric and yesterday's man.'

'To Olifarians it means a hero and a role model. Please, Steve, come to Olifa,' her smile was dazzling. She knelt beside him and placed her left hand on his knee while moving her face no more than an inch from his body. 'Come to Olifa. Do it for me.'

'All right, Maria,' instinctively he touched her head. 'Kirsten's going to make me go anyway. Yes, I'll see you in Olifa. I'll watch you and Emily sail and then I'll race in my event.'

Emily was waiting with their friend Andrea beside Maria's Laser. Maria saw them, waved, and gave the thumbs up signal.

'What did he say?' Emily asked.

'He will sail in Olifa,' said Maria. 'I made him promise.'

'Thank God for that,' said Emily. 'You twist men round your little finger. Will you share the secret with the rest of us?'

'There is no secret. I like gorgeous men, and your father is gorgeous and sexy.'

Emily grinned. 'All right Maria, but don't try it on with him too hard or my mum'll kill you.'

Maria smiled in return. 'No way; I am an honourable person.'

'I wish I could be sure of that.'

The following day, Sunday, Emily drove back to Hamble. She made a round of the sailing clubs and enjoyed meeting old friends. She asked the carefully worded questions she needed answering. Finally she made her way to Hamble Point Marina and there, alleluia, was the yacht and the man she had hoped to see.

'Young Emily Simpson, our Olympic hope,' he called out. 'How is your father? Come aboard, it's G and T time.'

CHAPTER 30

'These are the witnesses I'd like subpoenaed.' Emily handed the printed A4 sheet.

Paul Romero studied it carefully. 'All right, Emily, but remember this is a legal aid brief. You won't get paid for all this leg work.'

Emily shook her head. 'I don't care about that. I just want the right result and going round Hamble is no hassle. I love it there.'

'You want the woman called last?'

'The refuge manager has promised to bring her. The important thing is to get her there and then keep her out of sight. Her evidence has got to be the clincher. The police won't let me look at their exhibit so I'm playing that one as a hunch.'

Romero laughed. 'You mean it'll be the rabbit out of the magician's hat.'

'If it comes off, yes. If it doesn't, I'll look a bloody fool. But everything I've heard tells me my trick will work and the jury will love it.'

'But it won't be conclusive. The prosecution will still say, "It was the defendant what done it".'

'Let 'em and see what we ask the last witness.'

With Steve's mind finally made up, activity at Firs Farm had become frantic. Tomorrow the little 2.4 would be loaded in a container and on its way for airfreight to Olifa. The sails, the clothing and tools to be packed inside would all need to clear customs. Kirsten had once again taken charge. Her first task had been to fax and email Steve's acceptance to the Paralympic authority. The pile of paperwork could come later. Once the boat and gear were on their way she could relax and so, hopefully, would her fractious man. Kirsten had been determined that Steve would compete in Olifa, even if she had to drug him, handcuff him and put him on the plane. In the end it had all been too easy. She knew was that Emily had hatched a plan to catch her father off balance, as it were, and force his acceptance. Exactly how her too clever daughter had achieved this Kirsten had no idea, but it had worked.

The girls had already been kitted out in the uniforms they would march in at the opening ceremony. Emily was absorbed with this trial in Winchester, but she was still fanatical in her gym work and daily runs. Tom had earned a salary increase and once Emily started to earn her fees the young couple could look for their first proper house. In this they were determined to rely on their own resources and would not accept help with a deposit. Without that lump sum mortgages were almost impossible to obtain under the new rules. That cramped flat in Alresford was no place to rear children. Tom had the free use of the Duddlestone holiday cottage but that was so off the beaten track as to be impracticable.

Emily arrived at court. She felt anxious and confident at the same time. Her hearing was scheduled for two-thirty that afternoon, as long as the previous case did not overrun. Travis had told her that Mr Justice Groves was fairminded and not averse to women counsel. "Young and beautiful ones he's very partial to," Travis had laughed.

Emily almost shouted in relief to find that her key witness had arrived and was sheltering in the refuge manager's car. The dour taxi driver was already in the waiting room looking increasingly gloomy. Lastly, she saw her star witness parking his Mercedes. For the first time for real, Emily donned her gown and adjusted her wig. The prosecutor was an older and wizened barrister in his fifties. Emily knew little about him and had never seen the man in action.

At three o'clock they were called. Time was not on her side, and Emily really wanted the jury sent out that day. Mr Justice Groves took his place on the bench and the shrunken and white-faced Doyle was led into the dock.

The prosecutor outlined his case. Mr Walter Smidgin had woken on the morning of July the twenty-ninth to find his rigid inflatable boat and four boat engines had been stolen in the night. Mr Smidgin had been suspicious of the activities of the defendant, Doyle, and had suggested a search of Mr Doyle's house and workshop. The boat had been discovered there along with four boat engines, one of which was in the court as Exhibit (a). He pointed to a Yamaha outboard motor on a stand in the well of the court. As the jury would see, the engine had the distinctive plaque of Mr Smidgin's firm fixed to its casing.

Counsel then called his first witness, a local police constable from the Meon Valley. The officer reported being called to a workshop in the village of West Meon where he had found items corresponding to those missing.

The judge looked at Emily. 'Your witness, Miss Simpson.'

'No questions, your Honour.'

The prosecution called Walter Smidgin. Smidgin almost bounded onto the stand. To Emily he looked smug as well as confident.

He answered the prosecution questions reiterating the evidence already stated.

'Miss Simpson, your witness.'

Emily fixed an eye contact with Smidgin. There was no chance he would remember her as the little girl he had once enjoyed bullying. He stared coldly back with the sneer of the practiced chauvinist.

'Mr Smidgin, I have no doubt the boat is yours but can you positively identify the motors?'

'Course I can. They've got my logo haven't they?'

'We can all see that, Mr Smidgin. But could anyone else have a supply of your plaques in order to make that motor look legitimate?'

'Oh come on, Miss. No chance, I keep them in my safe and fix 'em on myself.'

'That's settled then. Tell me, Mr Smidgin, before these problems arose, how well did you know the defendant Mr Doyle?'

Smidgin's features darkened. 'He does bits around the Hamble.'

'I understand that, Mr Smidgin, but did you encounter him socially? I mean, do your wives know each other?'

'What you on about?' Smidgin's voice had turned to his bullying tone that Emily remembered so well.

'It's a simple question.'

'No comment.'

'Mr Smidgin,' Judge Groves growled, 'Counsel has asked you a fair question and you must answer.'

'Andy Doyle ain't got a woman. He dips in where he ain't wanted.'

Emily glanced at the bench. 'Thank you, Mr Smidgin. No more questions.'

'Do you have other witnesses?' the judge asked the prosecutor.

'No, your Honour; I think the facts are indisputable.'

Now it was Emily's turn. 'Call Andrew Doyle.'

Doyle left the dock and took the oath. He stumbled over the words and had the look of one who felt himself doomed. He repeated to the court the same story he had told Emily. Without the correct tools he had taken the rib and the motors to his own workshop.

'Mr Doyle, did you leave a note for Mr Smidgin?'

'I tried to reach him with my mobile but he didn't answer. So I put me head round the door and told his wife, Lucy.'

'Mr Doyle, you are a freelance marine mechanic. I would have thought that thieving boat engines would not be a smart move.'

'Too right, Miss. A lot of people give me work and Smidgin

knows that.'

'Tell me, Mr Doyle, have you done work for Mr Smidgin before?'

'No, that was first time. He usually does his own jobs. Got to hand that to him, he's good with engines.'

'Thank you, Mr Doyle. That is all.'

The prosecutor cross-examined Doyle on dates and time and other minutiae. The man remained unmoved and stuck to his story.

Emily glanced at the jury. They looked puzzled and slightly dissatisfied – good.

The judge looked around the court. 'We are proceeding on time. Miss Simpson do you want a recess or shall we continue?

'I have witnesses waiting, your Honour,' said Emily. 'I would prefer to press on.'

'Very well, call your next witness.'

'I would like to call Sir Roger Cornside.'

Emily heard the intake of breath and the subdued muttering. Cornside was a businessman and landowner and the current High Sheriff of Hampshire. Even the judge looked startled.

Cornside took the oath in a languid Etonian drawl and turned to regard Emily.

'Sir Roger,' she began. 'You are commodore of a Hamble yacht club and you are a well known figure in the local boat world.'

'Yes, you could say that.'

'I understand that you also had some motors stolen recently?'

'Yes I did.'

'Can you tell us the circumstances?'

'My main boat was moored at Hamble Point with our tenders lying alongside. In the morning we found all their motors were missing. It was particularly distressing because the little motor on my grandson's Mirror dinghy had been his birthday present.'

'Can you identify your motors for insurance purposes?'

'Your Honour,' the prosecutor intervened, 'Counsel is misleading the court by bringing in an unrelated crime.'

'Nevertheless, I am intrigued and I think the jury are entitled to see where Miss Simpson is leading us.' The judge nodded to Emily.

'Sir Roger?' she asked.

'My wife is a keen engraver and we marked the motors in an obscure part of the inside casing.'

This was the moment. Would her gamble work? 'Sir Roger, does the motor exhibited look like one of yours?' The whole room was hushed and Emily could sense the tension.

‘Yes,’ said Cornside. ‘I think it could well be my Yamaha four-stroke but I would welcome the chance to look closer.’

‘Your Honour?’ Emily looked at the judge.

‘Indeed, let the witness examine the exhibit.’

Cornside left the stand and walked to the engine. He released the clips holding the upper casing and removed it. ‘Yes, my goodness! There’s my postcode where Susan engraved it. Have we a magnifying glass? It’s very small digits but she’s clever that way.’

‘Sir Roger,’ Emily was overwhelmed with relief but it mustn’t show. ‘Sir Roger, did you buy this motor from Mr Smidgin?’

‘No, I did not. I bought it from Rawlins, the main dealers.’

‘Can you explain why Mr Smidgin’s company plaque is fixed to the case? Mr Smidgin has already told the court that he places all his plaques with his own hands. Can you furnish the jury with an explanation?’

‘I would prefer to leave that to them.’

Emily sat down.

‘Sir Roger,’ said the prosecutor. He didn’t look particularly put out and Emily guessed he had probably had enough of Smidgin. ‘Sir Roger, it is clear you do not know who stole your motors.’

‘Agreed.’

‘So it is not beyond the bounds of possibility that the defendant Doyle stole them before he stole Mr Smidgin’s boat.’

‘I really couldn’t say.’

‘Your Honour I have no further questions for this witness.’

It was Emily’s turn again. ‘Call Darren Smith.’

The taxi driver took the stand looking even more morose. No doubt he was calculating the number of fares he was missing.

‘Mr Smith,’ said Emily, ‘did you have a call to fetch a passenger from Harbour Close on the afternoon of July 30th?’

‘That’s right.’

‘Mr Smith, could you reply louder so that the jury can hear you?’

‘I said yes, didn’t I?’

‘Thank you. Can you tell us if there was anything unusual about this passenger?’

‘You bet I can. Lady what’d been beaten up bad.’

‘Did you know this lady?’

‘Not personal like, but she’s Smidgin’s missus, that Lucy, but we didn’t see her out and around much.’

‘Where did you drive her to?’

‘Just up the road to Wickham. She paid in twenties and let me keep the change.'

'Do you know of her connection to the defendant?'

'What, Andy Doyle? Yeah, Lucy's his bit on the side. Only a few weeks back Wally Smidgin found out. I heard him in the pub.'

'Mr Smith, this could be critical to the case in hand. What did Mr Smidgin say in the pub?'

'He shouted he'd kill 'em both. Don't know if he meant it but he sounded evil.'

Emily handed over to the prosecutor.

'Mr Smith, we may disapprove of Mr Smidgin's bluster and more so of his treatment of his wife, but I fail to see the connection with the defendant's thieving of his property. If he was angry with Doyle surely that was a more likely cause?'

'Sorry, mate, but it didn't seem that way to me. It was Doyle knocking off his missus that was aggravating him and I tell you something else. The barney in the pub was five days before Smidgen says his gear went AWOL.'

The prosecutor gave up and nodded to Emily.

'I would like to call my final witness. Mrs Lucy Smidgin.'

The atmosphere in the court could be described as electric without stating a cliché. Lucy Smidgin was a petite woman and would be pretty without her bedraggled state and the wound dressing over her left eye.

She took the oath with quiet confidence.

Emily addressed her gently. 'Can you tell us what happened on the 30th July?'

'The bastard beat the shit out of me. But I tell you all; he set up Andy with his lies. He boasted he'd get him sent to jail…'

'You deceitful little two-timing bitch!' Smidgin was standing inside the room uncalled for. He shook his fist at Emily. 'I wanted that Andy Doyle out of my hair and as for you,' he pointed at Emily, 'she's a bitch but you are a fucking witch.'

'Silence!' the usher roared.

'Officers,' the judge spoke. 'Remove that man.'

Smidgin was escorted from the court by police officers as he struggled and shouted.

'I am calling a short recess,' said the judge. 'The jury may withdraw and I wish to see both counsel in my chambers.'

Emily and the prosecutor followed the judge into his private robe room. The judge looked at the prosecutor. 'I intend to direct the jury to give a verdict of not guilty. Do you accept that?'

'Certainly, Sir; there's nothing left for me but accept the obvious.' He held out a hand and Emily shook it.

Judge Groves, fixed Emily with a quizzical stare. 'Tell me, Miss Simpson, are you quite certain that your father was not Perry Mason, because what I've witnessed this afternoon would perfectly match one of his scripts.'

Emily found herself shaking with the effects of the aftermath. She had won. She had laid down a spectacular marker for her future but she felt depressed and tearful. She had driven cross-country and had deviated from her route until she stopped on Old Winchester Hill. She was not far from the Sustainability burial wood where her mother had insisted her body must go when the time came. Emily didn't like to think of that. Dad might have narrowly escaped from his stroke but Mum seemed immortal. But none of them were immortal, and put into perspective Emily's own little triumph today looked pretty puny.

Smidgin had been arrested outside the courtroom. The man had shouted obscenities and threats at Emily even as he was being taken away. She was beginning to feel scared. What if he turned violent to both Tom and her? She wanted the comforts of parents and her old home. She returned to the car and drove down into the village of East Meon. Half an hour later she was at Firs Farm.

'Hi there, Sis,' Johnny greeted her. 'You're famous. Your case was on South Today telly.'

'What,' Emily was startled. 'How would they know about it?'

'I dunno, but they were full of it. Didn't mention you, but the police stood outside the court and made a climb down apology statement. It was a laugh.'

'At least they never mentioned me,' said Emily.

'Why not? Looks like you sort of scored the winning try and then kicked the points.'

'I know, but the man they've arrested for perjury is a nasty piece of work and violent. Quite honestly both him and the guy he was trying to stitch up must be pretty thick and it showed in court.'

'My darling, oh, we are so proud of you.' Mum had rushed outside and was hugging her and Dad followed grinning all over his face.

'Tony Travis rang us half an hour ago. The man prosecuting is a friend of his and he told Tony all about it. Emily sweetheart, Travis says you've got the whole bar profession buzzing. He said it might have been a small local case but you have made one hell of an impression.'

'Have I? Trouble is I had personal motivation. Do you remember that man at Warsash ten years ago? The one who yelled at me and Johnny and then threatened to punch you.'

'I'm not likely to forget. Your mother wanted to scratch his eyes out.'

'Well, Dad, it was the same man, Smidgin. The moment I heard it was him I decided to do my own sleuthing. They told me in the pub that Smidgin's wife was having an affair with the defendant and that she'd run to a women's refuge.

'Someone told me to find Roger Cornside and he told me about the outboard motors he'd had pinched and he'd actually seen Smidgin acting a bit odd. So, it's not me so much; it seems there were dozens of people out to get him, Smidgin that is, me included. And then I could hardly believe it when Smidgin forced his way back into court and admitted he'd set Doyle up and the whole thing was a con.'

'He really did that? Emily that's what used to happen in Perry Mason…'

'Dad, I wish someone would tell me who this Perry whatnot is. Everyone keeps mentioning him and old William idolised him. The judge today said I was like him but I haven't a clue who he was.'

Mum was giggling like a schoolgirl. 'He was on the TV in Denmark when I was a kid. The lawyer detective: American. Used to take on hopeless defences, then he would demolish the district attorney and the sheriff's case and the real villain would jump up and say: "Yes, it was me – I did it and I'm glad.'

Emily was laughing herself now. 'I can see why the judge saw a resemblance.'

Tom had left for Olifa yesterday to prepare for the team's arrival. Emily did not care to go back alone to the Alresford flat. That night she dreamed of Smidgin glowering at her. He was in the house, she could hear him clumping up the stairs. There was someone else with him and she could hear her muttering. It was the Larranaga woman from the fire siege.

Emily awoke, her naked body rigid with fright and oozing sweat. She sat up and looked around. It was yet another nightmare but she was safe in the familiar surroundings of her childhood bedroom. Years ago, in the aftermath of her abduction, she would have run to her parents for comfort. Not now, she was a grown woman with a career, a future husband and a goal to achieve in her sport. Quietly she slipped downstairs to the kitchen and made herself a cup of tea. Returning to her bed she slept undisturbed until the morning light filtered through her window to start another day.

The unwelcome phone call came just as the family were finishing breakfast. Kirsten took it in the office.

'I'm Peter Wilkins press officer RYA,' said the caller. 'I'm ringing to say, has Emily seen the article in the *Daily Postman*?'

The *Postman* was not a paper that Kirsten would normally have in the house. It was a far right tabloid, beloved of Middle England, with a constant xenophobic theme. As an immigrant herself, and one of Jewish extraction, the paper's carping at her and her like had always made her feel insecure. God only knew how the real ethnic minorities felt.

'Sorry,' she replied, 'but we don't read that paper. What's the problem?'

'There's an article attacking our Olympic team selection and Emily is mentioned. It's a rather silly piece and the British Olympic Association intend making a formal reply. Personally I wouldn't dignify the trash with one.'

Kirsten rang off and promptly left the house and drove down the quarter mile to the village shop. She returned with a copy of the *Postman.*

She found the article on page six,

HOW BRITISH IS YOUR OLYMPIC TEAM?
Michelle Le Bois investigates.

The article was pure poison. The writer began by listing athletes, some household names, who had African or Caribbean parents, and sniped at one girl born in Ghana. The writer was very careful not to use the word, *black*, Kirsten noted.

What has happened to the great traditions of Britishness laid down by Liddle and Abrahams? The rant continued.

Yes, thought Kirsten, Abrahams, who had been condemned at the time for his Jewishness by the same later pro-Hitler newspaper. She felt like spitting.

In no way is this opinion based on racial difference. Postman readers have no bias…

'Oh yes, and is the world flat?' Kirsten muttered.

'Look down there,' it was Steve pointing to the text. 'Where it says: SAILING.'

Take for example the three charming young ladies selected to sail for Great Britain.

Chloe Te-Koote, an ethnic New Zealander. Erin Walsh, born in Dublin. Emily Simpson of Danish and German extraction…'

'Bloody hell!' Kirsten clenched her fists and yelled. 'I'm not standing for this crap. Steve, it's got to be racial incitement…'

'It's a bit near the edge but it is opinion. I doubt we would have any legal challenge.'

'Legal,' said Emily who had joined them. 'What's all this about?'

Kirsten handed her the paper. She expected that Emily would react with anger but not this blazing fury.

'Bitch – dirty vindictive little bitch!' Emily hurled down the newspaper.

'What on earth…?'

'You see that name, Michelle le Bois, it's got to be the same one. Oh I wish Tom was here.' Emily picked up the paper and jabbed a finger at the thumbnail picture at the top of the article. 'That's her – I'd know her anywhere. Does the editor of the *Postman* know she spent three months in a French jail for sabotaging our boat?'

'Sweetheart, what are you talking about?'

'She's the same one we caught in Hyeres that night and that's not all. Tom was approached by this Michelle. She was with Sid Everett at the time, so I guess she is a journalist. It's me she wants disqualified from the Olympics not these other athletes.'

'That's crazy,' said Steve. 'The man got himself killed.'

'Tell you what,' said Kirsten, 'I've just remembered. Tony Travis left a message. Says he tried to reach you on your mobile.'

'Oh no. I turned it off.'

'Emily,' said Kirsten, 'ring him now and tell him about the paper. If we can sue this Le Bois woman we'll back you.'

'Tony's seen the article,' said Emily. 'He says it's crafty and nothing in it is actionable.'

'Darling, I'm so sorry,' said Kirsten. 'It's rotten the way the sun cult still follows you. How can that stupid woman think you had anything to do with that policeman being shot?'

'I know, but Tony says there's nothing she can do about the Olympics and everybody will forget it if we bring back a medal.'

'Em, is there something else that's wrong?' Steve asked.

'That's perceptive, Dad. I'm not sure, but Tony wants me to go over to the Island and go to Parkhurst Jail. There's a poor man in there who's been locked up for twelve years and now they've found DNA proof that he's almost certainly innocent of the crime he was convicted. Tony's his brief in the appeal next month. But it's not that: there's something else.'

'Go on,' said Steve.

'That horrible Joel Simons is in there and he wants to talk to me.'

'Good God,' said Steve. 'You don't have to do that. The cheek of the man after what he tried to do to you.'

'No, Dad, I think I ought to. Tony says the man has written a letter telling his fanatics that my DNA is genuine and I'm not related to Hitler or that Gobbles. Tony's been given a discreet contact to hand it to.'

The next day, Emily took the Isle of Wight Ferry and drove to Parkhurst prison. There, having completed the entry formalities, she was shown into an interview room. Emily had a cold reception from the prison staff. They had made it clear in so many words that the appeal was nonsense and, had her client been innocent, he would never have been tried. Emily studied the sad-faced prisoner as he was brought and seated opposite her. She wondered if this would in fact be a happy release. The man was wholly institutionalised. He had three meals a day, a tedious routine that he was accustomed to and even friends that he would miss. Justice was justice however and somewhere out there was the real murderer who had escaped retribution for far too long.

The man was escorted from the room and it was now that Emily began to panic. The prison authorities had agreed to Travis's request for Simons to meet Emily. Now she felt the claustrophobia of this place; the unique smell of prison and the echo of harsh male voices. Emily began to hyperventilate, she was about to meet the man who had wanted to mutilate her and ruin her life. Now she had just discovered that she already had the makings of the child inside her. She wanted to escape from this awful place and run out into the fresh air.

Simons entered, manacled to an officer. He looked older and

greyer than the man she remembered from the Haifa yacht club and the ill-fitting prison uniform was at odds with the elegance she had seen then.

'Simons,' said the officer. 'Sit down and be polite to the lady or we stop this interview.'

'Miss Simpson,' said Simons. 'You are older than I recall. I wish to apologise to you.'

'Whatever for?'

'I am now satisfied you are not who I supposed you to be. I will never apologise for the retributions I carried out against living Nazis, but to harm an innocent young life was unpardonable. I accept that you are innocent of any connection with the evil men.'

Emily took a deep breath. She fixed the man with her coldest stare. 'Very well, I believe you.'

Simons continued and Emily had to strain to hear his voice. 'There are others who do not accept the DNA proof. My only wish is to protect you from them. I have written this letter.' He held up an envelope. 'The authorities here have censored it but the meaning is still clear. I have addressed it to the lawyer Travis and he will see that it is delivered.' He passed the letter to Emily, nodded to the warder and was led from the room.

Somehow Emily found herself outside the prison walls and once more in the beautiful sunshine. She took her car and drove into Cowes. Here she walked along the sea front past the Yacht Squadron building and stood looking at the water. Now she wept, shaking convulsively and dabbing her eyes with a damp handkerchief.

'You all right, Miss?'

She looked round to see the concerned face of a policeman.

'No, I'm fine. I'm just being a bit stupid.'

'I should keep back from the edge there. You don't want to do something you might regret.'

Oh God, thought Emily, he must think I'm going to do myself in. The thought of the little germ of new life inside her jerked her into reality.

'I'm sorry,' she fixed him with a watery smile. 'I'd better get back to my car or I'll miss the ferry.'

Kirsten looked up in surprise as Steve clumped into the kitchen waving a cardboard packet. 'What do you think this is?'

'You know perfectly well what it is,' she replied. 'It's a pregnancy test kit.'

'And who is using it?'

'Well it's not likely to be me is it?'

'All right, Dad. It's mine,' said Emily.

'Are you telling me that you are pregnant and not married,' her father growled.

'Ignore him, Emily,' said Kirsten. 'He and I were coupling like rabbits for a whole year before we tied the knot.'

'We were careful.' Steve replied. 'Or at least I was.'

'Dad, we've been bloody careful for four years, but we're getting married as soon as we're home from Olifa. I think we can be forgiven one slip up.'

'Does Tom know?'

'He knows I missed a period. Actually he's rather hopeful that I am preggers.'

'Don't you realise you are about to sail in Olympic competition?'

'The doctor says that's fine. For Heaven's sake I'll only be six weeks or so when the competition starts.'

Kirsten intervened. 'I won my last big wind surfing trophy with you inside me.'

'Wow, Mum. I never knew that. Hi, extra ballast.'

'You were very tired all that week,' Steve added.

'I was knackered, but that was nothing to do with the baby and the exercise was just the thing.'

'What about morning sickness and all those sorts of women's things?'

'Dad, you are a chauvinist dinosaur. It's *morning* sickness. Even if it does hit me our races don't start till the afternoon session. Anyway, I may not get it.'

Steve sighed. 'I just do not know what society is coming to when in my young day…'

'Was that in Victorian times?' Emily spluttered.

'In Victorian times this nation was great, young lady.'

Kirsten changed the subject. 'Tom rang earlier. I was going to tell you but with all this shouting match I haven't had a chance. Well, he's arrived in Olifa and he says the match racing boats are there and the quarters in the village are great. He sounded pretty jetlagged by the way.'

'Good thing,' said Emily.

'Why do you say that?'

'He'll be too tired to jump into bed with Maria.'

Kirsten glared. ‘Do you think that likely?’

‘No, she fancies older men.’

‘What’s more important,’ said Steve, ‘did he say if my boat’s there?’

‘Yes, dear,’ said Kirsten. ‘Your boat arrived by airfreight yesterday. Tom says it’s there safe and sound as are all the UK boats. He made a point of checking.’

CHAPTER 31

'Jeez, what do I look like?' Chloe glowered in the full-length mirror and moaned.

'Never mind,' Erin grinned. 'Look at the label. It's high fashion; designed by Julian Paraquois.'

It was the last day of the assembly camp and the teams were donning their formal Olympic uniforms prior to the flight to Olifa. Chloe knew she must look something of a cartoon character in this combination of pleated blue skirt, white blouse, plus lurid red jacket and she hadn't worn white ankle socks with black shoes since she was a twelve-year old.

'I think you look rather sweet,' said Emily.

Chloe glared at the girl. 'I'd like to see you get into this rig in six months time.'

Emily's pregnancy, now medically confirmed, had come as a bombshell for Chloe. Not that she disliked kids; after all she was fond of her two nephews. But the whole messy business of conception and childbirth was alien to Chloe and to her sexuality.

The team medics had insisted the pregnancy was in too early a stage to affect Emily's crewing. Now Erin, who had just got engaged to her boyfriend, was becoming visibly broody. Chloe could only thank the heavens that they would all be in secure man-free purdah for the duration of the games.

'Say, Em, have you told your boss man?'

'About the baby? Yes, of course. He says get the family going and then the career. It's what Angela and he did. I can work almost up to the last minute, then take a break for the birth.'

Chloe wondered. She wished she understood the heterosexual world better. Emily's family was wealthy enough to hire nannies and all that and she couldn't see Tom staying home to mind the baby. Emily's rise to QC might take a year or so longer. Still, plenty of others had done it. Who was that woman business tycoon with a pliant house husband and six kids?

The three of them wandered outside onto the wide tarmac of the old abandoned airfield just as the team's coaches began to arrive to carry one hundred plus athletes and officials to Heathrow. This would not be as long a trip as the one to Auckland but heading west across several time zones it would definitely be an interesting arrival.

'This is a bit better.' Steve waved that morning's *Daily Postman*. 'The reader's letters are fantastic. Apart from one statement by the British Purity Party all of them have torn the Le Bois woman to pieces. Two people have identified Emily as the girl from the fire siege and they are pretty bloody angry about Le Bois's comments.'

'Good,' said Kirsten. 'And are you still angry?'

'Of course I am. What that woman wrote was dead out of order.'

'I don't mean the article, I mean about Emily and the baby. I told you I thought your behaviour was a disgrace. For God's sake you're going to have another grandchild.'

'I know. It was a bit of a shock that's all. But as they're getting married soon…'

'They've been together for over four years. They deserve to be happy. I'm going to make sure they have a beautiful wedding.'

'At a beautiful cost,' Steve grunted. 'That's the problem with daughters.'

'Remember when Sarah married it was all so low key. I think we deserve a real family occasion.'

Steve smiled and embraced his wife. 'It'll be two families celebration. Peter and Carol will have to be a big part of it.'

'Come on,' said Kirsten, 'let's drive down to the sail loft. We've got a really good order to complete and then it's off to Olifa and watch the girls in action.'

From the air conditioned comfort of the Boeing to the equatorial heat of the Enrique Castor Airport was a shock to Emily and every one of the athletes. They walked to the magnificent terminal building: all glass and copper domed with unusual sculptures on the forecourt. Even Chloe, used to the warmth of New Zealand's North Island, was not prepared for the humid blanket that enveloped them and the garish uniforms the girls wore did not help. Emily looked around and noticed others worse affected by the heat, including the red-haired Scottish cyclist, who with sweat pouring off his brow, swore softly in colloquial Glaswegian. The whole assembly passed through the entry formalities in the relative air conditioned cool of the terminal. The team was met by the British Ambassador and welcomed by the Olifarian Sports Minister. Other nation's teams were arriving by the hour and more diplomats were gathering as the British athletes departed to board their coaches for the Olympic village.

They drove along the highway towards the impressive city skyline with its glass and concrete skyscrapers. Emily had been warned by her mother about the shanty towns beside the freeway but it seemed these had been mysteriously cleared. Suddenly in front of them was the giant Olympic stadium, enlarged, shining and refurbished from its days as a football ground. Beside the stadium was a tree-lined avenue that led straight into the competitors' village. Village, thought Emily, was a complete misnomer. The place they were entering was a small town with seemingly miles of identical bungalows, mini villas and streets with familiar names: *Calle Carl Lewis, Calle Emil Zatopek, Calle Sebstian Coe, Calle Paavo Nurmi, Calle Mark Spitz,* and then, to Emily's delight, *Calle Ben Ainslie*. To her regret the coach passed it and shortly afterwards turned into *Calle Kenenisa Bekele,* which led to *Calle Stephen Redgrave,* which was to be the home of the Great Britain women's team.

The athletes climbed down from the coaches to stand once more in the stifling heat and near blinding sunshine.

'Christ this is hot,' said Chloe.

'I know,' said a tall young man who had overheard her. 'What's your sport? I'm in Pentathlon. We were pre-warned and a lot of us have been training in North Africa.'

'Don't blame you,' said Chloe. 'We're sailors and it's always that little bit cooler at sea. But this place is a sodding oven.'

'It's cooler at night I'm told,' said their new friend. 'Or I bloody hope it is.' Emily noticed that the man was looking with interest at both Erin and herself.

'Won't do you no good there, mate,' said Chloe. 'Both these two are spoken for and she's got a bun in the oven.' Chloe pointed at Emily.

The young man failed to take offence but grinned and made off towards his fellow athletes.

'Chlo', do you have to be so bloody crude?' Emily was not pleased.

'That's our Kiwi way. Tell it as it is.'

'We have noticed,' said Erin. 'Oh, look there's your Tom.'

Emily followed her friend's outstretched hand and, yes, there was Tom threading his way through the crowd. Emily ran, dodging the athletes, and grounded hand luggage to fling her arms around her man.

'Welcome, to Olifa,' said Tom. 'I've got your allotted house number. You're with a couple of badminton girls, but you can swap if you don't get on. Andrea and the other Brit girls are a few doors down. The lads are all in *Bob Beamon* street, that's a few blocks over there.' He pointed.

'Segregated are we?' said Chloe.

'You bet your life you are. This is a different world. No alcohol, no fatty food and definitely no sex!'

'We know all that already,' said Emily. 'That's the way it's gotta be if we're to win things.'

'You can go and have a chat to Maria. The Olifa girls are all in *Calle Garcia.* You can guess what Maria says about that.'

'That's not the Garcia we know?' Emily was surprised.

'That's him. He's the only Olifarian to win an Olympic medal since nineteen hundred and something, so they are all rather proud of him. Even if he did have a peek at your tits that time,' Tom smirked.

Emily fixed him with her practised courtroom gaze. 'What have you been up to with Maria?'

Tom didn't reply but grimaced at the other two girls. 'I helped her,' he said.

'Helped her with what?'

'I helped her lift her Laser off a car roof rack. It was a rather nice car as it happens. A genuine Roll-Royce Silver Shadow, mid-sixties, beautiful to touch – and her father was driving it.'

Having been mildly baffled at first by the whole circus, Emily was beginning to enjoy herself. By now the village was already filling with a thousand or more persons of every nationality, and the whole complex had descended into a Babel of languages from every corner of the globe. In some cases the pre-assumed stereotypes were true. Americans were noisy and swaggered, Spaniards were elegant and imperious, Australians laidback and untidy, Chloe's New Zealand Rugby Sevens squad silent and menacing, the Japanese smiling and polite, Chinese guarded and inscrutable, and so it went on. The Brits still retained an element of the old gentleman amateur's disdain for this cosmopolitan uproar. Emily and her friends knew this was false. Her fellow countrymen and women were as psyched up to win as anyone else.

The girl badminton players who shared their villa were initially as quiet as mice. The two well-built older teenagers had limited conversation only for their game. Emily came to the conclusion that these two were not the sharpest tools in the box mentally, however good their on-court speed and co-ordination. Their play venue was within walking distance whereas the sailors needed specially laid on mini-buses to run them the two kilometres to the yacht harbour. A pair of girl rowers in the next house complained that they had a five-mile trek to their lake. Everyone was tense and uncertain about the hours of standing around at the opening ceremony in four days time. After that, serious competition began for sports outside the stadium, including sailing. However all these events were scheduled to finish before the athletic finals the following week. Television ruled the timetable these days and all must accept that.

Having helped the girls to settle into their quarters, Tom had left for his shared room in the yacht club. An hour later Maria knocked on their open front door and Chloe called out cheerfully in welcome. An increasingly sleepy Emily had been desperate for a shower only to find the badminton girls had taken the bathroom as theirs and seemed unlikely to quit it for a while.

'Emily, I need to have a word,' said Maria. She looked worried, and not her usual blasé self.

Emily beckoned her to follow into the kitchen. 'What's the problem?'

'It's about that man you wanted watching.'

Emily felt apprehensive. 'You mean Hammersen?'

'Yes, our London embassy had already issued a press visa. He entered Olifa three days ago and he had a woman companion. They have booked into a hotel off the Avenida.'

'How come you know all this?'

'Emily, it is reliable information. My father traced it for me from the Interior Minister and he didn't come cheap.'

'You mean you bribed someone?'

Maria sighed. 'Emily, this is Olifa and the minister went to some trouble to please my father. This is not England. If you believe no politician ever sold favours in your country, then I think you are deluded.'

Emily was puzzled by the news that Hammersen had a companion, a female one at that. Not so surprising, the man was reasonably good looking, however mad.

'Do you know the name of the woman with Hammersen?'

'Yes, she's another accredited journalist: name Le Bois.'

Emily was in double shock. 'Maria, that is the woman who we caught messing with our boat in Hyeres that time. You must remember. She was jailed for it. Can't you expel her? She's got a criminal record.'

'Sorry, Emily, but this is Olifa, not the United States. We are welcoming by tradition…'

'I heard you sheltered not a few escaping Nazis,' Emily interrupted. 'Why doesn't Hammersen hunt them and leave me alone?'

'Because we know they are all dead, and a good thing too.'

Emily sighed, she still wanted a cooling shower, but even more she wanted to collapse on her bed and sleep.

David Manning was a sports journalist and proud to be one. In his homeland of New Zealand he had been a failed rugby player, a failed cricketer and an even bigger failure as an athlete. If the truth was told, he wasn't the right build and fitness for any of these sports and he didn't have the resolve to find the focus and do the physical preparation. Sailing had been the exception. He had scored modest success on the small dinghy circuits and had gained more prestige when he had sailed two legs of the Round the World Race as a crewman for a Kiwi national hero.

Following this minor triumph, Dave had decided, as so many sports journalists had before him that: "those who can, do, but those who can't write about it". New Zealand had been too small a stage for Dave and he had found his way to London. Another stroke of luck had been for Dave to meet his idol, the *Daily Banner's* Sid Everett. Sid had liked the writing style of his protégé and had found him a post as an international sports reporter for the *Banner*. Now he was on a mission, to uncover the human-interest stories: the triumph of winning and the misery of losing. But Sid had briefed him on a second mission and the potential story that would make his name. Sid was retired now but had made this story his own. Dave was proud and grateful that Sid had delegated the investigation and the possible glory to him.

Dave managed after half an hour to find an empty taxi and, with two other reporters, he had told the driver to take them to the press hotel that Sid had pointed him to. The place was a massive glass and concrete structure only a few blocks from the old colonial city centre. Dave had already prepared his spiel in his sketchy Spanish, but in the end he didn't need it; the receptionist spoke excellent English. A one hundred dollar bribe secured him the hotel register and there, yes, only two hours earlier were the two names he had come to find and to watch.

Following eight hours of sleep Emily felt better, although she still couldn't get to grips with the altered clock times. She wanted breakfast in the middle of the afternoon. Chloe, who seemed immune to jetlag, had been up for three hours and already had done a training run around the village. The kitchen and freezer were well stocked so Emily was able to grab something suitable to eat before the bus arrived to run the sailors to their boats.

The marina complex reserved for the games was impressive. Tom was already waiting for them and, with a couple of local men he had stepped the mast and set up the rigging. 'You'll have to do any tuning allowed on the water,' he said.

Emily really couldn't concentrate. The sun shone and she was becoming accustomed to the heat. The sea beyond the docks was blue: the inviting Pacific Ocean ready and waiting. In a week's time she would be taking part in the competition she had dreamed of and worked for all her life. She walked away from the others and stared moodily at the turgid water by the slipway. Tom had followed her and she could see the concern written on his face.

'Em, darling, something's wrong.'

'Tom, it's Hammersen, he's here in Olifa with Michelle Le Bois. Simons told me Hammersen doesn't believe the DNA results. He's convinced I'm descended from Hitler or whoever.' She collapsed and clung to him. 'Oh, Tom, if he's here it can only mean he wants to harm our baby.'

Tom had clenched his fists and she saw the anger wash through him. 'Are you certain that man is here?'

'Yes, Maria's dad bribed a government minister and he traced Hammersen to a press hotel. He's registered as a journalist and so is that evil little bitch.'

'Which hotel? He's better not show his face around here.'

'Tom, no! You are not to go and take the law into your own hands. This is South America – you could be in terrible trouble. No, we'll go to Maria and see if her father can have the pair watched.'

'All right,' he grumbled, 'but you will stick with the crowd and not go anywhere on your own. That shouldn't be difficult. This is different to Israel. That bastard Simons had it easy and you were caught off guard. This time is different.'

That evening Maria collected the three girls plus Tom and whisked them away into the countryside. The car was a four-year old Jaguar that Maria drove with a degree of Latin flair. Her passengers were glad that the country roads were empty apart from a handful of battered pickup trucks and cattle lorries.

Emily felt better for having told Tom of her fears. He in his turn had gone straight to Maria and given her the facts. Maria had suggested that they talk to her father, and that anyway they had a dinner date at the Olivarez family's estancia sixty kilometres from the city.

Maria's family home was a genuine Spanish colonial house of modest proportions but inviting and friendly. Her parents greeted them at the top of a wide flight of steps. Maria's father was a tall man of dark complexion with a neatly trimmed beard. Her mother was a lady of middle years who still radiated the natural dark beauty that her daughter had inherited.

The father held out his hand. 'I am Francisco. Welcome to our home, my daughter's friends are our friends.' He shook hands with each of them. 'And now meet my wife, and she also is Maria.'

The older Maria smiled. 'Come and have a glass of our own red wine. Dinner will be served in half an hour. I hope you will enjoy a consommé of our finest beef.'

Once again, thought Emily, here was an Olifarian family who spoke perfect English, learned presumably at British public schools. The younger Maria took them on a tour of the house. It was a nicely proportioned dwelling, far more farmhouse than mansion, but redolent of old money. The furnishings ranged over three hundred years covering the whole of the Olivarez family's involvement with Olifa. On one wall of the ground floor was a full-length portrait of a man in flamboyant military uniform. Here was clearly a family member. To Emily the resemblance was obvious.

Maria noticed her interest. 'He is General Olivarez, my great-grandfather. He is one reason, but one only, of why we wish no friendship with Garcia.'

'We find Garcia a bit creepy,' said Erin, 'and he ogled down the front of Emily's dress and mine too.'

'When was this?'

'At a reception in England,' said Emily. 'He's one of those guys you can sense mentally stripping you.'

'I know, he has tried it with me, but I would never let that man touch me. It would compromise our family honour.'

'What's wrong with him?'

'Many years ago his grandfather was one who destroyed the traditions of our nation. Let me tell you: the name Olivarez means something, my ancestors came with Pizzaro, and once we had brought order to these lands we provided stability and quality to affairs.'

Emily had no idea what Maria was talking about. Her friend had changed in front of their eyes into the Spanish grandee lady of old. 'Maria; my school teacher said you had a revolution and it was a good thing.'

'Revolutions are not good: reform yes, but revolution no. The mining companies were bad, they controlled their executives with drugs and they exploited our people. Had I been alive then, I too might have supported the revolution.'

Emily the barrister was alert. 'Maria, aren't you contradicting yourself. Either the revolution was good or it wasn't.'

'No, Emily, the intentions can be good but the results bad. The Garcias were nothing, but they profited by the rebellion and now things are little better for the indigenous people who work the mines. My great-grandfather was never involved in the mining, but he was a patriot and a soldier. He had to sign the surrender of the lawful government army, and he never recovered from the humiliation. He had to leave the army, and our family have been excluded from political life ever since.'

Maria had an expression of real pain and Emily regretted her probing. 'Maria, I'm sorry.'

'Do not be. These things happen. But our people, the old families, who are rooted in the soil are now ignored and Garcia and his like rule instead.'

Emily wondered. The Olivarez family even now were clearly wealthy even if they had been excluded from Olifa's governmental corruption culture. 'What's your dad's job now, Maria?'

Maria sniffed audibly. 'We are forced to engage in trade. Think of that, a family as old and honourable as ours. My father imports and distributes farm tractors and machinery.'

Emily gave up. Maria and her family seemed to live on another planet. 'Hey, where's Tom gone?'

'He asked to speak in private with my father. It is something to do with these people you wanted banned from Olifa.' Maria winked at Emily. 'If you will excuse me, I will go shower and change.'

'Mr Stoneman, what you tell me is so bizarre, but I believe it. I have seen many such things happen on every continent of this troubled world.' Francisco Olivarez poured a glass of wine and handed it to Tom. 'Very well, this man is deluded. You and your fiancée are my daughter's friends. That is enough for me to act. You have not met my son, Rafael, Maria's brother, but he is a captain in our national military security service. I will talk to him and we will arrange to have this Hammersen watched.'

'Thank you, Sir.' Tom was both relieved and worried. Being under the protection of the secret police in a South American country was a novel idea that he would rather not think about.

'Mr Hammersen and his colleague have valid press credentials. However, should either misbehave they will be removed.'

'Thank you, Sir.' Tom could think of no other reply but he didn't care for this man's inflexion on the word "removed". Removal in South American parlance could have several different definitions.

Through the house the mellow beat of an old-fashioned dinner gong sounded.

'Come, Mr Stoneman, let us forget troubles and enjoy some fine Olifarian cuisine.'

Tom could not take his eyes off the younger Maria. The girl had transformed herself in a brilliant red gown that clung to her slight form. A modest cleavage was enhanced with a bright diamond-studded pendant. She paused at the top of the broad staircase and, with a dazzling smile, she walked gracefully down to join them.

The older Maria had also transformed herself and Emily felt a pang of jealousy. She wondered if she would look as good in years to come if she had reared two children to adulthood. The food was delicious, tasty and contained nothing contrary to their training rules. Emily, mindful of her pregnancy abstained alcohol, but the other three girls confined themselves to one glass of red wine. Tom as a team supporter had no such restriction and consumed the best part of one bottle. He had no idea how severe were Olifa's drinking and driving laws, he whispered, and was pleased that it would be Maria who would be driving them back to Olifa City.

They gathered outside the house while Maria collected her car. Tom put an arm around Emily. 'Señor Olivarez is going to arrange for Hammersen to be watched.'

'I know,' she said. 'Maria told me her brother is on the case.'

'You will still have to be careful tomorrow night.' This was the evening of the formal reception for the Great Britain team, one of those tedious affairs that most would rather miss but couldn't. 'I can't be there to watch you. I'm only a supporter. I've no official status, but the press are invited.'

'No, Tom, I will rely on Maria and her brother. I don't want you and Hammersen coming face to face.'

Dave Manning had identified Hammersen within his first hour in the San Valentine Hotel. The man had been drinking in the central bar accompanied by Michelle Le Bois, the freelance who had brought such a storm down on the heads of the *Daily Postman*. He knew from Sid Everett that there was some sort of relationship between these two and it was less romantic than a shared dislike of Emily Simpson.

'Have one on me,' said Dave. 'I'm told you're English speaking journos.'

'Sure,' replied Le Bois. 'What are you, an Aussie?'

'Excuse me,' Dave adopted a pose of one deeply insulted. 'I'm from New Zealand. That's not the same thing at all. The name's Dave, Dave Manning: reporting for the London *Banner* and the Auckland *Sentinel.* '

'Apologies,' said Hammersen. 'What sports do you cover?'

'Well we've a Kiwi rugby sevens team and that's big back home, and so of course is sailing and we've big hopes there.'

Le Bois gave Dave a sharp look that could in other contexts have been rude. 'How come your best woman sailor won't compete for you?'

'You're talking about Chloe Te-Koote. She's permanently resident in Britain, serves in their army. We would rather she sailed for us, but there you go.'

'And she sails with a foreign crew,' Le Bois sneered. 'One's Irish and the other's a bloody German.'

Good, thought Dave. Now we are getting somewhere. 'I've met Chloe's crew and they seem pretty English to me. Anyway Emily Simpson's mum and dad both won Olympic medals. He's a Brit and she's a Dane. What's wrong with that if the daughter was born in the UK?'

Hammersen looked edgy, thought Dave. Le Bois was letting her malice show too clearly and the man didn't like it. 'No reason why not,' he said. 'The rules allow it. Simpson is an arrogant woman but she was born in England and her mother has adopted British nationality.'

'Just because her bloody mother was born in Denmark it doesn't make her less of a stinking German,' said Le Bois. 'As for that Emily, she deliberately gets kidnapped and then lets a decent man be killed trying to save her.'

'Seems you don't like Germans,' said Dave. 'Isn't it time we moved on? World War Two's been over for nearly seventy years.'

'It'll never be over,' replied Michelle.

Hammersen intervened. 'The Nazi regime was wholly evil, but that evil will not be over until we have seen every last element of it is purged. Once that is done the Germans and the rest of the world can start afresh.'

Any doubts Dave might have had over Sid Everett's claims had evaporated. Hammersen was a fanatic. The tone of voice and the look in his eyes had given too much away, and if little Emily was his target Hammersen would need watching.

'That Chloe told one of the athletes that Emily is pregnant. "Got a bun in the oven", he said.' Le Bois almost spat the words. 'How can she compete in the Olympics like that?'

'Lots of girls have,' Dave replied. 'It's safe in the early stages.'

Hammersen looked shocked, almost stunned. He seemed to have forgotten that Dave was there. 'Michelle. This is disaster. Why wasn't I told?'

The two of them began a slanging match, while Dave quietly withdrew.

Emily's secret fear of morning sickness had come to nothing. Of course the time difference between the UK and Olifa meant that morning to her was still mid afternoon and that was exactly the wrong time to be spewing up food. They had been bussed to the yacht harbour and taken possession of their allotted boat. It seemed well constructed and the sails, although not their preferred fabric, were well cut, and anyway all the competitors were identically equipped. They had their first tryout sail in a moderate breeze blowing in off the Pacific. It was good to be afloat again, working as a team and doing what they did best. Emily was able to forget, almost, the aggravations ashore. She was here to win a sailing regatta and that was all that mattered. If only she could concentrate on that and not feel this threat to herself and her unborn child.

They were not the only craft afloat; the seaway was crowded with other newly arrived competitors. They needed to keep all their concentration to handle the boat and avoid nearby craft and the launch-loads of inquisitive spectators. One of these came far too close and Chloe was not happy. Emily saw her friend gesticulate and shout a warning. Her tone suddenly changed. 'Hi, Dave. What are you up to?' she yelled.

A man whom Emily thought she had seen somewhere was perched in the bows of an enormous RIB. 'Chloe,' he shouted back. 'I wanna talk to you guys in private.'

‘Why?’ Chloe replied.

‘Nothing to do with your sailing but it’s important.’ He spoke with a Kiwi accent Emily noted.

‘We’ll be at this shindig reception. Talk to you then.’

The boat was close to them now and Emily could see genuine concern on the man’s face. ‘Emily, there’s a man asking questions.’

‘So long, Dave,’ Chloe called. She pulled the tiller toward her and Emily had to concentrate on the following gybe. Some of the magic of the day had gone. She thought she knew what this man was talking about. She wondered if she should tell Tom.

Chloe was glad of one thing. They were not required to wear the schoolgirl style uniforms to the press reception; tracksuit trousers and matching tops would be accepted. She didn’t want to go to this do, but their national coach had insisted that it was a must. Chloe was reluctant, but Emily seemed to be scared of the event. Emily was a party animal normally, but something was troubling her. The silly girl was sitting morosely in a corner of the tiny lounge in their villa. Sherrie, the sweaty badminton girl, had snatched first place with the shower again but that was not the reason for Emily’s grumps.

After ten minutes Sherrie emerged towelling herself. ‘Sod this place. I’d no idea it was going to be this fucking hot.’ The girl let her towel fall and was standing stark naked swinging her badminton racket. Chloe noted the tiny firm breasts and the exaggerated upper body and thigh muscles. The girl’s black pubes were a contrast to her dyed blonde hair. ‘By the way, they delivered some special food for you boaty lot. We put it in the fridge. Looks like yoghurt pots.’

‘Thanks,’ said Chloe. ‘We weren’t expecting it, but a drop of yoghurt might slip down nicely. We weren’t expecting extra food. Who delivered it?’

‘Local Spanish bloke, quite sexy – couldn’t speak English. It’s in three little boxes with names on them.’

‘What names?’

‘Yours of course and the other two.’

Chloe couldn’t make this out. They had a strict diet regime, and the team officials had already packed the fridge and freezer with everything the girls might require for themselves, as well as for Sherrie and her team partner Saffron. Emily was a bit snooty about those two, but Chloe rather liked them, even though she must not allow herself to be diverted by the shapely body standing in front of her. Emily had dubbed the pair “typical Essex girls”.

Chloe made her own investigation of the fridge. It was true; three trays of yoghurt pots were in place on a shelf. The interior light in the fridge had failed and the setting sun was blinding her as it shone through the kitchen window. Chloe reached in and grabbed a pot and one of the little plastic spoons that lay in the tray.

'I'd like one as well,' said Emily as she in turn helped herself.

'Chloe pulled off the lid of hers and spooned a helping into her mouth. 'I don't think this is so good,' she said. 'It's been sweetened and I don't think I like it.'

'This one's all right,' said Emily. 'Hey, that's odd.' She held up the lid. 'It's got Erin's name on it. What does yours say?'

'I threw mine in the bin,' said Chloe. She was more puzzled than ever but she fished in the waste and found her discarded pot lid. 'That's got your name on it. Here, let me have a spoon of yours.' Emily held hers out and Chloe dug in for a spoonful.

'That's odd, it's different taste altogether, really nice.'

Chloe seized both pots and stuffed them in a plastic bag. 'I'm going to pass these to that team diet geek. We weren't told anything about this stuff. Now it arrives out of the blue. There'll be hell to pay if someone's spiked them with steroids.'

'Why should anyone do that?'

'Remember what Maria said about Garcia's betting ring? Your Tom says there's big money on us to take gold, or a medal anyway. Where's that bloody phone list?'

Chloe retrieved her mobile phone and called their team coach. She hadn't known what reaction she would receive, but in this case the man was alarmed. He told Chloe to stay put in the house while he made contact with the team dietician. Twenty minutes later he called back. They must not touch the yoghurt again. The trays would be collected and taken for analysis.

'I told him about Garcia and the gambling but he wasn't impressed. They're scared that some other team may be trying to sabotage us.'

'Did anything happen?' Tom asked.

'Nothing, just a lot of old farts making speeches, and we were all good girls and stuck to the orange juice,' said Emily.

She and the others were standing in the early sunshine on the edge of the marina. Emily knew what Tom was worrying about. 'No sign of Hammersen or that Michelle, but I did see the Kiwi reporter, Dave Manning. He's quite nice really, for a journalist. Anyway, Sid Everett told him some of what happened in Haifa three years ago.

He's promised to watch those two for us.'

'Have you had the test results on that yoghurt?' Tom asked.

'Nothing yet,' said Chloe. 'If they find steroids we are in deep shit.'

'Just as well find the truth now than a random blood test…'

'If I'm slung out Emily will have to helm,' said Chloe. 'I still think Garcia has something to do with it. The team diet guy says the delivery wasn't authorised, and they've no idea where it came from.'

Tom looked shocked. 'Garcia's an Olympic sailor. Would he really play a trick like that?'

'From what Maria says – yes.' Chloe caught him by the arm. 'Come on, Tom. Help us get the sails on. There's a launch waiting to tow us out to sea.'

'Hi – are you Dave Manning?' Tom asked.

'Sure, mate. What can I do for you?'

Tom held out his hand, 'I'm Tom Stoneman. I'm Emily Simpson's fiancé.'

Manning gripped Tom's hand. 'I've seen you with those Brit girls, so I guessed a connection. Emily's a nice girl, so you're a lucky bloke.'

'Thanks, I'm here as a sort of unofficial team manager, but tell me – Emily's worried sick and I think you know why.'

'OK, we'll talk, but not out here. There's a sort of tapas bar up a side alley off Clanroyden Square. Some of the press guys discovered it, but the place should be quiet about now.'

Tom looked at his watch. It read 1400, so well into afternoon siesta time. 'Yeah, all right, maybe we can exchange information.'

The bar was within walking distance in the heart of the most affluent district of Olifa City. Tom was relieved to find the place was quiet apart from a few drinkers. These included a group of worse-for-wear sports journalists with Olympic IDs around their necks.

'Mad dogs and Englishmen booze in the midday sun,' said Dave. 'Should be Kiwis and Rumanians…' he pointed at the gathering by the bar. 'Hold on and I'll buy us a bottle of local vino; it's good stuff in here.'

Tom found a table by a tiny window. Fortunately, this superior place had full air conditioning although the room was dimly lit. He could smell a delightful aroma of slow cooking food. He hadn't eaten yet and this looked a good place to put that right. Dave returned with two bottles and glasses and slumped down in the seat opposite Tom.

‘What do you know about Hammersen?’ Tom came straight to the point.

‘I know what I’ve been told, maybe you know more than me,’ said Dave. ‘He wasn’t at the reception last night nor was the girl Michelle.’

‘Hammersen believes that Emily is descended from the leadership of the Nazi party. There’s not a scrap of truth in that but he’s convinced, and he wants to stop the line perpetuating.’

‘Yeah, I gathered that much,’ said Dave. ‘He wants to stop your girl … well to be straight, stop her breeding. I gather he’s a bit late.’

Tom was stunned. ‘How the hell could he know that?’

‘Sorry, Tom, but it seems Chloe dropped it in the hearing of a Brit athlete and he told Michelle.’

Tom remembered: the man in the street when the girls arrived. Well Emily’s pregnancy was no secret and it would be a smack in the teeth for Hammersen.

‘Thing is, Tom, I was briefed by a London colleague…’

‘Sid Everett?’

Dave looked surprised. ‘Yeah it was Sid. He gets emotional about the sun cult business and he doesn’t want Emily hurt. Anyway, I found Hammersen in the San Valentine. I was quizzing him when Michelle dropped the bit about Emily expecting. I can tell you Hammersen went apeshit.’

‘Good.’

Dave sniffed his wine and promptly swallowed the contents in one gulp. ‘I should be careful. I saw enough that time to convince me the man’s deranged. Watch your girl around the clock and I’ll watch Hammersen.’

‘Team boss man wants to see us,’ said Chloe.

‘Why?’ asked Erin.

‘I dunno’ he wouldn’t say. But we’ve got to be in the Yacht Club in half an hour.’

‘What you lot done?’ asked Saffron the badminton girl.

‘I guess it’s those test results.’

‘Look, we was here when that yoghurty stuff was delivered,’ Sherrie chipped in. ‘If some bastards’ve laced it, then it’s never your fault. Tell ’em to speak to us, we’ll back you.’

‘Thanks, Sherrie, we’ll wait and see,’ said Chloe. ‘Neither me nor Em had much more than a lick, but I tell you, jeez, the stuff I tasted was foul.’

Their spirits sank as they entered the private lounge in the Yacht Club Nationelle d'Olifa. This was the first time they had entered this building, and it was an intimidating place of heavy furnishings and whirring overhead fans. In the room waiting for them were their team manager and also Samira their team doctor. The latter carried a clipboard with a computer print out. Chloe smelt trouble.

'Take a seat, ladies,' said the manager. He walked across the room and shut the door. He nodded to the doctor.

'We have the results of the suspected contamination,' said the doctor. Her face was expressionless. 'The foodstuff was not authorised by us and we have no idea of its source. Have any of you?' She stared at each of them in turn.

Get on with it, thought Chloe. Let us hear the worst you pompous floosie.

'We weren't there when it was delivered,' said Erin. 'Our house mates signed for it.'

'Very well: I'm pleased to say we found no performance enhancing substances, but one set of pots was heavily contaminated. Miss Simpson, they were the four pots with your name.'

'But you've just said there weren't any performance drugs,' Emily sounded indignant.

'That's what we can't understand,' said the doctor. 'The pots in question had extra sugar and also a high concentration of the plant fungus, ergot.'

'What's that?' asked Emily.

'It is, as I've said, a fungus that grows on the ears of corn crops and mature grass. It's not a healthy substance but it's widely used in illegal medicine in these parts.'

'Miss Simpson,' the team manager sounded distinctly hostile. 'You quite correctly registered with us that you are in the early stages of pregnancy.'

'Yes, I did.'

'You are here to compete in the Olympic Games on behalf of your nation. There can be no greater honour…'

'Look, mate,' Chloe had had enough of this. 'I'm not a Brit, I'm a New Zealander by birth, but we don't' faff around. We tell things as they are. I'm proud to sail for Great Britain, but I am not having my girls talked down to by a Pom like you, whatever posh school expelled you.'

Thc man failed to take offence but even smiled faintly. 'Doctor tell them.'

'Emily,' said the doctor. 'We cannot have you making yourself deliberately ill at a time like this simply for your own convenience. You will let down your friends and your country.'

'What do you mean?' Emily seemed near to tears.

'Olifa is a Catholic country. Pregnancy termination is not encouraged and very hard to obtain except in one way and that way is the substance ergot, the same as we found in your yoghurt pots.'

'I'm not aborting my baby – never!' Emily was standing fists clenched, eyes blazing with fury.

'In that case someone is planning to do it for you,' said the doctor.

'And we know who that is,' said Chloe.

'If what you say is true, Miss Simpson,' said the team manager, 'then there can be only one suspect.'

'Maria, I've got to do something to stop Hammersen,' said Emily. 'I can't go on like this. I came here to sail and to race but I can't concentrate. I'm frightened.' The tears were flowing again. Emily had tried to stay calm but she couldn't. She was scared, and worse, she was beginning to wonder if the stress would cause her pregnancy to miscarry and save Hammersen the trouble of anymore ergot laced drinks.

Maria put her arms around Emily and whispered softly in English mixed with Spanish words. It was soothing and at last Emily began to relax.

'Emily, my brother has reported to the interior ministry. Two days ago Mr Hammersen and his girlfriend hired a jeep and drove three hundred kilometres to Tulifa.'

'Where's that?'

'It is a small town in the Gran Seco; that is the copper belt to the east of here. My brother had men trailing him. You see, he already knew things about this man. Hammersen has meddled in our affairs before. We do not want trouble from terrorists, especially at this time in our history.'

'Is Hammersen a terrorist?'

'On his last visit four years ago a young man was murdered here in Olifa city. He was of German descent and the son of an infamous war criminal who had been wanted for crimes in Norway in the war. We knew that, but the young man had proved himself harmless. He was an Olifarian citizen and he was murdered in cold blood.'

'Hammersen did it?'

'Nothing was proved but he was suspected of being implicated.'

Emily was angry again. 'Then why let him back in here?'

'He is an accredited journalist and as I said, nothing was proved. But it was enough for our interior police to watch him, and my brother is doing just that.'

'Do you know why he went to this place?'

'To Tulifa? My brother says his agent saw Hammersen in talks with a man he knows as a drug dealer. That is almost enough to have him deported, but we have no proof of why he wanted to meet the man.'

'To get the poison to kill my baby.' Emily's eyes filled with tears.

'Emily, I have a plan. Please listen. It is still two days before our sailing starts. Tomorrow evening we will all be at the Olympic opening ceremony. Then the next morning you will be too ill to practice with your friends. You will be very ill with an undeclared sickness and we will make sure that Hammersen knows all about it.'

Emily felt her troubles recede a little. She always knew her friend was devious, but this could be a brilliant solution. There was one huge drawback. 'Maria, we need the practise on the water, all three of us.'

'I have spoken to Chloe and she says not to worry, you are already a great team. The important thing is you all keep fit and focussed, but Chloe says on the water can wait until you are well again.'

'But I'm not ill. It's all pretence.'

'If Mr Hammersen believes you are ill by his hand, then he will think that he has won.'

CHAPTER 32

'Long live St Trinians,' Tom spluttered as he viewed the girls' uniforms. 'Your friend Sherrie looks really sexy in that rig.'

'And I suppose that we don't,' said Emily.

'You said it. Have a good ceremony,' said Tom. 'I've got to get a move on myself. I've a ticket for a good place in the stadium.' He gave Emily a gentle hug. 'You will be careful; you know all that standing around, in your condition.'

'God, you men,' she grumbled. 'Anyway I can sit on the grass. There's acres of it outside the stadium and it's dry.'

Tom didn't envy the athletes who would have to stand around for a couple of hours, but he was all set to enjoy the occasion. This would be a once in a lifetime opportunity to see an Olympic opening.

The Olifa Angelo football stadium was breathtaking in its scale and its one-hundred-thousand seat capacity. Tom was impressed: compared even to Wembley or Twickenham, it was well designed and the vast crowd of ticket holders had no difficulty in finding the correct entrances and gangways within. It took Tom less than ten minutes to enter and take his numbered seat. He found himself high in the upper echelons and just above a gantry of television cameras. Below these were seats reserved for the world's press. It was a good position with a clear view opposite of the entrance through which the competitors would march, and through which the marathon runners would enter in two weeks' time. Military bands began to play a medley of marching tunes, then, with a mighty fanfare a limousine drove around the running track. The speaker system announced in several languages the arrival of President Marco Castor of Olifa. The Head of State took his place in a purple draped box with bullet-proof screens in front, although Tom looking down on the man's head, would have had no difficulty in shooting him had he been so inclined.

Now came the preliminaries. A rolling sea of small children whirling coloured ribbons performed acrobatics, massed ballerinas pirouetted. Then proud and fierce looking Ameroindians performed a ritual. Tom thought they would have cheerfully speared the re-enacting conquistadors who followed them given a different time and place. Finally the whole cast gathered in the centre, and the president spoke a welcome in six languages. He formally declared the games open in English in an accent that could have passed for well-educated Home

Counties. Kirsten Simpson who had met the man three years ago had told him that the president was a product of Eton and Oxford and the great nephew of the famous El Liberator. The man it was said had recently bullied, bribed and intimidated his parliament into making him president for life.

Finally, the athletes paraded starting with a trio from Andorra followed in alphabetical order by the nations of the world from the small contingents to the massed ranks of Chinese. Then, "the United Kingdom of Britain", no "Great" included there Tom noted. It was good to see the union flag carried by Britain's greatest sailor: the man with already five medals won. The team followed him, shambling nonchalantly round the track to a most pleasing applause from the locals. At least the Olifarians like us even if no one else does, Tom mused. He searched the column for a sight of Emily. He saw Chloe, she was unmistakeable anywhere, and then yes; he could see his Emily. She was walking in the middle of her group looking from side to side and upwards into the crowd. Something drew Tom's gaze downwards into the seats below the TV gantry, the press section. A man was standing, leaning forward, staring intensely through binoculars at the British team. Now Tom knew him. It was Hammersen and he was staring at Emily.

There came a hush. Everyone was waiting for the arrival of the torch and the lighting of the flame. Next a surprise. The torch entered the arena carried by a very old man. Supported by two young athletes he walked stiffly and slowly but with a pride that left the whole stadium spellbound. The public address explained that here, aged one-hundred-and-four was the last living survivor of the revolutionary army. The Olifarian spectators went wild and the President stood and applauded. The old man handed the torch to a teenage girl athlete who sprinted away and up a long stairway to light the Olympic flame.

'I saw you march,' said Tom. 'Are you feeling OK?'

Emily hung her arms around his neck. 'The answer is yes, and no.'

'What, not that morning sickness?' Tom was worried.

'No, I feel great, I feel fit and I feel hungry, but officially I am laid low and ill.'

'Explain, I don't get it.'

'We want Hammersen to believe I'm miscarrying the baby. It's as simple as that. So go spread the news around the whole of this bloody circus.'

Tom still didn't understand. 'Why now?'

'You haven't told him?' said Erin.

'No.'

'Then it's about time you did,' said Chloe. 'The poor bloke's got more right to know than anyone.'

Emily pushed Tom away and stood staring at him. 'Hammersen is an inept idiot. If that stuff tasted as bad as Chloe says I'd never have touched it.'

Tom was still baffled. 'What's the man done?'

'He arranged for that food delivery to this place. The little pots of yoghurt with our names on them. That was stupid in itself. If he'd just supplied us all with the same stuff it might have worked…' Emily whispered these last few words.

Tom put his arms around her. 'So it wasn't drugs. Are you saying that Hammersen tried to poison you?'

'That's about it. The yoghurt with my name on it was laced with some stuff, can't remember what, but they use it in these parts to provoke abortions in unmarried girls.'

'Bloody hell! That's it. I am going to kill him.'

'Tom, no! You will do nothing. It was Maria's idea. If this bluff works then Hammersen will leave me alone.'

'Will you get away with this? What about those two you're house sharing with? They yap away the whole time.'

'No, Sherrie and Saffron are in on the secret. They are as bloody mad about it as the rest of us. Believe me they'll keep their mouths shut. We're friends and they are now part of the plan.'

Tom left them and thumbed a lift with the mini bus for the harbour. This morning there was less activity. Tom guessed the sailors, like all the athletes, were recovering from the previous evening. He saw no one he knew until Dave Manning hove in sight.

'Hi, Tom any news.'

'Not good. Emily's been taken ill.'

'Sorry about that, mate. What is it? A touch of the Mumbai belly.'

'The what?'

'Tummy trouble.'

'Could be something like that.'

'Tom,' Dave stared at him. 'Don't want to seem nosy, but Hammersen spoke to me earlier and he was sort of hinting about Emily. Asked how Chloe was and then he said one of the girls was poorly and might not be competing.'

Good, thought Tom. It's working. 'If he asks again you can be frank. Tell him Emily's a bit off colour but not enough to involve the team doctor.'

Poor Emily, thought Tom. Your hypothetical illness is going to get a lot worse in the next twenty-four hours.

'How did it go, Sherrie?' Emily asked. Their housemates had arrived back from their first match smiling and sweaty.

'It was a dream, really wicked. Polished off the Mongolian pair three nil,' said Saffron. 'Won't be so easy tomorrow. It's Anneka and Julie, the Dutch girls. They're tough.'

'Say, that guy out there in the street,' said Sherrie. 'There's sommink' weird about him and he's not moved for ten minutes.'

'Let me see.' Emily took a peek through the Venetian blind covering the open window. 'Oh, shit, it's him, it's Hammersen.'

'Right,' said Sherrie. 'Game on. Let's wind up the bastard.'

The two girls strolled through the front door into the street. Emily listened and watched.

'What do we do, Saff?' said Sherrie. 'She won't let us send for the doctor but I reckon she's losing it.'

'Yeah, that's a definite. Seen it before that time at school when Willow slipped her sprog in the playground.'

'Too right, just the same all that blood – not good.'

Sherrie spun round and stared at Hammersen. 'Oi, Mister. Your ears are flapping, nuthin' to do with you.'

'I'm most sorry,' he replied, 'but I couldn't help overhearing you.'

'Maybe, but there's nothing you can do. Our friend's in a bit of bother but we'll sort it, thank you.'

Hammersen nodded politely and sauntered away down the street. To Emily his back view said smugness.

Sherrie and Saffron returned indoors and collapsed in near hysterical laughter. 'Jesus fucking Christ,' Saffron gurgled. 'I reckon we could go for parts in Gravesenders. Hi, Em, do you reckon we fooled 'im?'

'Let's hope so. We've all got our events to win.'

'Mr Stoneman, I presume.'

Tom, absorbed in watching the yacht marina, had not heard this stranger approach. He turned round. The voice belonged to a middle-aged man. Tom had seen this character before but couldn't place him. He was a thin balding individual wearing white trousers and a British Olympic blazer. Too elderly and un-athletic to be a competitor, this was plainly an official of some kind.

'That's me. What do you want?'

'I would like you to accompany me to the yacht club. We need to have a talk.'

'What about?'

'You and Miss Emily Simpson.'

'Anything you need to say about Emily, you can say now.' Tom was angry. He took a step forward and it was nice to watch a flash of alarm cross the face of this seedy old fart.

'Please, Mr Stoneman. We are concerned about something and we think you may be able to reassure us,' a more conciliatory tone now.

'All right, lead on.'

Tom followed the man into the yacht club, across the foyer and down a corridor to a small office. Tom was ushered within to faced three more blazer wearers also middle aged and overweight. Tom felt a little better when he recognised one of them as Ken Littlecroft, a former sailing Olympian. But Littlecroft came from an earlier era; that of the gentleman amateur, selected primarily to represent the best of British and not expected to finish better than sixth.

Tom, not to be intimidated, took the initiative. 'What's this about?'

A man sitting in the middle of the group spoke. 'You are a friend of Miss Emily Simpson?'

'She's my fiancé, we're getting married in two months.'

'You know she's unwell?'

Tom knew now where this was going but he was not going to play the small boy before the head teacher. 'I think I am entitled to know who I am talking to.'

The man's expression changed from annoyance to indignation.

Littlecroft intervened. 'I cannot believe you do not know Oscar Priestman. He is the chairman and leader of our entire Olympic team.'

'All right,' Tom replied. 'I only remember a guy on the telly, in running gear, umpteen years ago.'

'A modicum of respect would do you no harm,' said Priestman. 'Let's come to the point. I think you have placed in jeopardy a likely Olympic medal.'

'I'm not a competitor. How the hell could I do that?'

'We have reports that Miss Simpson is ill. Someone infiltrated a noxious foodstuff into her quarters in the village. We suspect that you, Mr Stoneman, have poisoned this young lady, possibly with her complicity, in order to rid yourselves of an awkward complication.'

'I don't believe I'm hearing this. Look, Emily is expecting a baby in around eight months time. We are both looking forward to the event as the greatest thing in our lives. It's more important to Emily I can tell you than any sodding medal for you people to bask in and take all the credit for yourselves.'

'Careful, Mr Stoneman, that is slander,'

'Not half as slanderous as you implying we're deliberately aborting our child. Emily, you may not know, is a qualified lawyer. If anyone's going to face a slander trial it's you lot. If Emily wins a medal then that's more than any of you ever did. That hurts doesn't it.' Tom turned and walked from the room.

He somehow found himself once more at the waterfront consumed by the metaphorical red mist. He had wanted to shout the truth at those men and ram their false accusations back down their throats. He could not do that and jeopardise Maria's plan to force Hammersen to back off from Emily. It all depended on that man being convinced that he had caused Emily to lose her baby. The thought of that happening made Tom feel sick. He leant on a rail and glared moodily at the waters of the harbour.

'Please, Mr Stoneman, may I have a word?' It was Littlecroft. Tom had not seen the man leave the yacht club.

'I think you've said enough,' said Tom.

'Please, Mr Stoneman. I am really sorry if we caused you distress but we had to ask these questions. If neither Miss Simpson nor you had a hand in this matter, perhaps you could point us at who that person might be.'

Tom stared at the man. 'You mean you believe me.'

'Such was the force with which you spoke we could come to no other conclusion.'

'All right,' said Tom. 'I suggest you contact Captain Olivarez of the security police here in Olifa. His sister belongs to their sailing team. Find the man and tell him exactly what happened when you spoke to me.'

'Whoopee,' shouted Chloe. 'Here are the golden girls, or the bronze Poms.'

'How d'you know?' Saffron grinned.

'Satellite TV,' Chloe pointed at the big flat screen. 'You can watch us guys all next week.'

'Yeah, said Sherrie, 'but we've still got two more to go for the big 'un…'

'Or one for silver,' added Saffron.

Emily had watched the television with the other two, all three dancing around the room as their new friends smashed their opponents in the badminton quarterfinals.

'We've only just escaped the press men,' said Saffron. 'You wanna' watch out for that BBC bloke. I reckon he'd like to put his hand up me shorts and pull me thong off.'

'Tell you some more,' said Sherrie. 'That sneaky little Le Bois woman from the *Daily Postman* was asking questions about you, Em.'

Emily tensed. 'What questions?'

'Nosy little bitch. Said she'd heard you was ill, and would it affect your competition. Then she said could she speak to you.'

'Oh hell, what did you say?'

'I said you was ill, but you're feeling better but very down and you're not ready to talk to reporters.'

'Thanks, Sherrie.' Emily breathed an audible sigh and put her head in her hands.

Chloe was staring through the open door into the street. 'Here's Maria with a bloke. D'you reckon that's her boyfriend?'

Emily joined her. 'No, it's not one of her old men – he's too young, but tasty. What do you say, girls?'

'Wow, I'll say,' said Saffron. 'Real Latino sex on legs. Wouldn't mind a bit o' that.'

'Me too,' said Sherrie, 'but not until we've finished this tourno.'

'Hi there, Maria, come on in.'

Maria and the young man entered and were introduced to the girls. 'Please meet my brother,' said Maria. 'He is Captain Rafael Olivarez, and he is going to solve Emily's troubles.'

So this was the brother with a role in some obscure secret police. Emily looked again at the man. He was similar height to his sister and most elegant in white styled jeans, white jacket and white shoes. His open-necked shirt revealed a gold chain and an area of chest hair and tanned skin.

'Please, Miss Simpson, may we speak in private?'

'Of course, and please call me Emily.' She pointed him towards the tiny kitchen and shut the door behind them. 'Coffee?'

For the first time the man smiled. 'Thank you, but I had enough of your English instant in my school days.' Here was another Olifarian speaking perfect English.

'All right, Rafael, how can I help you?'

'It is more a case of how can I help you and your fiancé.'

'What have you in mind?'

'This morning I was approached by an official of your British Olympic team.'

Emily sighed. 'I can guess what's coming. Tom was rude. He told me.'

'Your chef of mission said your Tom was a most arrogant young man. They were offended but they believed him. So, this is our position. My sister has told us about the pressman Hammersen. We are aware of this person. He was implicated in the murder of an Olifarian citizen five years ago. He was not the one that pulled the trigger. We are sure that man is now in prison in England...'

'You mean, Simons.'

'Yes, but we are sure it was Hammersen who found and pointed Simons to the murder victim. So, we intend to deal with Hammersen. It was one of the reasons he was let into our country without questions and, now we find he is still creating mischief, the time has come to act.'

Emily was uncertain how to take this. 'What are you going to do?'

'We would like your friend Tom to identify Mr Hammersen as the man molesting you. We will then act.'

'Don't you know him already without involving Tom?'

Rafael shook his head. 'There are a thousand pressmen in Olifa for the games. Tom knows the man on sight and there must be no mistakes.'

Emily did not like this one bit. Here they all were in a strange country she had barely heard of a few years ago, and now she was being involved in something she didn't like the sound of. In that case it was probably better not to ask more questions.

'Miss Simpson, the eyes of the world are on Olifa for the first time since our revolution in 1927: in fact a very long time. We cannot and will not allow anything to besmirch the good name of our nation at such a moment as this.'

Emily was frustrated and fed up. 'Chloe, I can't stay in this house. We've only one more day to go before we start racing.'

'But you've still kept fit,' Chloe replied.

'Yeah, I've done hours of it; sit ups, push ups, running on the spot until I've almost worn a hole in the floor.'

Erin came into the room. 'Maria reckons you could go out in a while but you need to be inconsolable, which I think means look bloody miserable.'

'I feel more like punching someone in the face, that Michelle for starters.'

They were standing in the kitchen of their house with the overhead fan at full blast. It was hot and humid in what passed for spring on the equator. Chloe dipped a sponge in the sink and squeezed the contents over her head. 'At least it'll be cooler on the sea when we do start. It's this hanging around waiting.'

'It's all right for Saff and Sherrie,' said Erin. 'Their courts are air conditioned.'

'Someone mention my name,' Saffron had poked her head round the door. 'Oi, Em, you'd better watch out. There's an old guy outside wearing a British team blazer. Looks like they've come to check up on you.'

'An official?'

'Sure as 'ell he ain't a competitor.'

Emily wanted to hide. 'Oh, Chloe, what do I do?'

'Let's see what he wants first.'

Emily felt more apprehensive than she could remember, but followed Chloe into the front room.

Sherrie was looking through the window. 'That's the one – walks with a bit o' a limp like.'

Emily felt a wave of joy wash through her. 'Dad!' she screamed as she raced through the door and flung her arms around her father.

CHAPTER 33

Tom had good reason to be frightened. Being picked up by the police in South America was likely to mean trouble, danger or even death. He had been walking the streets not far from the yacht harbour when this car had drawn slowly alongside and stopped. The rear doors opened and Tom was hustled onto the back seat by two muscular white-uniformed thugs jabbering in Spanish. Neither they nor the driver seemed to speak English. Tom protested loudly but was ignored. The car drove through the streets of the city, siren screaming, and then took the same road that Maria had driven for her parents' house. After a few kilometres the driver braked hard and swung onto a concrete ramp that led through gates and a military guard post.

Tom remembered everything he had read about South American military cliques and their victims who disappeared never to be seen again. He could think of nothing that would make him the target of these people. He felt both defiance and despair. He thought of Emily and just how much she meant to him and he pictured her laughing with the sun in her hair, and then he thought of his parents in far away Duddlestone. Would he ever see any of them again? He looked out of the window and was surprised to see that this was not an army complex but an air base. He could see jet fighters parked, old types: Phantoms and Mirages, he thought, and on the tarmac in front of the control tower a modern helicopter with its rotors turning.

The car stopped and Tom was invited to climb out. He did so, relieved that none of the guards manhandled him. Instead they sprang to attention and saluted a young man in civilian clothes: smart all white casuals. 'Good morning, Mr Stoneman, welcome to the Archie Roylance Air base,' he held out a hand. 'Rafael Olivarez.'

Tom felt himself wobble unsteadily for a few seconds while he focussed on the man's face. 'You ... you're Maria's brother.'

'Maria is most certainly my sister and she is the friend of your fiancé Emily. We believe you can help us.'

Tom still felt insecure. If these people wanted him to help them it would pay him to agree. 'What can I do for you?'

'We are searching for one, Karl Hammersen. We want a witness who can positively identify this man.'

'All right, Emily and me have a score to settle with that guy.'

Rafael Olivarez nodded towards the idling helicopter. 'Come with me.'

'Dad, you look fantastic,' Emily laughed. 'Hi, you two,' she called out to Sherrie and Saffron. 'This is my dad and in fact he is a competitor.'

'Really?' replied Sherrie. She and Saffron had reappeared in running gear ready for a work out around the block.

'Yes, Paralympic single-handed sailing.'

'What the crips contest?' said Saffron. 'That ain't till next month.'

'Saff, do you mind?' Emily glared. 'I said Paralympics for the disabled and Dad won gold before in the main games…'

'A very long time ago that was,' Steve smiled. 'You're the badminton girls. I've seen you two on the TV. You're making quite a splash back home.'

'We done all right so far,' said Sherrie. 'Got the next big 'un tonight. Playing for silver against two Chinky girls. Dunno' much about 'em but they look good.'

'Don't let us hold up your training run then. Good luck.'

The girls took off jogging down the street.

'Essex girls,' said Emily. 'They're a bit blunt spoken but still nice.'

'Right,' said Steve. 'What have you been up to. How's the sailing going and are you OK with the baby?'

'Yes, the baby's growing fine but it's not all smooth. That man Hammersen's around and he's tried to poison me.'

'What!'

'Dad, where's Mum?'

'I last saw her down the street talking to Maria Olivarez. Maria wanted to tell her something.'

'I know what that is. Please Dad, when Mum comes I'd like to tell you what's happened.'

It was noisy inside the helicopter in spite of the ear protectors that Tom had been issued with. They came with a mike and earphones so he was able to hear Rafael's briefing to him and the instructions to the pilot.

'Below us is the Province of Gran Seco,' said Rafael. 'The name means "great thirst", and true it is short on annual rainfall compared to our coastal region. We have information that the man Hammersen has hired a four-by-four vehicle and, with a female companion, is heading for the Seco. We are not sure where, but the region only has one road in and a handful of towns and one city. We are confident our police will identify the vehicle.'

'What will you do when you find them?' Tom asked.

Rafael did not reply. Tom saw the pilot laugh.

A fresh voice, Spanish, was jabbering through the static of the radio. Tom saw Rafael frowning, trying to make out the message. 'Our men on the road have identified the vehicle with the man, the girl and one other male. They will keep us posted with directions.'

Tom had never been in a helicopter, although he knew that as a means of travel they were not the safest. The country below was wild and rocky with very few places for an emergency landing. Olifa City and the Pacific were far behind now, but to the east he could see the Andes stretching high and menacing.

Rafael spoke. 'That is El Pais de Venenos, or as you would say, The Poison Country.'

Oh, lovely, Tom thought. 'Why call it that?'

'Illegal cocaine growing.'

The radio crackled again. The pilot swung the machine through sixty degrees, so now they were heading towards the high ground. 'Hammersen has passed through Tulifa,' said Rafael. 'He is heading for El Tierra Caliente. It is a strange place and I have only ever been there once. It is bleak and infertile with no minerals. After the revolution it was given to the indigenous people as a self-governing province.'

'Sounds a bit grim,' said Tom.

'On the contrary it is mountainous and beautiful, but the people are tribal, secretive and stubborn. So they resent the coastal dwellers.'

'Sounds like Scotland,' said Tom.

'The road into it is rough but passable to a four-by-four. We will stop in Pacheco to refuel. If Mr Hammersen is heading for El Caliente he will have to pass through there and we shall be waiting for him.'

A whole three hours had passed since takeoff in Olifa City and Tom was beginning to feel nervous as he wondered what the fuel range of this machine ran to. At last, ahead of them, was a small town of sorts with a distinct landing strip. The pilot turned and headed for this and Tom sat back and for the first time that day he relaxed. The helicopter touched down in front of a drab concrete building with tiny windows. A painted sign on the wall announced that this was Pacheco Airport.

Rafael climbed out onto the ground: Tom followed him. The machine's rotor was still turning and instinctively Tom bending low crawled under it. Once clear he stood up and could see the pilot grinning at him from the cockpit. Thank goodness it was cooler than on the coast although the air was dusty and an odd chemical smell seemed to waft all around. A fuel bowser of World War Two vintage was rumbling across the field towards them.

Rafael indicated Tom to follow him to the terminal building. A lorry was parked beside it with a ragged platoon of soldiers relaxing on the ground dragging on cigars and cigarettes. A dust-covered Land Rover was also parked with two burly men beside it in lightweight clothes. Tom noted that both had pistols in their belts, and one had a high-power sniper's rifle slung over his shoulder. On the edge of the airfield was a road and along it at intervals passed groups of heavy lorries.

'Copper ore,' said Rafael, 'bound for the rail terminal at Tembequi. We have left instructions with the drivers. They are to radio us if they see the vehicle we are looking for. We have also posted watchers in the hills.'

'What happens next?'

'Come inside. It is cooler in there. We will wait and see.'

'It's funny,' said Steve,' but I always thought badminton was a high-class sport. I like your friends though; they're a breath of fresh air.'

'They were a bit of a shock to the system when we first met them,' said Emily, 'but we've really got to like them and they're bloody good at their game.'

'How did they get into it?'

'Saff says they went to a sports centre in Southend when they were kids and got hooked, or as Sherrie says that should be "Sairfaind". They're half-sisters. Their dad runs a couple of pubs. Saff says her mum was a model, but Sherrie says she posed for men's mags and did a bit of lap dancing on the side.'

'Never mind, they'll be household names if they win the gold, and so will you. By the way I've got this for you. He fumbled in his travel bag and produced a brown wrapped parcel. It's for all three of you but I expect you can open it now.'

Emily ripped the paper apart and inside was a tiny teddy bear with a card.

To you, all three.
See if you can go one better than us
Good luck
Love
Sammy, Tracie & Tanya.

Emily turned away and dabbed her eyes. She remembered all the hate and rivalry. It somehow brought her down to earth. This great sporting event was everything to her right now, but it was trivial in the greater scheme of things. Her baby was what mattered and her life with Tom. She had a wonderful career ahead of her. She wanted, desperately wanted, a medal this coming week but after that she did not mind if she never saw a boat again.

A mobile phone shrilled, making Tom jump. Rafael pulled it out of his top pocket and listened intently. Then he barked orders in Spanish to the two bodyguards who sat in a corner of the airfield lounge drinking iced coffee through straws. They left the building at a run, followed by Rafael with Tom a few steps behind.

'Hammersen has left the road,' said Rafael. 'He has taken a rough trail into the centre of Tierra Caliente. Quick, into the chopper! Go, go!'

Rafael sat drumming his fingers on a seat arm as the helicopter warmed up for takeoff. The lorry load of soldiers and the police Land Rover had left already and were turning onto the highway in clouds of dust. Now at last they were airborne and swooping low over some of the roughest terrain that Tom had ever seen. The pilot moved his aircraft from side to side while Rafael scanned the landscape. Below them ran a dusty track eroded by weather and the marks of vehicles.

'There,' shouted Rafael pointing.

Tom saw it too. A car was speeding along the trail swerving to avoid the potholes.

'Good,' said Rafael. 'That is the one that fits our description. Toyota Land Cruiser – colour red. There cannot be two such in a place like this.' He shouted more instructions to the pilot. The helicopter overtook the speeding car and crested a hill before slowly dropping to land on the road surface.

'We will get out here,' said Rafael. 'Tom I want you to put this on under your T-shirt.' He held out a tiny box with a length of wire and a little pendant shaped blob on the end.

Tom was uncertain. 'What's that?'

'It is a most sophisticated listening device. What in police parlance we call a wire. Tom, we will wait here for the Toyota. My men will also have caught up shortly.'

'What are you going to do?'

'Tom, I am going to ask you to speak to Mr Hammersen. We will listen to every word.'

'I don't like this.'

'I'm sure you don't. Just think of what Emily has been through. You act now and you will ensure her peace of mind and yours.'

'Is he dangerous? I mean would he have a gun?'

'We think it unlikely and remember my men will also be watching.'

'All right, I'll do it. It's almost history repeating itself.'

'How so?'

'Nothing really, only my stepfather did something like this to save me when I was a kid and in danger. And I wouldn't have it said I was less than him.'

They did not have too long to wait. Tom heard the Toyota groaning up the reverse side of the hill in low gear with its wheels spinning at times. He could see it as it lumbered over the top of the ridge and began to work down towards them. The driver stopped well short of the parked helicopter and sounded a long horn blast. He certainly wasn't intimidated. 'OK, Tom, go now,' said Rafael.

Tom walked slowly towards the Toyota. His nervousness was not improved by Rafael's instructions to keep his hands in view and away from his sides. He wondered how on earth it had come to be that, he Tom, a harmless British computer technician was carrying out a Bond style mission in a South American wasteland. His feet crunched over the road surface of small rocks and some sort of volcanic pumice. He could see the three occupants of the car now. The windows were dark tinted but it was Hammersen driving, with a girl as passenger and another obscure figure in the back seat. The Toyota must have air conditioning as the windows were still shut.

The driver's window slid down and Hammersen began to shout in disjointed Spanish with a sentence ending in "quito".

'Sorry, Hammersen, you'd better try in English.'

'English? Haven't I seen you before somewhere?'

'Yes.'

'Then get that stupid machine off the road and out of my way. I've important business and I'm late.'

'Business involving Emily Simpson?' Tom's nerves had vanished.

Hammersen's mouth dropped open.

'I know you,' it was the girl Michelle speaking. 'Tom Stoneman. You and the bitch have been screwing.'

'Hammersen, you are not going anywhere. I suggest you turn around and go back to Olifa City.'

'Stoneman, What are you doing here? Who brought you to this

place? You attacked me – an unprovoked attack. I was only trying to help you but it seems you are in the thrall of evil.' Hammersen had opened the door and left his seat. He was standing within a foot of Tom and his posture was pure menace. Michelle had also left the car and was standing on the far side, watching.

'Hammersen, please tell me what this is about? What is it you have against Emily?'

'She is spawn of evil. Have you no understanding of how we suffered in those years? That evil man set all Europe ablaze, even as far as my own country. My grandparents died in a labour camp. They died cold and starved. Now you want to be party to spreading that man's seed again.'

Tom was baffled. Hammersen's sincerity was obvious. Was it even possible to argue logically with such delusion? He must at least try. 'We have conclusive DNA evidence that Emily has no blood connection with any Nazi leader, and anyway, if you mean Hitler; he was incapable of having children.'

'What proof?' Hammersen's face was distorted and Tim took a step back. 'From the Russians. What proof is that?'

'The Russians suffered worse than anyone in the war. They have absolutely no motive in protecting the children of Nazis.' Tom was wary. The man opposite had changed. He was trembling, not in fear but with cold rage.

'Karl, kill 'im,' screeched Michelle. 'You gotta gun – kill 'im. Then we'll take that chopper and make the driver fly us the rest of the way.'

God, thought Tom, it's all happening again. Another crazed woman, just like Jolene.

'Go on,' Michelle screamed. 'Here, take this one.' She threw a black object over the car bonnet. It fell with a thud in front of Tom. It was a small automatic pistol. Tom dived for it grabbing it by the muzzle. But Hammersen was standing over him. Tom saw in his hand a larger gun. As he raised it to aim at Tom, Hammersen's body stiffened then convulsed as bullets tore into it. Hammersen was dead before he hit the ground. Tom heard Michelle give one more piercing scream. Then he too, for a few seconds, passed out. He was dimly aware that the ground on which he lay was baking hot and tasted chemical and gritty. He could smell blood, coagulating blood, and hear the buzz of hungry flies.

'Mum, I wish I knew where Tom was,' said Emily. 'It's not like him to vanish at a time like this.'

'Don't worry,' said Kirsten, 'he won't be far away. We'll find him and tell him off good and proper.'

'Come on, Em,' Chloe shouted, 'we're going.'

Emily looked round and sprinted to the boat. The tow launches were attached. This was the moment they had waited and worked for: the first race of an Olympic series. Tom should be here, but too bad. She would deal with him later.

The wind was blowing offshore a good twenty knots but shifting continually. Like all the meetings they had sailed the competition commenced with two round robin series: short two-leg races, one to one, with every team meeting every other team once. After that came the knock out stages. Twenty-three countries had reached the qualifying standard. The race committee had allotted two days to complete two series. It was going to be long and tough.

'Better watch it, girls,' Chloe called. 'One of the umpires is Ken Littlecroft. Well-named little shit and even if we are Brits, he don't like us.'

Emily was worried. They all knew they were a top crew who should qualify for the knockout series. Fear of failure was a driving force in every top sport and she was feeling it right now. 'Chloe, my dad's sailed this water with an offshore wind. He says there's a foul shift as soon as we get in line with those two skyscrapers,' she pointed. 'He says keep to starboard of that line.'

'OK, when was it he sailed here?'

'Three years ago when he came with the Olympic Committee.'

'Right, girls,' Chloe grinned. 'This is it. We want this one. The Slovenian girls are useful. If we beat 'em now it'll be one up if we race 'em later.'

Emily concentrated on the timer and the other boat. Chloe was trying to track them in the approved manner but the other girls were having none of it. They tacked away to their appointed port end and Chloe let them go. 'Five four three two one…' Emily called.

'Sheets in,' Chloe called. 'Top-speed. Wow I hope your dad's right. They're going port. Stand by to tack. Right – now!'

'It's working. They've hit one hell of a header,' Erin called back.

'I'm holding on for another minute,' said Chloe. 'Call when you think we'll lay the mark.'

'Now,' called Erin.

'Yeah, good call. Get ready with the kite.'

Emily looked back at the umpire launch. 'Reckon we could protest

Littlecroft? He's ignored the Slovenians and done nothing but watch us.'

'Get him over now,' said Chloe. 'We'll get better umps for the next few races.'

They rounded the weather mark, set the spinnaker and ran home to win by two hundred metres.

'Good start, girls, but we've a long way to go.'

Tom climbed groggily to his feet. His eyes stung with tears. He was a grown man weeping. He was the little ten-year old of nearly twenty years ago: the child running for his life while his future stepfather stood to take the fatal shot that never came. Now he stood here, his clothes covered in a film of fine grey dust. His mouth was dry, and he doubled up in a spasm of coughing. He became aware of the screaming. Michelle Le Bois was kneeling by the body of Hammersen and with every breath she screamed.

Now they had company. Rafael Olivarez and the two surly bodyguards were there and Tom could see the Olifarian soldiers in silhouette along the ridge crest. Suddenly he felt desperate for a drink of water. Rafael had walked to the rear doors of the Toyota. He wrenched one open and dragged out a person whom at first Tom took for a child. He was wrong. It was small man, little larger than a dwarf, but a mature adult. He was dark-skinned with a drooping moustache and jet-black hair. Tom's researches into Olifa told him that this was an Indian from the mountain tribes. These were a people who had managed to insulate themselves from the European settlers, at least in culture. The Indian was dressed in modern jeans and what looked like a stylish denim jacket. On his feet were rope sandals and he carried in his arms the most unexpected object: a child's doll.

Rafael relieved him of this and carried it across to Tom. Michelle had ceased to scream. Now she lay flat on the ground shaking.

'You OK, Tom?'

'I'm not sure. Was he really going to shoot me?'

'I am sure of it. He had a full chamber of ammunition and one shot in the barrel ready to fire. We were left with no choice and, remember; he would have been shot by firing squad in a few months for killing you, and for his part in the killing of an Olifarian three years ago. What has happened I would suggest was more merciful.'

Tom was looking at the doll. 'What's that?'

'You might call it a religious object. Our friend here is a shaman, a significant figure in his community. We had word that Hammersen had hired him and paid him many pesos for a special ritual.' Rafael tilted the doll towards Tom and pointed at the string of stone charms around its neck. On the largest was a single word: *Emmille.*

'What was he going to do?'

'This figure represents your fiancé: hence the name. No doubt the ritual would be performed and poor Emily would be taken ill. She would lose her baby and be unable to take part in her sailing.'

Tom couldn't take this. 'Oh come on, that's superstitious bullshit.'

'Do not be so cynical, Mr Stoneman. If you lived in this country you would not be. There are too many instances where these things have happened. However, good things can work as well.' Rafael handed back the doll to the shaman and with it a wad of folded bank notes. He spoke to the man rapidly in Spanish and then grinned and patted him on the back.

'Perhaps now Emily's luck will change,' said Rafael. 'This man's village is fifty kilometres away in El Caliente. Our military comrades will deliver him there. Hammersen was driving him home to perform his ritual but now the poor guy is stranded.'

'I only want a drink of water,' Tom replied.

'In the helicopter,' said Rafael.

A police Land Rover was on the scene, and the bodyguards were walking a stumbling Michelle to it with her hands secured with tape behind her back.

She turned and spat in Tom's direction. 'That's the second good man got killed for Emily Simpson.'

All Emily's suspicions were aroused. Tom had appeared and with him was Maria.

'Where were you when I wanted you?' her voice was deliberately cold.

'I've been for a ride in a helicopter. Not my choice.'

It was an odd reply and she barely recognised his voice. It seemed he had showered and put on fresh clothes, but she had never seen him so haggard and tired.

'It's all right, Emily,' said Maria. 'And don't look at me like that. You know I was sailing out there all day.'

'You tell her,' said Tom.

'My brother phoned me. Hammersen is dead.'

'What, how come?'

'He tried to kill me,' said Tom. His voice was so quiet she could hardly hear him above the surrounding chatter. 'Security forces took him out before he could pull the trigger.'

'When? How?' Emily flung her arms around him.

'Not now. Tell you all about it later. I want a stiff drink and a meal.'

Emily doubted if she would ever hear the full truth of what had happened to Tom in the Gran Seco. She might if she could one day coax him back to the place itself. But at the moment that was hardly practicable. Something was happening to her. If Tom was reticent and depressed, she on the contrary was finding a new strength. Where it came from she couldn't say. It wasn't entirely due to the demise of Hammersen. She knew anyone's death, even his, was not something to cry whoopee about. She felt relaxed, and she felt happy. Things were working out on the racecourse. In the following days they had swept to victory in match after match including defeat of some of their main rivals. They could go into the finals with a better than evens chance of a medal of some colour. Then Saffron and Sherrie had taken silver in their badminton pairs. They were young and glamorous of course, and their success had produced a feeding frenzy from the British press and TV. Sherrie had danced around the room waving a contract to advertise body lotion. Chloe had remarked sotto voce that it was just the thing for that sweaty couple.

But nothing that had happened helped Emily to understand this happiness that gripped her: the shadow that had hung over her life for five years was gone. But it was more than that, and she couldn't understand why she felt so liberated and why things were going so well. She only hoped that it would last a few more days.

'Maria,' Tom asked, 'what is your brother going to do about the Le Bois girl?'

'I think she is being held in the women's Magdalena jail. That's out on the road to the airport.'

'It's just that there are limits. I don't want to be responsible … I mean he's not going to have her shot is he?'

Maria delivered her most seductive smile. 'That could be arranged.'

'No, Maria. I wouldn't want it on my conscience.'

Now she laughed. 'Don't worry. Rafael told me she is going to be deported. But to do that she has to appear before the Central Security Court. I guess that will be a formality.'

So Michelle would be back in England before Emily. They could only hope that the horror she witnessed would turn her off any more vindictive adventures.

'Sorry, Maria, but all this has made me lose touch. How is your sailing going?'

She grimaced. 'As well as to be expected. We have three more races and I hope to finish better than ninth.'

'Emily's in the quarterfinals of her event. But your man Garcia is going to be in the umpire boat. You told me once that he had it in for the girls.'

'I don't think it's personal. We suspect he's worried at all the money being placed on the father-daughter double gold. What are the chances?'

'I wouldn't put money on it myself but Emily's team look set for a medal of some colour. No-one can see a better crew out there.'

'And Steve?'

'He's the oldest Paralympic sailor of all time, but he's easily the most experienced. He's already a gold medallist. A lot of the others have done far less sailing.'

'So it's age and experience against youth and inexperience.'

'That's about it.'

Steve and Kirsten had found places on an Olifarian naval ship that was patrolling the edges of the sailing courses. Steve felt a tiny bit conceited, as the invitation had come from the High Admiral at the instigation of the President's office. The sun shone as it always did and the sea was bright with short breaking waves. Both he and Kirsten were nervous. This was the time for the girls quarterfinal match and of all the races these must be the most tense. For the winner a bronze medal chance at least, or the frustration of finishing fourth in the sailoff. Forty years before, Steve had competed in the single-handed Finn event and won gold in spectacular fashion, in a race where he had been the survivor: the only competitor not to capsize. Now it was the turn of Emily and her friends.

The captain had invited them to watch the start from the bridge. Chloe and her team were matched against a Japanese crew whom they had already beaten in the preliminaries. Thc rival crew were bodily lightweights but that could help them if the wind blew less than twenty knots. They could see Chloe's boat now with the blue flag fluttering from its stern. That meant the crew were committed to approach the start line from thc port end.

Steve raised his binoculars. 'Come on you three; make it work,' he muttered. He watched as the umpire boat positioned to watch for any infringement.

'They're sailing round in circles, why?' asked Kirsten.

'This is match racing: nothing like our sort of game. Chloe's tracking behind the other girls trying to put the wind up. I'm not sure that's the right tactic: the Jap girls are too wise to fall for that.'

'How long to go?'

Steve looked at his timer. 'About half a minute. Now what's happening?' The two boats were almost still sails flapping. 'Don't Chloe, don't do it! Go past head to wind and you're on port tack. Oh no, they've got a penalty turn.'

'Do they have to take the penalty now?' asked Kirsten.

'No, they can choose the moment, let's keep fingers crossed and hope.'

He watched the two boats clear the start and begin the first long windward leg.

'They've got to do better; they've got to pull out a good lead now.'

They watched as the two boats parted tacks and saw Chloe cross the Japanese team and tack again. Shortly afterwards the penalty was taken and Chloe's boat was trailing. Both boats rounded the windward mark with the Japanese girls thirty seconds up. Steve lowered his binoculars. He'd never felt so miserable. 'It's over now,' Steve sighed.

'No it isn't,' said Kirsten. 'There's still another lap to go and four more races.'

Steve raised his binoculars. 'Wind's rising, and they've gained a bit. That could help.' The rival crew were all of a stone lighter than the British girls and the disadvantage to windward should be beginning to tell. The leeward mark was closing fast. 'Hello, our girls are dropping their kite early,' Steve called. 'Oh my God! The others are in trouble.' He could see the Japanese struggling to retrieve their spinnaker.'

'Umpire's given a yellow flag,' Kirsten was jumping up and down. 'The others must have hit the mark or done something and look – there's a red flag.'

'That means they did something really bad. I think they not only lost control they hit Chloe as she began to pass. They'll have to take a 270 right now before they get moving.'

'We've still got a chance,' Kirsten yelled. 'Oh come on my girls. You can do it.'

They saw the Japanese girls take the penalty. They were now

behind Chloe but only a few boat lengths. Chloe tacked away and then tacked again. It was classic racing, covering your opponents and locking them into your dirty backwind. Chloe rounded the windward mark and they saw Erin and Emily set the spinnaker. The Japanese crew were still a few metres astern but their spinnaker drill lacked the precision of the British girls. Very slowly Chloe was pulling ahead. Their rivals took a different line, an almost asymmetric semi-reaching leg. Chloe, anticipating did the same.

'It's going to be close,' said Steve. 'Too bloody close.'

The Japanese girls were now using their lighter weight to advantage. Their boat was planing and so was Chloe's but with less hull showing. Fifty metres to go Chloe was ahead but the other boat was closing. Steve couldn't look. It was Auckland all over again. He heard the finishing signal distantly, and then,almost instantly, a second one. He took a deep breath and dared to look. The committee boat was waving a blue flag. Their girls had won. The rest of the races ran to form. Chloe's team won two, mainly due to mistakes by the Japanese girls. The Japanese won the fourth, then Chloe and crew clinched the contest with the narrowest of wins in the fifth. As Steve noted they could, and must, do better if they were to even think about a gold medal.

It was a melancholy gathering in the Olympic village that evening. Sherrie and Saffron were sitting disconsolately, silver medals around their necks.

'We fucked up on the last game,' said Saffron. 'More or less handed it to 'em.'

'Don't be like that,' said Emily. She still couldn't think why she felt on such a high. 'You're silver medallists. There's not many can claim that.'

'I know,' Sherrie sighed. 'We've never beaten those Russian girls, but I really thought we were on our way to doing it. Oh, Em – never mind, give it twenty four hours and we'll feel better.'

'How did you guys make out today?' asked Saffron. 'You looked mighty down in the gobs when you walked in here.'

'Because we bloody near blew it too,' said Chloe. 'But we can't go on winning because of the other crews fouling up.'

'Chlo,' said Emily, 'I don't think you did go through onto port tack at the start of race one. I was watching and I reckon that was a bad call. And you know who the bloody umpire was? It was Garcia. He doesn't want us to take gold.'

'You can't argue with umpires or referees or whatever, and he did us a favour with that red flag.'

'He couldn't do otherwise, could he?' said Emily. 'Their double cock up was blatant.'

'Well, cheer up you lot for Chrissake,' said Sherrie. 'You gotta a bronze didn't you.'

'Not yet we haven't,' said Erin. 'If we don't win in the semis there's a shoot out for bronze. Loser finishes fourth and that doesn't take thinking about.'

Sherrie was looking out of the open front door. 'Cheer up anyway; here's your mum an' dad and your Tom. He's luvverly. I'll have 'im if you gets bored with 'im.'

'On your bike,' Emily laughed.

Dad had a bunch of newspapers under his arm. 'Hi there, I've just picked up these UK papers from the overseas club. They haven't got your race today yet but there's a piece in the *Daily Postman*. He spread one paper on a table.

CORRESPONDENT'S ORDEAL.
By Michelle Le Bois.

Two days ago I witnessed the bloody murder of a British man by the Olifarian secret police. For this I have been deported at twelve hours notice. Now I am free to tell the truth.

'What a load of crap.' Tom was angry.

I had been invited with fellow correspondent, Karl Hammersen to visit an Indian village in the mountain country. A few miles into our journey and we were surrounded by armed soldiers who forced Karl from our car and brutally shot him through the head. I was man-handled and feared for my life but I am British and would not bow to these uncivilised people. Twelve hours later I was put on a plane for home: no explanations, no choice. What will our government do now? I know what the British people will say. Withdraw our sports team from these corrupted games and do it now!

'This is lies,' Tom spluttered, 'it wasn't like that and she knows it.'

'I suspect our government knows it too,' said Steve. Read that.

This evening the Foreign Office issued a statement.

We have been in urgent consultation with the Government of Olifa and they have communicated this announcement.

The man Hammersen and his companion were in a forbidden zone. Olifarian law enforcement officers attempted a peaceful arrest but the man Hammersen produced a handgun and threatened officers attempting the arrest. In the resulting melée Mr Hammersen was shot dead. The government of Olifa very much regret this incident and send condolences to the family concerned.

'How accurate is that, Tom,' asked Emily.

'They're being economical with the truth. It's true Hammersen had a gun, but he was pointing it at me and about to pull the trigger…' His voice broke.

Emily wondered if she would ever hear what happened.

Steve opened another paper. 'The Times reports the same story and statement but they're a bit wary.'

Who exactly was this man, Karl Hammersen? Certainly he was not the sports journalist he claimed to be. Our investigators have discovered the secret life of a man of joint Norwegian-British nationality. Karl Hammersen was a writer with an obsession with Nazi Germany. He appears to have been a man of independent means with a mission to find and punish surviving wartime Nazis. Is that why he met his death in the secret interior of Olifa? Maybe we shall never know.

Other papers took a similar line, and certainly there was no support to be found for the *Postman's* demand to withdraw the British Olympic team.

That evening Tom met Dave Manning in the yacht club bar. He had left Emily and the girls fending off questions from two television teams. Thank heavens no one was connecting Emily with Michelle Le Bois and her allegations. Tom had a new longing that he knew he must fight: a longing to drink himself into oblivion. The aftershock was beginning to envelop him with a depression like nothing that he could remember. His ordeal of twenty years ago had been different. He had been a child with no real sense of death. Tonight he knew he was lucky to be alive, and that he would owe a lifetime's gratitude to Rafael Olivarez and his sharpshooters.

'Tom, mate,' said Dave, 'I think you know more than you're letting on about the Gran Seco. My sources say an Englishman was present and witnessed the shooting of that Brit journo Hammersen. Was it you?'

'Sorry, Dave. I know you've a job to do but don't push me because if I saw anything I'm not going to talk about it.'

'Off the record?'

'No, come back in a year or so.'

Dave stared at Tom long and hard. 'All right, mate. I can see something's hurt you. I won't lean on you.'

'Don't, all I want to do is drink myself silly.'

'Yeah, all right. Let's buy a few bottles of Tequila, it's the local brew and a lot stronger than the Mexican version.'

'Yes, Dave, let's do that but don't expect it to loosen my tongue.'

'Right,' said Chloe, 'tomorrow is the day. We'll settle it one way or another. We're up against the Polish girls, can't begin to pronounce their names. The Ukrainians are shooting off against the Yanks. If we win which do we want in the final?'

'Don't care,' said Erin. 'We've beat 'em both before. We'll do it again.'

All three had been heartily relieved to escape from the television interviews. BBC, ITV, Sky Sport, and then a New Zealand crew arrived with the entire Kiwi rugby sevens squad. The guys had picked up Chloe bodily, no mean feat even for them, and she had led them in an impromptu haaka.

'How do you feel, Em?' Chloe asked.

'I'm fine, never felt better.'

'You've looked a lot better since your Tom sorted out that Hammersen idiot.'

Emily shrugged. 'I say no more head to wind starts, particularly if Garcia is umpire. Go for speed off the line. I don't know about the Poles but I know we can beat the American girls.'

'Early to bed, all of us,' said Chloe. 'Tomorrow is tomorrow. We'll play things as they come.'

'Anyway,' said Erin, 'the Ukranians sail on the Black Sea and the Pacific here is nice and blue, so they won't be happy.'

'You'll never guess what I've been asked to do?' said Steve.

'I've given up second guessing you years ago,' replied Kirsten.

'They want me to go as a commentator in the BBC boat.'

'You!'

'Don't seem so surprised. I'm not doing the shouting – I'm supposed to be the expert who butts in with the finer detail.'

'But why you?'

'Pete, who does it has a tummy bug. I'm only for today. You see it's unique: every British boat has got a likely medal already so it's a hunt for gold in the finals.'

'Denmark aren't doing too bad either,' she reminded him.

'Not as well as the UK. People are going manic back home they say.'

'You can't be impartial with Emily out there.'

'They've already told me I've got to be.'

'Who is the mainstay commentator?'

'Jerry Blades.'

'The guy who does Formula One?'

Steve laughed. 'He's much better with his boat stuff now, or at least they've stopped him calling dinghies "dinggies".'

The commentary launch was a very large RIB with a protective cover for the transmission equipment and the TV monitors. The actual cameras were mounted on two heavier and slower craft, while a helicopter ranged overhead with an extra camera. In fact Steve was impressed with the Olifarian Broadcasting and TV services. All that he had seen on the previous days had been well covered, not just the sailing events, but for all the sports. Steve was more relaxed now following his briefing by Sarah the TV producer, a delightful blonde girl. It was going to be a nervous afternoon waiting for the women's match racing. First they had to cover the preceding races. A British gold in the Finn class was almost a tradition and it went where it had done for the last four games. The other British entries all looked good for medals. Now at last it was Chloe, Emily and Erin for their semi-final.

'Steve,' said Blades into his mike, 'I don't think it's any secret that you have a personal interest in this one.'

'Very much so, my daughter is competing,' Steve replied into his mike.

'Well, this team and everyone back home is rooting for her.' Blades certainly had a musical speaking voice. Steve had managed a year ago to kill off the fake West Country burr that the stroke had left him with, but he still had some doubts as to how he would sound.

'Here we go for the best of five,' Blades shouted into his mike.

'The five minute signal.'

'What are they doing now, Steve?'

'They're approaching the start line from their allotted ends. Our girls have blue flag again and that means they must enter the start zone from the port end – that's left hand side of course.'

'And the pre-start is almost as important as the race itself?'

'Yes, in a one-to-one competition like this it's vital.'

Steve switched anxiously between the TV monitor and the actual scene. He heard the start signal but it wasn't certain straight away who had won. The Polish boat was not looking for a close quarter duel but had swept away on a long starboard tack. Chloe had definitely cleared the start first and was moving well, and Steve dared to hope faster, but she was on port, give way, tack. Everything would depend on where the boats crossed. Once again the wind was a hot offshore blast. Would the Polish girls have learned the lessons of the foul shifts blowing from the city? It was so deceptive and so sudden and a crew could be caught unawares. Onshore winds had been the rule for most of the week: it might just work for Chloe.

'The British crew are crossing ahead of the Poles,' called Blades. 'Your views Steve?'

'I think they stay on that tack and not go too far over towards the high rise buildings,' Steve replied. 'And yes, there they go, good move Chloe – good move.'

It was a reprise of the first race of the series. Evidently the lessons had not been learned. The Polish girls sailed into the foul shift and tacked too late. Chloe rounded the windward mark while the others still struggled. Steve couldn't help but release a gasp of relief and delight, which he hoped would not be picked up on air. The race was won, provided nothing broke or the girls made a catastrophic error.

'Chloe Te-Koote and her crew are pulling away now,' Blades shouted. He was becoming genuinely excited. 'They are the world's number one and it shows.'

The British girls crossed the finish line half a leg ahead. The remaining races were much the same. Chloe and crew stayed well away from the negative wind shifts and took the next three races. Although the Polish girls had the consolation of a narrow first in the final race they seemed demoralised and to have settled for the bronze medal shootout long before the end.

The three girls huddled together as the sails slatted and the boat rolled gently in the swell. Emily felt both exultant and relieved. Their luck had held; their teamwork had worked, they were to take part in an Olympic final.

'We owe your dad, Em,' said Chloe. 'It's odd that no one else seems to have picked up that shift pattern.'

Emily felt sorry for the Polish girls. They had taken their failure with good sportsmanship, and that made things easier. Emily knew that without their own local knowledge it could easily have been they who would be facing a bronze medal shootout.

'Come on,' said Chloe. 'Job's not done yet. Sheets in – let's go to shore.'

'The other semi is near finishing,' called Erin from her station in the bows. 'There it goes, yellow flag. It's the Yanks we'll be facing.'

'Don't care,' said Chloe. 'Whichever – bring it on.'

'Hi, Maria, you did well today,' Steve wanted to be encouraging and not patronising.

'Sure, I was fifth,' she looked pleased. 'That's best I've ever done in an international fleet.'

Maria had emerged from the women's shower and changing area in the yacht club. She was carrying the large shoulder bag for her sailing kit, but she had changed into the same white sundress that he remembered her wearing at Branham. It was tasteful and provided a magic counterpoint to her bronzed shoulders and arms.

'How was your commentary?' she smiled.

'I think I got away with it but it was hard to be neutral with Emily sailing.'

Steve smiled inwardly. He remembered the story of the famous international rugby commentator who had described his son scoring a winning try without a trace of bias. That was professionalism of the highest order.

'So Emily is in the final?'

'Yes, one more to go.'

Her expression was serious now. 'Has Garcia spoken to you?'

'No.'

'Steve, be careful.'

'Why?'

'My brother tells me that big money is being put on the father-daughter double gold. A lot of it is going to Castinnio.com and that money is being staked from all parts of the world. Garcia is unscrupulous and he needs you to lose.'

'Are you telling me to watch my back?'

‘In a manner of speaking. I do not know how Garcia will react when you start winning.’

He had to laugh. ‘Maria, in nine days time I am seventy. What chance an old buffer like me doing much winning?’

‘That is not what your opponents say and it’s not what the gamblers think.’ She fixed him with her most devastating smile. ‘Steve, I believe in you, and I always will.’ She touched his shoulders with both hands, planted a kiss on his left cheek, and walked away.

Steve followed her with his gaze until he saw another person standing a few yards away. It was his wife and her face had an expression he did not care for.

Tom took the lines alongside the pontoon. He helped the girls ashore and gave each a hug and Emily a long kiss. ‘Go and get changed,’ he said. ‘I’ll bring the boat ashore and tidy up.’

‘Tomorrow is going to be much tougher,’ said Emily.

‘You can do it; now go change.’

‘Wait,’ said Emily. ‘Here’s Mum and Dad.’

Tom saw Steve wave as he walked across to them. He had a grin of delight on his face although Kirsten looked fed up about something. ‘Ladies,’ Steve called, ‘I saw it all. You were fantastic – great tactics.’

‘Thanks, Steve,’ said Chloe. ‘Any tips for tomorrow?’

‘Just concentrate and you’ll be fine.’

‘Mum, cheer up,’ said Emily. ‘We won. We’re in the final.’

The girls showered and changed, leaving Tom to see their boat ashore. They boarded a minibus for the village and arrived at their house to be greeted by Sherrie and Saffron along with several other athletes from their street.

‘We watched you on telly,’ said Saffron. ‘Couldn’t understand a word of the commentary, all in Spanish.’

‘Couldn’t you get the English version?’ Emily asked. ‘My dad was part of the commentary.’

‘We tried to adjust the thing but no luck,’ said Sherrie. ‘Saw you lot in your boat. Jeez, don’t like the way it tips up, I’d be sick. Think we’ll stick to our game.’

All three of them laughed. Emily knew they were riding on a high, but they would have to come down to earth. Tomorrow was the day and the final they had come for.

‘I know what you mean,’ said Chloe. ‘I’ve tried your game back home in NZ. I was bloody useless.’

Tom supervised the lifting of the boat onto its dockside cradle. He checked all the gear and smiled as he found an expensive pair of sunglasses that one of the girls had dropped in the cockpit. Finally he unrigged and carefully folded the three sails, putting them in their bags. Then he carried these and other loose gear across to the yacht club annexe where he placed them in the lock up box provided for each competitor.

He walked out into the early evening heat and there stood a familiar figure. It was Rafael Olivarez.

'Mr Stoneman, I have one more duty for you.'

'What?' Tom was tired and he wanted a beer.

'We have certain rules in our country. Two judges are on their way to the central mortuary. We need you to make a positive identification of the late Mr Hammersen.'

'Why? There's no doubt – can't be.'

'It is a formality only. After all dead men cannot bite.'

Tom looked at his watch. 'All right.'

This time he was not forced into an unmarked police car but was driven the few kilometres in Rafael's BMW. The central morgue was an unobtrusive building adjacent to a military barracks. Tom guessed this place was the final destination of dead bodies that the Olifarian government preferred to conceal from the world. The truth of this was made all too clear on their arrival. A small group of shabbily dressed men, women and children, was kneeling on the pavement outside the building's grim double doors. They were all Amerindians but with a white priest leading them in doleful prayer and singing.

'What's all that?' asked Tom.

'A man was executed by firing squad this morning.' Rafael sounded bored. 'His body is in there.'

'What did he do?'

'Trouble maker and gangster – waste of space.'

Tom left it there. He was in a country that seemed beautiful and welcoming but with a darker hidden side, and being indignant would solve nothing.

The interior of the building was brightly lit, spotlessly clean and smelt of disinfectant. It was all scrubbed floors and stainless steel benches. Tom was introduced to two smart-suited middle-aged men. Rafael explained that these were local court judges; Tom supposed the equivalent of magistrates. A forensic technician slid a body drawer open and he was invited to step forward. The corpse was Hammersen. Tom had only once before seen a dead body: that of mad Jolene when he was ten years old, and only then from a distance. This was the man who wanted to destroy Emily and stop them from having children. Tom wondered if he should feel hate but he didn't. The face on the corpse was relaxed. The body was just a shell but the personality, good or deluded, had flown. He wondered if there might be something in the religious belief in after life. This was hardly the time or place.

'Yeah, that's him – Hammersen.'

'Thank you,' said Rafael. He spoke a few sentences to the judges and then Tom was invited to put his signature to a piece of A5 paper that was clearly an official form.

They were outside again in the hot humid evening. It was growing dark with a vivid sunset out on the rim of the Pacific. The mourners were still there, quieter now as one by one they lit candles.

CHAPTER 34

The morning was bright and as hot as usual as Tom arrived at the marina. This was the final day of the sailing regatta. Three more gold medals needed deciding plus the bronze medal shootout in the women's match racing. That was to be the first contest of the afternoon so Emily and her crew would have to sweat it out until that was decided. Tom was still affected by what he had seen last night at the mortuary. He wondered who the execution victim had been. The crowd of mourners had seemed genuinely distraught: not the behaviour of people who had been the victims of gangland. Rafael had dropped Tom at the yacht club. The man had been even more evasive when Tom had questioned him.

Tom must forget all that. He must forget everything except today's contest. He was not a competitor, he never could be, but he had a part to play. He arrived at the dockside where the match racing boats were parked. The twenty-four teams that had started the series were now whittled down to two. By the end of the day there would be one gold medal winner. The concrete surface of the dock was already hot enough to fry an egg, and Tom knew his feet were sweating inside his sailing boots. The wind had changed overnight and was blowing onshore. This at least had some cooling effect. The dinghies and wind surfers had departed for their races. Now the mobile crane was beginning to move the match racers. Each boat in turn was due to be lifted from its shore cradle and placed in the sea. The crane, operating on electric motors, was almost silent. The Olifarians were very proud of these games as "the Eco Games".

Tom yawned as he watched the two bronze medal boats lifted and launched. Their crews were still changing. Secretly he wished the Polish girls good luck. They were an attractive trio and it was their mistake with the wind shifts that had gifted Emily and Co their win. The crane was moving towards the two finalists' boats. Tom wanted to be ready to fit the sails and sort out the gear as soon as the boat was in the water.

The crane rumbled past him. Different driver today he noted. The American boat was moved and launched. Now it was their boat's turn. Tom wondered why the crane had lifted the little yacht higher than the others, but he was unprepared for what happened next. This time no gentle lowering to the water. The release was the boat falling with a crunch onto the surface of the dock. Even from where he stood

Tom could see the damage was terminal. The glued fibre shell had shattered in two places and the light fin keel had broken.

Tom remembered little of the next hour, only the horrified faces of Emily and her friends. Chloe had been stoical, Emily and Erin had wept. The race was postponed while the race committee conferred.

They had watched while the officials had talked in a huddle.

'All bloody old fart men,' said Emily.

'Ken Littlecroft's there,' said Chloe. 'He doesn't like me but he'll stick up for the Brits.'

Steve walked across and his face mirrored his concern. 'I don't like this. If Garcia gets his way I'm going to the International Olympic committee.'

Emily clung to her father. 'Dad, what's going on?'

'I was listening, but when they realised, I was told to shove off. But they're divided. You see, it's all to do with the allocation of boats. Some of them say you can't change boats because the rules say the allocated boat must be the one used. Ken is fighting our corner. He's quoting some case law from the winter Olympics something to do with bobsleighs.'

'Steve, did you say Garcia was taking part?'

'Yes, he represents Olifa on the committee. I'm sorry to say this but he wants the gold handed to the Americans by default.'

'Oh does he?' said Tom. 'I saw that accident, only I don't think it was an accident. I know the driver deliberately let the hoist freewheel onto the dock, and who benefits financially if the Americans win? You tell me that.'

'Tom. I see where you are coming from,' said Steve. 'That's what Maria told me yesterday. Money on the double gold.'

'Hello,' said Chloe. She alone had kept her composure throughout. 'Look at that.' The impromptu committee meeting was dispersing. They could see Garcia stalking towards the yacht club.

Ken Littlecroft was walking to them with a grin on his face. 'Folks,' he said, 'you're on. The committee says you can take the first of the bronze medal race boats to come ashore.'

'What about the Americans?' Steve asked.

'They have been most sporting and agreed to the race under these terms.'

'They won't protest if we win?' asked Chloe.

'No, Chloe, and it seems, rivalry apart, that surprisingly they rather like you.'

'There's Maria,' said Tom. 'Just the person we need – excuse me.'

He sprinted across the dock and nearly fell headlong over a Laser dinghy mast. 'Maria, wait!' he gasped.

She spun round and stopped. Then Tom told her.

'That will be Garcia's work,' Maria almost spat the words. 'Tell me, Tom. You say you saw it happen?'

'It was blatant. Different driver from the last few days and he hoisted the boat a metre higher than the others and then just let it fall.'

'Were there many people around?'

'Hardly any. The Lasers and 470s had already gone afloat and the girl racers hadn't arrived.'

'Where is the driver now?' Maria was looking around.

'Can't say. Looks like he legged it straight away.'

'I saw Garcia here when I came. What was he doing?'

'They had a committee hearing right on the dock. Garcia wanted our girls disqualified and the Americans given the gold.'

Maria sniffed loudly. 'He is taking risks, or I think he is too confident.'

'Well it hasn't worked. They're letting Chloe have the first match racer to come ashore from the bronze medal race.'

'Tom, I am going to find my brother. He will act. We will not have Garcia dishonour our country.'

Maria left with her mobile phone clenched to her right ear. Tom felt both deflated and very angry. He wondered what a change of boat would do to the girl's chances. It really shouldn't matter. The boats were identical one-design, but the crew were in tune with their allotted boat and Tom had no idea how they would react psychologically. But there should be time to switch sails to their own with the GB insignia and flag. He ran into the yacht club store and recovered the three bags. He was surprised that the security man on the door was missing.

Tom left the store carrying the sails. The sun outside was momentarily blinding even with his dark glasses. He could see that a crowd was gathering around the wrecked boat, and this included press people with cameras: drawn like vultures to any disaster. Tom walked across and joined the throng. He picked out several scribes from the world of yachting, among them Dave Manning.

'Tom,' said Dave, 'there are people here who say you saw what happened.'

'Who says?'

'Couple of non-coms, just standing around at the time. Pointed you out.'

'Shit, I'd much rather not be noticed.'

'What's up, mate?'

'Dave, this is strictly off the record, for now anyway.'

'All right – go on.'

'I don't think this was any accident.'

Dave stared around and then pulled Tom away. 'Let's walk.' Tom followed him until they were standing at the water's edge. 'Tom, mate, I know it wasn't an accident.'

Tom put the sail bags on the ground. 'What do you know?'

'It's like this. The regular driver for that crane is a little guy called Pedro. He works for the yacht club. I was here early,' Dave checked his watch. 'About five hours ago I saw Pedro get bundled into a white van by a bunch of heavies. Little sod never had a chance.'

'An abduction?'

'That's what it looked like.'

'Dave, someone doesn't want the British girls to win gold.'

'Whyever not? Everyone loves them.'

'I think I know why. I'll tell you more when I find out more. This is still off the record – OK?'

'I suppose so.'

'Definitely. You can spin any conspiracy theory you like but I'd rather you kept what you saw for the police.'

A shrill voice was calling. It was Emily. 'Tom the boats are coming back. We'll want our sails.'

'Got 'em here,' Tom replied.

'Quick then, we haven't got much time.'

Tom picked up the three bags and ran with them. He could see the first of the match racing boats being towed into the dock. It was the Polish girls' boat and the crew were waving with joy. They had taken the bronze medals.

'Can anyone speak Polish?' Chloe shouted. 'They don't know about us, but we need that boat.'

'I speak good English.' It was Monika, the bow girl of the boat.

'Come ashore quick. We've a problem,' Chloe called back.

Monika and her crew climbed ashore looking puzzled and then astonished at the sight of the crippled boat on the dock. Chloe caught hold of Monika and in a few short words told her what has happened. Monika translated and her fellow crew almost fell into the boat and began to remove their sails. Emily and Erin passed down their own mainsail and jib.

'Hi, Tom, said Chloe, 'I don't reckon much on the way you've packed our kite.' She had opened the top of the sail bag containing their spinnaker.

Tom came over and looked himself. 'Hey, I never put it away like that. Someone's messed with it.' All of a sudden he had a bad feeling about this and he was right. Chloe pulled the head of the lightweight sail from the bag and then they saw it. A metre long vertical rip cut with some razor sharp instrument.

Chloe's self-control broke. 'Oh, holy fucking shit!' she screamed.

'You can use theirs,' said Tom. 'They're all identical.'

'No, you not do!' Tom swung round to see a small man with an Olympic ID badge around his neck. He also saw Maria speeding across the dockside towards them.

'No,' said the man. 'Me, I am official. You not go with wrong number on sail. You disqualified.'

'By what authority,' Tom shouted. 'I don't know who you are.'

The man stamped his left foot. 'Me official – you not to sail.'

Suddenly all was changing. Maria had arrived and immediately she began to yell in Spanish. The man shrugged and pointed at the ruined boat. Maria, still shouting, walked to within a foot of the other and delivered a stinging slap to his face. She followed this by pulling the ID square from around his neck snapping the cord that held it. 'Just as I thought,' she said. 'A forgery and not a very clever one.'

She turned back and gave the luckless man another blast in Spanish. Tom caught the name Garcia repeated three times.

By now a small crowd had gathered, applauding and laughing at Maria's assault. The alleged official, now red-faced, tore off his baseball cap and stamped on it drawing more merriment from onlookers. This macho Latino had clearly been deeply humiliated, and worse, by a woman.

Maria was looking at the torn sail. 'Garcia's work, I will tell my brother of this.'

'What the hell do we do?' Chloe shouted. 'The Yanks could protest us for a wrong sail number.'

'No, said Tom. 'In the store, there's some spares. Wait!' he took off at a sprint and arrived breathless at the store. Still no security guard. He found what he was looking for, and thank God, a box of stick-on letters and numbers. He ran back even faster.

'Here, use this one.' He poured the cloth on the ground and peeled off the Polish letters and flag. Then he sifted through the box. They were here: GBR. Within seconds they were on the sail, a bit lopsided but secure. 'No time to fold it,' he said. 'But it should work all right.'

The tow launch was becoming impatient. Chloe waited no more but jumped off the pontoon into the cockpit making the boat rock.

'Have you got the right flag?' called Tom.

'Yeah,' Emily held up the yellow flag and passed it to Chloe who fixed it on the stern.

Tom waved them off and Emily blew him a kiss. He realised that Monika and her crewmates were standing beside him. 'Thanks, Monika, and well done by the way. We'll see you on the podium come what may.'

He walked away from the scene. He was shaking and he suddenly noticed that his shirt was wringing with sweat. What would happen on the water? He couldn't say. Would the girls fight to the last? Tom knew Emily would. He was angry and resentful. He didn't know this Garcia character except as a well-known sailor from times past. That such a man should breach the Olympic ideal for his own selfish ends was incomprehensible. It was all in the hands of fate now: a cliché but bloody right. There was nothing he could do except find a cooling shower and a bar serving genuine English beer.

Two races apiece won. Chloe and the girls had won the first but lost the second with a penalty call on the start line. They had taken the third race with only metres to spare and had lost the fourth from a poor first leg. It was now or never: everything on this fifth and final race.

A few minutes short of the countdown Chloe let the boat idle with sheets loose and sails gently slatting.

Chloe spoke quietly. 'Guys, this is the big one. We've come a long way to be here, five years of hard graft and a lot of sacrifice. What's happened today hasn't helped or maybe, just maybe, it will. How badly do we want this? Or how badly do you want to stuff that man Garcia's dirty tricks down his fucking gob.'

Emily had never heard Chloe in this mood before. Minutes before she had been depressed wondering if they had been given a task too far even for them. Chloe's words had moved her and brought a tear to her eyes. Suddenly she felt that odd sensation again, that feeling that someone or something was riding with her. She resolved; if she never touched a boat again she would fight for this one with everything she had.

'Emily,' said Chloe, 'team coach says there's strong right-to-left tide near the line and it'll be starting about now. We don't want to be carried down below port layline at the start. Right, here come the

Yanks again. If they want a dial-up they can have one.'

Emily knew that meant an eye-to-eye staring match, boats a few metres apart: like boxers before a big fight. This time it wasn't like Auckland three years ago. The Americans were among their best friends on the circuit. The two teams went through the ritual staring daggers at other. Emily reckoned they won the dial-up so psychologically they were one-up.

Emily began the count down. 'Five, four, three…'

'Whoopee, we got 'em Chloe yelled. 'Luff 'em over the line.'

'Two, one, start!' Emily called.

'Blue Flag,' shouted Erin from the bow. 'They were over. They'll have to do a penalty.'

'At a time they choose,' Emily warned.

'Don't matter,' said Chloe. 'They're gone back for the re-start. Come on, never mind them. Get this boat sailing flat.'

That meant hiking, using their body weight over the rail to hold the boat to windward. Emily knew too well that temporary advantage they might have but this race wasn't going to be over until it was over. They were all three on the weather rail. Emily forgot everything, even the thought of the baby inside her. They had to keep their boat balanced and moving fast. Erin in front was catching the worst of the spray, but who cared. They were sailing fast, the wind was still rising, and the Americans were catching up. They tacked then they tacked and again and again. But so close were the boats as they closed the weather mark that the crews were briefly into a second dial-up. Maybe, thought Emily, they're trying to intimidate us into a mistake and a penalty. She hadn't time to bother with it. They were round the weather mark in front and – fantastic! The reserve kite went like the old one and a second quicker than the Americans.

Now for the downwind leg. They must concentrate, balance the boat, take the right line and build speed. It was a weird experience. She knew that they were all both nervous and at the same time loving it as they fought to balance and drive the boat. The downwind mark was coming closer. Emily glanced back; they had a lead, five boat lengths, but not enough to win the race. Now the next windward leg began. It was great the way the three of them were working and thinking as one. They tacked to cover and tacked again. Emily's nerves were jangling just as she knew the others were. Could they do it? Do the thing that would be with them for the rest of their lives? Yes, but it was going to be touch and go. One more tack, just one more and they would make the windward mark. Pray God, no foul shift.

'Tack,' Chloe yelled.

The mark was past them; they were on the final downwind leg. Three boats' lengths they led by, just three lengths. Emily found she was biting her lip almost to the point of bleeding. Just a race for the line and the Americans still had a penalty to take. The umpire boat was not far away and watching. The Americans were closing, inch-by-inch they were catching up and beginning to take their wind. Oh no, Emily could have sobbed. The Americans had picked up a freak gust and were slipping into their lee. Chloe was mentally locked into speed. Emily cried a warning. The Americans were going to luff. Emily screamed at Chloe who reacted but too late. They had not responded to a legal luffing manoeuvre. The umpire was showing a yellow flag. They had a penalty but by the rules that had only nullified the American penalty. It was evens.

'Keep your cool, guys,' Chloe shouted. 'Speed counts.'

The boats were level now. Which crew had the skill, the resolve and the bottle to make the difference and win? Those last few seconds were a blur that was to live in Emily's dreams for the rest of her days. It would be down to tiny helm movements, perfect balance, total concentration, and whoever made that last pump on the kite, that last surge that would take them to win. The finish was near, they were still level. Emily could see Chloe watching the gap between themselves and the other boat.

'The kite,' said Chloe. 'One big pump. Now!'

They did it; a tactic on the edge of legality, but a timed strong tug on the spinnaker and they felt the boat surge beneath them. If the Americans responded they were too late. The committee boat was showing the winner's flag. It was yellow. They had done it.

Tom didn't want to watch. He was too nervous, too depressed and too angry. He had stalked around the streets behind the yacht club unaware that passers by were staring at him and nervously avoiding him. Eventually he found himself outside the tapas bar again and, looking through the open door, he saw Dave Manning and some of the British contingent crowded round a television.

Tom pushed his way into the bar and joined them. Someone had managed to tune the set to BBC. He could hear the voice of Jerry Blades, and Blades was shouting at full throttle with multi decibels rising into a raucous scream.

'It's close, it can't be closer. All you Brits out there – watch the line on the screen! It's metres to go. Yes – yes – yeasss! Wow, a quarter of a length – half a second. Our girls have done it – it's gold for Great Britain!'

They fell in a heap clinging on to each other in the middle of the boat. Erin was crying, Chloe was whooping, but Emily was sick. It came on suddenly and just as she had been warned it might.

'Em, what's wrong. You can't do that – we've won.'

Emily retched again into a plastic bucket that the Poles had left behind. 'It's OK,' she said. 'It's the baby moving.'

'Oh, God. You haven't done damage have you?' Chloe's face was all concern.

'No, I'm sure it's not that. It's the morning sickness except it's mid-afternoon.'

'You're seeing the team doctor the moment we step ashore.'

'Hiya, you guys. Well done – what a party.' It was Amanda, the Americans' helm.

Emily was feeling better and a bit embarrassed. They had won, but what must their rivals be thinking? The two boats closed until their crews were hanging onto each other as the sea rocked their craft. Amanda, Leah and Colleen were their friends and maybe that helped.

'Guess we'll settle for silver this time,' said Amanda. 'Tell you something. They say the medals are the real thing. Seems they mine gold and silver in this goddam' stoopid country.'

'Sure thing, it's gotta' be true,' said Colleen. 'That creepy guy Garcia told me.'

'See yer,' called Amanda. The boats parted company and both sailed towards the distant shoreline.

Emily could hear shouting. A motor yacht with a British red ensign was idling not far away on their starboard side. A RIB full of applauding Brits was surging towards them.

'Dad, Mum,' screamed Emily. 'We've won – we've done it.'

She saw her father in the RIB clasp his wrists together above his head in a traditional victory salute. Her mother blew kisses at them; the others in the boat were waving. Now the tears flooded down Emily's cheeks as she waved back. The RIB drifted past and someone tossed them a bundle of cloth. Erin grabbed it and grinned as she unrolled a huge union flag. She stood and streamed it in the wind. Emily searched the faces in the RIB for Tom but she couldn't see him. She wished he could be with them now. They, the girls had won, but he too had played his part, along with Mum and Dad and Maria.

Colleen's mention of Garcia was the only negative in this moment of joy. Yes, they had stuffed him, but now the heat would be on Dad. In ten days time he too would be sailing for gold.

They picked up the tow launch, and from then on all was a blur. Emily had vague memories: their boat rocking in a sea disturbed by the spectator craft. Another RIB had come alongside and a commentator with a hand mike and a helmet camera had boarded them. They had all stammered some sort of answers to his questions. Minutes later it seemed they were alongside the pontoon again. The Polish girls were standing beaming, with genuine warmth. They helped them ashore clapped them on their backs while a crowd on the dock above applauded. It was all heady stuff especially when somebody handed Chloe a bottle of champagne, which she proceeded to spray over everyone in sight.

At last they could climb the dockside steps and there stood Tom waiting for her. Emily stumbled and fell against him crying unrestrainedly into his shirtfront. The American crew were standing by their boat. Emily felt a tremor of anxiety. She saw a man, his body language spelt anger as he leaned forward gesticulating. It was Garcia. Emily saw Amanda turn her back on the man and walk towards them. She was clearly upset, but not with Chloe's crew.

'That Garcia. What an asshole!' she snarled.

'What's up, Mandy?' asked Erin.

'He wants us to protest you. Fuck 'im – no way!'

'What about?' asked Emily.

'He says you pumped your kite at the finish. So what, we did too. Nothing illegal; you did it better. Fair play as you Brits say.'

'Mandy,' said Emily, 'you know there's a hidden agenda here?' In a few short sentences Emily enlightened her friend.

The three American girls were genuinely outraged. 'We'll take this to the highest level,' said Amanda. 'That shitass conman has no right to be on the Olympic committee. He's a dead man.'

'He's not the one presenting medals is he?' Chloe looked murderous.

'No,' said Amanda. 'It's Phillipe Castor, the president's son. We've seen him – he's a sex bomb. Leah fancies him.'

'The tradition is we hold hands and leap onto the top podium together,' said Chloe. 'That's what the three blondes used to do. But if we try that it'll be disaster. So, you two jump and give me a pull up when you get there.'

They stood waiting with the other medallists while two more presentations took place. The podium was set on the dockside and a huge crowd had gathered. Emily had only just been released by Samira, the team doctor, who had ushered her into a darkened room in the yacht club, and taken her pulse and blood pressure before listening with a portable ultra-sound. Emily had worried, but the doctor had declared her fit and well and the baby safe.

It should have been the most triumphant moment of her young life, but as Emily stood on the top step of the podium she felt only a strong desire to lie down and fall asleep. The president's son moved along the line dropping the medals around the necks of the winners. Why the hell should she see a flashback of old William telling how he'd once witnessed a hanging? She bent down to receive her own medal. The son was certainly a good-looking young guy but how could he survive on a roasting hot day like this wearing a dark suit and thick yellow waistcoat? They turned to face the flags as their anthem played. The crowd applauded and they jumped down onto the dock-side.

'That Garcia's full of bullshit,' it was Amanda. 'Real metal – my ass.' She held up her silver medal. 'Silver plate more likely.'

'This one doesn't feel too heavy either,' said Chloe.

Mum and Dad came to meet them. They hugged Emily, and then Chloe and Erin. Dad examined the medal. 'Two gold and a bronze in the display case.'

'Another medal to come?' Chloe grinned.

Emily couldn't help but look around the crowd. 'Was Garcia there?'

'I looked but I didn't see him,' said Kirsten.

'Dad, I'm worried. You'll be sailing next, and I doubt Garcia's giving up on his dirty tricks.'

CHAPTER 35

Emily hugged both her parents. ‘Oh, Mum, Dad. I wish I could stay with you.’

They stood in the departures area at Olifa Airport. Emily was dressed in her Great Britain tracksuit while around them the entire British team prepared to leave for home.

‘We’ll be fine,’ said Kirsten, ‘and you can follow your dad on TV.’

‘I know. Dad, I want you to win but I’m worried if you do.’

Her father bent down and kissed her head. ‘Go on, your friends are getting impatient.’

They could see Chloe and Erin standing with Sherrie and Saffron. Emily wiped a tear and then laughed. ‘Sherrie and Saff are due at a mayoral reception in Southend or “Sairfaind”. They’ve asked us to go along as well.’

‘Enjoy that. Goodbye then,’ said Steve. ‘See you as soon as we’re home.’

Emily had her mischievous expression. ‘Never mind, Dad. I’m sure Maria will look after you.’

Kirsten glared. ‘Go home you tiresome girl.’

They watched as the airliner took off and climbed away. Kirsten knew they felt both happy and empty. Emily was going home, but Steve was the one now with something to achieve. Tom was waving to them. He was standing near the exit gate with Ken Littlecroft and Samira the doctor.

‘What’s up, Tom?’

‘The doctor checked Emily again before the flight and the baby’s fine.’

‘I know; she told us. Thank God.’

‘There’s something else we’d like to discuss,’ said Ken. ‘I’ve spoken to the doctor here and she agrees that Steve here could help us.’

Kirsten already knew what was coming.

Ken looked at Steve. ‘You’ve made amazing progress in the last few years both with your physical strength and your sailing.’

‘I suppose so.’

Kirsten intervened. ‘Using one stick you can walk as fast as me. And you don’t get so tired.’

‘That’s just it,’ said Ken, who was clearly relieved by Kirsten’s support. 'The Paralympic opening ceremony is in three days' time. The committee are unanimous. They want you to carry the union flag.'

'Me!'

'Yes, you,' said Kirsten. 'The man who once won able-bodied gold is back at age seventy for a second time. It's a talking point all over the world and not just with sailing people.'

'It's a special flag,' said Ken. 'Lightweight fibre pole and light cloth.'

'You will say yes, of course,' said Kirsten.

'Put like that I daren't say no. Thanks, Ken. It's one hell of an honour. I feel quite emotional.'

'And you will be putting two fingers up at Garcia,' said Tom.

'Maria, I really need to talk to your brother,' said Tom.

'Why?'

'You know why. Steve could be in danger. Emily's won gold and Garcia must be worried about Steve.'

'My brother already knows all about Garcia. He told our father yesterday that it is impossible to link Garcia with anything that went on. The proper crane driver was found wandering in the countryside and he is too frightened to speak. The man who did the damage cannot be traced and the false official has also vanished.'

'Is anything being done to protect Steve?'

'Oh I think so, but I would not know what.'

'I would like to talk to Rafael.'

'No, Tom. I can convey your worries but my brother works for national security and often he disappears for weeks.'

Tom was not satisfied. 'What if Garcia decides to move from damaging boats to hurting the helm? Steve's a single-hander remember. It was different when the target was three girls.'

'Tom, I like Steve. He is a lovely man. I do not think Garcia will do anything stupid until he sees how the racing is going.'

Emily was not sure how she felt. She missed Tom, but at the same time she was glad he wasn't around fussing and trying to restrict her life. She had recurrent bursts of sickness since her return to England but these were less now. But her body was beginning to change; there was no doubt of that. All her energy had been spent in Olifa, and the consequences had been unsettling. The return of the British team to Heathrow had been a triumph and for the sailors even more so. For the first time in Olympic history every member of the sailing team had a medal. She had been plunged into a neverending round of interviews and television appearances. The media had already unearthed the memory of "little Emily from the fire siege" and the repeating of news reports and film from that time had been painful.

There had been the happy weekend spent with Sherrie and Saffron in Southend. The duo's family had overwhelmed them with hospitality. Emily, Chloe and Erin had been careful to keep in the background while their friends had received a hero's welcome in their hometown. Two days later the roles were reversed when all five of them had gone to Burnham-on-Crouch for a round of the yacht clubs.

Emily had finally fled to Dorset to stay with Tom's family. Suddenly, though extrovert by nature, she only wanted to hide: to find solitude and peace in walks along the coastal paths. If she met other walkers along the way they never recognised her. Sometimes she would take the family Labrador with her. He was good company. She missed her little cat, now with Sarah looking after Firs Farm, but it would be nice to have a sloppy passive dog to complete the family. Would her baby be a boy or a girl? In a few weeks she could have a scan and find out. Did she want to find out? Probably no.

Every night the family followed the Paralympics on television. Dad carrying the flag had been a huge shock. Mum had called and told her to watch the opening ceremony without giving a reason. Emily had been so proud of Dad, as still limping slightly he had carried the banner for the whole world to see. She worried for Dad. She wondered what Garcia might do to him should he start winning. Unwillingly she had been drawn to the internet. Castinnio.com had been offering odds of ten to one against the father-daughter double. If the amount of money being pledged was as high as Maria claimed then Garcia stood to lose out in spades. Emily knew to her cost what Garcia was capable of and she worried. In the event Dad, had made an indifferent start by his standards, with sixth, fifth, and second places plus a terrible twenty-third that the rules said he could discard. Then, out of the blue, he had won the fifth race elevating him to bronze medal spot. He had won the next race too. The gold medal was a possibility, and the wind was forecast to rise for the decisive last races. Emily had bad dreams. In the daytime she worried. Surely Garcia would not stand by and let it happen. Oh, Dad, be careful!

Steve was in turmoil. He was the undisputed bronze medal winner in the Paralympic single-handed class with two more races to go. But he had nearly, or so nearly, failed his beloved wife. She didn't know that yet but she would and then what. "Lead us not into temptation." He could hear and feel his late mother, austere and devoutly Catholic, hissing in his ear. 'There's is no fool like an old fool,' he mumbled. He only hoped Kirsten would link his odd mood to fixation on the next race.

Following the opening ceremony, Kirsten had gone to an all-women's cocktail party hosted by President Castor's wife. Steve had been at a loose end but had drifted back to the yacht club. The lounge bar was almost empty apart from Maria and her brother, Rafael.

'Steve,' Maria had called out. 'Rafael needs to talk with you.'

He had declined a drink, but had sat down with the two of them. Rafael had briefed him about action he was taking to protect Steve's boat.

'Our support is official,' said Rafael. 'What happened to your daughter is demeaning to my country. We will not let it happen to you.' Rafael had left with an old world bow, and Steve was alone with the delightful Maria.

They had talked at first about sailing and Olifa.

'Steve,' she said. 'Without your advice I would never have done so well.'

'I was so sorry you missed out on third place,' he replied. Not wholly tactful.

'No, Steve. I was never going to get near to those others. Do you know my rating when I came into these games?'

'No, I'm sorry.'

She smiled at him. 'I was thirty-eight in the world. So, fourth in the Olympics is one hell of an improvement and I wouldn't have got near it without your advice.' Maria stood up and moved to the chair next to Steve. They talked about Emily and about Maria's hopes to study art in England. It had all been harmless chat at first but almost indiscernibly the talk had become more intimate. Steve could, and he knew he should, have politely broken the relationship there and then.

'Oh no!' Maria was staring at the glass doors at the entrance to the lounge. 'It's no good – he's seen us.'

Now Steve saw him as well. Garcia was staring at them through the glass.

'Let's get out,' she said. 'I'm staying here tonight. Let's go where we can talk without that man watching.' She led out of the lounge into a service corridor with a lift at the end.

In the tiny bedroom they had sat on the bed and talked. 'Steve,

When I started sailing you were my hero.'

'Maria, you are a flatterer.'

She had snuggled against him, laying her head on his shoulder. Steve was losing it. He was falling for a girl half his age.

'Kirsten is so lucky,' she whispered in his ear.

The embraced and kissed as they lay together on the bed. 'Steve make love to me,' she pleaded.

He had never been so tempted in his life. He was aroused, he desired this beautiful nubile girl. It wasn't only lust, he really was fond of her, but it was a different affection. Over the months and weeks Maria, Emily's friend, had become more an additional niece or daughter even. Steve had never in twenty years betrayed his wife. He must be strong and he had a sailing challenge tomorrow.

'Maria, no – it won't do.'

She released him and rolled on her back and smiled a rueful smile now. 'Steve, I think you are right. Another time and another place it might have been.'

They kissed once more and then he left her. What did he feel? It was a mix of relief and deep regret. He slipped out of the air-conditioned cool of the yacht club and into the humid night air of the streets.

The experience had damaged his form on the racecourse. Most of the thirty contestants were people he had already beaten on the European circuit. A sixth place and a fifth scored in the first round, and then an unsatisfactory second and a humiliating twenty-third. It was his guilt that was destroying his sailing before a chance remark by Tom both hurt him and ignited his fighting spirit. Tom had been a godsend. He had supervised the launching and recovery of the boat and taken care of the sails. He had helped Steve to board and helped him out after the racing. Then, at the end of the second day, Tom had nodded at the burly man who had been hanging around the dock from day one. This Olifarian was dressed in baggy shorts and a shirt with a suspicious bulge under his left armpit.

'That's Rafael's heavy,' said Tom. 'Steve, if you don't get it together Garcia's got nothing to worry about.'

The implication from his future son-in-law that he was sitting back to avoid trouble was just the incentive that Steve needed. He sailed out to the start with a mental fire inside him. And it was easy. He knew his boat, the wind was offshore, and he knew its tricky shifts off the city skyline. He was sailing against helms he knew he could beat and he did. It was a decisive win by over one hundred metres. The second race was harder. He fought a windward duel with the young German Paralympian he remembered from Kiel when he, Steve, was felled by the stroke. In the end Steve passed him downwind to win by a boat and a half length. He couldn't now be beaten for the bronze medal. The next two races would decide the final placing.

He came ashore and, leaving the boat in Tom's care, he limped back to the hotel. He had chosen not to live in the village but had stayed on in the same hotel they had been in for a month. The bill was horrendous but the staff knew them almost as part of the family.

Kirsten was standing in the reception area. She greeted him with a glare that was hurtful seeing as he had done so well. He guessed what was coming and in a way he was relieved. It was better to get the revelation over and take his punishment.

'Come upstairs and we will talk,' said Kirsten.

Steve followed, feeling like an old time schoolboy on his way to face a caning. She said not a word as she ushered him into their room and shut the door.

'I would have thought,' she said, 'that in this corrupt country Maria would have chosen a better room for your fun and games.'

Steve said nothing.

His wife held up a DVD disk. 'Very revealing. This is a recording from the concealed surveillance camera that you never saw. Let's play it shall we?'

'I can explain…' he stuttered.

'Of course you can. You are a stupid man lured into stupidity. I do not blame the girl. She is a thirty-year old woman with a warped sexuality about older men. She would be much better looking for a nice cosy millionaire and stop behaving like a teenage temptress.'

'But … but …'

'Why the surveillance?'

'Well, yes.'

'Because among others there is one Grand Admiral of the Olifarian Navy who has been in the habit of taking the wives of his colleagues for a bit of hanky panky in the yacht club bedrooms. The manager tells me they've wired all of them, and he makes a lucrative bob or two by selling the evidence to the defaulters. If he was in England he could work for the *Daily Banner.*'

Steve said no more. He was caught bang to rights as the guilty party would say in fiction. 'Do you know Garcia saw us together in the lounge? That's why we went upstairs, but it was only to talk, or it was at first.'

'Steve, you are digging an even bigger hole for yourself. Do I need to embarrass us both by showing this again?'

'Oh, no, please don't, I'm so sorry. It'll never happen again I promise. I feel awful, forgive me.' For the first time for forty years his eyes blurred with tears.

'You will not have an opportunity to do it again ever. I shall see to that. For God's sake, Steve. I've already viewed this. You bloody fool. If you'd taken it any further you might have had another stroke. With that oversexed girl you're lucky to be still alive. At your age you are a fucking idiot. No pun intended.'

'Oh please, please. It never went that far. I promise you'

Steve felt embarrassed, chastened and more relieved than he deserved to be. His wife was angry, she felt horribly let down, but she was a Dane and understood better than most British women the weakness of men.

'Kirsten I still love you just as much as ever,' he was crying now as he fell to his knees. 'Please forgive me.'

She stood looking down at him before she delivered a stinging slap to his head that metaphorically sent it spinning. 'Get up, you! I feel like packing up and flying home, except that I would leave the field to that silly little girl. If you want me to even begin to forgive you; go out tomorrow and win.'

'You won't tell Tom?'

'I don't need to. I think he's already guessed. Being another bloody man he probably thinks you're the bees knees because of it.'

'I don't want Emily to find out.'

'I won't disillusion Emily; Maria's her friend. In spite of your idiocy I rather like her. She's welcome to visit us but if she does, I personally will pull up that stupid little mini-dress and clamp her with a chastity belt.'

For the first time in his life before a big race Steve took a sleeping pill. Without six hours' sleep he would not be in a fit state for his effort tomorrow. It made little difference, he could lie down and close his eyes but sleep would still not come. Kirsten had allowed him into the bed but had punched him when he snuggled too close to her. Half an hour later he heard her regular breathing and an occasional mutter from her dreamland. It was beginning to look as if he really might be forgiven, or on probation for his only lapse in over twenty years of marriage. But he would not and could not forgive himself.

The sleep remedy was beginning to take effect when he heard the sound: a gentle scraping and then a click. Someone was unlocking the door to the corridor. There was no doubt about it; they had an intruder in the tiny vestibule. He gave Kirsten a jab in the ribs. That was a mistake because she began to mumble. 'Wassa' matter?'

'Sssh – we've got intruders. Listen – don't turn the light on.'

She was sitting up staring at the open bedroom door. 'What do we do?' she whispered. 'No don't you move.' She slipped from under the covers and, still naked, tiptoed to the doorway.

Steve could hear movement in the tiny sitting room: the sound of a cupboard opening. That was it. They had a thief in the place. His wallet with his credit cards lay on the bedside table. He reached for it and tucked it under the mattress.

He could see now as a shaft of moonlight filtered through the open window. Kirsten was beside the bed groping silently in her handbag. She was holding her digital camera. Steve was alarmed. She was trying to repeat Johnny's trick but they weren't in rural England, they were in a strange and violent South American city. He was out of bed and on his feet. Even in the urgency of the moment he felt stiff. He touched Kirsten on the arm and shook his head. She shrugged and put down the camera. Instead she tiptoed to the bedside table and picked up a tiny object; it was a mobile phone. Oh no, the intruders would hear her. He tried to limp across but was caught short by a stabbing pain in his side and back. He felt a shiver of real fear. Another stroke? Was that the penalty he would pay for his stupidity? Kirsten was leaning through the open window holding the mobile at arm's length. She turned and sank back on the bed with a sigh.

She caught hold of his arm. 'Wait,' she hissed.

Five minutes later they heard it. It sounded like distant drumming. It was no such thing – it was footsteps running. Many footsteps. A stampede. He heard a voice in vestibule: Spanish but frightened. It might be a cliché but from that moment all hell broke loose. The outer door swung open with a force that nearly took it off its hinges. Voices yelled. Hard grating voices. A shrill scream followed by another. Then a frightening sound: batons striking human flesh again and again accompanied by screams that subsided into a mournful howl.

'What's happened?' Steve still whispered but louder now.

He could see Kirsten's wan smile in the moonlight. She held up the mobile. 'Panic button,' she whispered. 'Made to look like a phone. It came from Rafael Olivarez, but the person who gave it to me was … guess?'

'I've no idea.'

'It was your bit on the side – Maria.'

'I think I'll risk a look,' said Steve.

'Me too.' She started to move, remembered her nakedness, laughed and pulled on her bathrobe.

Steve followed her to the bedroom door. The lights were on in the vestibule, now filled with obese men in yellow uniforms. Comic they might have looked, were it not for the guns they carried: nasty little stub-barrelled carbines. One of these was pointed at two men prone on the floor, both groaning. A second man was cuffing their hands behind them.

'Signor and Signora,' a man, an officer judging by the braid on his jacket, saluted them. 'We catch them, bad men, very bad. They rob you?'

'Not sure,' said Kirsten. 'We'd like to have a look in there.' She pointed to the sitting room.

'OK, you looksee.'

The door of the drinks fridge was open. One glance and they could see the intruder's target. The soft energy drinks that Steve took with him to race were scattered on the floor. In a cardboard box was a second identical set.

'It doesn't make sense,' Steve muttered.

'To me it does,' said Kirsten. ' Remember Hammersen trying to poison Emily?'

'Hammersen's dead.'

'I've always wondered if it was really Hammersen who planted that yoghurt? When they caught him in the mountains he was trying to set up some voodoo curse against her.'

'I know, he was crazy enough to believe in all that,' said Steve.

'I would say Garcia's targeted you with something dodgy in those drinks.'

'Good God.' Steve was beginning to feel the full effects of shock combined with the sleeping pill. 'Sorry, I'm thick. Could it have been Garcia who tried to hurt Emily?'

'We'll probably never know, but Hammersen was definitely in the Gran Seco when the yoghurt was planted.'

'Signor, they steal things?' The officer had poked his head around the door.

'No, sir,' Steve replied. 'I think you arrived before they could take anything. We are forever grateful to you.'

‘That is good. Now we take away these bad men. Signor and Signora, please sleep well.’

The men left, dragging their wounded captives with them. Steve was relieved and grateful to their rescuers, even if as a Briton he was shocked by their brutality.

‘I must try and sleep. What should we do next?’

Kirsten looked out of the window. Steve was aware of the delicious scent of warm air and tropical shrubs. ‘Dawn’s breaking,’ she yawned. ‘First thing in the morning we’ll hand that stuff to the team doctor. Now get some sleep. You’re not due on the water until this afternoon, so this time I will allow you a lie in.’ She gave him a not so playful slap.

CHAPTER 36

'We've got the lab results from the analysis of those drinks.' It was Samira the team doctor. 'You are sure that they were planted?'

Steve was annoyed. 'You can be damn sure they were. I was there when it happened. The police caught the intruders and my wife is a witness.'

'All right, Steve, cool it. I believe you. You are absolutely certain that you never drank any of the stuff?'

'No, I was obviously suspicious. I may be able to tell you more when we see what the police have found.'

'Thank goodness you never drank any of it. Steve, someone wants you disqualified.'

'Doctor, I know that already.'

'The point is,' Samira continued, 'those drinks are laced with cocaine and the Olifarian officials are demanding blood tests on the first ten finishers after today's racing. That's almost unprecedented.'

'Which officials?'

'The chairman of the race committee is a distinguished Olympian and he authorised the tests himself.'

'Don't tell me. His name is Garcia.' Steve delivered a hollow laugh.

'Yes, that's right.'

'Tom is the boat all right?'

'The boat's fine, Steve. Rafael's doubled the security and I slept with her last night – the boat that is, not Maria.'

Steve was instantly suspicious. 'What about Maria?'

'What about her?' the lad smirked. 'I was only saying a boat wasn't such good company.'

Steve changed the subject. 'Did you know we had a break in last night?'

'No.'

'It was the same trick as happened to Emily. Intruders tried to switch the energy drinks in our fridge. Look – is Rafael around?'

'I don't know but Maria's in the yacht club.'

'No, Kirsten's forbidden me to talk to her.'

Tom smirked again. 'Well, that's odd. I saw them together. Your wife was delivering a bit of a lecture and the girlie was a mite tearful.'

Steve groaned. 'Tom do me a favour, find Maria and ask if I can get a message to her brother.'

'No need,' Kirsten spoke. 'I've seen her. Rafael told her the incident last night is under wraps. No one outside the security services knows about it. He believes that that includes Garcia. So, Steve, pressure's off. Go out and do your best and sod any drug tests.'

'Drug tests?' asked Tom.

'What if Garcia spikes my sample?' Steve asked.

'No chance. I've talked to Samira. She is entitled to monitor the test and anyway there are no Olifarians involved in the analysis.'

'Good.'

Kirsten dug in her bag and handed him two soft drink bottles. 'These are clean. I bought them in the bar. I would suggest you drink one very prominently in public.'

'What's all this about?' asked Tom.

'One of Garcia's dirty tricks,' she said. 'Tell you about it later, but first get this man afloat and racing.'

It was a sensation that Steve had felt many times before: leaving one's troubles ashore and escaping to sea.

For the final rounds of the event the course had been changed to a windward-leeward track, similar to that of the match racers. The wind had switched again blowing cooler air in from the Pacific and the Humboldt Current a few miles offshore. The pre-race briefing had estimated a maximum speed of twenty knots. Already a short disturbed sea was developing. Steve didn't mind that.

He looked around. He had three dangerous opponents. The Russian amputee, the German MS sufferer and the little Finnish girl with the spinal damage: he and they were the only four who could take gold. This was the wonderful essence of the Paralympics: young skilful helms could forget their disabilities and sail together on a level playing field. Young helms for God's sake? The average age of the other three was twenty something and he was seventy. Yes, the stroke had spoiled his reactions and his right side still didn't function fully without mental effort, but he was in his environment and he felt good.

It was a hard-fought race. Steve led from the start but lost that lead to the Finnish girl. He regained first spot on the fourth lap when his opponent mistimed a gybe and broached. The final beat to windward in a rising wind and breaking sea was a full- blooded contest between the two of them. In the end Steve had to yield to finish a narrow second. The two of them were now on level points for the gold medal. With the wind still rising the race officer called off a repeat for that day. A year ago Steve might have settled for a silver medal. It would have been a good culmination for a long career. No, the devious Garcia should be made to pay. Even if the man was safe from personal humiliation he could pay from his ill-gained fortune.

'We're going to guard the boat again,' said Tom. 'Rafael's got extra men on call should anything happen.'

'And we are not going back to the hotel,' said Kirsten. 'We've been given an empty flat in the village and there will be an armed guard outside.'

'How did the drug test go?' Tom asked.

'Fingers crossed they'll only find a residue of sleeping pill and Samira says that doesn't matter as it's vegetable based., and in the end Garcia, surprise, surprise, only wanted the first four finishers tested.'

Kirsten sighed. 'He doesn't give up does he.'

Steve laughed. 'Taking blood was easy but I was so dehydrated that I couldn't do the pee.'

'What happened then?' asked Tom.

'The doctor used psychology. He began to describe Niagara Falls, quite poetic. Then he ran a tap and that was a great mental trigger.'

'Are we sure Garcia can't get at the samples?'

'I think the Olympic committee suspect a bit of skulduggery. Actually, they took the stuff away in an armoured security van.'

'I've checked on my laptop,' said Tom. 'Castinnio.com have narrowed your odds to five to one on, but they will still catch a cold from the ante-post betting.'

'I feel sorry for the Russian lad,' said Steve. 'I've just had the results of the dope tests. They're coming down on him because he's been taking the wrong painkillers.'

'Are they disqualifying him?' asked Kirsten.

'Not this time. They've implemented some new rule I've never heard of. He's had six penalty points added. Bloody unfair in my opinion. Since when can a painkiller be performance enhancing? I suppose they think the poor sod should be able race when his leg stump is inflamed and giving him hell.'

They were trying to settle into their temporary home in the Olympic village. It was a dark concrete bunker of a ground floor flat which, during the main games, had housed two Peruvian boxers.

'Ha, ha, separate beds,' said Kirsten. 'Just right.'

'Not forever?' Steve looked pleading.

'No, be a good little boy and things may change when we're home.'

'What happened between you and Maria this morning?'

She looked at him hard and long. 'I think that is between her and me.'

'Tom told me she was crying.'

'Yes, she was. I think the remorse may even have been genuine. Now shut up and get some sleep for tomorrow,'

Strangely enough Steve did sleep, and without the help of sleeping remedies. Nor was he too disgruntled at being banished into a single bed. He was able to lie awake for a short period and, as in times gone by he used that half hour to formulate tactics for the morrow. He wasn't too sure about the guards outside the front door but at least there would be no more intruders.

He woke early. The sun was shining and even a few exotic birds sang in the trees at the end of the road. Steve guessed both trees and birds were a recent import. He reached the yacht club in plenty of time to have a high calorie breakfast and two cups of that superb locally grown coffee. The single-handed 2.4 class was to be the last start of the day following the three handed Sonar class. He went down to the dock to see Tom busy rigging the boat. The wind was still strong from the west but not as much so as yesterday. Other competitors were grouped around chatting while their helpers prepared the boats. Steve made his way across to Sonia, the little Finnish girl who was his rival for gold. She sat in her wheelchair, a pretty blonde with a cheerful if imaginative grasp of English.

'Steve, may your mast be broken,' she greeted him. Steve of course knew this old Viking greeting meant good luck.

'And Sonia, may your keel fall off,' he replied. They shook hands and as Kirsten was not around he gave the girl a kiss on the cheek.

An hour later the fleet of thirty was assembling near the start line. The first leg comprised a long beat out to sea to an orange inflatable mark about a mile away; then followed the long return leg downwind. This was to be repeated three times to complete a course of six nautical miles. Steve was happy, as this would be just about within the limits of his concentration. The timer on the front of the cockpit read fifteen minutes to the start. Surrounding them was a ring of spectator boats but none of them were intruding too closely except a single motor craft that he recognised.

It was a vintage PT: a Second World War US torpedo boat. Steve had seen it before in the fishing boat harbour with a trawling Registration number. He assumed it must have been hired as a spectator boat. He was annoyed to see that this craft was heading his way, and that the skipper had cranked up his engine as the boat surged onto a plane with a white bow wave. This was annoying as there was enough disturbed water already. The PT was heading straight at him. Hell, hadn't they seen him?

'Oi, slow down! Keep off!' his yell was futile.

The PT came within ten metres before it made a tight turn and roared away. Its wash enveloped Steve's boat, filling the cockpit to the brim.

'Of all the bloody fools,' he yelled.

He was wallowing in the waves with no more than a few inches of freeboard. In pain he heaved himself out of the cockpit and sat on the stern. That was it, he thought. His series lost all by the stupidity of some cowboy. The PT was heading away but not far. The Olifarian navy ship was moving to block its path and Steve could see a RIB load of uniformed men, marines he assumed, racing to intercept. Well that was nice of the locals but too late for him. A sound signal echoed over the water and a postponement flag was flying from the committee boat. Another RIB was heading towards him. Oh, not more wash. It was one of the rescue boats, humiliating but needed. If they were going to tow him to shore he would have to bale out half of this water. Typically, his electric pump had failed.

The RIB eased gently alongside. 'Steve, the race is postponed for fifteen minutes.' The man speaking was a Canadian official. 'Race starter thinks you're the victim of foul play. We're going to get you going.' A suction hose was dropped in front of Steve and he heard an electric pump whirr. Gradually the water subsided until his cockpit seat reappeared. He slid down into it and removed the last dregs with his hand pump.

He had had a reprieve. Foul play the man had said. If so, that would have been Garcia's last throw. Maybe the man hoped the incident would have put Steve off his game enough to stop him from competing properly. Well, sod Garcia. Steve was wet, his leg was stiff but he was going to give this race a go. So, what tactics? He had to finish in front of little Sonia and better than in tenth place. He could deploy the classic Ben Ainslie gambit. Lock onto ones' opponent like a limpet and cover-tack them into oblivion. Ainslie had been a young man in a high performance dinghy. Steve was an elderly man in a miniature keelboat. No, he would have to do it by speed alone.

The five-minute signal sounded. He took a quick sight with the little compass in front of him but could find no particular bias in either end of the line except that he knew a strong tidal current was running from left to right. Those who tried the far right hand end would risk being carried down to leeward of the top mark. He would go as tight to the limit buoy as he could and put in a long port tack and a short starboard to lay the mark. The other boats were packing the start line. He tried to find Sonia but couldn't see her at first. Now he could see her boat with the Finnish flag on its sail and she too was going for the left end. The time clock was counting down on the cockpit in front of him. Ten … nine … eight … He hardened in his mainsheet. He needed to build speed. Seven … six … five … four … three … two … Way across the water came the start signal. His timing was good but not good enough. Sonia was there and she had locked onto him. So it was to be a Ben Ainslie after all and he was the victim. But Steve knew a thing or two about yacht racing, experience picked up over forty years. Old and slow he might be but Sonia, young and beautiful, did not have his repertoire of tricks. He deliberately let her cover tack him for five minutes. Then he threw a feint, and she fell for it and tacked without watching him. Steve bore away for a fraction and then hardened up again. Sonia responded too late and now the position had reversed. Steve didn't bother to enter another duel; he doubted he could pull the same trick twice. It was going to be his boat speed plus his experience in this rising wind. He went back to his long port tack. He had moved a little off his predicted line but he could still reach the point where he would need to tack onto starboard. Playing chess in a racing car. That was how someone had once described small boat racing. He wasn't going to look for Sonia. No distractions, only concentration and boat speed mattered now. He could see a few other port tackers but well to leeward and behind him. They were going to be in trouble from the starboard advantage boats crossing towards them.

Just one boat needed watching. It was the German lad and he was going to be mighty close. Steve watched the gap. No he wasn't going to cross safely and he had made up his mind not to tack. A very slight tweak on the right hand steering pedal and Steve slipped under the other boat's stern with inches to spare. The German tried to tack on top of him but faded. Steve was on course and in clear air. He made the windward mark on his next tack with the German this time caught on port. He made a quick glance back. Sonia was third.

He rounded the mark and the thin line that poled out the jib ran sweetly. Whatever happened he must thank Tom who had so meticulously prepared the boat and her gear. Now he would watch the waveforms and feel the wind. He knew that no one in this fleet had his downwind experience. He was on a high now. Almost he felt like singing. Round the mark, not too close. Pole in. Sheets in. Now round. He had gained on all the others. Could he really clinch this one? He held his own on the next two legs: just two more to go. The wind was still rising and many of the competitors were in trouble. He could see the rescue RIB with its pump attending two waterlogged boats. He seized his own hand pump and worked it frantically until he heard the pipe suck air. Whatever happened he must stay dry. Read the waves, concentrate, keep the speed. The committee boat was in line for the finish at the end of the last downwind leg. Sonia had passed the German but she was fifty metres adrift in second. He would take this race as long as he kept dry and as long as nothing broke. The committee boat was close. He could see the watchers on her deck. He remembered that these Olifarians didn't have European inhibitions about guns. This race would finish with a gun and it did. The report was loud as he crossed the line, followed by cheers from the massive spectator fleet that had suddenly emerged, it seemed from nowhere.

Steve released the sails and sat with the boat rolling and drifting. He was shivering not with cold but a weird combination of euphoria and anticlimax. He had come a long way since he'd first sailed this lovely little boat at Kiel four years ago. Suddenly he heard that familiar voice, not in his imagination but loud and clear in his head.

'Steve, that was very well done. I salute you.' It was old Wolfgang who had left him this boat. Steve felt serenity then warmth, and now the tears came untamed and uncontrollable. His dear old departed friend had spoken to him from some dimension beyond his understanding.

Ashore everything was surreal. A huge multinational crowd had lined the dockside. The cheers were deafening, hands clapped him on the back. Everywhere smiling faces appeared and faded. Kirsten was there. She flung her arms around him as of old, all recriminations forgotten. Tom was there and gave Steve a huge bear hug. Little Sonia had struggled from her wheelchair to half stand and give him a full kiss on the lips. Lastly, and incredibly, Kirsten had smiled and pushed Maria towards him and thc two of them had exchanged a chaste embrace.

For the second time in his life Steve stood on the winner's podium while the gold medal was dropped around his neck. The band played the national anthem and the Union flag rose flanked by those of Finland and Germany. It had been a long and often challenging journey but he had come through it and won: won not just a sailing event but a victory against his darker inner self.

CHAPTER 37

'Tomorrow's the big day. How does it feel?' Steve knew he was repeating the silly question that Emily had been asked countless times already.

'I wonder what the vicar will think?' she replied. 'I haven't been in his church since Gerry's funeral and now he's marrying me with a great big baby inside me.'

'It's all right, Sarah's told him and he's OK. He may be a man of God but he served in the Army. He has a broad mind about almost everything.'

Steve had only just begun to recover from the fallout from the Olifa games. The medal winners had paraded through London on opentop buses. He and Emily had stood together, his arm around her. As the buses turned into Trafalgar Square the other athletes had moved back until he and she had stood alone at the front of the deck. The crowd lining the street, and watching from every vantage point, had gone wild. Everyone knew the story of the father-daughter double. Steve had been persuaded to wear both of his gold medals. One awarded to the energetic young sailor and the second forty years later for the grand old veteran.

Emily had now begun to enjoy her fame. Her appearance on the television programme *A Question of Sport* had seen her at her most sparkling. Soon she had resumed her career at law and had slipped back into her role as if she had never been away.

For Steve the outcome had been different. He had retreated back home to Sussex and had shunned publicity. That confidential letter from the Palace via Number Ten had not helped.

'Does this mean I'm going to be a lady?' Kirsten had giggled.

'You'll be Lady Godiva if you mow the lawn nude next summer,' he replied.

'Why not? I've always thought Lady Godiva must have been a Dane by birth. Can we announce it at the wedding?'

'No, it's got to be secret until next January first.'

Steve came back to the present. 'You happy with the dress?' he asked. 'He knew Emily's gown was a designer label, a gift from Tony Travis. Sarah was matron of honour and Christine, Chloe and Erin were bridesmaids. Johnny had refused point blank to be a page but had accepted the role of usher.

'I like it,' said Emily. 'It's nice and floaty and doesn't show my bump.'

'A very nice bump it is too,' said her mother who had come into the room. 'Your friend Saffron was on the phone just now. She and Sherrie took a wrong turn in Guildford but they'll be here in an hour.' She looked at Steve. ' Husband can I trust you?'

'Why?'

'Because if I allow Maria to sleep on the couch downstairs, I intend to see that you stay upstairs.'

'I can give you my word as an Englishman and a gentleman.'

'I don't know if that counts for much. I'll be bloody watching you.'

'Leave off, Mum,' said Emily. 'Poor Dad. He's learned his lesson.'

'We will see. Emily, never trust men. So keep that one of yours on a tight rein.'

Emily giggled. 'I once thought Tom was misbehaving with Alexia. You know at the reception she's going to play Charlene from Gravesenders one more time and Tom is going to try and be Mean Max.'

'Can Tom act?'

'No, that's why I trust him.'

It was a crisp late November morning. The church had attracted the media, not as big a showing as at Gerry's funeral but nine news cameras and two TV crews. Following the ceremony the newlyweds and their families had appeased the press and posed for over ten minutes. Then it was into the cars to travel the twenty miles to the Lakeview Hotel at Branham. Here all could enjoy the wedding breakfast and, later, everyone who cared to could dance the night away.

A sizeable crowd of locals and other bystanders had gathered outside the church. They applauded the happy scene and took their own pictures. One newspaper reporter at the rear of the crowd was not applauding. Michelle Le Bois stared at Emily. No one noticed her, or her expression of planned vengeance and hate.

Maria kissed both Emily and Tom. 'You are two lucky people,' she said.

'I am,' said Tom. 'I know that.'

'I will tell you something my brother Rafael told me,' Maria continued. 'You, Emily will be fortunate. Tom, remember that shaman you saw in El Caliente?'

'The funny little Indian guy?'

'That's the one. He had been hired to ill-wish Emily. Then Rafael gave him four hundred American dollars; for him and his people that would be like winning your lottery. Rafael told the man to hold a full ritual and he was to use it to bring fortune to a little English girl called Emily.'

'He hinted that at the time,' said Tom. 'I told him it was bullshit, but he seemed to believe it.'

'Tom, if you were an Olifarian you would never scoff. The Indians are a shrewd and ancient people with great knowledge. We see too many instances where strange things happen.'

'Tom, I think it's true,' said Emily. 'All that time in Olifa I had this feeling that someone or something was riding with me. I felt it during the sailing. It was going to be tough but we would win.'

'That confirms it,' said Maria. 'And what's more, Rafael told the Shaman he required the blessing to be for life.'

'Then I will do my best to see that that comes true,' said Tom.

THE END

EPILOGUE

THE FINANCIAL TIMES.
Collapse of internet gambling network.

Castinnio.com the worldwide internet gambling network based in Olifa has been declared insolvent. It appears that the concern offered long odds for ante-post betting on the Olympic Games staged by coincidence in Olifa City. It seems that these games failed to go to form in that fancied competitors failed to win medals while unexpected heavy betting on outsiders at long odds were successful. The network's losses covered almost every discipline and sport but the heaviest deficit is reported to be on one sailing event closely linked to a second in the Paralympics for the disabled. Heavy betting on a double win seems to have been the final straw that has destroyed what had been a profitable and popular international network. It seems that owing to its internet nature the network was unable to lay off bets elsewhere as the main stream bookmakers in the UK have done.

In a news conference on Thursday, President Castor of oil rich Olifa guaranteed that all debts and winnings would be honoured in order to protect the probity and good name of his nation. The president of Castinnio.com Snr Primo Garcia is believed to have disappeared but sightings of him have been reported in Chile.

By the same author

THE NEMESIS FILE

Professional yachtsman and Olympic medallist Steve Simpson has problems. His wife has died and his Chichester sail making business is under threat. When Steve and his daughter Sarah find the body of a young Dane in the sea off the Sussex coast they are inextricably sucked into an international blackmail and drugs conspiracy.

The story describes fourteen days in the late summer of 1990 that will change Steve's life. It is a test that leads him to new love and a rebirth of his hopes.

This tense mystery-thriller moves swiftly from Sussex to Copenhagen with interludes in Portsmouth, Italy and Scotland, and ends with a sea chase in a gale

ISBN 978-0-9548880-0-8 (0-9548880-0-6)

Available from Benhams Books
1 Fir Cottage, Greatham, Liss, Hampshire GU33 6BB

Reviews of *The Nemesis File*:

Journalist Pamela Payne: With locations as diverse as the South Coast of England, Naples and Denmark, *The Nemesis File*'s credible sailing scenes will either have you reaching for the seasickness-pills or signing on for a course; the sex scenes, however, are the most romantic I have read for along time. A great adventure story, which will delight both sexes – sailors or landlubbers."

Yachts and Yachting December 2004. "…Jim Morley is a sailor writing for sailors and his first novel is immersed in the South Coast yachting and dinghy scene…if somebody was going to write a novel for *Yachts and Yachting,* readers this would probably be it.

Yachting Monthly: 2006. Dell Quay based yachtsman Jim Morley has turned his hand to writing thrillers based on his sailing experiences of forty years. His first novel, *The Nemesis File,* is a murder mystery linking a Chichester sailmaker with a failing business, the corpse of a Dane found floating off Sussex and Nazi propaganda minister Josef Goebbels.

Reviews of *The Nemesis File* (continued):

Olympic sailor and coach: Cathy Foster, 11th Dec 2004

Rarely have I read such a racy book! It's carries you along at pace, and holds you fast until the very end. Just then, you think that maybe this is getting far-fetched, but the punch-line pulls you up short, and makes you re-assess the characters and their relationship to events. Suddenly the plot hangs together again in a very satisfactory way, just as good detective stories should.

Instead of long descriptions to 'paint a picture' of all the venues and situations, the writing is succinct and carefully crafted to give the maximum impression for the minimum words. This gives the book its fast tempo, yet nothing is lost because the accurate detailing of locations and action bonds the reader into plot. As a past Olympic sailor myself, I know the sailing venues described in both Chichester Harbour and Copenhagen well, and I can reassure any future reader that the author has definitely done his research. In addition, he's right – you do build life-long bonds with other British athletes and other countries' sailors when you are part of the Olympic team representing your country. It is a pleasure and highly unusual to read a book which describes the joys of sailing and racing so well. Yet it's not a book about sailing, full of technicalities of the sport. Sailing provides the background framework for a story of murder and blackmail where the investigation chases over four countries and three generations of lives. A thoroughly enjoyable read.

Cathy Foster went to the Olympics in 1984 (finished 7th and made history as the first woman helm since the 2nd World War) and competed in two other Olympic campaigns, the last being 2002/3. She's a freelance Coach who specialises in top level racing, including Olympic and Paralympic sailors

By the same author

ROCASTLE'S VENGEANCE

When out of work sea captain Peter Wilson takes a job as harbour master in the Dorset yacht harbour of Old Duddlestone, he is surprised to learn that his own father, James Wilson, was the harbour's wartime commander.

There are unsolved crimes involving this secretive community dating back fifty years. The deaths of the entire personnel of a research laboratory, then a rape and murder followed by a lynching.

Peter, aged ten, witnessed his father's suicide. Now he hears disquieting rumours about his father's dubious activities in Duddlestone. He forms a relationship with single-mother, Carol Stoneman. When Carol's ten-year-old son is abducted, Peter is forced into a situation that nearly bring his own destruction.

This mystery thriller is set on the Dorset coast in the summer of 1997, with a sailing background.

ISBN 978-0-9548880-1-5 (0-9548880-1-4)

Available from Benhams Books
1 Fir Cottage, Greatham, Liss, Hampshire GU33 6BB

Reviews of *Rocastle's Vengeance*:

Unsolicited comment on Amazon. *****
Wow! What a read. You know it is a good book when after a few pages you don't want to put it down, nor answer the phone, door or anything…

Bournemouth Echo, July 2006.
Novelist brings mystery to the coast.
Rocastle's Vengeance, James Morley's second novel, is brimming with references to Purbeck Poole and Bournemouth. The book recounts the tale of a harbour master who uncovers murky secrets when he takes a job in the imaginary village of Old Duddlestone…

Tim O'Kelly. Whitbread Prize judge southern region.
Jim Morley writes with skill and intelligence: a genuine storyteller in the finest tradition.

By the same author

MAGDALENA'S REDEMPTION

If an eight-year-old boy commits murder is he irredeemably evil? Can he ever be rehabilitated or will he kill again to preserve his secret?

Hampshire farmer, Tom O'Malley, finds the dead body of a young journalist. Not satisfied that she is a suicide he makes his own investigation.

Fed rumours about his friend and employer, Hollywood film director Gustav Fjortoft, he angrily rejects them. Yet all his inquiries into his friend's past seem to substantiate the rumours.

Following suspicious deaths in his own community, Tom's quest leads him the American West Coast, where he escapes abduction and near death.

Returning to England he finds the answers he seeks in a dramatic finale in his home village.

ISBN 978-0-9548880-2-2

Available from Benhams Books
1 Fir Cottage, Greatham, Liss, Hampshire GU33 6BB

By the same author

EMILY'S HOUR

Everything changes for the Simpson family when the dead body of an internet millionaire is found in Branham Lake and a close friend is falsely accused of murder.

It is 2004 and Steve and Kirsten, the central characters in James Morley's first novel, The Nemesis File are now married and have settled in rural Sussex with their children Emily 13 and John-Kaj 8. Steve runs the family nautical business near Chichester but teaches sailing at Branham Lake on the Surrey Hampshire border.

When further deaths occur, a police inspector facing a mental breakdown is convinced of his suspect's guilt. While Steve and Kirsten fight to clear their friend's name they have no inkling of the nightmare that is to engulf them. When Emily, along with an elderly war veteran, is abducted by a sacrificial religious cult, the family become the centre of worldwide attention.

Emily's Hour is a tense thriller, with a background in sailing that will engage both adults and teenagers alike

ISBN 978-0-9548880-3-9

Available from Benhams Books
1 Fir Cottage, Greatham, Liss, Hampshire GU33 6BB